WHAT DINAH THOUGHT

WHAT DINAH THOUGHT

Deena Metzger

VIKING

VIKING
Published by the Penguin Group
Viking Penguin, a division of Penguin Books USA Inc.,
40 West 23rd Street, New York, New York 10010, U.S.A.
Penguin Books Ltd, 27 Wrights Lane, London W8 5TZ, England
Penguin Books Australia Ltd, Ringwood, Victoria, Australia
Penguin Books Canada Ltd, 2801 John Street, Markham, Ontario, Canada L3R 1B4
Penguin Books (N.Z.) Ltd, 182–190 Wairau Road, Auckland 10, New Zealand

Penguin Books Ltd, Registered Offices: Harmondsworth, Middlesex, England

First published in 1989 by Viking Penguin, a division of Penguin Books USA Inc.

1 3 5 7 9 10 8 6 4 2

Portions of this book first appeared in different form in *Deep Down: The New
Sensual Writing by Women,* edited by Laura Chester (Faber & Faber), and *Hear the
Silence,* edited by Irene Zahava (The Crossing Press).

Grateful acknowledgment is made for permission to reprint
excerpts from the following copyrighted works:
The Bible Designed to Read as Living Literature, edited by Ernest Sutherland Bates.
Copyright © 1936, 1964 by Simon & Schuster, Inc. Reprinted by permission
of Simon & Schuster, Inc.
The Legends of the Jews, by Louis Ginzberg. Copyrighted and used by permission
of The Jewish Publication Society, Philadelphia.
Hebrew Myths: The Book of Genesis, by Robert Graves and Raphael Patai. By permission
of Doubleday, a division of Bantam Doubleday Dell Publishing Group, Inc.
Kabbalah and Exodus, by Z'ev ben Shimon Halevi. © 1980 by Warren Kenton.
Reprinted by arrangement with Shambhala Publications, Inc., Boston, MA.
The River of Light, by Lawrence Kushner. Reprinted with the
permission of Lawrence Kushner.
The Woman's Encyclopedia of Myths and Secrets, by Barbara Walker.
By permission of Harper & Row, Publishers, Inc.

Library of Congress Cataloging in Publication Data
Metzger, Deena.
What Dinah Thought / Deena P. Metzger.
p. cm.
ISBN 0-670-82750-9
I. Title.
PS3563.E864W4 1989
813'.54—dc20   88-40653

Printed in the United States of America
Set in Sabon

For Barbara Myerhoff
(1935–1985)
May our souls continue to guide each other

May this Midrash be in the service of Peace
and be an act of *tikkun olam*

Midrash is a literature that appears in the
spaces in between. After one word is done but
before the next one has opened its mouth.

—Lawrence Kushner,
The River of Light

Very special thanks to Michael Ortiz Hill, who was the first to read and understand the manuscript and who lovingly, generously, and most skillfully, undertook to help me with the very difficult task of editing the final work.

I am thankful to Nancy Bacal for her devoted companionship as we traveled through Israel together and I offer special thanks to Marc Kaminsky, whose encouragement and notes sustained me throughout the editing. Gratitude also to Naomi Newman, Diane Wolkstein, and Peter Levitt, whose readings and comments were of enormous help, and to Micha Taubman, who believed in the project.

My thankfulness is also extended to Ralph Abraham, who provided a sanctuary in a time of need so some of this manuscript might be revealed.

I am also grateful to the Virginia Center for the Creative Arts, where I found the solitude and support to write the first draft of this book, and to the Threshold Foundation, which also supported my work.

Finally, I would like to acknowledge Robert Graves, Lawrence Kushner, Raphael Patai, Z'ev ben Shimon Halevi, Merlin Stone, and Barbara Walker, whose books deeply provoked and nurtured my spiritual imagination.

Prologue

Dinah, daughter of Jacob by Leah, was ravished by Shechem, a Hivite. For that reason, and with the help of a peculiarly low cunning, Simeon and Levi, Dinah's own brothers, revenged the insult. What Dinah thought of the whole matter is not recorded.

—Ernest Sutherland Bates, ed.,
The Bible, Designed to Be Read as Living Literature

*My name is Dinah. It is a desert name. My father was Jacob and
I was his only daughter, the only soft flesh, the only breasts to
bud from his leathery hands. Who would have thought that he
could have a daughter, but it was in his old age when his limbs
were also beginning to soften as if they had been chewed, as hide
is, by the teeth of time. Because I am a woman, I was not taught
to kill. To everything that happened, until now, I have only been
a witness.*

And Dinah the daughter of Leah, which she bore unto Jacob,
went out to see the daughters of the land to dance and to beat
drums. And when Shechem, the Hivite Prince, the son of Hamor,
saw her, he was overcome with love and he lay with her.

*Do you know about names? Do you think a name is merely
sound? A name is alive, has a life far longer than a life. It persists
in its own form, drags itself through the centuries, cannot be killed,
rarely dies out. Dinah is the desert, is harsh, inhospitable, sub-
stantial, and enduring. Sometimes Dinah is tents and skins, sometimes she is the mercilessly shaped rock. Once I did not exist, but*

afterwards Dinah exists for all time. In those who are born of me,
I persist. You who come out of Dinah are Dinah again. Dinah is
irrevocably Dinah to the end of time. Our name means "well,"
means "water out of the earth, scarce but sweet," or Dinah means
"bitterness," or it means "judged."

Shechem saw her and he took her and lay with her and he defiled
her.

Dinah is the turned wine, the spoiled meat, the parched skin.
Dinah is the mirage and the dry well.

And Shechem's soul cleaved unto Dinah, the daughter of Jacob,
and he loved the damsel. And Shechem spoke unto his father,
Hamor, saying, "Get me this damsel to wife."

Dinah is the desert, the merciless sun, the grit.

And the sons of Jacob answered Shechem and Hamor deceitfully,
and said, "We cannot do this thing, to give our sister to one that
is uncircumcised; for that were a reproach unto us. But in this
will we consent unto you: if you will be as we be, that every
male of you be circumcised; then will we give our daughters unto
you and we will take your daughters to us, and we will dwell
with you, and we will become one people.

I am Dinah. I loved a heathen. My brothers killed him. It was
thousands of years ago.

And every Hivite male was circumcised and it came to pass on
the third day when they were sore that two of the sons of Jacob,
the brothers of Dinah by Leah, took each man his sword and
came upon the city boldly and slew all the males. And they slew
Hamor and Shechem, his son, with the edge of their swords. And
they took Dinah out of Shechem's house. And they spoiled the

city and even all that was in the house and took their wealth and their little ones and their wives.

I know what is happening and what is coming. This has happened before.

. . .

My name is Dina. It's the name my father chose in memory of his mother, Dinamira. He never told me it had another history. I'm an American woman although I've never felt as if I have a country. When I was a child, New York was country enough, but later the city was insufficient to create a ground for me. It has always puzzled me that I think of myself as a wanderer and found a way of making a living which keeps me moving. It was as if I had a history which I'd forgotten or which everyone who knew me had taken great pains to hide. I have always been self-conscious about my name. I liked it but every time I heard my name called, I was startled, as if I were an impersonator, or were expected to be someone else, or, worse, as if another person were going to answer.

You see, I didn't always know Dinah. To begin with, I postulated her existence just to explain a certain restlessness within me, an unusual propensity for trouble, a preoccupation with rape and violence, and a constant attraction to men who were utterly alien. Also, there was a lot of violence in my life, a disproportionate amount given my upbringing and circumstances. I couldn't explain it, not even psychologically, although I have always been willing to take responsibility for the circumstances of my own life. It was as if the nature of chance had been altered—there were too many effects seemingly without causes—as if some destiny was interfering with happenstance.

Then one day, I was suddenly aware of things I'd always known. Maybe I looked up the story of my name out of curiosity in that Book. Of course, I'd read Bible stories as a child, but Dinah hadn't been in any of them. She wasn't important enough. The first thing that struck me about her story was that she was completely alone.

Unlike many women, I like to travel by myself. I'll drive hours out of my way just for solitude. One night when I was happily lost, I came upon a white wall materializing out of fog as if it had been conjured. It spread as far as I could see in either direction. To convince myself that it wasn't a hallucination, I got out of the car and approached the wall to reassure myself by rubbing my hand along its incontrovertibly gritty surface. Then I noticed that the road curved slightly, following, I presumed, the contours of the wall to some gateway. I didn't bother to investigate; from where I stood the wall was endless and impenetrable and I like it that way. I drove off, the wall disappeared; eventually, I came to familiar territory and went on.

I decided that I had come to one of those remote prisons, detention or refugee camps which are, in themselves, small walled cities. Beyond that wall was another autonomous universe, complete unto itself, governed by its own law. Maybe, I thought, this was where they kept sexual offenders and the criminally insane or where they had isolated the Japanese or the German prisoners during what I hope will always be called "the war." Yet, it was clear to me that the world which loomed there and then disappeared as soon as I turned my back impinged upon me in some way. Surely the wall, and whatever mysterious world it enclosed, had impressed itself upon me even before I arrived at its perimeter. Had I never seen it, still it would have affected me subtly, silently, irrevocably. And hadn't I been drawn there to learn that, at the very least?

In the past when I found myself lost, somewhere unfamiliar on a road which was no longer on my map, perhaps not on any map, coming up against a stone blank wall, after some moments of amusement, I would wend my way back to where I had started to take off again in the right direction. But at about the age of forty, the concrete world was no longer as engaging as the invisible. By then I had adequately attended to the material circumstances of my life—career, security, friendship—so I could step out on the second half of the journey accurately delineated by any number of ancient maps: the Kabbalah, for example. I was becoming intrigued by what lay behind the veil—or the wall—that is, the frontier between the outer and the inner worlds.

It was time to investigate it—but with the proper credentials—posing as a reporter, as a concerned and upright citizen, as an honorary member of a grand jury—so that I could enter the confines, go and come as I pleased, without risk of incarceration. I still wanted to observe the life behind those walls; I certainly did not want to live there myself.

I had come to the time in my life when like Dinah's father, the biblical Jacob, I had amassed enough practical experience to justify establishing my own turf. He had had to be sufficiently skilled in both husbanding and animal husbandry before he could wrestle with the angel and change his name. And it seems to me that Jacob was also forty or thereabouts at that time, for he had come as a youth, let's say of twenty, to seek a wife, and had worked seven years for Rachel, and got Leah, and then again another seven for Rachel, and then again six more for the herds of cattle he had been promised, altogether then, twenty. So, forty years old when he set out.

So this time when I came to the wall, searching out the place which had stopped me earlier, I called it "Dinah" as one calls the unknown and impenetrable "God." I preferred to call it "Dinah" because that name contained more mystery and less will, was smaller in its proportions, and my heart could reach to her because she was a woman. The name served the same purpose as the name "God." The act of naming created meaning and so I was no longer up against the wall.

But still I was constrained to face the inevitable mystery. For having named the world on the other side of the wall "Dinah," and having agreed to pretend that the wall was not stone but a living membrane through which it was possible to pass in two directions, it happened that what I thought I had invented as a convenience of mind or spirit or as a balm for inadequate materialism challenged me beyond my expectations. It seems that when you name the gods, when you invent them, when you imagine them, no matter out of what childishness or desperation, they do appear. It seems that before we invoke the gods, they are ghosts. It is our desire, attention, insistence which gives them flesh. I thought it was clever of me to pretend the existence of Dinah; I was infatuated with the idea of her. Oh, I was more arrogant than Reb Judah Löw of Prague. I was going to create a living woman from the vapors of my apprehension and imagination.

And then, in fact, she appeared.

Dinah, the bitch, with her rage and wondrous knowledge, her fury and great love was within me. Many thoughts, instincts, responses, reflexes, emotions, rages I was assuming were mine were really hers.

> Regard not them that have familiar spirits, neither seek after wizards, to be defiled by them. I am the Lord your God.

. . .

Dear Shechem:
So far I have failed you. In the actual living out of events, I have not yet been equal to the task. And so I am beginning again, in the only way I know, to conjure a world. This story is for you. It is of the first order of magic: from my desire, I will conjure you; from my love, I will conjure you; in this writing, I will conjure you.

When I first went to Nablus—they have taken your name from the city and given it this modern name—you, the one I had gone to meet, were not there. Even as I disembarked from the airplane in Israel and, later, driving with those other two, Sybil and Eli, upon the dusty road to Nablus, I had thought it was hopeless. After all that effort, I was afraid even in my heart that it was madness and that the end of the journey would be only so much stone and ruin.

I have been trying to tell this story for months and at each turn I have undermined myself by not recognizing the enormity of the task. I have to tell it to you, and I have to tell it perfectly. What happened, what didn't happen, what could have happened, what needed to happen, what will happen, what must happen, must unite in the imaginal moment when I walk away from my friend, Sybil, and from Eli, the guide, through the archway in the ancient wall toward the altar in the center of Nablus, formerly Shechem. I stand there staring, faithless, as you come across the dry and empty earth, past the shards and fragments, the bits of temple and floor, and recognize me as certainly as if we have met before. As you walk toward me, your dark brown eyes stare into mine, equally dark.

Shechem, this task is exceedingly difficult; I think it is beyond me, not only in the realization, but even in the conception. But, Dinah, who is directing this, is not constrained by the limits of my understanding. She persists, that is, she insists I go on.

Sometimes, one tries to create a world. Of course, like God, we fail. Still, like God, we persist because it is in the moment of conceiving that everything comes to be. Something, Shechem, is to be rewritten, something is to be retold; something is to be relived. Somewhere at the end of this journey, something and someone will be altered. Even if I can't recreate our history while avoiding its consequences, I still must try to bring our story to another conclusion, so that at the end, Shechem, you won't die and I won't remain alone.

Now, I am beginning to realize how carefully I must tell this, how I must set down each word as an invocation, so that at the end, the very story which created us, which I have come to live again, will, indeed, be rewritten and transformed. Then my name will no longer carry this pain. I do not want to live out my name again and again. I want to be certain that all the Dinas who come after me will not continue to suffer Dinah's fate.

At first, I tried to avoid the issue in the simplest way: I changed the spelling of my name slightly, hoping that disguise would be sufficient. I should have known better; ignorance has never protected me. Also, a name is a name and cannot be set aside. Until this moment, all of us who have been fated to relive Dinah's life have lived out her life.

When I went to Israel, I was playing with the gods. I was playing with story as if it were a trinket. I went to Shechem, our city, and I put my feet on the same earth that Dinah had walked on and I meditated there and I wept a little, but it was a farce. I went to Shechem as one goes to temple these days, hoping in advance that it will be empty of God.

The truth is, I was entranced with the thought of going to Israel to visit the ancient site of my birth to encounter a dead man. I thought it made a good story. It was just as if Dinah, having gone to meet the daughters of the land, had minced about, parading her beauty and clothes as she is accused:

Dinah went abroad to see the dancing and singing women, whom Shechem had hired to dance and play in the streets in order to entice her forth. Had she remained at home, nothing would have happened to her. But she was a woman, and all women like to show themselves in the street.

—Louis Ginzberg,
The Legends of the Jews

And why would Dinah have paraded herself before those women—your sisters—but that she was so needy for the company of women who danced for the gods. Dinah had been kept from Rachel, who'd stolen *teraphim* from her father, Laban, and the only other women about her were her bitter, dry mother, Leah, and the maid servants. Dinah knew that the gods were not necessarily in those carved figurines, but she also knew that trees, the Asherahs, those sculptures with arms upraised, the idols, the temples to Baal, the kine, all reminded one of the spirits and that the earth is sacred and alive. Making a house, or being oneself a house for the spirit, is as close as we can get to the gods; then we must wait.

Maybe, Shechem, I thought you still lived in those stones and I was also hoping Dinah was outside myself and would walk across the site to put her hands in mine and then I could make a movie and the mystery would all be over. Oh yes, that would be far less frightening than the nightmare I once had when a shadowy woman swirled suddenly to confront me with my own face. At the least, I wanted Dinah to appear as a *dybbuk*—stylishly dressed, of course. I looked for you the same way. Perhaps I still want you, Shechem, to appear in muscle and bone, in khaki pants, sporting a dark beard, eyes piercing as date seeds, hair curling under your shirt about your nipples, startling me with your perfect, if gruff, Palestinian English, slightly British in pronunciation, saying, "Dina, it's me, Shechem, don't you remember? I've been waiting for you so long, it seems like centuries." Such a meeting would recompense me for all the years I already lived out parts of Dinah's story.

It was when I came home from Israel, I realized, despite our failure to meet, that something had been altered. I knew I would never be raped again. I would not call you to me in the way the story had outlined. Maybe I hadn't altogether forgotten what Dinah had understood so profoundly—that while stones, handfuls of earth, trees, wind are not god, still they are. And though you weren't there at all, maybe you were.

So, Shechem, at first I tried to accomplish this task by avoiding it. I went to Nablus and I came home. Now we begin again.

I am being harsh with myself. I didn't avoid you deliberately. I was only insufficient in my desire. If I accomplished less on that first journey than was appropriate, maybe it was only because something far greater is demanded now. And I am driven, even as I sit here, toward that demand, word by word, step by step. Now, Shechem, after all these years, I am drawn toward you blindly and without companion, as each and any of us may be drawn into the dark labyrinth.

So, I traveled to Israel, then to the West Bank, to find your ashes, thinking I was overcoming all odds to reach you. Standing, finally, on the very spot where we had last been together, I was distracted by a bull, sacred to Baal and Baalata and other gods we have forgotten, tethered to a fig tree which they say marks the entrance to the underworld. I was pulled toward the great slouch of its loose hide, the heavy slap of its prickly pink tongue as it chewed the few green grasses in its circle. When it lowered its head, the horns of the moon jutted from its fierce head. But even as I forgot you, it seemed I remembered everything.

We had detoured to Jericho, then driven along the olive-tree-lined road and Eli said some of the trees were old as Abraham, that Jacob, Dinah's father, and Dinah herself, had passed them as they wandered toward Shechem to pitch their tents. They say Dinah was kept in a casket lined with soft linens, the lid carefully fastened so as to hide her beauty from Esau her uncle, so he could not invoke his right to marry her. The thick trunks of the oldest trees were bent and twisted and the ancient irrigation walls bulged from the expansion of thousands of years of roots pressing out for food and water.

It was to this same city of Shechem that Jacob had come to plant his fierce god, not as one plants a tree as a gentle bridge between sky and earth, but as one plants a lightning rod to hold the wrath of heaven. And it seemed to me that Jacob, once he had changed his name, held God before him like a torch and the land was scorched in his path and nothing remained but this fierce god. Then there was no more dancing and the women planted their Asherahs as outlaws while the prophets called wrath down upon them for their vision of a sacred world. Afterwards nothing belonged to these women anymore. They were no longer priestesses in their own temple.

By the time we entered the site and walked across the dusty ground, not knowing what to expect, I was out of sorts. I could no longer justify why I had raised hell, as Sybil put it, to drag us to this isolated and unengaging spot, surrounded by rusting abandoned cars and strewn with the twilight blue plastic bags used to wrap bananas on the trees so they won't ripen prematurely. So I was shocked when Eli approached to identify the flat stone surrounded by a few standing but broken plinths as the remains of a temple to Baal.

Then, Shechem, a line of Palestinians walked slowly, as if attending a funeral, in single file around the perimeter of what was once the biblical city which carried your name. Eli rose to his feet and tucked his khaki shirt carefully into his pants so that he looked just like the young soldiers who had directed us to this site. He might have been Simeon or Levi, alert and apprehensive as your brothers passed by, circling the ancient encampment, as if they were coming back from their herds to the confines of your city walls. In each instance, we were the interlopers. I didn't pay much attention to Eli's gesture, or maybe I looked away, regarding the hand sliding past the open belt to smooth the shirt over the stomach and buttocks as performing an essentially intimate gesture. Then I saw that small handgun on his belt. I had had to choose to enter Nablus with Eli, even though he'd insisted on the pistol, or not enter at all. All the other favors I'd been offered had had military conditions, and I had refused them. I refused them even if it meant that we would never meet, that I would never come home. I was not going into Nablus with the army.

The men had parked a school bus above us at the upper edge of the minuscule crater which marks the old city, and left the engine running. Eli scowled. "Gas is cheap for Arabs," he muttered. Otherwise he seemed a kind man, more than that, even gentle and shy.

The men in their *djellabas* resembled you. I searched each face. You were not among them. They didn't look at us, and the leader— for it did seem that they were in some formation, the line was so exact, the distance between each of them equal—carried an enormous watermelon. Well, this was either a guerrilla action—in seconds we might have been the victims of it—or some religious rite of the absurd. I fantasized that they were comic priests bringing the red and white bountiful breast of the Great One, praise be Her name, to the kitchen altar in a nearby stucco house. My attention wavered again; it was destroyed in the gulch between the melon and the gun.

Then I became preoccupied not only by the bull, by the parade, but also by Eli and Sybil, the two who had so generously accompanied me—not without, as each specifically informed me, some risk to their lives. I never believed them for an instant, not because I'm naive, but because I know we call our deaths to us and death was not among us when we set out. Eli was redheaded and faintly soft, like a man who keeps his strength up by eating *challah* rather than meat. Perhaps it was the white softness of his skin which set my teeth on edge. Sybil found him attractive. His gun did not reassure me or enhance him in my eyes. Don't misunderstand; I liked him, appreciated his knowledge and the easy laughter he brought to dispel the fear he also collected about us. But it was Eli's task to distract me; he, like his namesake, Elijah, was still the servant of the one God. Sybil, my golden vole, she was afraid. So they unconsciously collaborated, partisans in the historic alliance against the infidel.

And Elijah said unto them, "Take the prophets of Baal, all four hundred and fifty of them; let not one of them escape." And they took them: and Elijah brought them down to the brook Kishon and slew them there.

And Elijah said unto Ahab, "Get them up, eat and drink; for there is a sound of abundance of rain."

There's a photo of the three of us smiling outside the wall, the oldest, or did he say, the most intact wall from biblical times? It was taken by a young Palestinian boy who sold us counterfeit Roman coins. I'm in the middle, Eli is to my right and Sybil at my left. Our arms are about each other and from the looks of it, we might have been anywhere, Knossos, Pergamum, Cheops, the Great Wall of China. We appear to be ordinary tourists amusing ourselves on the West Bank. Eli's shirt is draped, once again, over his gun belt. Three people on an outing, academic types, spending their summer vacation visiting the ancient ruins. Only we are on a knoll, surrounded, as I was told we were, by hostile and alien people, not six hundred yards from Joseph's tomb, where a young Israeli soldier squatted on the dome, automatic rifle across his knees.

Only Dinah gave it the lie. Though invisible, she was present, she was the same as she had always been, her character remained intact. Those of us who are alive like to assume that we're unique, originals. It's not the case, though over four thousand years have passed. Sometimes a name comes to the end of its line, but most often when a man or woman dies, the name does not die. Sometimes when a woman is born, or a man, a name is born with them, as the name Dinah was born with Dinah, but when she died, the name, its pain, did not die and the story that embedded itself in the name lived on. Because that is what a name is. A name is a story. Had Dinah known this would happen, would she have been able to live her life with more care? Could she have saved you, Shechem? Was that her task?

And your name, Shechem, does it continue? As a city, it has died out. Can someone with another name still carry your story within them, that is, still carry you?

And what about me? If I could erase Dinah's story, taking it with me, into the grave, would I? Is that what I was trying to do in Nablus as the three of us smiled, seemingly unperturbed, into the camera? Did I attempt to erase us with that image? Is the essence of this photo the fact that you are missing? Either way, in the modern world, it's embarrassing, whether I came to Nablus to avoid a ghost or meet a man.

When I was standing in that empty crater which had collapsed onto itself under the weight of history, in the bowl which had been our city, an area no larger than the foundation of a contemporary office building, I couldn't find you, not within me nor without. So at this moment, in the process of writing this letter, I come to the task of magic, the painstaking creation of a world through language. It's an old and precarious tradition, the alchemical task of transmuting base matter into gold. And Dinah, not this Dina—writer, journalist, filmmaker, U.S. citizen—but the other, the one you knew, the one I didn't find in Nablus because she was so deep inside me that even I couldn't find her, she's the one, Shechem, when I think I am moving my fingers and my lips, she's the one who writes this book.

This is what brought me to Israel but depending on whom I was speaking with, I pretended I had come to visit Sybil or to make another prizewinning documentary, while I told myself I missed my friend, needed a vacation, and was glad the network would pay for it.

You know what magic is, Shechem. It is the capacity to act on one plane and achieve results in another. It is the capacity to enact an event of the psyche upon the body, or to enact in the psyche an event of the physical world. Magic is the ability to fuse realities, to establish an effective and consistent action in all worlds. Through magic you can kill with a word, or you can breathe life into a stone; you can make the dead walk again. Dinah, the one you loved and married, Shechem, did she become a little dry and wrinkled woman, cratered with disappointment? Did she live out her barrenness among dozens of nieces and nephews? They say she was married off to anyone and everyone who has ever been scarred. They list her husbands as Simeon, your murderer, also Esau and Job. Or was it, as I have come to believe, that she married her other brother, Joseph, after Simeon and Levi killed you, and with Joseph she lived out a final heresy as an impassioned and devoted priestess in Egypt.

Events in the psyche are authentic occurrences. Story is alive and all the rest of what we consider reality, the circumstances of the material or physical world, that which the gross and awkward hand can verify, those are only so much illusion. Do I understand this correctly? If so, can we begin here to invoke another story, another grid, another original and unalterable mold? And who will help me? Who will come to play your part?

PART I

Two women in one body descended the airplane. One of us lost heart and the other, though also agitated, was most determined. Even before I could see through the neutral camouflage of the airfield, I realized I was in Israel as an old man, who was pushing so violently to the front of the line that the rest of us in the aisles instinctively pulled back from him as if an explosion were imminent, leaped down the mobile stairs and prostrated himself on the concrete. When Dinah passed the crouching man, rage rose in her. She wanted to crush him like a beetle under her feet. But as I passed him, I swore under my breath because my cameras weren't ready and I'd missed a great shot. I wondered how he would fare passing through the official corridor which was still to be negotiated. What did he expect on the other side? His ancestors were not coming on donkeys to meet him. Just as I reached the glass doors, I turned back and saw that he was on his feet staring into the sky, reading the clouds, waiting for his God to show Himself, to lead the way. The sun would be going down soon—a pillar of fire.

I also knew the border I had to cross to enter this country was the border of the psyche and across that barbed wire frontier there

would be no aid from passports, guides, or experience. Beyond
those doors there really was no disembarkation lounge, no loyal
friend, no car to whisk me to a comfortable hotel. There was what
story promised: danger, desert heat, treachery, and loneliness. This
country is called Israel. Israel was my father's name but, in America, he gave it up. I don't blame him for wanting a prosaic name
without a history.

Where is the border between past and future? Where is the spot
where the two coexist? I must be so careful with what I write,
Shechem. I am not attempting to be faithful to history as I have
no illusions that history can be recorded. But since whatever I set
down may become manifest, I cannot be arbitrary. On the other
hand, I am also afraid that what I set down will not materialize
at all. In either case, I must be ruthlessly accurate according to the
necessity of the imagination. One false word and everything is
ruined.

I had walked across airfields hundreds of times, wondering—
but without deviating—what would happen if I broke out of the
unmarked but still precisely indicated path and tried to slip across
the border in my own time and my own fashion. Might I then be
entering another country? By the time I got to the air-conditioned
lounge, before showing my passport and walking through the
swinging doors as if into another world, I was comforted by the
international customs which minimize the differences between one
nation and another, so that the largest and the smallest, the ag-
gressive and the colonized, each pretend to the same face. Shifting
my heavy purse and cameras from one shoulder to the other,
unwilling, I don't know why, to put them down, kicking the rest
of the hand luggage forward, I indulged my favorite line game of
counting and recalling in detail the number of identical airports
in other countries where I'd passed through the same two-story
rectangular buildings, observed the same signal men in jump suits,
the same metal stairs, the same doors that clamped shut behind
me like a jaw. I had never questioned the essential convention of

host and visitor, through which tacit agreements about the nature of reality are established and from which we develop and ratify a set of expectations and behaviors.

I was coming to find my lover. Not any lover. Not a lover. The purpose of this journey was to find you, Shechem. Greater than my inability to believe in your existence was my inability to believe in my belief and understand its relationship to desire.

Sybil was waiting some yards before me behind the closed doors. She was pacing up and down. I had felt her anxiety as far away as New York, her nervous pull, strong as any force field in the universe. Friendship was the device which brought me to her in the middle of what might change any minute from a routine skirmish to The Last War, everything tilting toward extinction. In the belly of the current hostilities was that ancient indigestible seed, passed on with shit and gore from one intestine to another, from DNA to DNA, code after code. There was a war and the war had a war and that war had a war and so on.

First Dinah's brothers killed the man who lay with her, whom she had married and whom she loved. Simeon and Levi, killed you, Shechem, at her (our) own wedding, not before, but after you were wed. They were protecting her honor, they said, as they took all your sisters as slaves and concubines. Levi, for his deeds, became a priest and the priesthood was passed on from him through his generations. Anyone born to his family became a priest. Any man, that is. My father says we are of the line of Levi which means I am of the brother who killed his sister's lover and I carry the priest and the killer in me as well. If I had sons they would be of the line of Levi and promised to that priesthood. As I don't have children, it must be Dinah who informs me of these betrayals.

After Shechem's death, I had sons with Joseph. My sons, the sons of Dinah, are Ephraim and Manasseh. When the sons of their sons returned from Egypt with my bones, they claimed my lands as their own. The lands that would have come to me from Shechem

they also stole. They refused to honor Shechem and they calum-
niated his gods.

That was so many generations after the massacre of the Hivites
and my disappearance to Egypt, after the famine and their reset-
tlement in Goshen, that it was convenient to ignore my maternity,
to contrive their ancestry with speculation and fantasy.

In the collective memory, Asenath, my daughter, is sometimes
given to Joseph as a wife and Ephraim and Manasseh are called
Asenath's sons. They received Jacob's blessing before he died. Had
Jacob known they were my sons, would he have blessed them so
generously?

The distraction of counting didn't work. Something was stirring
in me under the surface, and an unfamiliar wanting rose up in me.
I told myself it was my impatience to be with Sybil after all this
time, but it felt as if I were wanting a mother or wanting to be a
mother. I couldn't tell them apart. That's Israel for you, I sneered.
Within seconds I'm breathing in the historic urge to be a great
nation, to multiply. How different would things be if we had
named this the Land of Rachel?

Rachel, my mother Leah's sister, was also Jacob's wife. She was
the one who had wept and wept, who had died in childbirth before
she could bless me, leaving Benjamin, her second son, to me to
raise. Well, Rachel couldn't leave him to Leah, could she, when
this sister, my mother, was both bloated with sons and still dry
with envy? She left Benjamin to me.

In the last moments of extremis before Benjamin was born,
Rachel pulled me to her, and, gagging with pain, blurted somewhat
incoherently into my ear the location of the stone figures, the
teraphim, the little household gods, which had guarded her well
until then. Hearing these last bleats of the white ewe, Jacob broke
through the tent, threw everyone out, even, or especially, me. I
fled for the gods but could not find the teraphim *in time to save*
Rachel's life, while Jacob delivered Benjamin with great sweeps

of his thrashing arms. Then Jacob bellowed as Rachel left him. Deprived then of Rachel, and also of her blessing, I took the teraphim as my birthright, and placed the figurines alongside the gods Shechem had left me.

The men bless the men and the women bless the women. Asenath had my blessing. I taught her what I knew: stealth, deceit, pretense, patience and hope. I put them in her womb. They were the sure gifts. I could not guarantee her the speckled cows or the wells or the gnarled olive trees. So I taught her magic. I wrote it in her womb as well. I gave her dreams. She was my daughter. She was the beloved. Asenath had Shechem in her veins and when I carried her, he lived inside my body also, though he was dead. I carried him as I had carried her. Not before, but from the moment of my wedding night, I carried him within me. The dead never leave our bodies. I was his nest.

Yes, I could feel Sybil twittering behind the glass doors at the far end of the passenger lounge. Two years of separation do not weaken the knots that fasten one psyche to another. I sensed her small female anxiety, the wary, furry, tremulous desire to see me, her expectation that my visit—she had never alluded to this out-right—would also save her. But even as I ached for Sybil, saying she ached for me, I also felt myself resisting, withdrawing, wishing the airplane doors would slide open, as in a movie run backwards, so I could be sucked up into my seat, hoisted into the sky, to be deposited once again in Manhattan, spat out there on safer soil. I must have let people rush in front of me because when I looked about me at passport control, I was close to the end of the line. And it was almost the Sabbath. As I am a stubborn creature, I had chosen this ungodly hour to arrive, knowing full well the pre-Sabbath hours breed chaos and that afterwards, just when one is ready to go out on the town, the country falls into an unbearable stillness. The couple at the very end of the line muttered disgrun-tledly. The wife nudged the man so he pressed forward against the man who then leaned against me, as if there was something one could do.

Before I changed my name in an attempt to distinguish myself from my father, née Israel, by rejecting his patronymic, my initials were D. P., Displaced Persons. The exiled, expelled, imprisoned always guard the edge of my dreams. At night, I travel with wanderers who are not permitted to wander, who are circumscribed by cities, settlements, orange groves, until they find themselves fenced in by the outer perimeter of fences which have converged to form a compound imprisoning them, but in the daytime I'm an American, and in me, this protest is sentimental and romantic. Your people, Shechem, crossed the deserts for centuries, following clouds, water, and history in routes sacred to the gods of movement, worshipping fire, lightning, and wind.

Waiting on line, I was trying to divine the precise dislocation which was about to occur, for dislocation was inevitable. I was diving into story, and trying to avoid history, that is, its authorized version which controls me while it is also forbidden to me or omits me precisely because I am a woman and, by nature, a heretic. Also I was daring a clandestine action, to love "the other," the forbidden one, to search him out, even to resurrect him.

When the Code was established, a widow who wanted to marry out of Israel or Judah was called an adulteress and stoned for taking her land to "the other." A widow was always forced to marry her husband's brother. And today, in Israel, a rabbi cannot marry a Jew to a Gentile.

I knew, Shechem, that if I fell into history as it had been codified, I would be abandoning the living story and, therefore, permanently dislocated, would be absolutely restricted to my own inner landscape which according to religious and secular law should not belong to me either. Once you enter that history, nothing belongs to you. You can be forced to live in a camp. You can be surrounded by barbed wire. Your own passports are not honored. You can't travel at will. Your thoughts are no longer your own. You are a person without a country precisely because you claim ancient but coextensive rights. The Jews understood this as they returned to Palestine against the refusal of the British, but then, it seems, they forgot. I had to make a choice as I stood on that line in the midst of everyone's impatience, so I would know how to answer the unvoiced question: History or myth?

The man behind me was pressing for my attention, but I ignored him. Standing in that line, I was leaving my old life and listing toward yours, although I told myself that you, Shechem, were merely the excuse that I had devised to arrange a long-overdue visit with my dearest friend. I also told myself that Sybil was merely the excuse that I had devised to find you, Shechem.

Everyone waiting, but me, was irritable and restless. Oblivious, the officer meticulously scrutinized each document, questioned each passenger. We understood the concern with security but soon as first one and then another passenger was asked most politely, "Would you wait here for a moment?" another mood gripped all of us: tenacity, determination, righteousness. Each one of us who still remained wondered if he or she would be turned away. And each one, admittedly including myself, was ready to fight to the death, to storm the barricades, as if it was the Exodus that had brought us here.

Was it my photograph which so fascinated the officer that he took so much time with it? Was it the face of a woman disguised to appear optimistic and cheerful? Or did he sense the basic treason behind the smile? I had selected the photo with great care, choosing one that exuded confidence, wholesome well-being. Maybe it was just my name.

"You have a biblical name, but you don't spell it correctly." He acted as if he was personally offended. "And your last name . . . ?"

"As it's written: Z. There's nothing more to be said."

"You've changed your name?"

"It's not uncommon in the United States."

"Only among the women, I understand."

"And refugees. We can only stand so much history." I gave him one of the dazzling smiles I practice in the film business.

"No stories, please. We have enough storytellers in Israel. This passport was issued recently, do you have your old passport with you? Why was it just issued, did it expire, did you *lose* the other?" He was examining each page of my passport, checking the dates of entry and exit, trying to determine, I assumed, if I had managed to slip into a forbidden country without having it noted. Even without formally crossing the border, only the white line freeing me from everyone remaining in the coffle behind, I was already under suspicion. I had, in my life, managed to enter forbidden countries several times without my passport being stamped, only to discover I had fooled no one with my stratagems as my entrances and exits were always duly recorded in an official file.

"Have you been to Egypt? Have you been to . . . ?" He reeled off a list of enemy countries. I felt Sybil straining toward me, her loneliness seeping through the doors of this anonymous, low-ceilinged entry lounge. I focused on the green seats I had last seen in the Athens airport, the carts like those in London, the pale green paint, scientifically determined to be soothing, the color which also covered the walls in thousands of hospitals and mental institutions.

"Why have you come here?" Everything he said sounded like code. Was he only pretending to be speaking the official language of bureaucrats and frontier guards or was it only my imagination that heard other questions beneath his questions? Exhaustion could do it, exhaustion and excitement could strip the insulation from the everyday exposing the numinous or the dreadful.

So, I thought, this is the first station of the journey: Passing the inspection of the record keeper. His job was to inscribe the names of all the returning prodigal children in the Holy Book. He had a lean, self-satisfied face, a moustache just outlined the shadow of a sneer and he wore his light blue short-sleeved Dacron shirt and navy blue tie as a priest, not as a rabbi, wears his dark cloth as a sign of service to the One.

Studiedly casual, I tried the official half-truth. "I'm making a documentary. This round is pre-production work, research, interviews, site location. . . . The impact of history and myth on people who reside on or near holy sites. . . ."

"Do you have all the permits?"

"Would you like . . . ?"

He did not like. It didn't matter. The week between Rosh Hashonah and Yom Kippur had just passed. For the next year, I had already been written in or out of the Book of Life. According to traditional belief, the Hebrew god had already settled everything and this angel's will—even my willfulness—meant nothing. If I were to live out the year, my fate was already decided and this officer was only a scribe; he had no power, though he was acting as if the decision was his. So if I were to meet you, Shechem, if you were alive, and if I were to remain alive for us to reenact our lives, it would be with His blessings. That caused me no small alarm.

My passport said, Dina Z. Birthplace: U.S.A. Address: New York City, N.Y. The officer examined it again and again. He looked up numbers in a black looseleaf notebook. He studied the other documents I put before him: forms, permits, letters of recommendation, invitations, financial statements. In not one of the documents would he find a trace of my ancient sojourn in Egypt. Now I was beginning to worry because I felt anger rising in me and it was not mine; it was within me, my heart beating, my face reddening, but it was not mine. Containing it was probably beyond me and I hoped Dinah would be tactful. I was coming back as one comes back from Egypt, hopeful, despairing, enraged.

Suddenly there was a turnabout. The angel glanced at the clock, decided he couldn't or wouldn't postpone the Sabbath, closed the documents, and handed them to me.

Then, Shechem, I walked slowly. This was not a moment which should be rushed. I could feel Sybil urging me on, quickly, more quickly, but I crossed that anonymous space, hesitated, rearranged cameras, purse, books, coat, allowed them to slip from my shoulders, and then rebalanced everything. I stopped to return my passport to its case, zipping it slowly, then deliberately fastening the bulky black leather purse. I was not trying to protect my valuables. I was stopping time. Then I walked across the line and returned to the country where my name and history, and therefore my psyche, was formed, where the history of almost everyone I know was formed originally. I felt a blast of ancient wind as I stepped forward onto the pedal hidden under the rubber mat which opened the automatic door and sucked me up into the maelstrom.

And there stood Sybil.

I had come back as if return were an ordinary event. There were tears in my eyes when I saw her. I gave myself over, letting the coat, bags drop to the floor. I fell upon her but even as I felt the joy of our meeting, I felt the enormous grief outside the terminal and my body recoiled from the soil itself. Through the glass sheets, I could see that it was almost sunset. The air was quivering with the blood of the sun running from the pursuing dark. They say She, the Shechina, the female aspect of God, descends in the blood time of the Sabbath.

Sybil held me up, then she pushed a cart toward the turntable. Soon my numerous cases tumbled down the shoot. Then we stepped into the damp twilight and made our way to Jerusalem. Sybil nestled into my arm, my elbow against her rib cage, her blond curls against my dark hair and we were the same girls we had been twenty years before when we had first met. Her nose twitched in the air, saying, "September, falling leaves, earth colors." Tomorrow, I expected, she would pull on her boots, shrugging apologetically, murmuring, "Fall." I knew it would be too hot for boots tomorrow, but she would persist and then, soon, in fact, it would be cooler.

Jerusalem is cooler than Tel Aviv. A climatic belt lies in the hour between the two cities. But it would not be cold, it would not snow. In New York, Sybil and I had often snuggled against each other in our second-hand beaver coats, walking in snowy weather from the Cloisters to the Village. I would come into her apartment, red-cheeked, like some peasant girl who'd been tending the cows in the icy barn, so exhilarated I could smell the dung on my fingers. Sybil was pale, white, snow itself. With her blond hair tightly curled about her head, she was the fine lady I was bringing milk. Then Sybil's hair had been a prim and orderly cap, but she had let it grow full and wild and it surprised and delighted me now. My face was lost in her hair; it was like a thorn bush. As Sybil moved us toward the car, I detected only the faintest signs of her usually cautious nature. She is one of those creatures that moves out nose first, sniffing danger, but something had altered.

Dinah pulled at me so I stopped to take a deep breath and I must have looked lost immediately, because an Israeli man stopped and asked, "What are you looking for?"

"I'm not looking for anything." I was startled to be noticed.

"Everyone who comes to Israel is looking for something." It was a casual remark and he walked on.

"That's the way they talk in this country," Sybil laughed and pointed to the car. "A station wagon. A big fat American station wagon. You must be an important lady."

"We are. We're making a film."

We were the last passengers to leave the airport. The sky was cobalt blue, intense, chemical, modern. The few pink clouds, the flounced hem of the Lady, the Shechina, had almost disappeared. The land was flat, the highway virtually deserted. Driving from Tel Aviv to Jerusalem was like passing through a war-torn country with everyone hiding indoors, yet the female god was everywhere. When we came to the city, we saw a few men walking to or from synagogue. From the road, I thought I could hear the hum of prayer. Nablus was off limits, almost behind barbed wire. When Dinah had left Shechem she traveled south through Jerusalem, Hebron, Beer-sheba to the desert. She'd never seen this road, had never been so close to the sea. I rolled up the window of the car; it was good to be inside with Sybil, close and safe.

I didn't recognize the hills. There was a tank on the side of the road which had become a memorial from an earlier war. The memorials are not dead monuments, they are living things. "Remember!" they demand. Memory is more than scholarship, it is an art and an obsession in this country. I was trying to remember something that had completely vanished.

There were four of us in the car. Sybil, myself, and two dead men. Sometimes people thought Sybil and I were lovers and now we had only these two dead men in the car to contradict that. You were there, Shechem, rammed among the luggage. And next to you was the stranger I'd never met.

Jeremiah Abazadik had brought Sybil to Israel through his death. They had been casual lovers when she'd been covering a human interest story in Boston for the newspapers. A fling, she'd called it. He was very skittish and she'd speculated he was married, "to at least one woman." Only she hadn't known him as Jeremy then but as Charlie, an odd name for someone with his accent, but he was always mysterious about his origins. She used to say that he pronounced his name like a boy imitating the sound of a rifle. Ch-arlie. He was attending a technical college at the time and then he disappeared or she returned to New York and he didn't write or call. One day she read in the newspaper that an Israeli folksinger returning to the Golan had stepped on a mine and died. She recognized him from the photo and fell in love. She went to join the groom. "It's a story, a great news story. You see, it's suicide. It's a damned good story and only an outsider can tell it," she said before packing her tape recorder and dozens and dozens of tapes and a few of her favorite clothes.

I felt Jeremy's breath in the place where my shoulder was almost touching Sybil. He was leaning forward. She leaned into the steering wheel and listed toward me a little. He wanted her and he was dead and she wanted him and he was dead. I could feel their mutual wanting. Sybil hoped that my coming would ease her. I knew it wouldn't; longing would awaken with her every morning, hard as sunrise.

"I have to go to Nablus."

"That's what you said in your letter. It's off limits, restricted to military personnel."

"I know. Still . . ."

"Be patient, Dina. We're not even in Jerusalem yet."

I laughed. Sybil laughed. It was the Sabbath, then it would be Sunday and I was crazy out of my mind with traveling and jet lag. My hair was disheveled, my face was dirty. I was both stuffed and famished, filled to the brim with that terrible airline food which is served as a distraction. I wanted a drink, a good meal, talk, sleep. I didn't even know where we were going. Then, maybe, it would be Monday.

"I haven't seen you in two years." I squeezed her arm. "Tell me everything."

The two of you shifted uneasily in the back seat. I didn't know how to tell Sybil about you, Shechem. I didn't even know what to call you, your name was so awkward on my tongue. I don't speak Hebrew, Aramaic, Arabic, not any Semitic language, though you wouldn't know it to look at me. My face is the same as Dinah's was—don't you think?—except for the modern expression, that determined, brazen look, my habit of staring. I was nervous about Jeremy. I didn't know how we'd get on. Charlie, I could handle, I knew about *puers*, but Jeremy. . . . Jeremiah had announced the victory of the Babylonians, had castigated the Israelis, had declaimed against the priests of Baal. I didn't know if the two of you would be friends or enemies. We hadn't asked your permission to cart you about so unceremoniously in adjoining seats or coffins, tightly packed between equipment designed to record what would soon disappear precisely because of how we were attempting to preserve it. As a documentary filmmaker, I was certainly guilty.

"What do you think, Sybil, how are people affected by living on a historic site?

"No. No. No shop talk. No work until Monday. It's against the religious laws to work on the Sabbath."

"Tomorrow, then."

"No. No. It's still the Sabbath. Monday."

"Sunday."

"It's against the secular and the Christian laws. Don't you understand the Sabbath starts with the Arabs on Friday and goes through Sunday in this country. There's no relief from rest and contemplation for three days."

"I have to get to . . ."

"Nablus. I know. Immediately. Yesterday, if possible. That's what you wrote. Didn't you come to see me? Can't you pretend you did?"

The car accelerated. The men lurched backwards onto the luggage. She recovered from her pout. "You're exhausted and a little mad, dear friend. I'm not going to tell you anything, Dina, because you'll forget it immediately. Your memory, you may remember, or you may not, is not the best under the best of circumstances."

I leaned back against the seat. "I love you, Sybil."

"I know you do."

The robes of the Lady were black, sequined with lights and stars. In a moment I fell asleep and I couldn't remember what I dreamed even as I dreamed it.

I was the one who had traveled for so many hours, but Sybil was
asleep long before me. I had insisted on unpacking my clothes
immediately, which amused Sybil who knows that I'm in the habit
of living out of suitcases. "Afraid, Dina, you'll leave in the middle
of the night?"

"Something like that. You've divided the drawers meticulously."

"I wanted to be sure you would have every incentive to stay."

"But you didn't install a private phone."

Sybil rolled her eyes in mock outrage. "I want you to give up
your bad habits and have a vacation."

I sat back in the somewhat easy chair and looked at Sybil as
she climbed into bed, but she lay down so I knew we weren't going
to talk. When she closed her eyes, I thumbed aimlessly through a
few travel guides. "Go to sleep," she mumbled and then she was
breathing deeply. I padded very quietly about the room, running
my hands over the surfaces of the furniture, fastidiously avoiding
her desk, looking in all the other drawers, in the closet at my
clothes and Sybil's, fondled the little objects she'd placed about
the room, even arranged our toothbrushes in the bathroom in a
favorite cup I'd brought, tried her new perfume, straightened the

towels, and put my hand-loomed shawl at the foot of my bed to accompany the russet silk scarf she'd draped over the desk chair. Trust Sybil to attend to all details. She'd gotten us the largest room in the hospice and had had an extra desk installed, one for each of us, under the windows. My desk top was still bare. Sybil's, of course, was not. There, just as I'd expected, was her journal, open as it had always been for me when she'd been in New York.

"Don't ask me," she'd insist. "If you want to know, read, but then, don't say anything to me about it, just pretend you don't know a thing." I glanced over at the open page and found a card on it: "Welcome Dina. It's been lonely without you. I've been talking to myself for too long. But go to sleep now, it's probably quite late." So I went to sleep too, leaving everything as it had been.

When I awaken . . . When I awakened . . . ? Is it past tense? Have we already met, Shechem? Is this a record or the original moment? I can't be certain which. I mean, have we met for the second time? When I awakened in the Scottish Hospice, I was not writing to you yet. The fiction of your existence hadn't insisted itself in my imagination the way you exist there now. Do you, at least, understand this layering of time?

"What time is it?" the pilgrim asked the great hermit living in isolation on the great mountain. "Time is strudel," the great one answered. "Strudel?" The pilgrim was devastated. The great one was silent for a long time, maybe eternity, then spoke again, "You mean time isn't strudel?"

I don't believe we can ever meet in this hospice, which is so plain and tidy. I only want/wanted to go to Nablus to see a few graves. And, of course, with all my protestations, I couldn't leave the filmmaker at home. I mean, I pretend it was a ruse that brought me to Israel, but, to be candid, I'd gone through hell to organize the making of that film. Dinah was the one who brought me there for her own purposes, using Sybil, film, and god knows whatever other pretenses and devices. Maybe she's always had her fingers on the strings of my psyche; she knows how to make me dance. But I barely detected her presence until I came there. It doesn't mean she's subtle. And it doesn't mean she's barely here. It only means I am/was dense.

Am I writing to a corpse? Not even a corpse anymore, not even bones. To an idea of a corpse. To an idea of bones which existed once. What kind of fool am I, sitting at a typewriter, pretending to be writing to a dead man although I know you can't call a man who's been dead over three thousand years a dead man. He's only an idea of a dead man. He's not even dust. I mean he's dust that's already become worms, oaks, roaches, jackals, linen, men, women. He could be me. It may not be Dinah at all, but Shechem himself, yourself, tangled in the DNA, directing everything not by direct transmission but through atoms, molecules, and cellular matter which has somehow acquired consciousness and wants to go back and look in the mirror. What if I looked in the mirror and saw your eyes? Anyway our story, then and now, is all a myth, isn't it? Even the Bible is the work of a superb storyteller, or a team, to be accurate. Storytellers don't limit themselves to authentic materials. I know that much about storytelling: if you want to tell the truth, you've got to lie.

When I awakened it was just dawn and I stood before the window for more than an hour, looking outside and then back to Sybil, watching her breathing in, breathing out, wondering if the window also breathed, or the table, or any of the small stones she had gathered from holy places. The plane is much faster than the spirit and though my body arrived, my understanding remained behind. That's jet lag, the body traveling on one wave and the psyche traveling on another. Sybil was probably dreaming of Jeremiah and his great rage. I stood beside her quietly inhaling her white breath. The sunlight was modest. When she turned, I was afraid she would awaken before I was ready for all of her. But Sybil, like other animal creatures, likes to sleep, her head on her paws.

I had fallen asleep eventually, agitating for the first hours, as one does when exhausted, between sleep and sleeplessness, and then I crossed that border too, visited by indistinct ghosts, visions, and phantoms. Maybe they were more of an odor, a smear of jasmine or rot in the air. Then, after a few hours I was awake again, wondering if it had only been a night that we had passed in those exceedingly narrow single beds.

Sybil, curled about herself in sleep, reminded me that certain tribes in Africa customarily offer an elderly woman a child to warm her bed. They believe no one should sleep alone, particularly the old. I've become used to it, own a wide bed, sleep with legs spread out, sometimes use satin sheets for my own pleasure so when I pull the pillow between my thighs, it feels like another thigh. Sybil slept soundly, her mouth partially open, a soft animal gurgle issuing from rounded lips, while her hand disappeared under the white pillow pressing it against her crown of blond curls.

I located myself by stating simple sentences. "I am standing by the window. Below, the garden is orderly, though the flowers grow in profusion. I cannot tell if the thick beds of marigolds or the tangle of tomato vines are tame or wild. I hear traffic, and a train and then the incongruous braying of donkeys." Soon, I hoped, I would feel at home without the need to identify the world.

Everything is in order. I don't know what is coming. Maybe there is something more to the Sabbath than a day of rest. Maybe, as they say, it is a time when one can enter this country of mind where, paradoxically, nothing can be known and also all knowledge, all time, all space coexist. Here, I must continually remind myself that I can't, mustn't, predict what is coming. There is a danger that I will avoid the real adventure—if there will be an adventure—by pretending that everything has already happened, by pretending that I know everything, when I don't know a thing. It is one thing to tolerate innocence within myself, but I must not be ignorant during this crucial time.

When the Israelites came out from the Wilderness of Sin . . . and encamped at Rephidim, . . . there was again no water. This brought out once more the cry of protest. Moses replied, Why do you quarrel with me? . . . 'Why do you try to test or challenge YAHVEH?' . . .

According to rabbinical commentary, when the Israelites failed to keep up their study and practice of the Torah or spiritual teaching, there appeared to be a lack of water. The people, not being able to discern there was a connection between performance and result, immediately projected their inadequacy on to their leader, saying in their ignorance that it was Moses who brought them out of Egypt and put them in this impossible position. Now the word ignorance can be seen to mean 'ignore,' that is, to turn away from what is known, which is a condition quite different from innocence which is not to know. . . . Those who are spiritually awakened or have experienced the miraculous, as the Israelites, can distrust, doubt or become ignorant.

—Z'ev ben Shimon Halevi,
Exile and Kabbalah

Despite the sounds from the city, there was a remarkable stillness as if the worlds I had known had entirely disappeared. I walked about on tiptoe but not only to keep from awakening Sybil, but to keep from awakening myself.

I am trying, though I've desisted, to introduce the present tense because I need, continually, to remind myself that I know nothing of what is coming. It is not tense, but time which trips me. In fact, already caught by one current, then by another, I cannot quite keep the decades and centuries discrete. I was a bit unnerved, more than could be attributed to traveling. Listen, when I arrived, Shechem, I could not distinguish what should have been so distinct—your imagined breath—from the breath of Jeremiah hot upon my neck as he leaned forward wanting Sybil. Did you want me, Shechem, as any human being wants another—as I want you now—or am I alone in this?

*You wanted me once and took me as if I were one of the speckled
kids my father, Jacob, wrested from Laban, my grandfather,
through trickery and magic. My father was wily but not wily
enough to do it without God. Since your death, I carry this wanting
in me; it increases and multiplies like Jacob's speckled flock. Wanting, wanting, wanting has been multiplying for centuries. How
can a woman as delicate and frail as I am, small-boned as a thrush,
you said, carry such great longing? When you took me, unlike the
goat, I was of slightly more value innocent than bearing. Nevertheless my life had been and was to be of no great matter to anyone.*

No greater reproach attaches to Bilhah than to Tamar seduced
by Amnon, to Bathsheba, seduced by David or to Dinah seduced
by Shechem. Hebrew myths treat women as fields to be ploughed
and sown by godlike heroes—passive, and thus necessarily guilt-
less if the wrong farmer should enter. Sexual prohibitions in the
Mosaic Law are addressed to men alone; and though proof of
adultery sentences the woman as well as her lover to death by
stoning, she is punished as an involuntary participant—like the
luckless animal with which a man has committed bestiality.
　　　　　　　　　　　—Robert Graves and Raphael Patai,
　　　　　　　　　　　Hebrew Myths: The Book of Genesis

I wanted to be alone, to be with Sybil, but also to be alone with
you, Shechem, and with you, Dinah, damn you. It was the first time,
Dinah, that it occurred to me that we might actually speak. When
I opened the window onto the English garden Sybil admired so
much with its pastel petunias, looking to the simply dusty orange-
petaled zinnias and the bright little white metal bench under the
willow, onto the carefully maintained walks through the abundant
vegetable and flower beds, everything arranged so thoughtfully, I
felt overwhelmed. Too much of a breeze. I closed it again. The
garden was empty and safe; why, then, did it disrupt me so? Hadn't
I been careful enough to avoid looking too long at the wall of the
Old City where life was already teeming with anger and chickens?

There was Sybil's journal on the desk top and this time I couldn't keep from turning a few pages. She had never used a loose notebook before and scattered among the pages in her own handwriting were very carefully typed pages, with an odd title.

I thought I'd known what Sybil was up to, but I hadn't. This Ch-arlie she'd talked about had meant more to her than she'd ever admitted. And he hadn't appeared in her journal at the time she knew him, at least not any journal that I had had access to. And still she'd claimed her life was an open book. But now he was more than a name, or a potential—lover? partner? spouse? What had she been wanting so strongly that had caused her to hide him away in the back of her mind? Jeremiah. I had not been wrong, there had indeed been two dead men in the back of the car.

THE TESTIMONY OF JEREMIAH ABAZADIK
A Posthumous Autobiography

I was born Jeremy Ezra Blazer. "My Jerry" is what my mother called me. I gave up the name Blazer as soon as I could because my mother wanted me to be a great fire on her horizon. I think she would have called me Moses if she wasn't afraid the name would also keep her from the holy land. When I was a kid, she lullabied me with heroes' songs to inspire me to great deeds. I was her Messiah, her Moshe Dayan. When I said I wanted to play the guitar, she bought me a toy rifle. Later when I insisted, she agreed because, "King David played a stringed instrument." The Nazis hadn't broken her; they had filled her mouth with the gold teeth of the dead. She had a nasty bite.

You want to know where I came from? Everyone always asks, "Where are you from?" They don't ask, "Where are you going?" I'll tell you where I'm going, where we're all going. To hell and to die. The question is—"When?" In good time.

I don't remember my father. As they took him away, he left me his shoes. I thought of dipping them in bronze and making bookends of them.

My grandfather taught me to sing all the songs he thought God wanted to hear. If I were to satisfy both my grandfather and my mother, I'd have become a ritual slaughterer.

My mother won't tell me how we escaped. My grandfather only sings, will not speak of Europe, Nazis, or boats. Whenever he gets tired of the enemy, he sings, "Oy veh." When the angel of death will come, he'll still sing, "Oy veh, darling, oy veh."

There are many secrets in my family. I had a girlfriend when I was twelve. Her name was Tamara. I watched her breasts grow in. Every day, she would take me to the niche between our two houses and open her blouse so we could measure the growth from the night before. When the first hair grew in my groin, I plucked it for her and she put it in her locket.

Did I want to be a singer? No, I didn't. But if you have a voice, you use it. It's simple. If you have a gun, you shoot; if you have a voice, you sing.

.   .   .

Then Sybil stirred. I held my breath until she burrowed back down into the dream again. Then I decided to brave it and went downstairs to the white bench to sit quietly until I could hear the clink of silver on porcelain and glass which would mean breakfast. From the bench the view ended at the stone wall about the British Embassy. The flag was up. Oh yes, this was Sybil's turf. She found it reassuring, like tea and friends returning, the perfect antidote for Jeremiah. Sybil had once mentioned in a letter how much she liked Anne MacDowell, who, just as I thought of her, was turning the corner to bring me morning coffee in a flowered china cup, as if life were ordinary and reliable.

"Did you sleep well?" She offered cream and sugar from silver servers on a lacquered tray. There was only one cup on the tray. "I hope you closed the windows, the donkeys are enough to wake the dead."

"This is an idyll. How do you manage to make Great Britain here in this country? I'm not surprised Sybil makes this a second home."

"Yes she's here whenever she's in Jerusalem. It's quite restful to chat in English and have a cup of tea, don't you think? Isn't it lovely here? Even though I've planted the garden, I still marvel at it."

"It is so well maintained, is that true of the rest of the country?"

"Well, we patched all the bullet holes; there were quite a few. Unlike others in this city, we don't care to remember their location."

"A little whitewash?"

"Yes a little whitewash is very satisfying. Come in for breakfast whenever you like until nine-thirty. If Sybil is in form, she will trip down the stairs at nine twenty-five."

Sybil was in form. I was waiting for her in the octagonal entry hall, doors, stairs leading in all directions when she tripped down the stairs, her eyes alert for the first glance of me. Her dress was copper colored and, surprise, no boots. Sandals on her feet.

"You've hardly slept. You can't be rested, you'll be crazy all day," she rebuked me.

"It doesn't matter, there's nothing we can do today."

"All the worse for me, having to put up with you." She hugged me, "You're always so difficult, Dina. Welcome to Jerusalem. I bet you ate it up through the window while I was sleeping. Thanks for keeping the window closed."

"I did open the curtains."

"Well, I was prepared for your bad habits. Let's eat, you're famished."

"I'm famished?"

Sybil laughed. We sat down. I wanted to talk to her about Jeremiah and I wanted to tell her my dreams immediately. I had been so lonely without her. But when I examined her face illuminated by the light reflecting upwards from the white tablecloth and silver, it occurred to me that she was lonelier than I was and I held back. Jeremy, Jeremiah, whatever his name is, had been no one to tell a dream to, dead or alive. After the first sip of tea from the shallow, round translucent tea cup, she plunged in, "Well, what did you dream your first night in Jerusalem?"

I was suddenly shy.

If Sybil were to tell this story, how would she remember our meeting? She'd invited me. Each letter ended with a demand that I visit. In the last letter, however, the excitement over my visit seemed tempered by allusions to her work. She was glad I was coming, but she had a schedule to keep up and she'd had experience before with my agendas.

"I've changed," she had written. Something made me uneasy. What was the change? She looked so very bright and cheerful, why did I repeat that phrase in my mind as if I were writing a novel, " 'I've changed,' she said mournfully." I wondered what she was thinking at that moment, how she would have breakfasted if I hadn't been there. How would she remember it later? Really all we had in the world was each other. And now we were together for the first time in so long. The fact of the breakfast made it seem so very familiar, so very ordinary. We were eating a thoroughly English breakfast, white toast, gooseberry jam, eggs, bacon, everything as Sybil and I had always done it. As if we weren't in Israel, as if we hadn't been separated, as if everything was as it had been. As if Dinah hadn't been there as well. How clever of Dinah, to sneak in so innocently, to dissolve herself in the familiar steam of coffee and eggs. Were she and Sybil in cahoots? Fat chance I had of putting out my hand to your hand, Shechem, which was hard, dark, and strange, when almost everything I encountered that morning, even the light, was so very familiar, everything arranged so that I'd feel perfectly, dreadfully, at home. And the braying donkeys? They were behind the wall.

"Well, if you won't tell me your dream, tell me what's going on? Is there any romance on the horizon? How's Anatole?"

Though she seemed genuinely interested, Sybil was also slightly distracted. She opened her eyes widely, stared determinedly into mine, but when I returned the look, she was not quite there.

"Anatole and I have had a sort of falling out, Sybil. You're not surprised, are you?"

"I always found him self-centered and ambitious. Very cute and very, very vain. What happened?"

"Oh, the usual, I got needy and didn't want to talk politics in bed. It's bad for my libido. He wanted 'to be friends,' he said, whatever that means. I think it meant sex and no involvement. Entertainment. Or it meant I'd be his media advisor and no sex. He didn't want to 'take advantage of me.' "

"Are you bitter?"

"Probably. I couldn't remember what I was getting out of the connection with him. He'd leave messages on my phone machine telling me he was thinking about me all the time. He'd never call back when I was home. I was always relieved."

"That's more than a warning sign."

"Look, he still took me to the airport. And was very loving! Do you think it was because I was really taking off? I think everyone is taking off. You're gone, too. It's an international plague."

She looked dismayed and turned her attention to placing the yolk of her fried egg on a square of toast. Then she sliced it precisely in half, the yellow flooding onto the plate. "No, I'm not gone, I'm having a book; it's like having a baby. You know. I can barely think of anything else. That's why I've been so hungry for you to come here. I couldn't write to you about it, it is hard enough to write the book. Though I'm grateful for what got into the letters. Writing to you was like keeping a journal. Whatever I know, you know."

She didn't blink an eye as she said that and continued blithely as if nothing might contradict the huge chasm I now felt yawning between us. "I found out things I never knew typing those voluminous sheets to you at three in the morning," she continued. "Did you mind? Did you read them all?"

"Every word. Twice, sometimes. I have missed you. I'm glad you wrote long letters. I'd tear them open at the mailbox and then, remembering how much they meant to me, I'd tuck them in my purse, zip it up so I wouldn't cheat, go inside, pour myself a sherry, sit down and then I'd read them slowly. But no matter how detailed your letters were, I never knew what country you were living in."

"A passion is another country, isn't it, Dina. You always said that. Whenever you worked on a film, I'd want you to send me a telegram telling me you were OK. Even if I was sitting across from you in your own living room, I didn't know where you were."

"Well, imagine what it was like thinking of you in Israel. I couldn't imagine it."

"I sent photos."

"They weren't enough. They didn't help."

"No, they wouldn't. I'm luckier. I know what your bed and office looked like."

"Are you coming home?"

"I don't know."

"After the research is done?"

"Maybe. I don't know."

"Do you like it here?"

"I don't know. The question doesn't make sense to me."

At the next table, a man tipping a brass coffee pot some height from the cup watched intently as the dark liquid streamed out of the bird's beak. He was tall, thin, white-haired. Danish, I fantasized. Seated, he looked like he might be seven, eight feet tall. There goes the imagination. I guessed that he was there to climb some of the Biblical mountains. I liked his face, the cheekbones were the polished rock he would edge up, his hands and fingers tense against the surface. Under other circumstances, I would have pictured myself climbing his body looking for handholds in the hidden crevices. I was staring and so he looked away; I do stare.

I didn't think he was you, Shechem, though you could have been even more disguised than I am, a completely foreign body. You might be a rock, a wet and salted limb of granite, the orange, delivered daily from the West Bank or Jordan, luminous and innocent in the blue china bowl in the center of our table. I could have bitten into the peel, eaten you whole, and gotten it over with.

"Your dream?" Sybil persisted.

I felt as if I were opening a wound. I'd become accustomed to not being known. No one has ever known me as well as Sybil has. When she was gone, I'd had to do without.

"I didn't have time to dream."

"A lie. I know you dreamed, you always do."

"I had a baby but got distracted and forgot about it. Though it was just born, it slipped from my mind. Neglecting to nurse it, my milk dried up, and by the time I remembered the child, it was too late. I couldn't nurse it any longer. I did put my nipple into its mouth. It had become permanently elongated and hard, but, for all the infant's sucking, nothing came of it."

I should have gone across the field to find Joseph, who was always off by himself. My brothers hated him, thinking that by God's trick, or Rachel's witchery, he would get everything and they would have nothing, although Leah was so vigilant everything already belonged to them. "An ugly woman must be well cared for," she taunted Jacob and he didn't dare argue with her. Her body compelled him. He couldn't distinguish his need for her angry hips from his need for sons. To tell Joseph my dream I would have had to acknowledge my new breasts to him.

"When you neglect others, your own source dries up." Sybil looked at me with tears in her eyes. "When you're not dreaming about vagabonds, drifters, and wanderers, the lost ones, you're dreaming about children. Maybe all your dreams have children in them, children being born, again and again, infant upon infant, and you never remember." She looked away and then the Dane caught her attention, his eyes dropped over her body, and afterwards she seemed more animated.

I also couldn't avoid seeing the age lines about Sybil's otherwise stately neck. I know where the lines are on my face. There are some about the jaw because I grind my teeth at night and set them determinedly during the day. And there are lines about my eyes and about the mouth. I like to think some of them are laugh lines. Children? Neither Sybil nor I have children. Maybe in a few years. She has more time than I do, all things and biology being equal, which they aren't. I fantasized the child she could have with the Dane. The child would be so very white. I don't know how many years I have. I'm not Sarah or Rachel. Modern medicine doesn't match God's ability to prolong or extend fertility.

Dinah was fourteen when she married. And I was fourteen when I took my first lover. When we met again, ten years ago, he marched confidently into my apartment to stare at me as if I were a statue which had been stolen from his collection. To verify my authenticity, he asked, "It was real, wasn't it, what we had between us?" I considered returning myself to him on loan. He doesn't have children either. Jeremy had no children. Maybe no one has children any longer. *Fin de siècle.* Does one stop having children when one realizes it is the end of the world? You hope you will die before the bomb goes off but you can't be sure you can protect your kids from that ending and it's too awful to risk. Is that what the dream meant? Children? I can't think about them.

I only remember one of your brothers and sisters, Shechem. There were flocks of them. You were the oldest. Bonah was the third. Her eyes were as dark as mine. We thought we were the beginning of the world. I was Jacob's youngest, except for Benjamin whom I suckled.

Joseph and I were born within minutes of each other with Jacob waiting outside the two adjoining tents listening to the two sisters screaming. My birth was of no concern to him. Leah had so many sons, I could have been another lamb breached in the field, but this was his first by Rachel whom he loved. Imagine the scene: The two tents are adjacent because the two women cannot be apart though they hate each other. Outside Jacob is standing, facing the tents, listening to the groans, pretending that they are equal, but there is only one cry he wants to hear and then he hears it. It's Joseph. I must have heard him as well through the last crunch of muscle bearing down upon me, for they say I was born to Joseph's piercing screech. They say that I was silent, that when my mother, Leah, the bitter one, took me up to nurse me, I turned away.

Leah was the chronicler of dissatisfactions. She always reminded me that it was hours before Jacob came into her tent and that he reeked of Joseph. Lifting me out of my linens, he outlined my belly and the delta beneath, as Joseph and I later, as children, had the habit of touching our bodies as if they were maps drawn with a finger in the soft riverbank clay. Awkward as a boy with his first woman, my father pressed me against his chest; I was cradled within his robes, naked against his ribs, my mouth against his dry nipple. He rocked me until I finally began to cry and Leah turned away and Jacob gave me to Zilpah, her handmaiden.

Jacob carried both of us like twin towers on the stone wall of his shoulders, Joseph on the right and me on his left. He took us over every dunnum of land, teaching us both the name of each plant. When spring was tender, he took us to the cows and ewes and guided our hands so we could lead the calves and lambs out of the bloody sockets. Leah screeched at him, said he was mad, tried to keep me home.

When you died, Shechem, it was the end of your pure line. Levi killed everyone, even the old men, including your father, Hamor. And all the boy children, even those who were young enough to make good slaves. That was the beginning and now we're at the end.

Would you like a cup of coffee, Shechem? I can ask the young Arab boy who is waiting tables here to set an extra place for a dead friend who might arrive.

"Do you remember my dreams, Dina?"

"That doesn't seem half as difficult as remembering my own. I remember your night dreams and your day dreams. In the night, you dream about horses, stampeding horses, fabrics tearing, things falling apart. Once in a dream, you were circling your neighborhood until you came to a round room, or a round house, or a gazebo where all your relatives had gathered for a formal dinner or a funeral. No one spoke and no one noticed you. Sometimes in your dreams everyone but you is deaf. The furniture is highly polished. That's a common image, you are always hoping your dream maid will come into your real life. Once a light was shining so brightly, the stairs went up in flames. Then the attic was on fire. Also the mountains. You didn't want to save anything. Your pockets caught on fire and you thrust your hands into them. Soon your body was burning. You felt no pain. You could see no ashes, only the flames. In your dreams, everything is always on fire."

"You know me better than anyone else." Sybil lowered her head to her tea, breathing in the steam.

"What does my dream mean, dream teller?"

"You neglect your instincts, Dina. They're fledgling to begin with and even so, or because of that—I can't tell which—you ignore them. There's nothing to feed them and so they die."

"The child didn't die in this dream."

"It's not going to live long without food. What is it going to get out of a hard, swollen, angry teat?"

"Whenever I follow my instincts, you discourage me."

Sybil mocked me with a patient, long-suffering look. Then she put her hand on my arm like a good mother and chided me. "Instincts? Instincts have to do with survival, self-preservation, attending to basic needs. They have to do with food, clothing, and shelter. They do not have to do with hunches, wild intuitions, fantasies, adventures. They do not have to do with risking your life; they have to do with preserving it. Give the kid a chance, huh?"

I knew why Sybil was crying.

"If I lose you, there's no one else. I've no one left in my family, Dina."

"You're the one who's moved away."

The Arab boy brought more hot water in one silver pot, coffee in another. I wanted the coffee in the brass bird, but the boy didn't speak enough English for me to make the request. Anne MacDowell hadn't anticipated that an American woman might want Turkish coffee. Sybil was very specific that she wanted everything the way it was at home. We heard the gentle crunching of a car slowly driven over the gravel to the embassy next door. A rooster crowed out of tune.

"What's the gossip, Dina?"

"Well, I do have money to make this film. It's not enough, but that's usual. I wrote you in for a small salary—we get all our meals and accommodations paid and, best of all, I return in a few months to shoot. So we get two visits at least."

"I won't have to do anything? There has to be a price."

"You get me to Nablus without my having to go public to arrange it."

Breakfast did not give me energy. It tired me and we went back to the room. Sybil was ahead of me by a few stairs, and both of us were sliding our hands up the polished white bannister wondering if the other one wanted the Dane. I lay down on my bed to rest and pretended to sleep while spying on Sybil through partially closed eyes. At first she sat quietly on her bed, arranging pencils, smoothing scarves, fingering the bedspread, smoothing ripples, until everything was orderly, though she was not concerned with fabrics, but lost in the pale yellow hue of her dreams, lost in Jeremy Abazadik. She glanced over toward me, disappointment showed on her face. My arrival had not rescued her from her obsessions. Even as we breakfasted, I could see that Jeremy would not let her alone. He filled her thoughts, he nagged at her. As much as she loved him, it was not sufficient for him; he wanted to possess her totally. I had known that yesterday as I felt his breath upon her, although when he'd been in the flesh he had seemingly not wanted her at all.

I didn't stir; she observed me for awhile. I could have tried to read her thoughts precisely, or spoken openly to her, but I didn't want to abuse the privileges of friendship. She would tell me everything in her own time. In the meantime, I was wondering why I had come.

Suddenly my thoughts scattered, or rather there was an explosion or a burst of electricity. I could feel the neurons firing, a sensation of brilliant sharp white light—felt rather than seen. Afterwards, there was nothing, emptiness, then a voice, autonomous and confident. Dinah was talking bitterly. She did know everything I was thinking, no matter what I said or did. I wondered if Jeremy was the same, if Sybil who was sitting there with similar outward calm was being assaulted by an inner barrage.

In your heart, Dina, you are not capable of belief. You don't believe in me or in Shechem. You act as if you are making him up. What will you make him up with? Even God had to use clay. It is said that women were intricately carved, patiently fashioned, the finest scrimshaw on live bone that breathes, has marrow and blood. Do you think you can make a man out of words or clay or bone? You will have to make blood, heart, sperm, fear, all of it and you haven't even learned to conjure. You're not a witch; you're only a woman harboring a witch. I'm the witch. There is no way you can make a man. When you meet him, if you meet him again, it is because I will bring him to you in the flesh.

Dear Shechem:

Sometimes when I'm alone, I think I hear Dinah's voice. I dismiss her pretending it's my own cackling. I'm lonely. Even in company. I live under enormous pressure. Naturally, the mind develops fine line fissures and cracks a little. So, when I hear her voice, I assume I've cracked. Then I hear her again. I complain. She laughs at me.

Dinah was lamenting in my ear, telling another one of her stories I didn't want to hear. It sounded like it was Dinah speaking but then I knew it had to be my grandmother, Dinamira.

I lived in the last stone house in the crooked street that was permitted to the Jews. On humid nights, we could smell the pigs from the neighboring village. One night, the Cossacks pulled the women out of the houses, ripping their shaitls *and* babushkas *from their heads, to tear at the stubs of their hair as they trampled the women in lust in the fields. Your father knows nothing of this, he was an infant. Your grandfather was away. That was the only sign of God's grace.*

When he returned, I lied and told him that I had hidden successfully under the children's bed in a pile of urine-soaked rags, so the Cossacks thought I had already been taken because all the children were naked and screeching. He asked me why I hadn't hidden the boys before I hid myself. I was silent. That night I told him the terror had brought my period on so we slept in separate beds until I went to the mikvah *weeks later after the blood really came. Without telling him, I washed in the river each day though it was winter. Had he known what had transpired, he never would have slept with me again even though he wanted more sons. I made sons the way cows make butter. My neighbors did not betray me, and I did not betray them. The women, I mean, we did not betray each other. We knew what kind of men we had. They were moral and holy men and such men are not necessarily kind.*

This is a form of the madness, Shechem. Other lives bubble up into mine as if they are mine, dark iridescent bubbles rise through the centuries as through a pool of tar. Then I am forced, also, to remember my own life. Dinah is harsh. She does not comfort me.

Why do you shudder, Dina? Why does this story alarm you so? When you were raped, my dear, did your kind lover take you in his arms and stroke you tenderly, washing the rapist's sperm from your mouth with his own tongue? Or did he look at you from that day on with scorn, having decided that now he would never have a child with you? Once a bitch has been spoiled by a mongrel, they say, she will never have a pure litter. How did you feel when he mounted you, laughing, "When you fall off a horse, you've got to get in the saddle again." When you awakened in the morning,

you didn't feel clean. He could have wet his fingers in his own
mouth to clean you of the gun and of the sperm.

Shechem, whoever you are, in whatever form you have, does it
happen to you, I mean, does he come to you the way Dinah comes
to me? Did she set up these rapes so I'd know her life?

You think I enact these stories in your life. You want to think you
do not suffer them on your own account. You want to keep think-
ing we're separate. We have one life, lived again and again. It gets
translated into different centuries, different languages, seemingly
different characters. The same structure, my dear, the same story,
again and again. You think you ought to live a protected life, free
of bitterness.

    You have to know the story as you're not immune to it. You
say you are possessed, that I bring this darkness to you, otherwise
you would always live in the light. Even at fourteen, I was not so
innocent. It's easy to accuse Dinah; it's easy to accuse a woman,
isn't it? An old habit.

    I wasn't raped by Shechem. After Shechem was killed, Simeon
took Shechem's sister as his booty and there was rape forever in
the world. They say I married Simeon. Imagine that horror—
Simeon writhing on me while Bonah, Shechem's sister, who is
forced to wait on us, kneels at the foot of our bed and both of us,
women, with our eyes open.

I was back in the room watching Sybil through half-closed eyes.
She began to leaf through manila folders she retrieved from under
a champagne silk slip and very sheer pale stockings at the bottom
of her suitcase, which was serving as a file drawer. Then like a
gypsy preparing to read cards, she took out photographs from her
desk and arranged them about her in a half circle as she sat crosslegged on her bed. Sybil is a little girl who must touch everything
she loves in order to feel safe.

    Propriety demanded I keep my eyes closed, but curiosity over-

came me. Was she still pretending to herself that she'd come here
to work, using Radio WAAA as her cover? She held up a photograph. I could see by the way she stared, then touched his face,
that Jeremy had her.

I'd have had to come here even if Sybil hadn't blazed the trail—
or gotten lost—whichever it was. If she'd been in New York, I
would have wanted to bring her with me even though I always
travel alone. I have four suitcases—winter, spring, summer, fall—
packed on standby; I am ready no matter what the weather.

Everyone is brought to Israel by the dead, who want to control
everything. History is simply a euphemism for that tyranny.

I'd lost control of my direction. Here I was apparently mid-road,
asking as everyone inevitably does, "Is this it? This? *This* is *it?*"
Nevertheless it seemed it was precisely *it*. I could recite the formula:
There is a call, a going forth, a getting lost, a need to sacrifice. . . . Like everyone else, I refused the call at first. So there was
another call, more insistent. Jeremiah had also tried to get away,
saying, "Listen, God, I'm just a child. I can't speak." After I said
repeatedly, "Not me. I'm the wrong one. I've no interest in such
things," I found myself on the road. It was no big deal.

For a long time, Sybil sorted those photographs, newspaper clippings, notes, transcripts, I don't know what else, clearly all related
to Jeremiah Abazadik. She wrote intermittently, reshuffled papers,
lost herself in thought. There was about her again that air of
efficiency which I always relied upon. Sometimes she turned away
from the pages and stared out the window and then played with
the photographs, arranging them and rearranging them endlessly.
Her journal was nowhere in sight. It seemed to me she was trying
to retrieve something she had lost. I felt as if she was trying to
reconcile what she was learning with the little bit she knew from
the flesh she'd held, from the brief conversations they'd attempted
over cold coffee in all-night coffee shops. He always met her on
street corners at odd hours and never took her to his house. She
would have believed him if he'd said he lived on the street. She

would have believed anything he said. "This relationship—it's no relationship—will come to nothing," she confessed the one time she'd mentioned him. "He's a man without a country. He's jumped ship without a passport. You can't ever get a handhold when there's no ground beneath a man's feet."

I wanted to tear the papers out of Sybil's hands and berate her as a proper older sister would: "You have your entire life ahead of you. What are you doing here? Your career is going to hell. Live, damn you." That or something else equally patronizing and banal. She continued to tell her fortune with the photos and I pretended to be asleep or maybe I dozed.

I had no sister except, briefly, your sisters, Shechem, who oiled my body before we married, stained my fingernails with red berries, and braided my hair in flames as if it were the sabbath candles which are lit when the sun goes down. After you were killed, they reviled me when I passed in my brothers' fields. Their magic had had no power against Levi. Their berries had not kept away the evil eye. Still it had been more appropriate for them to bathe me for my wedding than for my thin, bitter mother to give me as a gift. When she turned from me in the birth bed, she turned fully and forever. I could feel her spirit curdling as my approaching wedding day reminded her of her own humiliating wedding when she had had to dress to disguise her eyes. Unlike my mother, I knew I was the chosen one. You had already seen my face, Shechem, and knew my body. Asenath was already within me, already named. You had pulled me down on the earth among the gods as the goats couple, as the ram insists himself upon the ewe. Then your sisters had come out of hiding, surrounded us, drumming. Afterwards, you went to my father and requested my hand. We had arranged that between us in advance.

I opened my eyes and sat up in bed. Sybil had removed her blouse, revealing her soft full breasts, the ripe, fragrant oranges of her body which Charlie had clearly never fully appreciated. It was going to be warmer than we had expected. She put on a robe.

"I'm going to tell you a story," I said.

"I like your stories." Sybil pretended to be relaxed as she carefully gathered the remaining papers and put them out of my sight.

"The last time we had dinner together, we met in that little Italian restaurant on MacDougal Street you always choose for formal occasions, celebrations, and announcements. I didn't know what to expect. You were so calm it was unnerving. For a long time you seemed to have nothing to say while you carefully aligned and realigned the heavy silver knife, examining the width and sharpness of the blade. Then you giggled because you had a date and you were going to be very late. You kept saying you would call him, but you didn't."

"It's good to be reminded. I'd forgotten it all."

"You said, 'I'll call him in a minute and tell him I'm midway through taping an interview, and can't stop.' After all the years of friendship, I was still flattered that you'd rather be with me than whoever he was. I asked you whom you would say you were interviewing.

" 'Someone important. Yasser Arafat.'

" 'He's in Lebanon today.'

" 'Are you sure? Someone else, then. I'll think of it when I'm on the phone. Listen, he won't know where Arafat is.' "

"Did you ever call him, Sybil?"

"I never called."

"We went on with the meal. Anchovies and peppers, garlic soup, scampi, pasta, tortoni for dessert, lots of espresso. It was a perfect celebration except I didn't know why we were there. Then you picked up the knife, carefully wiped the blade, put it down, wiped the other silver with your napkin, reset the table. You were admiring your golden fingernails. You looked at your ring, the same one you're wearing now, moved it from one finger to another. 'Pretty, isn't it?' you asked."

"You're making this up, Dina."

"You said, 'I was reading the paper yesterday and came across an article about an Israeli singer. I don't mean he was born in Israel, they don't know where he was born, or how old he was, forty I imagine. . . . Did you see it?'

"I remember your words exactly, Sybil. After all, they changed my life. You were speaking suspiciously matter-of-factly as if you were telling me about a radio program you were going to do."

"I was."

"I knew better. You're a weasel. 'He was a singer,' you continued. 'Did I tell you that?' That was the clue. Years of radio training kept you from ever repeating anything, also always brought you right to the point. 'It seems he disappeared for some years. He was in the States. He'd had quite a reputation in Israel and Europe. It happens that we were lovers in Boston. Remember I'd told you about a short-lived affair with a man who'd never sleep with me on Friday nights? I knew him as 'Charlie,' an inappropriate name for him. My guess had been he was from Hungary or Czechoslovakia. Well, the paper said he returned to Israel a few days ago, went out into the Golan where he had once served in the army and, knowing the land, had walked very deliberately onto a mine and blew himself to heaven.'

"You continued as if we were talking about a routine assignment. 'I'm going to Israel tomorrow. Will you take me to the airport? I want to meet him.' You did laugh nervously at that slip. 'I mean, I want the story,' you corrected yourself. And then you asked me to send a few of your things after you."

"You're the best wardrobe mistress I've ever had."

I closed my eyes and fell back onto the pillow. For awhile I didn't say another word.

"You went home and were waiting for me in the lobby when I arrived in the morning. At the airport you insisted I not see you off. You'd been silent for the entire ride. I assumed you'd be home soon, until the letters came. When I entered your apartment to dispose of your plants, as ordered, and pick up your bills, etc., I saw the evidence of the last night: one pillow still horizontal at the head of the bed on the right side where your lover had slept and your pillow, vertical lower down, as if you stuffed it against him where his belly and arms might have been. I guess he wasn't a light sleeper. Your note to him was crushed into a ball on the floor beside a few broken cups, plates, and glasses. I heaved them all into the incinerator. Weeks later, according to your instructions, I sublet the apartment. Then I packed up your clothes, keeping the few I admired for myself, some books, and that antique bronze coffee pot I'd bought you some years ago, exactly like the one they serve Turkish coffee in here. Some stuff I sent, some's in my apartment, some's in storage."

"You are a dear friend."

I sat up straight, got off the bed, went over to the photographs, picked one up.

"What do you know about this man after all this time?"

Sybil turned to me in her most confident manner. The rabbit was gone, the journalist installed.

"To be brief: Jeremiah Abazadik changed his name from Jeremy Ezra Blazer. Occupation? Singer. Marital status? Single. Birthplace? His mother won't say, won't even reveal his birthday. I think she was in the States when he was born and then made a tactical error, went back—to Europe—in the early thirties to be with her family and then . . . ! Political affiliations? None. Cause of death? Explosion. Cause of death? Suicide."

"You're writing a biography, just as you've indicated in your letters?"

"Yes, the only *and* the definitive story of his life. If anyone else were thinking about doing it at the moment, I'd have heard by now. I've contacted everyone." She drew out "everyone" so that I knew that she meant it and also that everyone knew that she was claiming this territory.

"A straight biography?"

"Very straight. It has to be—he was such an odd man."

"Anything else?"

"A lot. A little."

"There's more, Sybil, I know there is." That was as much as I could say.

"I'll tell you bit by bit, Dina. I don't want to blow my story. I'm going to make some calls."

"On the Sabbath, Sybil?"

"I do have a few unorthodox friends."

When I was in the car, I wanted Sybil with me just as much as I
wanted to be alone, if the state I was in could be called being
alone, beset as I was by two voices, two inclinations, two perceptions, two different sets of knowledge and experience. From the
moment I left the hospice, Dinah would be looking for someone.
Were you looking for me, Shechem, as I looked for you, did it
even occur to you that we existed or don't you give a damn about
history?

The Old City has been destroyed at least twice. Outside its walls
the new city spreads out and spreads out and spreads out like
linen. The new city has no walls about it. What protects it? you
ask. Guns.

I tried to concentrate on the streets, but I was preoccupied. I
wondered if Sybil had caught me eyeing the Dane as I'd caught
her and whether she could imagine that I intended him for her. In
the past, we had tossed coins and said, "No hard feelings: go for
it!" This Dane was of no account. He could not have separated
us the way Jeremiah—or was it Shechem—was already keeping
us apart. That was why I couldn't get close to her: Jeremiah had

imposed himself between us. A tall, white-haired man who knew about mountains would have been a relief, even a stockbroker or an engineer, someone who built bridges and other real things.

I'd been in the country less than twenty-four hours. I'd seen nothing yet except the few blocks I was driving about. I already hated the country. There were quite a few soldiers carrying sub-machine guns. I could have had a son the age of those boys in uniform who were gathered on the street corners not unlike the way my friends and I used to hang out beside the candy store in the summers before I was fourteen.

I began to pay attention. It was like pulling myself back into time and place; it was comforting to focus. Then I was pulled apart. The familiar—the shape of a loaf of bread, a deli that could have been in Brooklyn—soothed me, just as the equally familiar whiff of ancient incense I'd never encountered in this life made me distraught. I was drawn and quartered, my memory, my heart lunging backwards as my mind raced ahead, each loathing the other for its affiliations.

Shechem, can you understand what it was to be alone in the streets of that too familiar, too strange city in a country I had always refused to visit? My father's entreaties to 'go back' had always set my teeth on edge. I looked at my reflection in the store windows, trying to place myself among the shimmering green plates, the romantic odalisques leaning one onto the other, the silver wine goblets, the ubiquitous filigree hands set with blue stones against the evil eye. I was pretending to myself to be interested in the merchandise, the shoes, the unstylish dresses, the jewelry, even the reflections of the soldiers, lounging but alert, at the street corners. But I was trying to catch my own eye, I was trying to make a stand, here, in the fourth quarter of the twentieth century, in Israel, née Palestine, in the second half of my life, on Saturday, among sponge cake, jewelry, sponges, and guns.

Soon I was driving up and down, up and down, strange streets, trying to figure out the traffic patterns, imagining the deserted-Sabbath streets filled with cars, struggling with the alphabet, trying to read the Hebrew letters even though I didn't understand their meaning. The street of the queen . . . the street of the king . . . that's all I managed. Felafel stands, jewelry stores, bakeries. . . . I was beginning to see.

What was I doing? I was learning to drive in that country on the Sabbath. Even as I settled down, I heard myself think, "A mad country." And then I felt the madness. It was in the wind which had come up, in the humidity in the air, in the silence, the ancient angry heat. I could feel disembodied temper everywhere. They built with stone to hold it in. That's why they have so many holy days— to ease that fever.

I wasn't a stranger to madness, to this kind of possession. It attacks like a virus, is accompanied by the same fever and dizziness, sensitivity to pain, wariness, weariness, dislocation, and self-absorption. An affliction as ordinary as a cold. I parked the car and got out, wrote down exactly where I was vis à vis the hostel, knowing it was forbidden to write on the Sabbath, and realized I was totally lost.

Then a story came to me. A story can sometimes be a map and a location.

According to the Baal Shem Tov, there was a king who was advised that all the wheat was poisoned, and everyone who would eat it—and there was nothing else to eat—would go mad. Confronted by this disaster, the king's ministers suggested they set aside for themselves the little remaining unblighted wheat so that they could continue to rule as sane men. But the king refused. He insisted that they share in the general plight. However, on the eve of destruction, the king called his ministers together and marked their foreheads and his own with ashes. This was the only quarter he granted them: when they saw the mark they would remember they were mad.

I thought of marking my own forehead, Shechem.

Perhaps the wheat never improved. Perhaps the plague never subsided. Perhaps the king and all his ministers and all the citizens, being permanently maddened, pass the madness on. When one enters the country, as I had, even on the Sabbath, on the holy day, one takes in the madness through the pollen, by breathing it in.

Was Sybil mad? Underneath her pleasure in seeing me, I detected an insidious exhaustion and mournfulness. I wanted to know everything and was afraid of opening the box of evils, loosening what she so carefully contained. I was already tired of the dead, of my sense of Sybil's discreet weeping. I could smell the redness about her eyes under the carefully applied mascara, could smell the damp of the rooms she lived in when I wasn't with her.

I began to be impressed with Israel, the extent of its influence. In such a short time I was driving around cursing, talking to myself aloud, pretending to read street signs, having a conversation with Dinah, even with Sybil while she was sitting on her bed telling the photographs like Tarot cards.

And I had this corpse in the car. It was more than three thousand years old and I hoped to resurrect him, in the body, you understand. I was going to create a *golem* for my own use. I had inflated ideas about altering history. I didn't even know if he had ever existed, but this lady inside of me, who talks all the time, she said he existed, and she's been dead almost the same number of years, so she ought to know. And I love him. Even then I loved him.

As I was driving about Jerusalem, I was thinking of getting to Nablus. Everyone, Christians, Muslims, and Jews come to Jerusalem as if they're coming home to heaven and here I was near the heart of the holy city, thinking of a minor archaeological site on the West Bank where no one in her right mind wanted to go. What anyone who was sane would have characterized as enemy territory, I thought might be home. There I hoped to touch an old wall which had the sweat of my hands in its bricks. Nablus. I couldn't yet use the ancient name, couldn't say "Shechem," not even to myself. I needed Sybil to help me and I didn't trust her—hadn't she taken up with Jeremiah, with someone from the enemy camp? On the other hand she was more loyal and more loving to me than I had ever been to myself.

> For of old time I have broken thy yoke *and* burst thy bands; and thou saidst, I will not transgress; when upon every high hill and under every green tree thou wanderest, playing the harlot. . . . But thou saidst, There is no hope: no; for I have loved strangers, and after them I will go.

I parked the car. I was somewhat wary of leaving the camera equipment exposed when all the shops were closed. Sybil had said there was relatively little theft in Israel, but I didn't like to count on the presence of soldiers. I especially didn't want to empower them with my hopes. When my father maintained that Jews didn't steal or commit crimes, I listed the Jews in the Mafia and recited them to him, endlessly, like a litany: Meyer Lansky, Louis "Lepke" Buchalter, Moe Dalitz, Lewis Rosenstiel, Mickey Cohen, Allen Dorfman, Sam Blum, Bugsy Siegel, Arnold Rothstein. . . .

I was standing still, trying to get my bearings, when a tall man appeared wearing a blue and white striped *djellaba*, his head covered by a checkered cloth under a twisted rope. He could have been you; you could be anyone. I felt myself drawn to him, would have followed had he crooked a finger. I was willing to believe on the basis of my own longing that he, if he had noticed me, felt the same pull. Then he disappeared and the streets were deserted again except for the young soldiers on patrol.

> And Hamor said unto Jacob, "The soul of my son Shechem longeth for your daughter: I pray you give her to him to wife. And make ye marriages with us, and give your daughters unto us and take our daughters unto you. And ye shall dwell with us: and the land shall be before you; dwell and trade ye therein and get you possessions therein."

And Hamor and Shechem, his son, came unto the gate of their own city and communed with the men of their city, saying, "These Israelites are peaceable with us; therefore let them dwell in the land and trade therein; for the land, behold, it is large enough for them; let us take their daughters to us for wives and let us give them our daughters."

What does it do to the mind when history converges, when what one has associated with the lost and irreversible past appears most naturally upon the pavement, shopping bag in hand? The longer I stayed, the less certain I would be of what was extinct, what had survived, what would return.

Suddenly the breeze was carrying the smell of all those who had died since sundown and who, by law, religious and secular, could not be buried. Suddenly it seemed that under the scent of rosemary and thyme, under the spices readied in the synagogues to be inhaled at sunset, under the clove and myrrh, under the frankincense, as under the skirts of a bride, there hovered that other scent, lethal and animal, gamy as the flesh of the skinned and spitted deer, the demanding, even seductive odor of death.

Sometimes, Shechem, when one is in a certain frame of mind, when the window within has been thrown open and the lace curtains torn from the cornices, it is possible to see what has been rendered invisible through the years. I'd never thought that *dybbuks* could be so subtle, that their presence might be only an odor. Now it seemed to me that I was walking in air as divers walk through water, through the luminous gliding bodies of all the soldiers of the Yom Kippur War, of the Six Day War, of the War of Independence, of the wars and skirmishes of the Turks, Romans, Babylonians, Israelites.

Dinah was advancing; I was certain of it. She knew about corpses. She had prepared them, had washed the dead, first as a young girl and then she had wrapped the bodies in white linen and ointments in Egypt. When you died, she prepared your body though that task was usually reserved to women past menopause. But she was a widow, just having been a bride. She had lived her entire lifetime in twenty-four hours. It had aged her.

Shechem and his father went home thereafter, satisfied with the result achieved, and when they had gone, the sons of Jacob asked him to seek counsel and pretext in order to kill all the inhabitants of the city, who had deserved this punishment on account of their wickedness. Then Simeon said to them: "I have good counsel to give you. Bid them be circumcised. If they consent not, we shall take our daughter from them, and go away. And if they consent to do this, then, when they are in pain, we shall attack them and slay them."

> —Louis Ginzberg,
> *The Legends of the Jews*

. . .

I sat on the stone floor so that I might be as cold as Shechem and waited until the city was totally silent, until all the men were dead and the women extracted from their rooms, until the goats and sheep clustered soundlessly in the corners of the walls, herding against the smell of blood. Then I slashed the belt from about his hips and opened his robes to examine his body. I had never washed a corpse, nor seen it done. I was only fourteen. I cut the hem from my wedding dress, wet it and ran it over his skin. It was not different from washing Reuben's child. When he was an infant and lay in my arms, I had cooled him with wet linen, singing a little song so that the two of us fell asleep in the reverie of the warm afternoon, bees, and water. I washed Shechem's throat, removed the snakes of congealed blood from his shoulder. I laid him out carefully, then sat astride him, staring at his closed eyes. Lifting his stiffening hands, I passed them across my breasts. Then I slid down onto his thighs, took his phallus in my surprisingly steady hand, saw where he had cut the skin with a dagger: It had been my bride price. I picked at the red scabrous line beneath the glans, then licked it clean where he had been sore, as I had watched animals lick their genitals. Then dropped it hopelessly.

· · ·

That was the time for someone to shout, "Never again." But instead that was the moment when a story was born. And a story wants to be repeated; that is its nature.

And Dinah refused to bury you although she knew the slanders that were coming.

How can it be, Shechem, that you don't know anything about my life, that I have to tell you everything? When I was in Chile in 1973, I was viewing an exhibit of photographs in the National Museum. There were only two of us in the room; I did not know the man. The museum was exceptionally cold, we both wore gloves. The photographs were mounted with thumbtacks and Scotch tape. The Chilean stood behind me as I turned to see a life-size photograph of an American soldier standing over the body of a Vietnamese child. The child lay in the dirt where it had fallen, its hand was severed from its wrist. I reached back to the stranger to steady myself. He whispered to me so very quietly, "How do you account for the behavior of your brother?"

I hear Dinah grieving as I write this, Shechem. She says, "The story repeats itself."

The antechamber where Dinah slept with Shechem became their tomb. She wanted to wrap him in living linen, the strips of one warm body upon the other cold body. When she washed his body, she washed her own body, and then she folded herself upon him as if she were a cloth.

When her brothers entered for the second time, they were looking for booty and did not expect to encounter Dinah. They had forgotten about her altogether. As she was simply a girl, they assumed she had been herded back with the other women or that

Levi had killed her as was customary under the circumstances. Or that Reuben, who was sentimental, had spared her and taken her back to the tents though she was gravely dishonored. But when they entered, they found her in Shechem's embrace, his yellowing hand upon her shoulder. Her head was upon his scarred chest, the wounds in his neck unhealed. Her right leg was thrown across his thigh and her hair covering her face was like a shovelful of earth.

She rose slowly from the dead man and retreated to a dark corner, pressing her body against the stone. Their breath offended her. Her body closed against them, but her eyes were open, they were pits of grief extending to the other world. Her brothers felt they would die if they looked into her eyes. The flesh had fallen from her body but the bones were shining so that in her darkness there was a light. And Shechem was shining too. The two of them were the light in the room. Then she became a great bird of prey, so when they tried to remove the body, she came toward them with great webs of darkness hanging from her arms. She was the fire falling from a burning tree. She was a blight. She was a spray of ashes.

She stood over them, and she cursed them. She cursed them as the vulture curses, as the burning tree curses, as the slaughtered lion curses, as poisoned water curses. She gathered to herself all the curses of the felled, poisoned, and slaughtered, all those which had already occurred and those which were coming and she heaped the curses upon her brothers and her brothers' generations. Until that moment, she had not had such power, but Shechem had taken her into his life and then into his death. In the time since he had died, she had become an old woman, and her breasts were withered grapes. These brothers who had never seen her naked, saw only bones.

"I will bury him," she said. They did not challenge her. But she didn't bury him. She placed him in the hollow trunk of a dead tree and she burned him. When she went to Egypt she took his bones and ashes and left the curses behind. When she first appeared to them she was like a tree burning in the night until there is as

much light as there is darkness. Then she was a hag, was only smoke.

For days the air was filled with smoke and the ashes fell on everything even as Jacob and his sons and their wives and the newly acquired sheep, oxen, and cattle, and the eighty-five captive virgins, prepared to leave. After the first days of the fire, Jacob came to her, asking that she sacrifice a lamb on the altar to appease God for him.

"If you offer a sacrifice of peace offerings unto the Lord you shall offer it at your own will." She turned to him with her dark face smeared with charcoal, her eyes a black fire in the fire, a darkness within the darkness and she laughed as only Lilith might have laughed when she confronted Adam. It was laughter that could set fires. It was the light in her.

"I am your father."

She was feeding sticks to the fire and when she turned to him again her face was a scorched branch. "I don't kill living things except to eat."

"It's for God."

"Is God still hungry? Let him kill whatever he wishes to eat. I am not his handmaiden."

"And didn't your Shechem's gods demand sacrifices?" Jacob sneered. "Did Shechem refuse to make offerings to his gods? Is that why he died?"

"We don't speak about this. But I dance for his gods. Do you want to watch me dance?" She made him watch as she danced a twisted dance, leering and awkward. As she bent down, she took charcoal from the fire and rubbed it on her body, on her face, feet, hands, even sucked the charcoal stick so her lips, mouth, and tongue were blackened. Then she tore her clothes and inserted the stick beneath the rags and darkened herself there. And everything turned black before Jacob's eyes. When she tore off her dress altogether, Jacob saw that her still-white breasts were covered with bloody streaks. He turned away, vomiting, and then he left her. Even from a distance, he could hear her deranged singing.

The ashes fell for days and later when the tents were opened, ashes were found in the creases and folds. The cheeses were darkened and the milk was gray. The wool of the animals was smudged so that everything woven had a dark pallor, and the water, even the wine, had ash in it. And no matter how far away they traveled, and they traveled far, they could not get clean and for a year they lived with Shechem in their mouths.

When they opened the camps of Sabra and Shattilah after the Falangists had entered, the Palestinians were spread upon the dirt like Hivites in the last days of Shechem. Like all the bodies of my beloved.

I will bring evil from the north and a great destruction. The lion is come up from his thicket; the destroyer of the Gentiles is on his way; He is gone forth from his place to make thy land desolate; And thy cities shall be laid waste, without an inhabitant. . . .

Therefore behold . . . the valley of slaughter: And the carcasses of this people shall be meat for the fowls of the heaven and for the beasts of the earth. Then will I cause to cease from the cities of Judah, the streets of Jerusalem, the voice of mirth, and the voice of gladness, the voice of the bridegroom and the voice of the bride: for the land shall be desolate.

Jacob's God was stronger than your gods, Shechem. And the little *teraphim* that Rachel stole and hid between her legs from her father, Laban, who wouldn't dare be soiled by menstrual juices, they didn't save Dinah. And afterwards God blessed Jacob.

And Jacob said to Simeon and Levi, "Ye have troubled me to make me to stink among the inhabitants of the land, among the Canaanites and Perizzites: and I being few in number, they shall gather themselves together against me, and slay me; and I shall be destroyed, I and my house."

And they said, "Should he deal with our sister as with a harlot?"

And God said unto Jacob, "Arise, go up to Bethel, and dwell there: and make there an altar unto God."

And God appeared unto Jacob again, when he came out of Padan-aram and blessed him. And God said unto him, "Thy name is Jacob: thy name shall not be called any more Jacob, but Israel shall be thy name."

I was fourteen at the time we left Shechem, came out of Padan-aram on the way to Ephrath where we settled. On the way, our daughter, Asenath, was born, but the place and time was not recorded. When we were at Bethlehem, Benjamin was born and Rachel died.

Two years after that, Joseph was sold into slavery and I followed him. I was always with him. When he went to tend the sheep, I was behind him, and when they put him in the pit, I kept a vigil near him, and when they sold him, I followed him, and when he was in Egypt, so was I, and when he told the dreams, I told them with him. When he was in prison, I was the pile of rags outside the prison, and when he was a Viceroy, I was a priestess. However they speak of Joseph in Egypt, they do not mention me; after Shechem, they do not speak of me. And when Joseph died, I died. And when his sons, who were my sons, brought his bones back to Shechem, they brought back my bones as well.

Joseph forgave his brothers before he died. I did not.

I remembered that I was to return to the Scottish Hospice by four, and hoped that we would eat dinner there because Sybil had assured me the food was ample, wholesome, tasty, with a choice of vegetables, the kind of food I usually disdained, but needed now. I wanted something very simple. Still, I wasn't ready to return to our room, and I felt uncomfortable walking the streets. I had no issue with death; it was, to the contrary, as if everything was alive. The letters of the alphabet looked like flames. I darted into the lobby of the King David Hotel, walked across the carpeted vestibules, up and down the dimly lit arcades grateful for marble, leather, pearls, gold leaf, shops, pottery, and suntan oil. The hotel was fairly desolate as it was Saturday and the guests were probably sleeping or fucking—the latter is allowed, even prescribed—until the Sabbath was over. I found myself in a dim corner near the silent elevators, standing before another frame, another gilt-framed mirror, covered with rosettes, cupids, rather, cherubim, and trumpets, and before I realized what was happening—it seemed so natural—I was talking aloud to God.

The inner harangue absorbed me as I swayed in the darkened hallway of the King David Hotel. It was not an inappropriate place to pray; my father had always asserted that money was the real synagogue of many latter-day Jews and a friend had once taken me to the Hilton to meet two gentlemen cowering in his hotel suite, who, he announced, had blown up the King David and the British during the War of Independence, so I felt connected to the surroundings. It was exactly the kind of hotel anyone from New York or Miami would build to satisfy all needs, particularly the one to avoid the unfamiliar while away from home. Luckily no one came down the hall.

I wanted to know what He intended with all the dead. Sybil and I were trying to solve the population problem; we'd taken up with dead men. At best our unlikely progeny might only live half time, being half dead at birth—or would they live forever, being fathered by immortals? We didn't want to birth a child for Moloch, which seemed to me to be one of His disguises. I looked about. I was spent. The hallway was no haven, and the long, deep, carpeted view toward the lobby where cocktails were being served irritated me. Had I stayed any longer, Dinah, given half a chance and plastique, would have blown it up again. And this time my brothers would not have thought I was a hero.

Outside the walls of Shechem, Jacob tore his clothes in shame and fear of reprisal. He turned inward, became like stone inside. When he looked at his sons, he questioned progeny, fertility, all the increase which was fundamental to his life. Even the flocks failed to divert him. What did flourishing mean if it could be overthrown in an instant? In the heat of the afternoons, he raked stones from the fields with his bare hands.

Then I could have brought Jacob gods to hold in his hands to comfort him, could have shown him how to carve, loosening the gods which slept in limestone and bone, awakening spirit exactly in the gesture which awakened form, but he would have despised me; like Rachel I had to remain silent about the mysteries. I studied them with Joseph and sometimes my Hivite sisters, who, except for Bonah, forgot their bitterness and taught me well.

Miracle of miracles, after Asenath was born, Rachel became pregnant again and Jacob reaffiliated to his flock. When Rachel swelled with Benjamin, he was reconciled, turned to the herds, chatted with the herdsmen, named each one of his animals once again. Leah cursed him, cursed Rachel, and cursed me. She buried herself in her sons; they surrounded her like an army; I had had my daughter in secret so my father would not be present; I would not let Jacob claim her as if she, half Hivite, were also his booty to be bestowed upon one of his sons. Now, like Adam, Jacob practiced the giving of names and so I had to keep Asenath from him. Each day as he prayed to Jehovah, he named his enemies and he blessed his sons. Jehovah was a great light in his life and every-thing was certain and known.

You were at home, Sybil, in one dream, and I was out trying to escape from you in another dream. Had we been lovers, we would have managed better—the urgency of sex might have bonded us and I would not have left your side until we had negotiated some sort of union. I always regret that limitation of friendship; it doesn't have the necessity of chemistry. We were choosing not to drown in each other's sorrows.

If Sybil had followed me, she would have seen nothing but a delicate, small boned, even fragile, American woman casually dressed in a white sleeveless dress, with an openwork bodice of blue and red flowers, strolling through what we can call downtown Jerusalem, her hands in her pockets, a purple fabric purse slung over her narrow shoulder. But if I had filmed it, a close-up would have revealed hands so tightly thrust into my pockets they trembled when the soldiers passed me and when I stepped to the side for the Arab to pass.

Now and then it felt as if I'd forgotten Shechem entirely. Or that I forgot myself. Maybe it was that Dinah was occupying all the available neural transmitters; having just returned to Israel she was absorbed in her own history. She had been an independent woman, a priestess with her own ambitions and prejudices, a woman by her own right in her own body, separate even from Shechem and Asenath, from Joseph and Benjamin, separate even from Rachel who had taught her surreptitiously what Shechem's sisters had passed on openly and with joy. And, like any modern woman, Dinah not only wanted her man, she wanted her territory. And she was in me, the bitch, sniffing; the stink of her was everywhere.

I walked for a long time. The neighborhoods changed, became poorer. There were fewer stores and those were the smaller ones that attend to daily needs. Apparently not only prayer, but the heat and the hour emptied the streets. For blocks at a time I saw no one, so I was startled by what seemed an apparition, the appearance of two Hassidic men walking in my direction. When they clearly edged toward the curb to avoid me, I unwittingly pressed myself against the wall, matching their recoil with a countermove. It was not that I thought to protect them from my touch, but their engrained religious fear or distaste aroused an internal reflex of shame and the need to be invisible. Turning to watch them from behind, I saw them arc back to the center of the sidewalk, the gesture flowing as from a dance, the curve of the initial sidestep equal to the returning curve toward the center, they had done this hundreds, thousands of times, to avoid even the tip of my breath which might have blood on it.

And if a woman have an issue, and her issue in her flesh be blood, she shall be seven days in her separation: and whosoever toucheth her shall be unclean until the even.

The two men strode athletically away from me, their long black coats flapping between their legs about their linen breeches covering their pale white buttocks, slightly flattened from much sitting at study tables; to discomfit these men to the fullest extent possible, if only psychically, I vividly imagined their naked asses. Too bad you weren't there, Sybil, we could have tossed a coin: heads the one on the right, tails, the one with the bushy tail. Without you,

I misbehaved; I couldn't resist. I put two fingers in my mouth and let loose with an ear-piercing whistle which forced them to turn around and see me laughing. When I got to the end of the street, it was barricaded against cars, but I continued walking.

Zion spreadeth forth her hands, and there is none to comfort her:
   The Lord hath commanded concerning Jacob, that his adversaries should be round about him:
   Jerusalem is as a menstruous woman among them.

. . .

As I entered Mea Shearim, my mood changed and again the men who might have been even more prominent in my thoughts and angers slipped from my mind altogether. Perhaps it was because I was thinking of my grandmother and that made me lonely for Sybil, for some inner kindness. She had attempted to be tender with me and I had not permitted it. Even though we'd nestled against each other, I maintained some distance from her. Well, she had left me, and without notice, and now she expected me to pick up with her as if I hadn't spent two years without my dearest companion.

I'd always thought of Mea Shearim as a woman who demonstrated the final orthodoxy of submission, both passion and defeat, by shaving her head. It was afternoon, the Sabbath Bride had become the Grandmother. I wanted to settle under Her skirts. Hours have their moods. High noon is argumentative but the hours before dusk contain a certain forgetfulness and one could say that torpor saturated the air. It was the time and season when the birds sleep and people sweat through the last twist of their afternoon naps. The curtains were drawn everywhere. A few young boys lounged here and there against brick buildings, whispering to each other in the narrow streets. Soon it would be time to return to synagogue for the evening prayers. I wondered if they felt stifled by Her heavy skirts. In a short while She would braid up her hair in light once more and leave. The neighborhood is old, the streets huddle into each other as if they remembered how to lean, as if they were shoulders pressing against each other. I wanted to lie down also, to put my pillow next to another's. It was the time of day I could have forgiven anyone anything.

As I passed an arched doorway, a brace of girls burst forth, then, seeing me, stopped short in a flap of wings, not expecting anyone to be a witness to their giggles, which disrupted the dignified departure of the Shechinah. They walked slowly behind me like pigeons, then flew in front so when I stopped again to glance about me, they flocked together in their new location, fluttering. There was no one else in the street—the boys I had passed originally had disappeared—but these girls twittering and cooing in the shadows. As I came nearer to them, a few stepped forward, and one, in particular, caught my attention. She was taller than the rest and in her face I saw the onset of aging so that as I examined her face, I could not tell exactly if she was fourteen, as I thought at first, if only because of the clear ages of the others, or whether she was already a woman, perhaps even a mother. The photographs of Israeli women I'd studied before I'd come revealed how quickly they slide into plump matronliness from the lithe and beautiful girls they had been. Though she was thin, I detected the same resignation that I'd seen in the photographs. Her dark eyes were very full but slanted down at the sides so that her face, at rest, had a gloomy expression. She saw whatever she saw openly, but it weighed upon her. I couldn't disengage myself from her eyes and then was even more intrigued when I realized that she had not looked away either, not for an instant.

As she moved to the front of the group, she did not release my eyes, yet she clasped her hands behind her, almost shyly. An ill-fitting brown skirt, rather too warm I thought for this time of year, covered bony knees in white stockings, and her long-sleeved white blouse had a bit of very worn lace at the wrists. She wore the clothes as if they happened to her like a random event. It did not seem to me that she had chosen them, that she could imagine choice. There was something so familiar in her outfit, I slowed my pace because I didn't want to pass her without identifying it, and then it seemed to me I recognized her vest as one which had been mine. A modest gray garment, cut much like a man's vest, with a bit of dark leather on the pockets, one of which was frayed, the color rubbed out, because I had had the habit of keeping my keys there, and a bit of change. In the other pocket, I always stored a folded dollar bill for emergencies, so I was careful not to reach into that one very often. I had given the vest to my mother with other clothes. She demanded an inventory of my wardrobe twice a year in order to send whatever she thought appropriate to Israel. Just as I recognized the vest, the girl raised her arm as if to stretch, the vest unbuttoned, as I'd known it to do—she had also been too lazy to sew up the buttonholes—and opened her palm to show me the stone in her hand. The other girls yelled in Hebrew; I couldn't understand them until it was impossible to avoid the understanding that came from their hands pointed at my bare arms. Instinctively I crossed my arms and covered some of my forearm with my fingers as the girl carefully let the stone fly toward me. It almost hit me. She could have hit me if she had tried. The other girls bent down; I suspect they had a cache of pebbles in the doorway. "You must not," was what I said. That was probably what they were shouting to me as well: "You must not!" Then I dropped my hands to the crooks of my arms and stared at them with my arms folded.

After she threw the stone, she looked aside and I couldn't engage her eyes again. She and the other girls shuffled and bumped against each other, looking down at their feet and at each other. Yes, she was obviously fourteen. I wouldn't be fourteen again if . . . I remembered the terrible menstrual pain, chafing pads, abrasion of the dry blood, that flat fungal smell which increased in the heat, that improbable mangy smell, comprehensible in the barn but so startling and inappropriate to brick houses and paved streets. In the privacy of my room, I would put my fingers in the blood and carry them to my nose trying to learn the smell, wanting it to be familiar. At fourteen I already had a lover, it made it easier, I began to learn the blood from his mouth. When I was with him I did not feel so odd a creature as when I was alone.

> For the life of the flesh *is* blood: and I have given it to you upon the altar to make an atonement for your souls: for it *is* the blood *that* maketh an atonement for the soul.
> Therefore I said unto the children of Israel, No soul of you shall eat blood, neither shall any stranger that sojourneth among you eat blood.

My girlfriends and I never spoke about this. We wore cotton panties; I could never fully wash them clean of the monthly dark brown stains.

> And everything that she lieth upon in her separation shall be unclean: everything also that she sitteth upon shall be unclean.
> And if any man lie with her at all, and her flowers be upon him, he shall be unclean seven days: and all the bed whereon he lieth shall be unclean.

Still staring at the agitated covey of adolescent girls, unwilling to walk past them or turn away, I put my hands in my pockets, my two fists pulled the fabric of the dress down so I leaned against it, my pelvis swaying forward. Girls will throw stones; they don't mean any harm by it. There isn't much they can do in the world and fourteen is an awkward time between one confinement and another. I looked at my adversary steadily and she caught my eye again to observe me as if I were not a person but simply a phenomenon; she stared at me as if it were her duty—she was the leader—without letting me engage her. Her eyes were fully open and blind to me at the same time; I turned slowly away.

One of the girls yelled after me in heavily accented English; I don't think it was she, the voice was too high pitched, not how I imagined her voice. "What's your name?"

"Dinah," I answered over my shoulder.

"Dinah what?"

"Dinah."

"Dinah, where are you from? Are you American?"

"I'm from over there." I looked back to the east and then at the pulsing cluster of little birds, and then away, forcing myself to walk slowly without looking back, looking instead at the street which, though a city street, curved slightly to accommodate to the irregularity of the land. I carried with me the last image of her, her arm raised again, the shoulder of the gray vest hitched up and bunching about her neck. The stone hit me on the heel; it was the only one to make its mark.

I hesitated for a moment when I felt the impact and then, without turning toward them, bent down and picked it up. Back at the room, I wrote the date and place on it, to keep it with the other stones I'd collected instead of postcards and other souvenirs. I always carried stones, smooth stones from riverbeds and bits of walls.

When I was nine, I had organized my classmates to adopt a war orphan who had been liberated from Dachau and sent to an orphanage in France. I didn't have a sister, and this girl became the sister for me, one who had been saved from the dark throat of war. At night when I was lonely, I pretended she was in another bed—the trundle bed I slept in opened for her—and I whispered to her late into the night. The whispers were translated into letters—I wrote to her regularly—and my mother and I almost as regularly wrapped small packages of used and new clothes, toys, perfumes, soap, dried foods, mirrors, stationery, other inexpensive female delights, and human necessities in sturdy cartons and shipped them to the orphanage. After some years, we received the astonishing news that her father had also survived another camp, (his wife had died) and had, as the legend went, literally walked across Europe looking for his scattered children, and finding Edka, apparently the only other survivor in the family, brought her to New York.

One Sunday in August, her father, short, stooped, bearded, with what seemed to me wholly unremarkable feet, brought Edka to my house. I drew her away immediately into our room, sat her next to me on the bed, and compared our feet and hands. Satisfied we could be sisters, I stood with her facing the mirror to find the similarities in our features, then I divided the room in two, emptied half the drawers, she would take the top drawer of the maple bureau and I would take the second drawer because those knobs were loose. I gave her my coveted black patent leather shoes as a preliminary gift. I had fought long and hard for shoes which were without arch supports and, according to my mother, not sensible. I would not get another pair. It was as if I was gathering a bride price. I would have given her everything I had. When she left that evening, I assumed it was to gather her clothes and return. A true miracle, I thought, that this man had searched her out and brought her to me.

After this visit, she didn't return again. Whenever I telephoned her, I was told she would call me back, that she was out, that she couldn't speak to me, finally that she had moved. My mother and father both called but could not tell me when she would come to visit though they tried to explain to me that she would not ever come to live at our house. I began to think she was dead and mourned her irreconcilably. Finally, my mother told me what her father had said:

We were sinners; we were the scum of the earth; we had turned from God; we were the cause of all the destruction in Europe; we had effectively killed his wife and children; we wanted to destroy Edka as well. We were not orthodox. I had worn a sleeveless blouse, my elbows had been uncovered. We were a plague on the universe. He had burned my black patent leather shoes in the street on a pyre of newspapers and dry leaves.

Coming back to the car, I had had enough time to climb out of my anger and when the Sabbath had passed, I was soothed. Relief filled me as soon as the sun fell behind the buildings into the prosaic night. Somehow I felt I had a chance of success if I only had to negotiate in the secular world. And meeting Edka, for that is the name I chose for the already burdened young woman who had hailed me in my own vest, seemed too much like a portent which I could not decipher.

It was well after six when I came home. Sybil was seated at the desk she had made out of a low bureau, typing on a portable typewriter when I returned. I had hoped to find her differently occupied. I wanted to find her with her sweaters, silk blouses, sashes, amber beads, earrings, calf's leather belts spread out on the bed looking for just the right stone or amber to reflect the velvet skirt, to contrast with the crinkly sand-colored crepe blouse, working the colors—which was one of her great gifts—so that they would rise up and reflect on her white skin, so that her hair would shine in companionable light. I had always loved watching her dress, beginning the afternoon modestly as a hearth fire, a small safe flame, knowing that by the end of the evening when it would be dark, and she was seated among the candles, she would begin to burn like a torch. I longed for her preparations and her beauty; I thought it was an homage to the gods.

But she was seated astride a bench before the bureau, a pencil in her unkempt hair, wearing a pair of old jeans which were already faded and baggy when I knew them in New York.

I wanted Sybil to distract me, to stroke me, to tease me, to chide me for being late, to spill out a hundred different plans for the evening, to run a bath for me and send the anger down the drain with the bubbles and perfume and herbs. There was not enough water in all Israel for a proper bath.

Whenever Jacob came to see his son, Dinah placed Benjamin on the ground and hid herself in the tent until Jacob left and then she took the boy inside and washed her father's familiar smell from him. As she breathed it in, she remembered how she had also lain against him wrapped in his robe, breathing in the safe air.

On the bed there were some photographs, not only those from newspapers, but several she had taken of a cemetery and a headstone. "I was at the unveiling," Sybil commented as she saw me pick one up.

"They let you in?"

"The book."

There were several photos of the grave in different seasons with different flowers, light, atmosphere. "You seem to be the chief mourner." I was thinking of the woman who mourned Valentino leaving a single red rose on his grave each year. Sybil read my mind immediately.

"I understand all kinds of mourners. The dead demand a kind of devotion which may not be possible for the beloved or the family. The dead don't ask for a great deal—it isn't grief they want because grief is a concern with oneself. When I think about Jeremy, when I am doing my work, I reach out of myself, dissolve in part. He takes on what I give up so we meet someplace which is between here and nothing."

"But you hardly knew him. You complained that he never revealed himself to you. His withholding, as you put it then, embittered you. Remember you left him because he gave you nothing."

"Now I know him better than anyone else; he does reveal himself. It's as if I've found the way into a sacred text. By the time I finish, I'll know him better than he knows himself."

"How long will you give it?"

"I'll even know how he smelled the moment before he died."

So, I pulled my suitcase out from under the bed and opened it to give Sybil the black mid-calf-length woolen cape I'd bought because I had known she would be staying and would want something elegant and warm for the winter.

"I don't look good in black," she murmured as she stroked it admiringly, as she swirled it in a dramatic turn about her shoulders. She had always looked good in mourning clothes.

"The book?" I could see that she didn't want to tell me anything more than she'd already said.

I fell silent. I could hear her laugh nervously, caught between fear and loneliness, the sound she made was more of a grunt, more of a "hu, hu, hu" than a human laugh. To protect her from myself, I held Shechem in my heart. Sybil picked up the manuscript and brought it to me, sat down at the edge of the bed, putting it down beside me. I only had to read the title to understand. She cried and I held her.

"I did read some of your journal." I felt I had to whisper.

She put her finger on her lips and shook her head for me to be quiet. Then it was as if she'd never heard what I said. That book was her secret, her talisman, it had the power of a secret name which must never be revealed.

How she is become as a widow! She that was great . . .

When I picked up the manuscript to look at it, she left my side, threw the cape in which she had fully wrapped herself onto a chair and sat down again to the bureau as one sits down with a straight back to confront a fatal disease.

How doth she sit solitary, that was full. She weepeth sore in the night and her tears are on her cheeks. Among all her lovers she hath none to comfort her.

Only all her beauty had not departed.

After a few pages, I needed to scurry back into ordinary life. She was certainly thorough, but I was reading between the lines. When I looked at her, I saw everything she wasn't writing in the book. The air hummed with magic. I could not breathe. I didn't know if my mind or heart were breaking.

"Have you met his mother?" The sun had gone down. On the Sabbath, the river between earth and *gehenna* is stilled so one can cross over first to one side and then back again. One may not remain in Eden. It was dark. We were in the slot between holiness and holiness. For Arabs and Jews alike the Sabbath was over. For Christians it would not begin until dawn. We were pulled back onto this side of the bank. We were on earth again, on solid ground. The curtain of unconsciousness, opaque as night has ever been, fell from a great height and whatever stars fell with it, wrapped in its heavy folds, were extinguished as a comet burns to ashes or falls like stone as it enters our atmosphere. I itched for the relief and distraction of the ordinary.

"I am the chief mourner. There are his fans, of course. His mother keeps up the public posture whenever necessary or when state occasion requires it. When I interviewed her neighbors, one quoted her: 'I'm so ashamed. If he was going to kill himself, he should have taken a few Arabs with him. That's whom the mines were meant for.'"

THE TESTIMONY OF JEREMIAH ABAZADIK
A Posthumous Autobiography

I needed a new devil's chord and couldn't find it. I would have made a noose with it. I would have been satisfied with just the edge of dissonance, just a tone of doubt to dislocate the order, but this is a century already so dissonant and yet so very orderly— think of the Nazis and all we can learn from them. I needed to learn set theory. My instructor advised, "Practice." I studied demography while my mother sneered, "So now he wants to be a sociologist." She wiped her hands on her blue and white plaid apron. "If God wanted you to be an organizer, he'd have made you an ant." I thought he did.

Making mines is very meticulous work. My fingers were trained to the finest wires. I could make a mine that would vibrate to the human voice, to the note A440 which is basic to a scream or to GG which is the sound of fear. When the mine heard these notes, it could not contain itself. I signed each mine as if it were any gift and I directed it specifically to this set of bones, that ganglia, that neuron display, whichever wanted it. I could smell the desire for death as easily as a dog can smell the sweat of a man's feet through his shoes. I thought everyone I touched should take it personally: "This is for you, my dear, this is for you."

"You don't have to do this bloody work," Nahum said, "you can play music for us again." But whenever I played songs, everyone got into line and marched off to war. I wanted to write another chord, something erotic, but the marching song was in me just as gunpowder was in the mine and any tremble set it off. I was called up. I wrote marches. I asked for different duty. When I made mines, I picked them off one by one, or a very few at a time. If I was unlucky, I got a bull's-eye with a bus or tank, but with a march or an arpeggio, I killed hundreds. Everyone who learns to march continues marching. It is good exercise. I looked for a small element, a single tone which would disrupt everything. I looked for a virus to set into my music to create a small infection.

Nahum went into the army as easily as he put on his underwear, shit stains and all. "Why wash them? I'll only get piss on them in the afternoon.

"Jerry, what is there to know? What is there to know? You think your mother has a right to live here and make chicken soup on Friday? You want to get married and have your own chicken soup? Do you think you can cook chicken soup under the sea? Do you like life? Fight!"

It is our considered opinion that Jeremiah Blazer Abazadik is one of the natural resources of this country. It would not be too much to add that his presence and gift is a sign that we were meant to return to Jerusalem at this time. With music such as this to guide us, we can secure our homeland forever.

Thus spake *Zeitung*. So I did my own little diaspora and scattered myself about the face of the globe.

For a few days we were tourists and girlfriends; I even forgot you, Shechem, for hours at a time. Sometimes, even when I write this, I forget you. Forgetting is a serious issue, perhaps the most serious issue of our time; we spend so much time remembering, recording, we forget everything that is essential. One of the small angels of forgetting was Anne MacDowell who hovered solicitously about us. She had a deep maternal or sisterly love for Sybil which she expressed by preparing the most extravagant English menus for the evenings we ate at home. One morning she managed croissants and a berry jam that was very French; "Contraband," she joked. Usually she served the guests fruit or ice cream for dessert, but when Sybil ate dinner there, rich and sweet desserts from East Jerusalem and the Old City appeared as if by miracle, though they seemed tamer, less full of life than when we gorged ourselves at the source. In her sitting room amidst the pale gray upholstered furniture, amidst the petit point, they became exotics. At night if it was not too late we sipped cups of tea in the drawing room, served from an elegant silver service Anne had brought with her from Scotland. In the mornings, after I'd made my preference known, I was served coffee from the brass bird I loved so much.

I met some of Sybil's friends and of them all I liked Joseph ben Yacob best. He appeared first and foremost to be a sincere man. The irony of his name struck me immediately and before I could comment, he said, "We can be brother and sister," but I understood by the way he held my hand when we were introduced that it was not what he had in mind. Exactly what unnerved people about him attracted me to Joseph. As a prominent attorney, he often wore the hat of a professional mediator or an ambassador without portfolio. He was the diplomat of diplomats; prominent though he was, he was always working secretly behind the lines. Joseph was not accommodating but he had developed the habit of biding his time and this, with an instinctive love of the unexpected and a modesty one finds only among the extremely intelligent, made him seem removed if not dispassionate, free of the frailties which plague the rest of us. He thought there was a value to every situation and he was willing, if not eager, to see all sides. This did not, however, keep him from taking a stand. He had a reputation for being an extremist which was balanced by a similar reputation for being uncompromisingly ("infuriatingly," Sybil said) rational.

"Dina, you and I will also have to deal with history." He held onto my hand so that the handshake which had been perfunctory and formal meant something quite other by the time I was released. Joseph was not a cautious man, that is, clearly not fearful, he enjoyed every detail of discovery. Before the handshake was over, he had traced the lines on my hand, thoroughly examining my palm, then reached for my other hand, held both in his two hands, testing my receptiveness, sensitive to the minutest indications of responsiveness, submission, or withdrawal. I put my hands in my pockets.

We met some days after a major peace demonstration supporting Palestinian rights on the West Bank. In Nablus, martial law was continuing while the land was expropriated from the Palestinians through one means or another. Afterwards, he was understandably tired. He had been responsible, if not entirely for its organization, for its energy and many of its principles and demands, and though he had declined, strategically, to participate as a featured speaker, he assumed responsibility to see that something concrete came of it. Sentiment was a habit in Israel, but sentiment is not politics. Joseph believed in politics; he believed in getting something done. Mass protest, he was known to object, too often served the incumbents, providing an atmosphere of dialogue and the pretense of pluralism, when, in actual fact, there were no consequences but the expenditure of emotion.

Dinah and Joseph set themselves behind the caravan for Beth-El and when it stopped, they placed their tent in the farthest corner of the field and when they traveled again, they followed, but always slowly and at a distance. After the first months, when she had recovered in part from her exhaustion, Dinah went to her brothers' flocks and took some cattle, lambs, and goats which had belonged to Shechem, for she said that everything of Shechem's belonged to her. She did not want more than she could care for with a broken heart; still, she took the best. Then she called Shechem's sister, Bonah, the one that Simeon coveted although Levi had stolen her for himself, and who was close to her age, and she gave her earrings which she had retrieved from the pits where Levi and Simeon had buried them and offered to bring the girl to her tent though she knew she would have war with her brothers about it. But she would not speak to Dinah even though there was no safer tent for the girl and no one would be kinder to her. The two women, for they could not be girls any longer, were silent with each other from then until the moment when Asenath was born. Then Bonah helped her and when she first held the child, examining her features, she said, "This is indeed my brother's child." Only then she taught Dinah and Joseph everything she knew.

Joseph was a painstakingly determined and dedicated negotiator. "Someday I'll take you on a tour of monuments to my work," he smiled wryly. "I can name each crater and the agreement I forged that it broke. When I die, Sybil, I expect you to bury me in any one of a thousand holes in the ground blasted open on my behalf. It's the great promise of democracy: everyone—Jew, Israeli, Palestinian, Lebanese, Saudi, Egyptian, male, female—has the ability to make a bomb."

As with the Dane, I wanted Sybil to love Joseph. It pleased me to imagine his sensitive and long-boned hands on her body. Sybil, similarly, hoped that Joseph and I would become lovers.

Joseph and I began talking and Sybil faded out of the conversation. She stared blankly into the street from the patio of the small Arab cafe that Joseph had led us to. She sat almost immobile, endlessly stirring her coffee until it cooled and then she set it aside. Still, she glowed from some faraway inner light, as if Jeremiah brought light to dense tissue, as if she were becoming a light herself even as she was being extinguished. I examined my own face in the compact mirror but saw no changes since I'd arrived. When I looked up, Joseph was staring at me. I was flustered. "I'm trying to get reacquainted with your face; it is not as familiar to me as you are. Let me order for you. It's not only that I speak Arabic, but I'd like to see if it's true that I know what you want because I've known you all my life."

"You should have been a sculptor," I said, watching Joseph's hands test the cutlery, arrange the plates, examine the physical world. His gestures were so much like those of the old Sybil. Leaning back upon the patched oilcloth-covered chairs, Joseph was more comfortable, despite his suit and white shirt, than he would have been in one of the elegant restaurants in the wealthier parts of the city. He was not discomfited by differences, but clearly energized by them; where there was differentiation, he felt at home. I did not share his experience, quite the opposite. I was also comfortable—for the first time since I'd arrived—but it was not difference which interested me but familiarity. The *suk* was bustling with white-robed men and dark-robed women. I had never been in this part of the world before; I was completely at home.

"A sculptor? I did think of that when I was younger. I could have easily become an artist, I had a certain talent for color and composition and the knife. I always know what to cut away. But, I thought, the communication of the artist was painfully slow and tentative. I had the fantasy when I was younger that words could be used efficiently and effectively. And if one were good with them . . . and I am . . . well, then. . . . It was one of the persistent sweet illusions of youth. Now,"—he stared at me directly—"I am looking for a beautiful woman to be the artist for me."

I stared back at him. The remark was deliberately flirtatious, challenging, and insulting. An almost intimate moment vanished as a stone falls away into water.

We pushed the plates aside, sat silently for a while in the mid afternoon sun. Around us, vendors, tourists, donkeys, pressed uncomfortably against each other. Young boys balancing tea glasses on engraved circular bronze trays darted through the dark stream of people and animals toward the shops. Peace existed within the triangle we formed. Sybil got up after a while to go inside to talk with the proprietor; Jeremiah and the rotund man whose apron was smeared with *hummus* stains had exchanged songs.

We stood up with her. I wanted to stop Sybil, had some premonition that as she began eyeing the dark entrance to the restaurant, some parting was occurring between us, though who was leaving, she or I, was unclear. The labyrinth of the *suk* wound through other dark, mysterious archways in all directions. Urbane, Europeanized, assimilated, modern Jews and Arabs trafficked amidst their unassimilated relatives. Every century was represented as if Jerusalem were itself the fecund crease in time, the *ur* point of coexistence of all futures and all pasts. Is this why it is the holy city?

A man passed passed who might have been you, Shechem. Then, examining his features, I realized he as easily could have been my brother.

"It's not differences they can't tolerate," I said to Joseph. "It's familiarity. This is a family fight, internecine warfare, the rivalry between brothers that precedes or follows the killing of the father. What else can it be? It's the most primitive blood feud."

"Close your eyes," Joseph urged, "then open them and begin speaking. Tell me what you see, as if you've never seen this before, have never been here, have never heard of this spot. Imagine you've been teleported here without expectations or prejudice, what is before your eyes? What do you see?"

"History."

"What do you mean?"

"All of it at once. Anyone who sees it as it is goes mad. You have to pretend it isn't all happening now, but it is. There's only the present, and so we're torn apart by all the warring elements, the contradictions, the impossibilities. . . . There has to be some control on living in several centuries at once. My brain may be up for it, but the rest of my body hasn't the capacity."

"But you aren't torn apart." Joseph understood. His voice was both cautious and concerned. So that's how he negotiated so well; he was privy to all viewpoints; they lived in him and he sustained them. "There are two creatures of history, those that history bites and inflames and those that swallow it. Tell me what you are thinking, Dina."

"I am thinking about the West Bank. I am thinking of Shechem's betrayal."

Sybil, who had joined us again, did not recognize the name and turned her golden face to me in puzzlement, but Joseph interrupted before I could give her an explanation.

"Betrayal? Whose? Shechem's or Levi's?"

"I don't think Shechem betrayed Dinah. I think Levi betrayed everyone."

"That's what I suspected you'd think. The women here, of course, have another interpretation of the story."

"I know, but it is constructed from the present. The story of Dinah's rape and Levi's heroism is politically correct, particularly for these times. I know that from my own life. I know all too well about rape." Joseph leaned toward me about to interrupt, slow me down, but I had to avoid him. "But, unfortunately, their interpretation also helps the Zionist zealots."

"So many unlikely bed partners in the modern world."

"You know that better than I do, Joseph." He could have taken the conversation to politics, but he didn't. He waited for me to finish. I waited also and then continued, "The problem is that the story they tell about Shechem isn't true. The O.T. cleverly leaves out the essential elements."

"How do you know?"

"The only way I know anything—little birds tell me."

"What are you two talking about?" Sybil was becoming restless.

"The Old Testament."

"You never knew anything about that."

"I had to do my homework, didn't I? Even if the film was a ruse to see you, I have to know something to make it plausible."

Joseph and I turned toward the street; Sybil stepped into the dark restaurant again, calling for Mansur. I was wondering, Shechem, if I had found us an ally. I was coming to believe I could trust Joseph, I did not want us to be alone in this country. I was not even as prepared as Dinah had been. I needed an advocate and advocacy was Joseph's work.

"We'll return for you in half an hour," Joseph called after her just as she was vanishing. His tone was casual again as if nothing had transpired between us. "You haven't been through the Old City yet, have you?" He was leading me deftly through the crowd, his hand barely on my forearm, but still firm in his attention. "The first time you walk through the city you must be alone or with a native, otherwise you'll never see her as she wants to be seen."

"Were you born here?"

"And my father and mother as well."

"Isn't it odd then that you do this work. Sybil says you're always accused of working for the Palestinians."

"Odd? Everything in this country is odd. But who else would know compassion but someone who's lived here all his life." Later I learned that Joseph had sold the land he'd inherited from his parents to a Palestinian family. It had caused quite a disturbance.

He steered me from stall to stall, greeting many by name and all in their own language. I didn't imagine anything would surprise him, especially the commonplace, but as a squat middle-aged woman walked or floated through the crowd balancing an enormous tray of fruits upon her head, Joseph grabbed my arm and turned me toward her. "Isn't she wonderful, isn't she wonderful?" he whispered in unselfconscious admiration. "I wish I could do that. I've practiced. I've practiced a good deal, to be honest with you, and I can't do it. My failure almost causes me to agree with the conservative bastards who say the differences are in our genes." He danced about me. "My posture's good; my balance is excellent. My teeth are better than hers. Why can't I do it?"

"Because you're not a woman and you have no need," I offered casually, but Joseph caught my eye and held it, before he responded deliberately.

"You're right, you're absolutely right." He danced about me again balancing an invisible burden upon his head, then placed his palms on his slender hips and examined them with dismay. "How fortunate I am to have met you; you've saved me from a terrible political decline."

It is exactly when there are no words that moments of understanding occur suddenly and unexpectedly, when alliances are made that are not reasoned or calculated, when one experiences the ease and then the affinity that causes one not so much to know the other as to know oneself more deeply. A snatch of conversation suddenly blazes with implication, illuminating the dark and forbidding cave within and the stranger who has stumbled on this inner chamber senses that this is the place where one, oneself, has gotten lost and remained so, afraid to explore further, not knowing how to return. Because the stranger is innocent, he comes in with a torch, and the two, the lost self and the stranger, hover together in the warmth of the new fire.

"Do you carry history in your hips, lady?"

"No. In my heart, Joseph. Where do you carry it?"

"In my head. That's the trouble, isn't it?"

"Your reputation says you carry it in your heart, otherwise you couldn't do your work."

"Oh, there's heart, but it's a motivating principle, not yet a principle of thought. I mediate between men, you see, and I must always speak their language. That's why I like . . ."

"To be around women! It won't do, Joseph, I won't be your muse."

"Are you certain?"

"I'm afraid so. I gave that up eons ago."

"Where does that leave us?"

"I want you to help me."

"I will serve you with devotion." He indulged himself in a mocking, gallant sweep of another invisible headdress.

One morning Dinah came to Joseph with a dream. They had arrived at Ephrath after burying Rachel at Bethlehem. Asenath was nine months old, Benjamin was three months, and Dinah had nursed him since he was born.

"This is what I dreamed, Joseph. A man who had been slaving in the field suddenly placed his fist in the overseer's mouth. The overseer was a brutal man, brutal as summer heat. Forced to leave the field, the man could take only a few sheaves of the wheat he had cultivated; they would not see him through the winter. His friend ran after him, his own arms filled with grain. 'I can't protest this injustice,' the friend cried bitterly. 'I have a wife and daughter to feed.' The first man did not answer but stumbled forward like someone who had not had any water to drink since high noon."

Joseph looked at his sister with his eyes filled with tears. "I am not able to protect you." Because he couldn't see, he stumbled over the words. Even though a young boy, he knew the disorder that lay between intention and action. He took her in his arms and Dinah felt how soft he was compared with Jacob; when they slept together, she sometimes wrapped herself in him as if they were both women. It was not that softness which was between them now but the knowledge that he could not rely upon his will.

Dinah didn't have this dream. I'm not certain of that. With certainty, I can say she wasn't the only one to have this dream. I also dreamed it. I didn't recognize any of the characters, not the man, his friend, nor the overseer. I've never seen that field. When I awakened, I felt as if I had drifted by accident into another person's dream, even into another century of dreaming. I told Joseph the dream, but he didn't find it odd.

"Don't you recognize it?" He seemed genuinely surprised.

"It is a familiar story, but as a dream it's odd."

"I hear it every day." Joseph was weary.

"Dreams are personal," I insisted. "What do you think the dream means for me?"

"There are no personal dreams in this country. We only dream our reality. What we fail to understand in the daytime, we have to learn at night. There is not much time."

"All right, Joseph, wizard to the Knesset, since you're an expert in these matters, what does the dream have to say to me? What did I have to learn during the night that I'd ignored during the day."

"We . . . I . . . may not be able to protect you. There have been so many I have wanted to protect and I haven't been able to. You'll find it a terrible injustice, but I won't be able to help myself . . . help you. . . . Maybe that's why I never married. This damned country is more of a burden than a wife."

"Well, you're married to it."

"Yes, and it's a good marriage. There is even love in it."

———

There is a certain tone, Shechem, in which conversations take place, which allows for an event to occur that is not contained, may even be contradicted, by the words which are being spoken. I am trying to isolate this tone because I am not certain that we will speak a common language when we meet, and, in order to speak, I shall have to hum to you. But the tone, I find, cannot be isolated from the words even though it is not embedded in them. This is mysterious. Perhaps the tone is external, perhaps it enters us of its own will and our task is to acknowledge its appearance. Perhaps that is what happens in such moments between people; perhaps a third, invisible companion appears.

In that moment of communion, a permanent bond is established between people as if they had saved each other's lives. The two may never meet again. But afterwards, there is never permanent darkness. It is as if little bits of light from the stranger's torch adhere to the walls, as if some unique phosphorescent material is forever activated. At such moments, I give myself over to the gods. This is when I refuse to pray and try to learn praise.

If I were to play back the film of the meeting with Joseph, we would see nothing. Still it is all there beyond the reach of the camera, just under the moment when he took my hand. He knew it before I did. Familiarity is not part of his persona. People say he is a shy man, observant but unobtrusive in social gatherings, and he never dances.

"Did you like him?" Sybil asked hopefully as we were settling into sleep after we'd both written a bit by hand in our journals. I hadn't seen Sybil at the typewriter since I'd arrived, but it was always ready, with a clean white paper waiting in the roller. I liked this ritual between us, the quietening down into ourselves so as to be prepared for sleep or dreams. We had turned out the light in the room, and could see Jerusalem sparkling through the windows. "What did he say to you?"

"He said I couldn't go to Nablus, that it was off limits, that martial law had been imposed. I pressed him to let me accompany

him when he returned to work there, but he said he wouldn't
risk it."

Sybil was smiling, self-satisfied. I knew she was smiling though
I couldn't see her face. She was smiling because she didn't say
anything, was waiting, strategically, for me to continue. She didn't
want to be the one to keep me out of the West Bank. That is, she
wanted to appear innocent. So I remained silent too.

"Joseph will arrange our trip to the Sinai," Sybil said, delight-
edly. "He will introduce us to anyone we might want to meet. I
told him we would be ready to leave a week from Wednesday, I
imagined you'd be weary of Jerusalem by then."

"I may not be ready to leave on Wednesday."

"Are you going to be difficult?"

"No. Only pigheaded, not a kosher style in Israel. But I won't
leave until I have found out when and how I will get to Nablus."

THE TESTIMONY OF JEREMIAH ABAZADIK
A Posthumous Autobiography

You don't ask anyone to sing a song. A song is a bodily function, like a fart or a sneeze. It seizes you and has to be expressed. So if you ask, what you get is an actor, a simulation, a fake. But sometimes someone looked at me and the song emerged from that glance. They didn't have to say anything. "Here we are," I'd think, "two birds in the same tree," so I'd sing. I didn't like to sing in my own language. I always liked to sing in a language I didn't know, so I could pretend it was someone else singing and listen to it myself. Why shouldn't I have the joy?

Nothing gave me more joy than watching Mansur sing. He sang with his hands, with the soapy water, with the dish rag, with his dirty apron, with his fat face, with his eyebrows. Even his hair sang. First he spat into his handkerchief to clear his throat, then he prayed to Allah for a clean spirit, then he turned to the east, then he picked up his glass to the light and said, "May I be as clear as this glass," then he sang. That was a song!

I'd come in fifteen minutes before he closed the restaurant. Exactly fifteen minutes. Why? Because I could only stand fifteen minutes of paradise. If I was with him another second, my heart would break. How did I know when to arrive, since he closed at a different time each night? He thought I was a prophet. Maybe he sang for me because he thought this scoundrel was a holy man. But it was simple to tell time by Mansur. I could read his internal clock. When he got tired at night, and didn't want any more customers, he turned on a lamp he had over the sink. It had a terribly bright bulb that announced the cracks in the walls, the indelible smears, the resistant poverty. He didn't know he took this last good look at reality each night before he went home. But when I saw him examining the world, the filth, sweat, and hopelessness of it, I'd say, "Jerry, it's time to go in to distract Mansur with a little remembrance from his grandfather."

"And what do *you* remember from your grandfather?" he'd ask and before I could answer he'd put his hand on my arm and say, "No prayers." So I'd sing him any little Yiddish song as long as it had no rabbis in it, or I'd invent a Polish song my grandfather never knew to sing, about love.

· · ·

It seemed to me that weeks had passed, but it was only a week since I'd arrived. It didn't seem I going to be ready to leave on Wednesday as Sybil had hoped. Some time was spent, of course, aranging for the eventual shoot, interviewing production people, looking at their work, but I pursued that within the same reverie which characterized this time, except when I was trying to find a way to visit Nablus. Sybil didn't seem to mind the change from my usual pace; she had, herself, it seemed to me, become a dream animal, nocturnal, enigmatic, torporous. Perhaps our entire lives were entering the dream and Sybil's disintegration, which probably started long before I came, was the physical evidence that we were living on another plane of existence where the material world manifested, rather than disguised, the state of the psyche. Not a reversal of reality, only a reversal of habits of disguise.

I tried to keep up appearances—I telephoned New York every other day, spoke to my staff, dissembled perfectly like the great poseurs, the men who invent degrees and become surgeons without any training at all.

Joseph was also a dreamer, living a dream despite all his portfolios, briefs, and credentials. "Do you imagine you'll make any progress mating these two antagonists, these Arabs of yours and these Jews?"

"An event of the imagination is a real event," he said solemnly.

"Do they know you're mad, Joseph?"

"But am I mad enough to be able to imagine peace?"

My conversations with the contacts I'd been given were increasingly disturbing. No matter what ruse I used, anyone willing to accompany me to Nablus offered to do it only with enough fanfare to terrify all the inhabitants. So far, I could find no way to slip behind enemy lines. But in order to find you, Shechem, to conjure you, to mate with you, I have to enter your world, and by that I do not mean Nablus alone. And it was this other entrance, without knowing it, for which I was preparing.

To enter your world I do not only mean passing through security, defying martial law, settling down in a Palestinian village, or learning Arabic. The task is greater. The impassable barriers—another station of the journey—are not only political but psychic. The question is whether I am really willing—and able—to pass over into another world and whether, like Sybil, I am willing, if required, to look the fool.

As never before, some of Sybil's shoes were run down at the heels, her colors didn't quite match. Sybil, who usually managed costume with so much drama, in a certain light looked sometimes to be in a state of disarray, as if her mood caused her hems to droop, buttons to pop, skirts to unfasten, as if she was literally coming apart at the seams.

A bag lady, I had thought when I was supposed to meet her in a restaurant to comfort her after the end of a disastrous interview. But the woman who approached the table was no derelict, no down and outer, but my own distraught Sybil. It was not her clothes actually—perhaps she was as stylish as ever—but the cast of her, how she sat in them, an aura, not quite disheveled but definitely of dishabillé.

I am hoping vanity will save me because, unlike Sybil—dying for Jeremiah—I intend to meet you in the flesh.

Almost everything between us was different than it had ever been, though on the surface it seemed the same. The great difference, however, was our failure to speak about it. Perfunctorily, I added Sybil to the list of characters with whom I now had extensive conversations in my mind, although it would never have occurred to me before to exercise the kindness, or betrayal, of looking away. Was that the treason between us? Not my love for a man which distracts me, but the astonishing synchronicities of our parallel adventures with the dead. We were both mad women and I said nothing. All of civilization hangs on this decorum.

Clinically mad, I thought, as I pursued my obsession, yet sane enough to avoid a *folie à deux*. I relied on the silence between Sybil and me in more ways than one: she was my cover.

"When you went to see Mansur in the restaurant the other day, did he remember Jeremiah?"

"If you met him once, you'd never forget him. That's what everyone says, Dina.

"Mansur remembered Jeremiah walking into his restaurant at the end of the day when everyone had left, so no one would ask him for an autograph, and he'd lean over the counter just as Mansur would be scraping the yogurt from the bowls, washing up the last glasses, and then Jeremy would ask in precise and hesitant Arabic, 'Wouldn't it be easier if you sang while you worked?'

"Mansur showed me a photograph of the two of them together which Jeremiah agreed to have taken as long as Mansur promised not to hang it on the wall. It's one of the rare ones of Jeremiah smiling. Jeremiah, Mansur, and teeth. I'll show it to you when we go back some other time for lunch."

"Is it on the wall?"

"Oh no, Mansur's an honest man. Jeremiah was consistently accurate in his judgment of character."

———

Envy, Shechem, not jealousy. I wouldn't take from Sybil what she has, but I would like as much from you as well. A photograph of you, for example, proof of your existence, a curriculum vita, fingerprints, a police record, anything.

I attend to this task of conjuring, and then I forget. I am not trained or I have forgotten the means, forgotten for centuries. And it is not only that I forget, but that dedication is not sufficient, caution is of the highest priority. What if I conjure you with a vital organ missing, if I forget a blood vessel, the semilunar valve, the aorta, or even your heart? It is not only history that has to be rendered here, but history made whole. What god has sundered, let me join. Joseph says the task of the imagination requires infinite, painstaking patience.

"Why don't you just imagine world peace and be done with it, Joseph? Okay, you're not so ambitious, how about something modest, like peace in the Middle East."

"Gross acts of the imagination are relatively easy and somewhat utilitarian, they promote a moderate change in the political climate, but for the task we're considering, they are ineffective. You have to imagine each event in its entirety, all past and future, all that leads up to it, all the implications, each and every detail."

"Do you know this Buddhist story, Joseph? A peasant's horse broke its leg. 'What a shame,' his neighbor said.

" 'Maybe,' the man answered.

"The next day the army entered the village to requisition all the sturdy horses. 'How fortunate,' the neighbor said.

" 'Maybe,' the man answered. Soon the horse's leg healed and the peasant's son rode him but was thrown and injured.

" 'What a shame,' the neighbor said, but within hours the army returned for recruits . . . and so on. Is that the idea, Joseph?"

"Maybe. I only have the capacity for something small."

"What is small?"

"Imagining a sincere exchange is possible between an Arab villager and an Israeli settler."

"When?"

"Tonight."

"Can I come?"

"No. They are already too uncomfortable and endangered as it is."

"Another time?"

"I can't imagine it yet, but I will try."

"I can imagine it."

"Well, then certainly it will come to pass. You have training at this."

"Until now all my films have been about what exists, not what is coming."

"That's not your reputation, Dina."

"Maybe. I forget who I am."

I have something else to tell you, Shechem. I have stopped loving you. That is, I have stopped loving you in the form I expected you to take when you appeared. I was imagining a virile man in an olive verde uniform, a fierce primitive shepherd with rough hands, all fire and intensity. I imagined all the prejudices of my parents for whom 'terrorist' is a comparatively kind word. They believe you are all born with bombs emerging for tails. As I was looking to heal something, I was also hoping you'd explode my life open with a mortar shell. There are so many centuries and wars and deaths between us. It may be Dinah's curse, but it's not her doing.

I give up all fantasies, so you can emerge as who you are. I even give up the one of your almond skin and your nipples like burrs.

My hair has a little silver in it. When you knew me I was a young girl. My breasts were small, each one the size of your palm; afterwards they withered and then they swelled with milk, so they came to have all the lines of age and motherhood on them.

After Shechem's death, even the reflection of my face in a pan of water terrified me. How could a fourteen-year-old become a hag overnight? And if I did not trust water, I had to trust my own eyes alighting on what I could see, the wrinkles about my belly, wrist, thighs, the calloused skin about the toes. Perhaps my body had gone all the way to death with Shechem and then something, his gods perhaps, gripped me, and made me turn back. I could not take my own life, not even through sorrow. In time—days, weeks, months—I don't know how many moons passed—I had stopped counting moons and was living only between the waxing and the waning—my skin smoothed again, and the muscles returned, supported me once again.

One day, I saw a young pregnant girl in the river. Her belly was smooth, very round and pulsing. I sat with my belly resting on my palms; Asenath twisted, frolicking like Leviathan within me. When Joseph used to rest his head against my breasts, which were soft as clay that had been worked a long time, and the sadness of our lives was in their droop, I used to ask him if he wanted a young girl who was still firm as oranges. It was the custom for the first wife to offer her husband concubines in her stead, a convention that preserved the line, territory, possession, and power. But I couldn't do this. I was willing to share him with Bonah whom I loved, though—but then she still despised us both.

How will you recognize me? When my father named me Dina, did he imagine this? Your name, Shechem, what is it?

Eye of adder, hair of wolf, jackal's tooth, mandrake root, tongue of eagle: because they are so hard to come by, because the gathering requires so much attention, persistence, and cunning.

I sit in a small room like a woman bewitched. I look out the window. Do you have a window, Shechem? I do not know where you live, but I know that in order to reach you, I must pass through Dinah. She is the window, the wall, and the road around the wall.

Outside this window there is a garden where I can see, though it is past noon, a single drop of water remaining on the rapier tip of a blade of grass bobbing in the sun like a semaphore. We used to know this language. May it be sufficient.

I pretended to myself that it was Sybil's too-obvious anxiety and disapproval of my desire to go to Nablus that prevented me from saying more than necessary about my inner life. I insisted without explanation that the film could not be made if that site which was off limits was eliminated from our shooting schedule. However, implying that the government might become alarmed, I maintained the necessity of discretion, even with her. Sybil, seeing I was obsessed, but having no way to know its source, attributed it to my characteristic bullheadedness, which she knew had served me so well professionally, if not in my life. She tried, as had always been her habit, to deflect me without precipitating a direct confrontation. She spoke persistently, even reverentially, of the beauty of Sinai, of our upcoming vacation, the opportunity for us to be together in a very different way. Perhaps, she did so not so much to distract me as to escape, herself, from a preoccupation which was no less intransigent than mine.

As the days passed without visible progress on my mission, I became more and more irritable and Sybil, of course, was the focus of my displeasure. We looked at each other, shook our heads, our eyes wide open, needy. Once we stopped in the middle of the street just as the sun was setting and everything in the city seemingly at peace. "What is wrong between us, what is it?' I asked hopelessly.

"What is it?" she repeated and we walked back to our room.

When Joseph telephoned to ask us to dinner, I accepted; but then Sybil declined, claiming an interview she had scheduled could not be postponed. "I always have to respect your work, your deadlines and unreasonable demands, you have to respect mine." She was quivering. I had never seen this emotion in Sybil. It reminded me of the fear of a very small trapped animal, the fear of someone who could not run.

"Don't leave me so alone," I begged her. "The work be damned, my work, your work, all work."

Joseph cooked for us and we drank too much wine. It was a relief to giggle and tease. At least for the evening, Sybil was fleshy again, and carefully dressed. When we slipped into our narrow virginal beds, Sybil did not immediately dig into the blankets but propped herself against the pillow and asked for all the gossip. "Catch me up on the last months." For a while we were reconciled.

I asked Sybil to walk through Mea Shearim with me. It was a weekday afternoon and people bustled in the streets, attending to their daily secular life. There were no little girls with stones in their hands.

With stones you can contain a fire, with five stones you can mark the corner of your field, with more stones you can build a house and secure a roof and a grave; it takes any number of stones to kill a woman. Was it a miracle that Dinah wasn't stoned? Or was she stoned and the Testament is simply silent about it? Are the rumors of her alleged husbands glossing the presumption that she was a spoiled woman and was, therefore, killed, and Asenath with her?

If she were stoned, it could have been your doing, Shechem, your calling to her from the dead. Your unbearable loneliness could have raised the hands against her. One of her brothers would have carried her lifeless body into Leah's tent and laid her down before that bitter woman who had to bring her husband to her bed with mandrakes.

"Like mother, like daughter," they said about me for centuries. Simeon and Levi account for themselves this way: "Should he deal with our sister as with a harlot?"

"Dinah is a Hebrew name." The woman who opened the conversation at one of the gatherings Sybil had arranged so I could meet her newly acquired countrymen and countrywomen brought me a glass of wine as I was admiring the *Suka* on the roof, a canopy of branches and palm leaves hung with grapes, esrog, and oranges to celebrate the holiday of the fruits of the field. For seven days, Jewish families eat within these reconstructed fields on rooftops and porches.

"It is also a Greek name." I was trying to avoid the inevitable discussion.

"I don't think you're Greek, are you?"

"American."

"Of course, but you're Jewish."

"That's true." She'd led me immediately to what she considered essential, as one tended to do in Israel.

"It is a terrible name," she persisted. "The bastard raped her. Things haven't changed much. We need a few Levis and Simeons around to take care of women. Don't you agree?"

I looked out over Jerusalem. The lights were just beginning to come up across the city. The grapes and leaves swayed gently in the evening breeze.

"I've forgotten your name," I confessed to her. I knew she would continue talking and I wanted to take the focus away from me. I saw her nature was to talk.

"Miriam. Her brothers, Dinah's brothers, Levi and Simeon, they've been slandered." She was indomitable. "When I was growing up, my brothers protected me all the time, but that was before the war."

"Which war?"

"For independence, of course. I'll tell you something." Miriam leaned toward me conspiratorially, her wiry bird-like body quivering. "Do you want to know the real story of Hanukkah?

"When the Syrians under Antiochus Epiphanes ruled Palestine, they imposed that custom we now call the *droit du seigneur*. You know what I mean. Miriam, the sister of the Maccabees, stood up in the bridal hall after she was married and slowly dropped her bridal dress to the floor in front of all the guests, including the local despot who'd claimed her. Her brothers yelled, 'Shame,' and tried to stop her, but she held them off until she was naked. 'The shame is the *droit du seigneur*,' she said, defiantly. *That* was the beginning of *that* war!" Miriam settled back with satisfaction, her wings folded.

"Do you have any brothers?"

"No."

"Well, then, you can't quite understand. Do you want any more wine?"

I did and she brought it to me. "Too bad you can't go to Nablus now. Then you'd see how they still are. You would see how they live around that site. It would be a great scene for your film. Pigs."

"I would like to go. But I can't seem to get there. Do you have any ideas?"

"Come back in a few months, when things calm down. Anything could create a terrible incident now. They're always looking for some excuse to stir things up." She paused. "What's your full name?"

"My grandmother's name was Dinamira."

"Yes, Miriam the prophetess. She was another fighter. If you'd been here during the war. . . . The boundary lines were in the middle of the streets. The bastards shot right into our bedroom windows. They even shot through the hospital when my sister was giving birth." Someone called to Miriam from the other room. She put her hand on my arm. "You've got a good name. A strong name. But, beware, it also means 'bitterness,' " she added brightly over her shoulder as she left the room. "Wear it well."

Twice bitter then.

I drifted into the other room behind her into the discussion about the news, the latest devaluation of the pound, the deteriorating economic and political situation, oil, energy, the lack of it, and we went home.

I was giving no thought to leaving. Sybil and I spoke less and less and felt more and more uncomfortable in each other's presence. Now we walked arm in arm, if silently. Our room became a joint office, amplified by the little alcove at the head of the stairs which we soon adopted as our personal phone room. I'd offered to put in a private phone, but Anne MacDowell was horrified and Sybil laughed at both of us, I think.

We worked side by side for hours, Sybil writing or transcribing an interview, sorting papers, while I read, arranged notes, plotted the film and a means to Nablus. Sometimes, now, I saw her at her typewriter, but she was never writing any of the pieces which I was reading regularly in her journal and there was no indication that anything in her journal affected the manuscript which she regularly asked me to peruse.

Within a week I had exhausted all my contacts and all those Sybil was importuned to offer. I had implored, tricked, lied, cajoled, bullied her into giving me the phone numbers of all her influential acquaintances, though she maintained the right to call them afterwards and implore them not to help me in my quest. It was never necessary. Most people said no outright but as my contacts became higher and higher in the government, several offered to take me into the area by military convoy, by jeep, with a few soldiers, with even a captain or Pasha on parade. After a while people started calling me back with the names of heads of local battalions, captains in charge of training and recruitment, with air force colonels and experts in interrogation. I kept a careful list for Joseph. It amused him. As I gave him my daily tally, I ritually requested, "Joseph, you take me in."

"With your 'crew' and camera." The 'crew' was understood to be soldiers in civilian clothes.

"No, Joseph, I have to get to Nablus as a private person. I simply want to see the place where my name was born. You travel there all the time. You work there. Why can't I go with you? Isn't Israel supposed to be my country too? Why am I suddenly an American when most of the time it is most convenient for everyone to insist I'm a Jew?" When I threatened to go in with Moshe Dayan if Joseph refused me, he only laughed, "You'll see, he's not as charming as I am."

He did lose patience with me once. I was pressing him mercilessly, and having come to care for me a great deal, he found it difficult to refuse the only thing that seemed to matter to me.

"You damned Americans," I thought he shouted but actually he never raised his voice over an enraged whisper, "don't understand what it means to be at war. You think we're playing games here and you treat this like a high society outing. American women are the worst. Did you bring some designer Stay-Prest battle fatigues?"

"Correspondents go behind the lines. Even women correspondents. Are you so afraid I'll be injured? I'll risk it." I did feel absurd, whining like a spoiled child.

"I am not overly concerned about your welfare. It's your life, throw it where you will. But it's not only your life that is threatened by an incident. You're not innocent, but others are."

I told Joseph that I'd dreamed I was in trouble and saved myself at the last minute by making the sign against the evil eye.

Joseph regretted that there was no conclusive military evidence that the sign was as effective as a gun. As with the peace sign, he said, he hadn't found it too effective in negotiation. He admitted he hadn't found anything too effective. We were friends again.

And I was still outside the wall. I was afraid Dinah would

become even more restive. By now, I had to go to Nablus because I'd never been there and Dinah wanted to go because she had.

What of you, Shechem? We talk of you as someone to be awakened from the dead, as if Dinah is the active principle and you lie in state like some moribund Osiris without hope or will. Surely this is not the case: someone leads a donkey through via Dolorosa, someone plants a bomb in a bus station, someone harvests oranges, someone negotiates with UNRWA, and one of them is you. I envy Sybil. Her lover is identified.

Sometimes when Sybil was out for the evening, I lowered the blinds, locked the door, took off my clothes, and called you, Shechem, to me with my body. Is that what Sybil did with Jeremiah when I went out? It is a form of fidelity. As Shechem you can't desert me, you are my captive, you have no will of your own yet, while I can be unfaithful in all the ways it is possible to be unfaithful. I can even go to Joseph and bring you to me in my mind so that you witness my betrayal. Or I can disappear from you into myself as women have done for centuries, busying themselves with oils and furniture polish, diamonds, a variety of gleaming surfaces. Still, I do not go with Joseph when he asks me to spend the night with him. He does not press me too strongly and I refuse him by referring to Sybil, which he understands. Joseph does not understand why I call Sybil my little squirrel, or my piglet, my chick, my bobcat. He says he cannot find the animal in her. I want to buy Sybil everything that gleams, anything of silk, all the unhammered silver and copper so she will look like my Sybil again. She says she prefers these work clothes, the ragged sleeves, even when she offers to cover me with small bells. Yesterday we drove toward the Arab city of Ramallah but at the outskirts we got scared and turned back. Maybe we'll go again another time.

In the hills, I heard the bell of a goat. There was only one mournful deep tone and no answering tones. It was dusk, the animal was climbing slowly up into the hills, further and further from us, until the sound disappeared in the distance or it was stopped as we had and was also listening. My fingers do not feel like your fingers. I think of cutting my nails to further the deception between my legs, but the tips of my fingers are round, and your fingers, I am certain, are square.

Something changed. I was spending more time alone than I had ever done in my entire life. Sybil was grateful for my growing need for solitude. She followed me through my moods, suggesting we were finding ways of being together that we had never experienced before. We had never lived together, and now we lived together as lovers often live together, in the unspoken heart of what we were doing. I needed to be with her at night. She did not need to speak. I needed to breathe in the air that she breathed out. The comfort was not in our activities nor in our talk; for the first time, these were entirely irrelevant. I watched her dress or undress, I accompanied her to parties, we walked in the garden, we exchanged small talk and memories. For days at a time we wanted nothing from each other. It was so easy, we could have been trees.

Once I commented that I was hardly dreaming anymore. She revealed that she had also stopped dreaming. "Jeremiah is the dream," she said. "And yours?" She did not press me for an answer.

She received a letter from Jeremiah's mother. Fortunately, I was in the room when it arrived. She read it aloud:

Stay away from my son. There's a stiff penalty for anyone who digs up graves to take what was buried with the dead. Whatever was buried there was buried for good reason. His remains belong to the state.

Sincerely yours,
Anna Blazer

I learned where to walk, wandering in the ordinary residential sections, avoiding the shops, hotels, museums, and boulevards and daring the Old City only occasionally. When I visited Joseph in his apartment, I insisted he meet me at the Eastern Gate of the Old City to walk me through the streets, my fingers firmly clenched about his arm. I preferred to be where nothing would startle me, though everywhere I found the air thick with everything that had ever been born.

For balance, I turned and turned about the same blocks of undistinguished apartments and small houses fronted by ragged gardens in the neighborhood of the hospice. We could say that I walked the streets. In the modern world that has sinister implications. Today when a woman wraps a red thread about her wrist, tosses a garish flounce of red dyed ostrich feathers over her shoulder, or sits in a window under a red light, legs crossed, wearing stiletto heels, she is not seen for her service to the goddess.

Levi was afraid that Dinah would become a harlot. Did he mean he was afraid that she'd slip into the other camp? She could not be a priestess in her own home. Rachel had had a red string about her wrist when she met Jacob at the well. But Leah never wore a string; she was determined not to be in anyone's service. When she married Jacob, she took his god in as easily as she took in his food and his body. What remained in her of the old gods was fertility; she wanted as many sons as there were sheaves of wheat in the field; she wanted to see herself spreading out across the horizon. Rachel continued to pray through the trees and Jacob, without acknowledging it, prayed through the kine.

The white stone from which Jerusalem is constructed soothed me more than the cedars. I made a friend of an elderly lady who opened her front door at 9 A.M., precisely, to water her roses with dish water carefully saved in a yellow pail. We exchanged greetings. She spoke no English. I didn't accept her offer to tea. We looked at the sky together and commiserated about the weather through elaborate hand and facial gestures. I waited for her most mornings, trying to be regular in my devotions.

The weather was erratic. After a cold spell, the humidity rose again suddenly and I expected it would rain. When I passed my friend's house in the evening, I saw she had left the bucket beside the front door to catch the rainwater. If the rain was heavy enough I could wash my hair in it.

What am I doing? I asked myself. In the States, I would have diagnosed a depression and prescribed a bout of disciplined work, exercise, movies, or a jaunt at a fat farm. I assured myself that Dinah was teaching me patience. Walking became a practice. I turned the block again and again. My life emptied. Sybil and I spoke less and less. We were closer than ever before. I threw the diaphragm, which I had inserted each morning ritually for years, into my suitcase so I would not be tempted by Joseph. Then I withdrew it from my luggage and inserted it again.

"Do you miss me?" Sybil turned to me sweetly, apologetically.

"Not as much as I would have predicted."

"Where do you go?"

"I walk a great deal."

"Where?"

"Anywhere."

"In the Sinai, it will be different."

She returned to her notes. There was a thickening sheaf of papers on the bureau. My presence was at least good for something; she was getting a lot of work done. When I looked through them, I did not find her, except as the most neutral, competent journalist.

In the past, she'd always ridiculed the dispassionate reporter she seemingly had become.

"I've never known anyone like Jeremiah," I tell her.

"Neither have I."

Levi always stank like a bear, but Joseph was thin as a dream. I could see through his bones to the dream filter at the back of his eyes. His irises were sometimes green, sometimes mauve; before night they turned blue as the sky faded. When we traveled, Joseph put me on a camel or an ass and walked beside me. Fur was beginning to grow on his chest, but it never whorled or matted. When the birds over our heads were flying in formation, Joseph knew what dreams would come. He said dreams had to fly and that anything could kill a dream. I asked what dead men dreamed because I was afraid of what had happened to Hamor and his brothers as Levi had put out their eyes. "Color and song," Joseph assured me. I closed my eyes and rocked on the camel as Joseph sang. We went on this way for days, swaying in the heat and, for all that time, I kept my eyes closed and did not look where we were going. Sometimes the sounds we heard were so loud they wounded the air and I put my hands over my ears to keep out the din of language, the complaints of cicadas, lizards, earthworms, and crows. It was difficult to dream when the crows followed us: crows are always death. I had learned to trill and whistle so as to call living creatures to me. Snakes slithered silently about me but never did us harm. Sometimes Joseph sat behind me, his hands crossed over my heart or on my belly. I was relieved that Asenath would have a father.

I had not been a love child, but Jacob had carried me under his cloak. I was a rage child. Jacob had pummeled Leah until she bleated in delight, then he pulled his strength back into him, left the bed, and threw himself at Rachel. Like a great ram, he entered the white ewe thighs of Rachel that same night. So Joseph was also my younger brother. He was conceived second but born first.

Then it was Simchas Torah. I asked Sybil to go to the Wall with me, thinking to please her and, surprisingly, she objected. Every seventh year there was a fertility ceremony and this was the seventh year and I wanted to be there because I have been childless. I have always said it is by choice, but it turns out that when a species is overcrowded, rats, for example, or wolves, the creatures become sterile, decide not to breed. Although I always said I had chosen my life, I may have been programmed to respond to conditions I only remotely appreciated. The Dane left the hospice; Sybil was not going to have tall, white children, would not have red-legged stork babies.

Sybil admitted that she had never been to the Wall. To avoid the Wall while spending time in the Old City is not easy. "Wailing? Don't I know everything there is to know about wailing? Do I have to ritualize it?" Everyone in Sybil's family is dead. Even her friends die prematurely and I have had to promise her I will live a long time. I didn't worry about going to Nablus, neither Dina nor Dinah will die there.

"Who is refusing to go to the Wall? You or Jeremiah?"

"That's an odd question."

"Don't you find you grow into him a little?"

She held a photo of a dark, gaunt soldier next to her face and glanced in the mirror. Sybil has large, round, soft deer eyes. The newsprint managed to capture the sneer and threat, the jackal, in Jeremiah's eyes.

"Well, are we alike?"

"He seems such a harsh man. What attracts you to him?"

"When he first left the country, he put on a Groucho Marx disguise. Imagine that in the airport in Tel Aviv. False nose, moustache, fake glasses, the entire obvious masquerade. As he went through passport control, one officer, who was not reassured by his performance, by his comic sauntering through the airport, his little charades for the children, or his public clowning, jumped to stop him. Jeremiah leaned toward the officer, 'You know who I am. The stewardess is my wife. We just married secretly,' he whispered conspiratorially. 'She thinks I'm at the front. Please . . .' He lifted the false nose as a gesture but not far enough to be seen by the crowd. Later, when he was interviewed, the officer said he'd been enchanted, that he would have done anything for Jeremiah Abazadik. Had he taken off the diguise, he would have been stampeded. An Israeli Beatle. Everywhere I go, someone knows him. He blew himself to a thousand pieces and everyone wants a souvenir. They didn't even find his watch intact."

"I'll take a prayer to the Wall for you."

"Look who is becoming religious, Dina!"

"Only trying to play my role as a tourist. Will you give me a prayer?"

"I'll take it myself, thank you." Sybil managed to refuse and acquiesce at the same time.

You write a prayer on a sliver of paper and slip it into one of the cracks of the wall. Kissing the earth when you come to Israel is one way of receiving a blessing, praying at the Wailing Wall is another. I spent a long time trying to find the right words, then I wrote them down in my smallest possible hand so neither Lucifer nor God could read them. I wrote, "Let Shechem be alive. Let us meet. May I not be afraid." Perhaps I asked for too much. I believe that greed should interfere with luck, though I've never found evidence for that in the world.

"I know what you wrote: 'Let me get to Nablus.' "

"You're right. Would you like to have a cup of tea?"

"Yes, a cup of tea with English cream and a . . ."

"Trifle." It was perfect. Sybil ate the trifle while I watched her, my fear of greed greatly reduced.

A wind ripped across the large square before the Wall. The children ran into the sudden blast. The square was filled with its presence. Between the Wall and the specially erected bandstand where a military band with much brass embarked on a program of marches, an unofficial small square was created through the instinct for the sacred. In order to reach the Wall, we had to cross this area where so many were crowded about the band. A rope reaching to the bandstand unequally divided the Wall in two. Men prayed to the left on the northern side, women to the right. The men stood some small distance from the Wall, grasping their prayer books, bending back and forth in the rhythm of devotion, while the women climbed the wall, pressed against it, caressed it with their hands, wept, their faces grinding into the stone. The wind was strong and gusty. It whipped at their clothes. As we approached, we heard the murmurs, whispers, and soft cries of the women praying, their beseechments and demands. Some scraped their hands across the stones, careful not to dislodge the thousands of scraps of paper jammed into the cracks. A few pounded the walls with their fists, others treated the stone as a lover, as safety, as escape.

As we passed through the sacred space, Sybil quivered with irritation. She dislikes crowds, brass bands, and patriotic music. "This isn't right," she hissed into my ear. But I am stubborn, so she did not try to convince me to leave.

"I'll put the paper in the wall for you; then it will have the strength of two prayers, yours and mine."

Within me, Shechem, I could feel you hold back, even recoil. Ours was a smaller wall and your people had built it. My people built other walls in Egypt. Since then we've all become experts in walls and fences. There was a wall about me even as I approached the Wall. I had forgotten the most common prayer for my father's and my mother's health which I could have slipped into the wall with ease. The music was blasting in our ears and the military rhythms, so precise and arousing, conflicted with the erratic wind and graceful sweep of dust and odd papers through the air.

I hesitated, but then I was attracted to the women weeping on the Wall. I wanted to weep with them. It would have been as if I were in the fields again with the daughters. Their skirts whipped about their delicate embroidered breeches. They were mostly immigrants from Iran, Egypt, and Syria, other Arab countries, the newly arrived and newly disdained. The white cloths on their heads covering their hair slapped about like rags of clouds.

Later, we saw them standing in small groups, husbands and wives outside the Wall of the Old City, the women dancing their little dances in the street, white handkerchiefs alive in their fists. Outside there was no music except for the music they made, singing and clicking. First the women danced alone, then the men joined them, one hand behind the back, head erect, both gripping the white cloth. They danced on one corner then on the other. Sybil and I stopped to watch them and I danced a little in response from across the street. They waved us to join them, but I was too shy. So we stood and watched and then we applauded them and then we clapped our hands so that we could add to the music, but from a distance.

But this, Shechem, was after the Wall.

We approached the Wall and though the women were preoccupied with their grief, they sensed our presence. Crowded though they were—the men had twice as much space and there were fewer of them—they yielded a bit of Wall to us. Sybil approached as someone who had seen a ghost, touched the Wall briefly, mumbled something, dug her white paper into a crack, and retreated, sniffing the air for danger. To the south, tourists, children, and a few soldiers were perched like prairie dogs on a clay slope which was marked "Off Limits." Sybil smiled graciously when the soldiers insisted she could not mount the hill and, pretending not to understand Hebrew, she grasped the extended hand intended to shake her off and pulled herself on to the higher ground. The soldier, nonplussed, tried to rebuff her again but she only grabbed his wrist again, smiling gratefully, and pulled herself to an even better vantage point. Then the soldier, having no jacket he could give her legally, offered her a large square of newspaper while finally escorting her to the best spot of all.

Meanwhile, I leaned my head against the Wall, praying and eavesdropping. I tucked three pieces of paper into a crack as high as I could reach so that they would not be dislodged. Some of the weathered papers deep within the Wall must have been there for years. How long did the Wall require to answer a request? When did one give up hope? In the third paper, I had asked to meet you, Shechem, in the second paper, I did ask to go to Nablus. And in the first paper—I confess it, Dinah—I addressed God directly. After all, I was in His Temple and in God's Temple, one cannot pray to the trees or the snakes. In any temple one must propitiate the presiding deity. In the first paper, I asked God to protect us.

I fell into reverie, hypnotized by the litanies of pain expressed in English, Yiddish, French, Spanish, Hebrew, Arabic, Russian, Farsi, Ladino. The whispered complaints from all the soft women's mouths overcame the harsh brass sounds from the band. With my ear against the Wall, I was able to concentrate on the brush strokes of their hands and bodies and the little cries of loss, separation, desperation, illness, hunger, fear, dying, regret, loss, separation, despair, I beg you . . . I pray you. . . . My eyes closed, I could have fallen asleep in the warm afternoon sun, when I was startled by a long loud wail of someone overcome. I shuddered at the sound as it was followed by another wail more like a howl and then some distinctly female cries of protest. A woman was being pulled off the Wall by a stocky, gruff, dark man in a rumpled uniform. Had she prayed too long? Was there some secret time one was permitted, were there rules posted somewhere of which I was not aware? I closed my eyes again trying to pray in case the time was limited, but I was taken into the prayers of the Sephardic woman next to me who tapped her forehead against the stones while the edge of her yellow scarf tapped my face. She turned her face toward me briefly. Beneath her eyes were grey runlets where the grit of the stone had mixed with her tears. I swayed slightly, rhythmically, my knees also rocking toward the Wall as I braced my arm against it. Behind me there were the ongoing rhythmic murmurs of men reading from the prayer books. My body swayed even as their bodies rocked and swayed. Then there was another howl, then men's prayers continued undisturbed, and I saw that another woman was fighting a soldier who was pulling her away from the

Wall, placing her behind a barrier which had just been erected so that the sacred space I had had to cross was now officially secularized. After the soldier left the woman, he turned around again, raised his finger commandingly, "Don't move!"

The soldier returned to the Wall and then another joined him and together they pried off the next two women, then the next, but the first returned, yelling words I somehow magically deciphered. She had traveled from Morocco to be there. She had not been able to conceive and her husband was ready to leave her because he wanted a son. Then more soldiers entered, urgency expressed in their rough movements. I didn't understand a word of what was being shouted at us but it became clear that the women were being removed, all of us, and my turn was next. Behind me the men continued praying; there were no soldiers on that side of the Wall though I assumed they were next.

I closed my eyes again, pretended to pray and then, I was praying. Then I felt a soldier's hand closing on my wrist, wrenching me from the Wall. As I opened my eyes, I saw that the men were no longer praying, but were watching with great attention though they did nothing; they did not protest, even when the men were touching us roughly with their bare hands. I said, "I am praying," but the soldier, though more gentle with me after he heard my American accent, was still insistent. I thought of sitting down, but I saw this fracas was being observed by the crowd and was afraid of how they would respond. There were now thousands of people filling the square pressing up to the barricades and their bovine intensity frightened me even more than the soldiers. I had never, until that moment, been touched by a soldier, not even in love. I did what I ought to have done, originally. I stood erect, took the man's hand from my arm, which he permitted because it did not seem likely I would pray again, while rummaging in my purse for the other kind of papers which always answer prayers, saying: "I am an American journalist. I do not understand what is happening here." I found my credentials and the requisite pad and pen and waited. I was the only woman remaining at the Wall.

In broken English, the soldier informed me that the Head Rabbi of Jerusalem was about to perform the fructification ceremony. Looking up, I saw a dark portly man in black robes and a tall black priestly hat on the bandstand, surrounded by shorter similarly bearded, robed men within a golden fence of horns and tubas. The soldier was patient and careful because he saw I was writing and did not see the Rabbi's impatience. "This is a very joyful occasion, but very solemn," he explained. "It is performed only every seven years and it must be done well for our economy depends on its success." Then he lowered his voice. "You understand that the Rabbi must not be distracted by the presence of women. He must be able to pray with a clear heart."

There were some shouts from the bandstand and the soldier bristled, and pulled me not to the barrier but to the clay mound where Sybil was watching. I was the last woman to leave and as soon as I was out of the square, the men who had been waiting for this moment raced forward across the rope to take up our places on the Wall.

This wall is all that remains from the Second Temple, which the Romans destroyed. After the destruction, the Jews were dispersed. The Wall symbolizes both exile and return. When the temple was destroyed, the worship of Asherah ceased also. It is not commonly known that the worship of Asherah continued until that time.

Sybil insisted that the Wall, like every holy place, speaks to whoever comes, saying what he wants to hear.

"What I want to hear or what is to be heard?" I asked her. "Did the Wall say anything to you?"

"Nothing. I said nothing to it; it said nothing to me."

But that, Sybil, is a sign.

Two weeks had passed. We had taken the room in the hostel for a month. When Sybil smoothed a sheet, or aligned the crocheted scarf on the end table, she reassured me with the gesture that there was love in the universe. Each morning she went to the garden and picked fresh flowers for the two small vases beside our beds. Increasingly, she treated the material world with respect again, as if each object was a sacred container; the vase contained holy water, the flowers were the eyes of god, the crocheted scarf was a hermetic script.

Always at a good distance, so as not to be discovered by Leah, I followed behind Rachel as she took Joseph through the fields. Joseph always knew when I was there, we had the second sense of twins. I think we had the same scent, the animals who preferred me preferred him as well, though we had been born from separate wombs. Like twins, we had been born a few minutes apart, only the sound of a cry separated us, but it was enough to make a difference in the stars. Rachel walked so slowly across the fields, she resembled the planet that takes a lifetime to cross the con- stellations. Walking that slowly she saw everything and taught it to Joseph, how one leaf differed from another, which berries were used for medicines, which roots alleviated pain, how to use figs in potions. Afterwards Joseph taught me what he had learned, the names of plants, their uses, the names of stars, their influences. Then I dreamed the teaching and made the knowledge mine. What he learned from Rachel was not different from what I learned later from Shechem's sisters. Leah taught me about lentils, olives, and barley; Rachel, through Joseph, taught me about the gods.

Joseph and I were always set apart from the others. At first I thought it was because we were the youngest, then because I was the first girl, but finally I realized it was because Jacob loved us. The other sons resembled Jacob; they worshipped as he did and were equally fierce and stern, but we were the beloveds. Even Leah, to his regret, came to be more like him each day. When they came to die they were two branches of the same twisted wood. But Rachel was slow and soft, spoke to the trees and nuzzled with the flocks. When Jacob came to Rachel's tent, she made him dance for her and afterwards he was ashamed and lay next to Leah's hard body so he could sleep without desire. Jacob said Rachel nursed Joseph far too long, that it would make him soft. I weaned myself from Leah's breast but it was not long before I learned to suck the cow's teats when I wanted milk.

Joseph approved my sloth. Though everyone bustled about him, though Israel itself beat with the frantic rhythm of a very small bird, Joseph believed in stillness. "At the negotiating table," he maintained, contrary to his colleagues, "it must always seem that there is an infinite amount of time so that every decision is thoughtful and considered. The opposition must have sufficient time to reconsider so that agreements cannot be abrogated because they were made in haste. When those he negotiated with finally signed a paper, they had a remote feeling of friendship though they were still committed enemies; they had known each other such a long time.

I was amused to think that I had come to understand the adage "Time heals all wounds." I even gave up my ferocious determination to visit Nablus. I went through the motions of trying to get there, but some days I forgot my need entirely. Perhaps I fell under Jeremiah's spell. After a while Jeremiah was no longer friction between Sybil and myself. I began to accept his presence. "That is a pretty skirt, I think Jeremiah would have liked it on you," I said one morning. "Jeremiah would have yogurt for breakfast," Sybil answered. "Jeremiah never voted. . . . Jeremiah spent the Sabbath sharpening knives. . . . Sometimes Jeremiah gave his entire salary to war widows—on both sides. . . . I don't think Jeremiah would mind this weather."

THE TESTIMONY OF JEREMIAH ABAZADIK
A Posthumous Autobiography

Go to the Golan if you want to see trees shaped like wire, a landscape of metal, earth like gunpowder. Go to the Golan if you want to see the palette of war in mud and underbrush. That was my country; it took the softness from my voice and where I needed a rasp, it gave it to me. I went back to it, the way you go back to a gun, lovingly. When your hand itches with necessity, you stroke the barrel, saying, "This goddamnfuckingmother will get me through." My life was a time bomb, someone set it ticking, then gave me the guitar to muffle the noise.

A singer has to have twenty-twenty vision. They don't tell you that in music school. He has to see over the barbed wire. He has to be able to see to the next hope. Singers die early, earlier and more violently than poets, and just as often by their own hands, voluntary and involuntary suicide. If you're a real singer and you live in this world, either you commit suicide, or you're a fraud.

My grandfather bought me a guitar. He bought it because he wanted me to play the violin. He gave me my first cigarette and my first glass of schnapps. "The only thing I don't permit you is a lie." He lit the cigarette, passed it to me, watched me inhale and then he stood over me and prayed. When I finished, he took off his *tallit* and lit a cigarette as if he smoked every day. "I don't want you to think I am a holy man. God is holy. Men are men. Try your best."

.   .   .

Jeremiah was with us all the time now. He had become another side of Sybil; he amplified her and brought a new dimension to our lives. For the first time, I could discuss politics with Sybil, who had always been disinterested. One day, we walked through the Arab section of Jerusalem and, inexplicably, I burst into tears;

holding me, she asked no questions. Later she said, "Jeremiah also wept." But when I tried to speak to her about the other Jeremiah, the one in her journal, she looked at me as if I were mad. Naturally, then, I didn't try to speak to her about you, Shechem.

When I was ill for a few days, drinking orange juice, sometimes moaning, Sybil attended me, saying it softened me, that I had come with a hard, determined edge, but the illness had taken it and chewed me as if I were a cud. "You were so willful when you came, so determined about Nablus and Simchas Torah. Israel's finally broken your damned will; New York didn't do it. I thought you were doomed."

I began to keep my journal conscientiously in order to try to understand Dinah, or articulate the affinities between us, also to create an inner order. But I did not give Sybil access to it, and she never asked. Whenever Nablus was in the news, I felt obligated to save the clippings.

There was another sniping incident in Nablus against the Palestinians, followed by retaliations against the border kibbutzim. The mayor of Nablus was under house arrest. There were rumors of atrocities by the Palestinians and torture by the Israelis. A bomb exploded in Haifa. Joseph had just been to Nablus—would tell me nothing. I refrained from pressing him to take me with him. I knew he saw my desire in my eyes. I was not trying to disguise it.

I knew I couldn't stay in the hospice with Sybil indefinitely. I seemed to be settling into a disconcerting inertia, but couldn't imagine doing anything but what I was doing. Sometimes I imagined living by myself, finding an apartment or taking a room with cooking privileges in someone's house, the way my parents took in boarders when I was young. Huddling in the little nook by the telephone, looking out over the sleeping city, I sometimes imagined myself desolate and exiled in a small and shabby kitchen with an old gas stove set on four metal legs between a window which old paint had sealed and a chipped sink on the other side. There would be a brown stain where the cold water dripped because no one bothered to change the washer until no washer could repair it anymore, even though such neglect is a crime in Israel. Two steps from the sink I saw a small gray formica table, with tubular aluminum legs, stained and chipped at one edge. Very thin and absorbent paper napkins were aligned with the core of a plastic apple slit down the middle. Bread crumbs dropped onto the table through the plastic bread basket woven to resemble straw. White rolls hardened into stone each night. Once a month, the cleaning lady, a recent Russian immigrant, would clean the kitchen, but afterwards, the linoleum would look the same. In my imagination, I slept on a sofa bed without bothering to open it unless Sybil was spending the night. I didn't do much with my time.

In reality, I stayed with Sybil quite happily except when I spent the night at Joseph's house. I wrote home again saying, "The truth is I'm not really working on the film yet. Need a few more weeks, even some months off. Very tired. Can't concentrate."

The office answered. "We've got our hands full dealing with distribution on the old stuff. Don't do anything new yet. Anyway we could live in your elegant apartment forever. Where are the instructions for the microwave? We never knew we couldn't live without a Cuisinart. Are you sure you can get rest in Israel? Have you thought about Bali? We've gotten the funding for the film. They're ready to roll when you are but in no hurry. J. Productions wants to know if you'd consider the same approach in Egypt? We said, 'Yes, after this one is shot,' but also told them you're incommunicado for a while. You know how they are, made them even more eager. Early first snow. Bitter winter coming. Great Impressionist show at MOMA. Rumors that your last pix will get an award. When you're ready to work WE'LL COME THERE—it's too cold to meet here. What's the equivalent of a dacha on the Black Sea? How *is* Sybil? We hear rumors. . . . We all love you."

I read the letters again and again to remind myself of my past. The imaginary kitchen became more real. In my mind, I would tiptoe about my boarding house room or lie in bed trying to remember my dreams while waiting for the landlady to go to work so I could have a bath or shower with more water than was allowed. My room had a private entrance but the landlady listened carefully to footsteps. The rule was "No overnight guests." Sybil was an exception because they knew she had been a friend of Jeremiah Abazadik's and she promised them a photo or some other memento when she got around to it.

"Are you lonely, Joseph?" We enjoyed walking through the Old City late at night when everyone but the residents had deserted it.

"Very lonely." From the windows of his very contemporary apartment in an elegant gentrified Jewish area we looked out over the closed stalls of the *suk,* listening to the night singing of the donkeys.

"And you never married?"

"Never. I could never marry a foreign woman and any woman would be foreign to half of me. I have to marry someone who is absolutely loyal to both sides. I try to imagine her: she has an Israeli mother and a Palestinian father, or is the more ideal, more unlikely combination, an Israeli father and a Palestinian mother? Ideally, I should marry a woman born in 1947 on the border partitioning Jerusalem, whose parents, Palestinian and Israeli, stayed together during the war and were completely loyal to their people and to each other. You see how impossible it is? Find her for me and I'll marry her sight unseen and give you the matchmaker price. Agreed?"

Some nights we drank *arak* in his other small apartment in the Arab quarter of East Jerusalem. He was never comfortable for long in either place. Two apartments were an extreme indulgence, but he had many guests so one or the other was always being used by someone else.

"If I find her, she'll be a madwoman, Joseph."

"Then she'll be right for me."

His colleagues didn't trust him. The Palestinians didn't trust him either. But they had no one else.

Sometimes we lay beside each other embracing for hours without moving. I thought making love with him would be so tame, that in time our clothes would dissolve so our naked bodies could press against each other and after another millenium our bodies would penetrate each other, all without movement and without sound.

"Are you lonely, Joseph?"

"Very lonely. Are you?"

"No. No longer." And I wasn't.

PART II

*In the beginning there was sound, a strange whirr, a subtle hum-
ming, a single tone . . . song. There was one song from one end
of the universe to the other. Even across the sacred river, there
was only this one sound, and the sacred river was also song. There
was no separation between the worlds, there was only one
world . . . the cadences rose and fell . . . it was always the same.
It was always singing.*

*Once in the singing unto itself, song came out of nothingness
to meet it. One tone filling the universe in the one direction and
another tone filling the universe in the other direction, each called
out of nothingness unable to resist the singing.*

*The tones met within themselves, each exactly the other, and
each totally distinct. . . . Trembling, they were drawn together into
one note, met violently in themselves, and shattered.*

*. . . Once there had been one song and no loneliness. Now when
they were two, they were shards of song, they were splinters among
silence. They brought their brokenness together, they heard each
other for the first time, they listened, but they could not join.*

Listening was a great light, a great darkness, and a great fire.

The fire became smoke, it was falling into water, it was rising to be mist, it was the wind burning . . . it was the world. . . .

Because they were broken, they sang to each other, one singing and the other listening, astonished by their differences, then the other singing and the one listening . . . wrapped, each of them, into a moving braid of longing . . .

. . . And then they slipped from each other, were pulled apart, to the far ends of the universe, to the edge of nothing from which they had come . . . the song became fainter and fainter, the pulses of the universe barely audible; it was almost winter . . . still.

In the beginning there was silence and it lasted forever from the beginning. It was absolutely silent from one end to the other— there was only silence and nothingness. . . . Inevitably, there was loneliness, there was longing, once more. . . .

. . . the silence on the edge of nothingness began to sound, began the one tone, a faint hum, increasing in speed, pitch, intensity until singing met itself violently in its core, in the very point of sound, the entire universe pitching, weaving, vibrant and one. . . . Forever. There was nothing else . . . two chants . . . inseparable and indistinct . . . a great implosion of song . . . they could not contain it. They held it forever. The world disappeared. . . .

So it came to pass again as it must when nothing changes and everything must change, they shattered again, were broken, became two, became one, separation and unity, motion and stillness, song and silence. They went toward their brokenness joyfully, singing and listening, with as much longing, need, and sorrow as they had gone toward their pointedness out of silence. Once more they were splintered and intertwining, were wrapped within a moving braid of longing, became a great dancing braid of light, the strands misty and shining, became time and space, particles of water and pieces of wind, night, and darkness, they were the serpent and the tree, they were the moon . . . they were the darkness about the light, they were . . .

There had been the one sound, it was dance and song, it was the world. Out of it came earth, a great luminous egg, it was a stone, breathing.

... From the beginning when men and women were apart they sang to each other ... created loneliness ... created longing ... and the song which made them one. ...

These fragments, these bits of knowing, did not come in words. The knowing came through the body, as if a great light penetrated my skin, I don't know from where, from very far away, perhaps the stars. It wrote itself everywhere, even in my heart, and when I awakened I could read it, or words would come to me in part, afterwards, as if I were running my fingers over the new small wedges in my flesh which were an alphabet made by stones and axes. I could never make up all the words, but this did not prevent me from knowing. It was only that I couldn't speak fully about my knowing to anyone, not to Shechem, not to Joseph, not to the sisters, not even to myself. I couldn't receive their knowing fully either, even when they had words, because the knowing was not in words either. The words were a code, they only pointed a direction. I was told that I would know it all but it would take a long time. I would have to learn the code first. After the code, I would learn the stories, that was the second stage of learning. But finally all the learning came through the light which entered my body. Joseph and I practiced dreaming, lying under the stars, holding hands, falling off together into another world, letting the dream

enter us at the same time. When we did this we always had the same dream and we knew we were opening.

I do not know what happened after Shechem died. It is possible that I learned nothing after that, that I was no longer a great tent of skins with the wind as a guest, but I was a withered hide hanging full of holes and could contain nothing. I looked at my brothers, they were so full of God and were so empty. They looked like my mother, Leah, her dry breasts filling again and again with milk, feeding nothing. I watched my father, Jacob. Sometimes he was full of knowing, but only when he was also full of God. When knowing slipped from him like an earthslide, he shone through the mud like the great tree shines through her bark, putting up her arms, reaching toward heaven. Once after both Asenath and Benjamin had been born, I came upon Jacob by himself in the field at night secretly shining as a man shines, not like a tree shines but like lightning or a great ladder, and I asked to climb the light with him. I offered to show him the dance I knew that could bring fire.

But he growled at me, "What can your gods do? They didn't save Shechem. They brought shame on me through my sons. I had to leave my lands. They betrayed me through their impotence. What else can they do?"

I said, "They do nothing. The gods are only the way to the gods. Nothing else." I didn't know what I meant. I meant something like the god was the ladder or the tree, it was the tendril of light, the luminous vine of beans he was climbing to the stars and emptiness.

Rachel must have taught him that for I had seen her dancing with the teraphim. *Jacob lowered his eyes. When he looked up at me, the ladder was gone, obscured by the great storm in his face. "There is only one God," he snarled at me, "even Rachel knows that now. I have taught her more than Laban ever could teach her with his clay dolls. I teach her with words, do you understand? Words. God gives me the words and I give them to her, and to*

Leah and to my sons, and I would give them to you and Joseph if you wanted to hear."

"It isn't in the words," I mumbled. I didn't have words to match his words. I only said, "It doesn't matter if you say there is one or many gods." I tried again but he was not listening and I didn't understand my own words. I knew only through my body that the words were leaves in the wind, they showed me the direction.

Before Shechem's death, I asked Joseph if he would come with me to see Bonah. I wanted her to teach him as I was learning to teach, not with words, but with my body. As I was learning to be water, she would teach him to be the snake. But he wouldn't come. "I want to be the first man you teach," he said. Then I knew that he had never been with a woman. But the first one I taught was Shechem. I had already promised that to him.

Naturally, the Museum Secretary was polite. My reputation had preceded me, either that I was a friend of Joseph's or that I was making a film, or both. Still he saw no way that I could go to Nablus, all archaeological work had ceased in the West Bank and though Joseph's tomb was still under Israeli control, the site at Shechem only some few meters away was in Arab hands. "It's become a dump," he added belligerently.

I backtracked, hoping that if I presented scholarly intentions, he would be more inclined to help me. So I inquired about the small Asherahs which had been removed from the museum case. He was as impatient with this inquiry as with my other request.

"You're not the first to want to see them this year. They were gathering dust for decades, but now every foreign woman wants to look at them. Imagine, some woman came here to do a dissertation on Asherah, trees, and snakes. What's next! Most of them have been destroyed, of course, through time, though it is still exaggerated how important or interesting they are. Feminist scholars are making too big a deal of them. I'd be happy, too, if more had been preserved. The large ones which stood outside the temple were made of wood and those, of course, disappeared. But I'm certain that the smaller ones were out of use for centuries before that. It isn't as if we destroyed them, you know. The women threw them away. The women did not continue to worship Asherah. They freed themselves from that primitive belief system as soon as Abraham received the Word. They threw it away quite voluntarily with other trinkets."

"Don't you think the Asherahs survive in the Cross," I persisted, "in the way that Demeter worship probably survives in the taboo against pigs, in the way that what is prohibited or altered refers to an underlying preexistent recognition of power?"

"No, I don't think the Cross is a variation of the Asherah." I hadn't found the right subject at all and it was too late to step out of the conversation. The Secretary wasn't much interested in tree imagery, in world tree myths, in the *axis mundi*, not even in the tree of knowledge or the Kabbalistic tree of life.

I saw quickly that he found the discussion boring. "There aren't many trees in Israel. Maybe you haven't noticed since you haven't been to the Negev yet, have you? Frankly, when I think about trees, these days, I think about planting them. I'm sure there are some trees in Israel with your name on them, aren't there? Were your parents Zionists? Do you want to see your trees? Most Americans come to Israel with a plot map of their contributions. It wastes a lot of petrol running around from grove to grove."

I assured him that this was not my interest.

"What is your interest?"

"Nablus."

"Nablus and Asherahs, right? You know, I planted an entire orange orchard myself and now I add a tree a year for myself and each member of my family. It gives me an odd satisfaction to interrupt this work of preserving ruins to put a spade in the earth."

I was in my great darkness and lay against my own belly as if it were a boulder I could not dislodge. We had been traveling south, away from Shechem. When we passed Beth-El, I felt as if I was

choking with weeds and mud. I was heavier than stagnant waters.
There was scum over my eyes and nothing stirred me. But after a
moon and then again two other moons, I woke up wanting to
wash my hair. Joseph poured water into a basin and helped me.
I knew that Shechem had given me into Joseph's hands so I might
reawaken.

I think the Secretary was embarrassed by his domestic revelation
about planting trees because he launched into me again. "Who
knows what those little figurines were originally. We don't have
any texts about them, so we can't speculate and create a fantasy
history that we want to exist. These figurines left no traces because
they'd had little import. Don't you understand the simplest tenet
of Judaism—you are Jewish, aren't you?—Jews worship one God.
They don't have idols. That's it; that is Judaism. There isn't any
more to it than that.

   "I am always amazed at how secular American Jews are. Judaism
marks the end of fetishism. It was/is the apogee and perigee of
human thought. Everything follows from it. Look what happened
when the Jews went to Egypt. Joseph even converted the Pharaoh.
Do you think Amenhotep would have become Akhenaten without us?"

Asenath was born as if lightning married the lake. I sat in Joseph's
lap so that she would exit from the two of us and he could say,
"This is my child," as Rachel had claimed Dan who was born
from Bilhah in Rachel's lap. Asenath was the last born this way
from the double lap. Afterwards the women forgot the practice,
my brothers kept them apart from each other, forbid them to speak
their own languages. It was up to me, therefore, to remember. So
few of us remembering so much through the centuries.

The meeting was clearly over, Shechem, but I wasn't going to leave.
Joseph had impressed me greatly with a story, and I took it to
heart in this moment and fell into silence.

"What's your most developed diplomatic skill?" I had asked Joseph.

"Silence." He was proud of it.

"How do you manage it?" I asked. It was a pragmatic question.

"I'll tell you a story. During one of the worst meetings, when the rebuttals, crossfire, accusations, had reached an unbearable pitch, my turn came to speak. My aide hastily passed me some notes that our team wanted translated into an eloquent and succinct volley. Everyone was impatient, wanting to speak himself, including the restive members of my own delegation. In the odd way that sometimes happens, when we intend one thing and another happens, I was suddenly back in my childhood when I'd been a serious stutterer. It was humiliating. I was stuttering again. I had always been able to imitate stuttering, but this wasn't an imitation. I couldn't loose myself from it. I interrupted my direction, stammering, 'F-f-f-forgive me. I m-m-m-m-must collect m-my thoughts.' We sat quietly. Naturally everyone was embarrassed and feeling generous. I deliberately engaged each person's eyes so that no one would think I was yielding my turn, then I lowered my eyes and meditated. I don't know how long we sat this way together. The others followed suit, many are, you know, on each side, in their ways, religious, even spiritual, men, so they have the habit of meditation. Rumors say we sat for an hour. I doubt it, but it makes a good story. Afterwards, not wishing to take up any more time with words, I said, 'Thank you very much gentlemen. That's all I have to say.' We adjourned at that point. In the morning we proceeded with less madness."

I continued sitting in the Secretary's office quietly, longer than it was polite to stay. The phone rang. A blessing. He finished his conversation in Hebrew and we were staring at each other. I had to get up and I couldn't. I wouldn't, which was even more disconcerting. Then the door opened and a man entered. The Secretary turned to him as I stood up. Defeated once again, about to leave, I was unwilling to go through any more useless formalities, but the Secretary introduced us: "Dina Z., this is Jamine Amouri, perhaps he can help you. He comes from that area."

I followed Amouri to his office, though I did not find his manner inviting. He had very dark eyes. Bitter, I thought. His jaw was clenched and there was a scowl on his face. It was evident that he didn't want to be bothered with a female American tourist. Furthermore, the simple fact of a woman making a demand or asking for help seemed grossly irritating to him. So, in the way bureaucracy usually operates, I felt I was being sabotaged in the very moment of the pretense of being helped. Normally, I would have fled, but I willfully suppressed my discomfort. Or Dinah, insensitive or ignorant of such clear signs, persisted stubbornly.

I didn't attempt any conversation with him as we walked down the corridor to his office at the other end. I wanted to be as unobtrusive as possible. It could have been administratively appropriate that I was referred to him, but more than my intuition, the evident irritability in his back, the slight twitch of his shoulders as he adjusted a posture, told me he felt he'd been given another task that his superior found distasteful. So, in a moment, I would be disposed of again. The Museum Secretary had found the right lackey to do this work.

Amouri sat down behind his desk and perfunctorily motioned me to a chair while he perused papers. Finally, without waiting for him to look up at me, I said, as openly as I could, trying to keep the demand from my voice which for an American woman is difficult, "If it is possible, I would like to be helped to go to Shechem."

"You'd like to be helped or you'd like me to help you?"

"Either way."

"Of course, it's not personal."

"It's very personal, Mr. Amouri."

"Going to Nablus is personal, is it? You're a filmmaker, aren't you?"

"Yes, but no. I want to go to Shechem, and the truth is—no one knows this but you—I want to go for myself."

"Are you looking for revenge?"

He didn't give me the courtesy of looking at me while we were speaking, but continued to shuffle papers, only extending arrogant inattention to me. I concentrated on setting aside the part of me who was unwilling to appear a fool. His professional demeanor, theatrical as it was, did not at all disguise his hate, but he had not yet refused me.

As quietly as I could and as slowly, feeling quite foolish, I managed to say, "Not revenge. Love." My heart was pounding and I flushed.

"There is no love in this country. Go home. It's not possible."

"There's no love in my country either."

"We know. 'No love' is one of your subtlest exports."

"I can't go home until I go to Shechem."

"Well, then, ask the military, they're very accommodating, especially to American . . . women."

"I know. I refused them."

"Well, then, we can't help you. They have everything to offer these days. We have nothing."

I don't know how to explain what happened next. It seems like such a cheap shot, a common ploy, but it was not calculated. I sat still and then, having retreated to my obsessive thoughts and strategies, I became aware that Dinah was crying. She wept quietly, wanted nothing from me. When she composed herself I wiped her tears and blew her nose, continued to sit without impatience.

"Come back tomorrow. In the afternoon. At three-fifteen."

"Thank you."

"Forget it. Isn't that, Ms. Z, or shall I call you Dina, what you Americans say, 'Forget it'?" He emphasized my name by pushing the 'd' through clenched teeth.

"I won't forget it."

"That's what the Israelis say."

I hesitated. "Maybe, Mr. Amouri. But I can't forget it."

"Neither can we, Dina."

Down the hall, a door slammed, the shock reverberated through the wood partitions.

"When you leave, see if you can close the door gently."

When I arrived at three-fifteen, Jamine Amouri was not in his office when I knocked so I opened the door, went inside, and sat down in the same molded plastic chair. He followed me almost immediately, and smiled or snarled a fleeting flash of white, even more cutting than his formerly dour countenance. He looked directly into my eyes. It's the interaction I am most sensitive to, because I stare at people, I suppose, or because I am determined to be acknowledged. "American women take everything for granted. It's quite a passport you have, gets you in everywhere."

"I thought you were expecting me. I didn't think you'd mind if I waited in your office, there was no place in the hall and I didn't want to see the Secretary. . . . I'm sorry if I offended."

"I'm only envious. I don't have such a passport, you see. Point of fact, I don't really have a passport. No matter. It's not your problem, is it?"

I sat quietly.

"Please sit down," he mocked me.

"Thank you."

"You have a guide. His name is Eli Cohen. He's an archaeologist. He'll take you in exactly three weeks. He's worked in the area. You'll stay one afternoon. He charges $100 in American dollars. You might want to give him more . . . in dollars." He leaned forward aggressively. "Don't offer me any money, thank you. I don't take tips. Eli is currently in the Sinai, his wife is expecting a baby, they can use the money. He won't ask you for it. Eli will return just before he'll take you in. I'll give you his telephone number at that time and you can make the final arrangements. He'll need a car."

"I have a car."

"Yes, I assumed as much.

"You can bring in one still camera, no movie equipment. He'll carry a handgun. It's not only to protect you, don't worry. He carries it whenever he's in the West Bank. It makes him nervous to be there otherwise. Well, it's his privilege. You're still going with the army, you can't escape that, my dear, even with your very fine sensibilities. Every Israeli adult is either in the army or in the reserves. Except for us Palestinians, of course."

"Can I bring a friend? Sybil Stone. She's an American, but has been living here. It's Sybil that I came to visit."

"I thought you came to visit the archaeological site?"

"Yes, I did, I told you, I am interested in my name."

"Are you going to do a heartbreaking, romantic, tender commercial film and make lots of money, a *Romeo and Juliet,* Israeli style?"

"We'll see. But can Sybil come with me? She can play the nurse."

"Let me find out. I'll try to arrange it. It's difficult."

"How did you manage it? I'd given up. Last night I knew you were my last hope."

"Well, you know, we're not entirely, how do you say it?—emasculated. Sometimes we are allowed the means to do a small favor for a pretty woman. Gives us a sense of power. Keeps the natives quiet."

"Is there any way I can thank you?"

"I doubt it."

"I did think you were my last hope."

"No, you are very persistent. You have quite a reputation around here. It's just, my dear, that no one else was willing to bother."

"And you? Do I assume this is a personal favor, not a courtesy of the Museum?"

"I also have quite a reputation here. It amused me to work this out. You can say I will find a way to have it serve me. Also there is national pride. We like to show our war memorials and battle wounds like everyone else.

"I'll find out about your friend. And I'll confirm this with Eli. You're agreed? Come back tomorrow to confirm everything."

"Can we have coffee?"

"We can have lunch. Come on Monday, instead, at noon."

Now I wanted to weep, but Dinah was exultant. Standing up, as much to balance myself as anything else, I extended my hand, then, not knowing if that was polite or proper, I withdrew it. Amouri laughed then and offered me his hand. I felt a surge of hope, Shechem, hope. Hope is like lightning, it is so sudden.

"Now—" Jamine kicked a brick against his cubicle door so it would stay open—"you've arranged everything and you can let yourself be afraid."

When I reached the hospice, Sybil was also just entering the garden. We stopped under the trees. "I'll ask Joseph to arrange the Sinai trip for us."

Sybil looked relieved. "So you've finally given up. You're so difficult to be with when you're determined to have everything your way."

"I'm like everyone else, Sybil, it's a very willful century."

"Yes, and you rail against willfulness more than most. You hate it in everyone."

"I'm contradictory. And I hate it in myself. Actually, my little muskrat, I am about to disappoint you. It seems I didn't give up. It seems I'm going to Nablus."

"Joseph . . . I don't believe it. You've worn him down, what no Israeli or Arab or foreign country has been able to do. You should have gone into the diplomatic service."

"Not Joseph. He won't be pleased." And then I was afraid. "You won't try and stop me?"

"Stop you? It would be like trying to interfere with the forces of nature. I give in. I submit."

That was the beginning, Shechem. That was the first sign of coming home. The garden was still gold with the last of the flowers. Spring blues and pale pinks had yielded to the russets, the dark blood flush which foretells winter. Hope, Shechem, is an emotion like love. The past stretched out before me open as the future. Dinah was appeased. It was the time of day when the light changes rapidly and time falls at the same speed. The leaves were falling. It was autumn.

Joseph wants to talk to me about history. But I am not interested in history. "Tell me your dreams," I counter. But he insists he doesn't dream. Yet he understands dreams, even dreaming.

"We have to choose," he says, "dreams or history. They're in essential conflict."

But one can choose them both, Joseph—if one has courage. Otherwise, like most people, one has nothing. Jeremiah? He chose the dream. But to do that alone in this country is to commit suicide.

"What am I choosing, dream or history, Joseph?"

"You're beginning, just beginning, to choose the dream."

"How do you know?"

"I am watching you fall into a sleep."

"What does that mean to you?"

"The start of another loneliness."

I told Joseph that I was indeed going to Nablus.

"When?"

"It's a secret." He thought I meant I hoped to go, that I was expressing my determination once again.

"Is there anything I can do to persuade you not to persist in this?"

"No."

"No matter what the consequences might be?"

"I've never been a selfish woman. I don't think this is a matter of willfulness. Quite the contrary, I must go, no matter what I wish to do. This is completely beyond my control. Don't you understand?"

"No. If you live in history, you don't understand such things. Well, it doesn't matter."

"What do you mean?"

"It's foolish of me to think one incident or another is going to make any difference. It's all in the cards already."

"What is?"

"Our stupid, mutual destruction."

When he left the room momentarily, I went to the window and stood there with my arms raised.

"You don't believe in fate, do you, Joseph? I would hardly think so."

"No, not at all, I believe in inertia, recalcitrance, and assininity. For example, it's a totally stupid idea for you to go to Nablus. I know it and you know it. It will only make trouble. I know that and you know that. And you will go anyway. You think you have a higher purpose. And I think you're an ass."

"But do you love me?"

"I love you. Let it be known by all and sundry that Joseph ben Yacob loves an ass. I bet there is a fairly tale about that."

"There is in Grimm's."

"Well, then, I'm not the first."

I asked Joseph to tell me what he thinks history is. "History is what we remember or what is recorded, one way or another, deliberately or by default, of what men do."

"Is that it?"

"History is also what we don't remember."

Is that it, then? Should he have said, "History is what men do?" Then I could have asked, "Isn't there more?"

When I sit here and do not move and say nothing, seem asleep, is that part of history, Joseph? I sit here with my eyes closed, without moving, seemingly idle. I am observing, in the reality of my mind, a young girl dragging a hollow tree across a field. Under normal circumstances, it is far too heavy for her but rage and desperation have temporarily given her inhuman strength. I say this is part of history. Both the woman and my vision of her. In another culture, a bard would say, "She gathered the ants to help her," or, "The night jackals set their laughter against it and it rolled." I say it is Dinah dragging the dead tree through the centuries, her arms as withered as its branches and her hair full of moldering leaves and her eyes blind. I sit here and watch. I see every sinew tearing with her effort, though she is oblivious to pain and exhaustion. I sit with her for as long as it takes her to burn her dead husband in the tree which was once a god. When I open my eyes, it is as if I open them to a film, because what I saw in my mind is more real than your tie, Joseph, or your Dacron shirt or the jacket woven in the Philippines, which doesn't fit you well. Is all of this part of history?

Now, stay with me, Joseph. If as a result of all this which I see, I dial the telephone, agree to a request that has been made of me, let's say to buy a bus ticket for myself or for someone else who must not buy it herself, or if I accept the charge to place a suitcase in a public locker, or I buy a gun, let's say one identical to the one Jamine says Eli will carry, if I perform these acts which can be witnessed, they will be part of history, right? Only if a man does them? If I refuse to do anything which had to do with a gun, will that be history?

I would ask Joseph these questions if I knew how to speak to him about Dinah. But what could I tell him or anyone? There were already two Dinahs. There was the Dinah I had been watching in my mind, she did not know she was being observed, she did not know of me at all and never would. Then there was another Dinah, not separated from me, as the first was, by about 3,330 years, but by each one of those years individually because she was always present and still present, coexistent with me, conscious, willful, active, alive. I have to assume she had always been with me, if only just coming into voice or action. She is pulling her story into my life or my life is being pulled into her story, as determinedly as Dinah dragged the tree to the pyre. The second Dinah is watching me, reassembling, revising me.

A story has a thousand variations. All of them are true.

How can these stories be part of history? How can they all be true? Only one happened.

That's logical, but it's not true.

I call the actor in my life 'Dinah' but how do I know it's Dinah? Can't it, equally, be you, Shechem, pushing at me from the outside as Dinah pulls at me from within? Or maybe Dinah does not exist at all and this is your creation entirely. And why do I feel Dinah is alive and you, Shechem, are the dead man in the back of the car? Why do I ascribe consciousness, will, vitality, to her? Who is engaging in magic?

What's the difference between false magic and true magic?

False magic wants to control the world. False magic is pure will. And true magic?

True magic is the attempt to align oneself with the gods and do their will. Sometimes it is easy to identify false magic. The person who makes a voodoo doll or throws a hex is engaging in false magic.

Are you sure?

It's close enough to be a working definition.

What about the one who does a rain dance?

Harder to tell. Is it in the service of herself, himself, the people, the animals, trees, and of the gods? Only the gods have a universal perspective. Also you have to know the shaman's state of mind, which can never be known. Unless she's pure, she's never pure enough to know if she's pure. Circles.

What if she's pure . . . what if he's pure . . . and still she errs? What if she enters the service of the gods with an open heart and the false gods enter without her knowing it? Can't false gods enter a pure heart? It's happened a million times. You're too naive, you haven't studied Kabbalah.

There's a way out of this dilemma, but I'm limited in my understanding so I'm going to settle for belief in the security of a pure and conscious heart.

What about the unconscious?

I'm going to be simple; I'm going to suggest that consciousness, alertness, and a pure heart guarantee . . .

Pure heart? Guarantees?

. . . OK then, I want to be a pure heart, a vessel for the gods to enter. I want to be that vessel for Dinah. Sybil says that I am willful, by which she means stubborn, spoiled, uncooperative, inflexible. I am all these things, but there is another side to this. To be willful is to be infinitely, exquisitely malleable because it takes great will to serve the gods and one must give up one's will entirely to do it. But what if Dinah isn't god?

Why do I ascribe all this to Dinah? Because I can't yet feel you, Shechem, not with all my conjuring.

Once, in Mexico, I was assaulted by a man very different from myself. He lay on top of me, allowing the knife to fall to the floor beside the bed. He could reach it in an instant and he had the strength to hold me by his weight alone. With his free hand—the other rested alternately on my breast and my throat—he reached into a drawer in his bedroom, where he had brought me at knife point, and extracted a photograph. What did he see on my face as he proudly showed me the face of his daughter? She was three in the photo in which he was holding her so tenderly. I would have said, anyone would have said, according to the image, this is a model father. He remained, uninvited, in my body as he described his great love for her. Then he added, "I love you, Dina."

Was this the reliving of Dinah's life? Was this you, Shechem, again gaining a wife by force because language and custom keep us apart forever? Did I fail to understand who he was when he said, "I love you," with tears in his eyes?

Which belongs to you, the tears or the knife? Perhaps I will never meet you again. Perhaps we only have one opportunity per lifetime and the test is always to see through the distortion to the essential form, and neither Dinah nor I were sufficiently awake and everything we are attempting now is belated and ludicrous. Maybe Dinah knows this, knows, bitterly, she has always been blind at every opportunity. Had she met you in the fourteenth century, for example, we might not have to go through this now.

So, Shechem, that tall, blond Hidalgo rapist with blue eyes whom I met on the street in Oaxaca, who was born in Mexico of a French mother and a Mexican father, who spoke Spanish, French, and German and enough English to convince me to have dinner with him, was that you? Was that your clumsy attempt at a meeting? Am I wasting my time here, shall I go back to Mexico to find you? And if I try to ally myself with you, are you god? Or were you the rapist, pure and simple, Shechem? Did you first appear carrying a gun and then reenter my life a few years later carrying a knife? Was that you, each time I was raped, brandishing a weapon against me, pretending to be a stranger? Was there no love in it? Were you laughing at me, Shechem? Is that why Jamine advised me to learn to be afraid?

The holy time was finally over. I was tired of piety and restriction. I admit I had hoped that I would be caught by it again, as, on occasion, I have been caught, while taking a walk, by a brief penetrating glance of a passing stranger. Jerusalem was even noisier than it had been, was returning completely to the province of men who were making up for lost time. The visitors who had come to Jerusalem to celebrate the High Holy Days thronged the Old City buying *mezuzahs,* silver hands against the evil eye, blue stones, anything to protect them from these times. But as they bargained, argued, handled the cloth, silver, copper, anyone could sense their fear (any minute a bomb may explode—this shopper, shopkeeper may be a terrorist), one eye always alert to the future death while the other eye scanned the past, the fingers clutching the purse, death looming in all directions, and they didn't believe in the talismans anyway.

I came back to the Wall one morning to see it without the crowds and brass bands and fanfare. Joseph and I separated as each of us approached "our" side of the Wall and then we signaled to each other across the great chasm of gender and prayer. "Are your prayers still in the Wall?" he asked.

They weren't there. I knew exactly where I had placed them and they couldn't have been dislodged without effort. "Not a single one is here. A *dybbuk* has stolen them."

Joseph was scanning the wall, reading the little desperate flags and putting them back. "There aren't any *dybbuks,* but don't worry, all the prayers are the same, nothing changes, yours can be included in anyone else's."

"You think history is a straight line," I shouted to him.

"What do you think it is?" He didn't wait for me to answer. "History is a wall. This is it, run your hands over it. Ignore the little pieces of paper. History doesn't grant favors, it makes demands."

Sybil was amused and pretended not to know us. She didn't join us but sat on her little mound like a chipmunk, drawing.

"It's not as neat as all that."

"Oh, you want blood and birth. That's also a straight line. I'll show you." He called Sybil and then the three of us raced to the Muslim holy place, the Dome of the Rock.

"Here," Joseph said, "on this very spot, out of this pregnant belly, on this navel the size of a drop of blood, have stood Adam, Abraham, Isaac, Christ. No women, sorry. I regret it, but that is how it is, how it happened, like it or not. Mohammed rose from this pregnant rock through the dome to heaven." We walked further, he ran his hand down an undistinguished piece of masonry. "Here you can see the scar of the Greeks, Babylonians, Syrians, Romans, Turks, English, Arabs, Jews, Palestinians, Israelis. A nick, a stain, a scratch, a bullet hole for each layer of the dead."

"One dead for you, Joseph, one dead for me, one dead for you, Sybil."

"I have enough dead, thank you." Sybil did not disguise her impatience.

"We must begin again, then," Joseph insisted. "Most people think that there aren't enough dead to go around and are always trying to get more."

"What I would like . . ." Sybil began.

I interrupted, "Is to go to the Sinai."

"Yes, but not this minute. Is for you two to be more serious and less so. I want to walk by the ocean, look out at international waters, and forget Israel. We can go to Tel Aviv, pretend we're in Paris, and act like tourists. Agreed?"

"Agreed. But now I have an appointment, so you and Joseph are going to have to tryst by yourselves."

"How will I manage outside my ménage à trois?" Joseph asked ruefully.

"Do you like triangles because you like conflict or do you like conflict because you like triangles?"

"It's the strongest form, Dina."

"That's another one of the lies people try to live by," Sybil said.

We sauntered toward the gate closest to the Rockefeller Museum. Above the buzzing ominous undercurrent of history, the prosaic babble of commerce was reassuring. At the exit, we went in different directions. I crossed the street, and Joseph and Sybil, arm in arm, turned inside again.

I visited the exhibition hall just before it was time to meet Jamine. I had been careful to arrive early enough so I could look in the display case for the missing Asherahs though I knew they would not yet be returned. Among the ones which had not been removed, there lay one of clay, the size of my thumb, a clay Y, a tree, a woman with her arms raised. I couldn't quite make out the gesture—praise? request? demand? invocation? It reminded me of the Cross but the arms were lifted in ecstasy, not death. Woman as tree. Tree as woman. Crude as it was, I could still see the dance in it. I had a stong urge to lift the case cover to hold the Asherah, rub it between my fingers, feel the pulse of sap and blood.

There are two stone tablets in the temple at Shechem, the covenant which Tiamat the Goddess Mother, (Dia Mater) who divided the Deep, Tohu Bohu, into heaven above and earth below, first gave to her son, king of the universe. [Tiamat is Ishtar and Ishtar is Asherah.]

Asherah is the semitic name of the Great Goddess, possibly from Old Iranian asha, Universal Law. Asherah was "in wisdom the Mistress of the Gods" . . . strength of all things. The Old Testament "Asherah" is translated "grove." In the matriarchal period, Hebrews worshipped the Goddess in groves,—

> For they built them high places, and
> images and groves, on every high hill,
> and under every green tree
> —1 Kings 14:23

—later cut down by patriarchal reformers who burned the bones of Asherah's priests on their own altars.

The Goddess's grove-yoni was *Athra qaddisa,* "the holy place" (literally, "divine harlot") sometimes she was called simply "holiness" a word later applied to Yahweh. Canaanites called her *Quanyatu elima,* She Who Gives Birth to the Gods or *Rabbatu athiratu yammi,* Lady Who Traverses the Sea. *Rabbatu* was an early female form of *rabbi.* Some called her "Great Lady of Ashert, The Lady of heaven, The queen of the gods." For awhile Asherah accepted the semitic god El as her consort. She was the

Heavenly Cow, he the Bull. The marriage rite seems to have involved the cooking of a kid in its mother's milk.

—*Barbara Walker,*
The Woman's Encyclopedia
of Myths and Secrets

When I arrived at Jamine's office, he was out once again. I did not go inside this time but waited in the hallway, trying not to look impatient. I knew that my instincts and intuitions were not serving me in the least. When Jamine came down the hall, he took in my presence without any visible effect, as if I were the doorknob on the open door. The thought that I was invisible entered my mind and persisted. Wasn't it possible that Dinah, having invaded, had, like all other imperialists, imposed not only her need but her form, and replaced my sentient being by her ghostly presence, so that through her appearance I completely disappeared?

"You could have sat down and waited. Surely you didn't presume I wanted to keep you standing in the hall? Do you think we're so barbarian we have no manners? Is that what you're taught?"

"Easy. I can only answer one question at a time. I feel like I'm under fire." I returned the volley. "I know words are the only fire you're allowed."

"Sometimes not even words."

"I was trying not to offend you again. But more to the point, I was actually wondering if I hadn't made up the whole thing—the possibility of getting to Nablus, your help, etc."

"Yes, I think all Jews wish that the Palestinians were imaginary beings; I'm sorry to disappoint you. I do hope that next time you will feel free to sit down. Don't presume that I desire to limit your freedom, just because mine is so curtailed. Or do you believe the rumors that we treat our women like animals and slaves, that they don't sit while the men stand."

I'd always liked banter in New York. You couldn't survive there if you weren't good at it, but here it mattered more, was not only about the war between men and women, but about the other war. I didn't want to risk it. "I'd like to take you to lunch to thank you for your efforts."

"Ah, Ms. Z—is it Ms.? Or is it Mrs.? Miss?"

"Yes, Ms., it's never been Mrs. You called me Dina before."

"Did I? How rude, Ms. Z . . ."

"Can't you call me Dina?"

"Of course, if you like. I'm afraid I'm about to contradict myself because I must, forgive me, explain Mideastern manners. You see, in this country, or among my people, since we have been denied our country, we are dependent upon protocol for coherence. You said you didn't want to offend me, therefore I will take you to lunch."

"Well, I can manage lunch but what can I offer in return?"

"Your intelligence." Was he mocking me? "Your imagination. I'll bring mine. I think we may match each other. And if you have some humor, because I don't anymore, then you might bring that. I will consider it a great gift."

Another lesson learned as Jamine outlined the current political conditions on the West Bank from his perspective: I was not going to be able to avoid Nablus when I went to Shechem. I might even find Shechem through Nablus. He was not at all interested in limiting our conversation to ancient history. "You want history? Myth? It's happening right now, you'll see. Be sure Eli takes you through the town as well. He'll try to avoid it."

I would have to learn to see very well, to read the negative and transparent. The food appeared. All the food I was coming to appreciate, first the small mixtures of cucumbers, yogurt, mint, eggplant, and *hummus,* and then a wonderful chicken smothered in onions and cinnamon which smelled of paradise. Before the meal, the waiter offered me a warm handtowel dampened with rose water, as if eating were a sacred act.

————

One of the steps on the journey is sacrifice. It was time to prepare myself. There are many forms of sacrifice necessary to propitiate the gods. The first is the offering up of what one loves best. I thought I had made that sacrifice; I had offered up my knowledge. Compared to Dinah, I know nothing. I have given up my old forms.

But what if I have not offered the most beloved? What do I do next? What if you, Shechem, are the most beloved? Am I to offer you up? To give you up in order to gain you. To offer you up is to give up the journey altogether. I gave up the journey once by simply pretending to set out. But now, how can I give you up when we are so close?

The second sacrifice is the offering of a gift. What is appropriate to bring to this altar? I give you my life.

The third form of sacrifice includes the taking in of the god. Jamine did not eat pork. He ordered most carefully and though he talked throughout the meal, I noticed that his attention was also to what he put in his mouth. Food is one of the first forms of god. One of the Asherahs remaining in the case had exactly the same attitude as Demeter at Delphi, each god with her hands to her breast. Demeter is the pig. If the god isn't taken in, it is difficult to manifest. I want to eat what Dinah ate, to devour Dinah. If she is not in me yet, I want to take her in, even if, as I've said over and over, "I am afraid."

"To be cut off from your land is like being cut off from your mother," Jamine said.

"Why do you stay here?"

"Because the mother is kept from us, is that a reason to leave? You know the custom of wet nurses. The poor woman earned her living by nursing the rich woman's child. Sometimes she didn't have enough milk for her own baby. Should the child have turned his back on his mother then?"

"Are you waiting for the nipple?"

"I'm waiting for the mother to come home even if I'm grown

when she arrives. I am waiting—impatiently—for the sweet milk of political change. What would you do if you had lost your mother? Run to an orphanage? A camp in Lebanon?"

"I often feel, Jamine, like I don't have a country."

"You have something even better than a country; you have a passport. You not only have a place to be, you have a place to leave. You have the biggest, reddest teat."

"Well, if I do, it is because my father got his ass out of the country where they didn't like the physiognomy of his cock. I'm asking you again, why do you stay?"

"We stay here because we stay here. Myth keeps us here. It grabs you, a lifeline and a noose. It keeps me here like it brings you across the world, resisting coming but unable to resist. What are you doing here, Dina, turning all of Israel upside down to get to a pile of rubble where you won't ever be permitted to film anything."

I didn't know what provoked him, maybe everything provoked him. There are people—I had thought they were only Jews—for whom argument is a daily exercise. But Jamine enjoyed it as much as anyone I knew. And I liked listening to him, there was a rhythmic swack to his sentences, like a hard black ball regularly swatted against a wall.

"I tell you you'll be in Nablus for only one afternoon, you don't complain. I tell you it will cost you a hundred dollars, you don't complain. I tell you not to bring a camera, you don't complain. So what do you want there? Myth, that is what you want, everyone who comes to Palestine comes for myth."

"So then we're very much alike, aren't we, Jamine?"

"Alike? We're the Jews of the Arab world. Do you think we're not as flexible as you are, that we couldn't also make a great triumph out of exile? We're more like the Jews every day. We're the best educated people in the Mideast except for the Jews and we're also displaced. We rise to the highest offices in foreign countries and then we're equally mistreated and disenfranchised. Educated and wandering. Doesn't it sound like your song?

"I can survive anywhere. I could live in Egypt, Lebanon, Jordan, France, England, even the United States. Why not? Do I need the little plot of land which was stolen from my father? Do you think I can't plant an apricot tree somewhere else? As for the bones, that's what you've come for, haven't you? You should have come earlier and we could have gone out together digging with a little spoon for gods. You could have bought a piece of land and a trained archaeologist and his pissing pot for your hundred dollars."

"Jamine, please, I didn't come to make a war. Not even to finish one. Not even to get the spoils. Do we have to talk politics? Isn't there ever anything else to talk about in this country? Why don't you tell me how this chicken is prepared. Tell me a story. Tell me the myth your mother told when you were born."

"I told you, we don't have a mother, but, you're right, we're not discussing politics now, we are discussing myth. Men and women shouldn't discuss politics. Don't misunderstand; I'm not, as you say, a sexist. It's just that politics insists on establishing differences and men and women—well, they're so different, it's nice when we agree. No one should discuss politics, it tears us all apart.

"Come, if you want myth, I'll show you myth." We hadn't really finished eating but he leaped up, motioned to the waiter who nodded, and, without even paying the bill, we were in the street. Sometimes you don't ask where you're going. Sometimes someone takes the lead so suddenly and forthrightly that the hesitance which accompanies mere curiosity can sabotage the moment. The *suk* was filled with people, but fortunately Jamine was tall and when I couldn't keep up with him, I could see the dense curls on his goatlike head above the crowd. He never turned to see if I was behind him. Then he turned a corner, I turned after him, and he disappeared. I stopped and just as I decided to go on, assuming he would appear again in the same direction, a hand reached out from behind me and pulled me back into a little stall. The hand was his.

"What do you think?" The owner of the shop emerged from the cloth and embroideries and scrutinized me. The very small shop could not be distinguished for the dresses, weavings, blouses, and other embroidery that hung everywhere or were folded in great piles on the floor. Linen, wool, goat hair, leather, the animal or plant still alive in the fabric. The stall was pungent with animal spices. In the distance a rooster crowed as if the call was yet another scent.

Jamine handed me a dress. I said nothing. I saw that a few dresses suspended from the ceiling made a private room. I knew about these dresses. A Bedouin girl learns to embroider when she is very young. When her skill is sufficiently developed, she begins her wedding dress. First she embroiders the bodice so that her to-be-formed breasts will be covered with shiny threads, colors of pomegranates, sky, almonds, and milk. Then she embroiders the sleeves to cover the lust of the elbow and wrist, finally the hem to cover the seduction of the ankle. If there is time, the needle dances over the entire fabric. She spends years embroidering her wedding dress, wears it for the ceremony and, afterwards, it is her daily garment. These dresses smell of camel and tent, of sweat, perfume, and flesh. The smell never disappears no matter how many times they are cleaned. You want to buy an old dress, though it's always patched, one with the shape and scent of the bride in it. First you examine the stitching and then you press it to your nose to be certain the life has remained in the heavy black linen weave.

When I emerged, Jamine propped a narrow mirror against the wall so I could see myself. We looked at my reflection together. He stood behind me and covered my head with a piece of dark linen edged with red and purple cross-stitching. With his hand lightly on my shoulder, he turned me about so that the shop owner could see the dress. I understood I was not to ask to see another garment. The dress fit. It was almost completely covered with exquisite handwork. A museum piece. The work of a lifetime.

"Well, was I right? Will you sell it to her?"

The proprietor examined my face carefully, did more than stare. Running his fingers along my cheekbones, he gave me a black kohl pencil: "Darken your eyes."

Sometimes my face does not belong to me. While some people belong to their times, I don't. I have often been startled when passing a mirror because my face is odd to me, I have not been able to adjust to the discrepancy between what I imagine and what I see.

In the glass, I saw a small, dark woman, smaller than I expected, in a black Bedouin wedding dress, a linen covering her hair, her eyes outlined in kohl. Above her was a fierce and Levantine man with a dramatic sharply angled nose, a determined jaw, and a full sensuous mouth, almost camel-like. His black eyes, hard as bitter pits, stared down into hers. Her face belonged to another woman, another time, and other sorrows.

A reflex from childhood caused me to pass the linen cloth under my eyes, veiling half my face. It seemed that Jamine shuddered. Our eyes locked. There was nothing in the mirror but these two sets of dark eyes which could not disengage.

And then Jamine's eyes vanished and I saw another terrifyingly familiar pair of eyes in the mirror. I remembered what I hated remembering—when I had seen a very different pair of eyes in a mirror. They were fearfully blue. And I was shaking as I had shaken when I saw them that time, when they'd appeared suddenly in my hotel room, through a window, without any warning. The eyes that, with all my practice of forgetting, I knew I could never forget.

I can pause here and refuse to go on. I have refused before to remember how it was when those blue, killer eyes locked into mine ten years before. At each step there have been places where I have waivered. I can repress the insistent memory. I insist that I am free to reject anything that is coming to me. If I am even trapped here, obligated, by the necessity of whatever presents itself, how can we ever get free? How is it possible to direct this myth to its neces-sary—no, desired—conclusion? And worse, how do I know that this act of recording, even of a fantasy or momentary aberration, let alone a memory, will not, itself, generate the tragic repetition of that very story I have set out to alter? Can't I be selective? If everything I am trying to do is inspired by the idea, the hope of creation, isn't there a filter that distinguishes good from evil? Aren't we ever free of history? Is there no hope?

Invasion, Shechem. In the very moment that is so pure, an uninvited element enters and taints it. We know this story—one of our brethren asserts his will on our lives as if it were his own.

In film, images can be superimposed one on the other. You place one negative over another, moving one feature slowly over another feature until you're satisfied by the blend. This time slide of time causes me so much vertigo.

I looked up at Jamine as he looked down into my eyes in the mirror. But I couldn't keep his face, his eyes, in focus, something else imposed itself. In reality my face was covered with a black linen cloth but when I looked at it I saw that my face was bare, my mouth trembling. There was a soiled white handkerchief about the man's muzzle. We were both reflected in the mirror. When I looked up, he said, "You will never forget these blue eyes." His voice crunched, his larynx was metal. "Don't lower your eyes for an instant. I want you to see nothing but these blue eyes. Never forget them. Never describe them. Now, as you keep your eyes focused, take off your clothes." From behind, he bent me into position against the mirror. "Slowly," he ordered and though I was shaking, I was obedient and removed my clothes as quickly, as slowly, as I dared, closing my eyes, until he insisted again that I open them. With one hand he directed my rhythm, did not permit me to tear the clothes awkwardly off me. "Slow, you damned bitch, slowly. Entice me. Let me watch you while you watch me." He forced me to stand with my naked back against him. I let my forehead fall against the glass. Then he pulled me back so that he could watch me watching him. I tried to remember his eyes because I told myself I would testify against him. The barrel of his gun was braced against my skull. I saw a snatch of eye, like a snatch of sky in a prison window, a sky that is made of metal or other dead matter.

Blue eyes, blue as nightshade, were superimposed upon another set of eyes, upon Jamine's black eyes, as if they were the other eyes in the mirror. Then fucked in the ass like an animal. Injunctions against sodomy. I can see into the barrel of the gun as if it is another eye. After the explosion, the mirror will shatter. "Slow down, you damned bitch in heat, you donkey, you asshole." I hadn't moved. "Move, you bitch, slowly." I moved. I slowed down. I jerked forward. I caught his blue eyes in the mirror. They were vacant.

I am trying to learn about necessity, Shechem, not the necessity of character—character is mutable—but the ghostly image that asserts itself from the lithostone despite all attempts to remove it, despite its invisibility to the naked eye. Do you understand that I cannot impose another version of these events, cannot erase the memory, even when it seems that would be in the greater interest? Even in this work of imagination, I cannot sidestep the confluence of history and desire. Each is independent of us, has its own riverbed, is a living thing.

You must understand, Shechem. I have no power in this, though I know your life is at stake. Even as I set myself a deliberate task, I cannot simply conjure you arbitrarily. Even as I set this task for myself, I must submit to other forces, must attend them devoutly as a priestess, to the necessity of imagination, or to memory, or personal history. I have learned that I cannot sidestep what the imagination offers and I have no right to judge it. My personal will must be abandoned. I can only be mindful, though I admit I long for you and also for some final redemption, and further, I confess, I want you to save me, as I am trying to save you, from the agonies of my own life.

Dinah wasn't raped, despite the testament. Still, rape entered the story and once admitted could not be excised or denied, the truth and the lie cohabiting in a permanent marriage. Whatever became part of the story continued whether it was a true story or not.

Do I trust you? How can I trust you? How can you trust me?

Do you think that this Jamine didn't frighten me? I was scared to death taking off my dress in a makeshift dressing room in a close, smelly stall.

I'll tell you the rest, Shechem. What difference does it make what I tell you, you're a dead man. I've never told anyone before.

The man leaned so heavily against me as I leaned against the mirror, I was afraid the glass would break and the splinters would enter my hands, face, and breasts. He closed his eyes only for a minute, then caught mine again by tugging at my hair to pull my head back. "Never forget these blue eyes and never betray them, or I'll kill you next time." There was a shuffle outside the door, footsteps or a hand scraping against the wall. I was standing with my clothes in a pile at my feet and his sperm stinging me. He was startled by the sound, zipped up his pants rapidly when someone gasped in a female voice, some alien sound tearing out of my throat released from fear by the sound outside. "Get out of here. Save yourself," I croaked.

What possessed me? Was I thinking of you, Shechem?

What was I doing undressing in that stall with those two potential terrorists no further away from me than the thickness of a skirt? I'm a Jewish woman, an American, I could also have been carrying a bomb. No one is clean. What does Dinah want? Does she think there is nothing else between us, no other history between her story and this story? Does she really think it's all her story?

"Well," Jamine whispered. "It is odd what the veil reveals, isn't it?" He passed it through his fingers as I've seen magicians readying themselves for a sleight of hand making red silk into carnations and rabbits. He turned away. When I came out of the makeshift dressing room, the dress on my arm, he took it and folded it carefully, saying, "We've agreed on a price." Turning to face me, "I've bargained very well for you." He looked like an ordinary man except for his dark eyes, both piercing and tender, and the slightly scornful or bitter round sensual mouth. I searched my purse for the money and he passed his hands along the camel belts hanging from the ceiling, jangling the small brass bells tied to multi-colored tufts of wool. As we were leaving, he turned me toward the mirror again, taking the opportunity to put his hands gently on my shoulders. "You were completely transformed," he smiled. Perhaps it was the first smile he allowed to rest upon his mouth. I would have paid any price he asked for the dress.

"It was very odd," was all I could say to Sybil.

"A steal," Sybil said approvingly as I modeled the dress for her, surprised to find the headdress had been tucked into its folds. I draped it about my hair and face. "What do you think?"

"You have old eyes. Everyone tells you that."

Oh, Sybil, I was beginning to be weary. I was so weary of the silence between us. We had come to such an unpredictable and terrible intimacy, telling all and telling nothing.

"Do you know"—she was pensive but not withdrawn— "there are some people who never really live their own experience."

"They don't have a history, then."

"They refuse a history. Still, sometimes they're trapped by it."

"Do you mean Jeremiah?"

"Don't you think so, Dina? What are you thinking?"

"I'm not thinking. You tell me nothing . . . about him."

"There is nothing to tell."

"When I come back to shoot the film, let's get an apartment in the Old City. I'm tired of living here in the English quarter as if we were still living out colonialism."

"It's not quite that bad. You're not going to live in the Arab quarter, for god's sake, are you, Dina?"

"Well, let's not argue that now. The fact is that I've got the opening scene of the film beating against my temples. It's much better than what I thought I had lost, that old man beating his brains out in gratitude on the concrete in the airfield. I want to follow an old man as he brings oranges from the West Bank to Jerusalem."

"Anything to get to the West Bank. This old man changes your point of view, doesn't he? He's an Arab, that's much different than following a Jew, isn't it?"

"I want to film him getting up in the morning, coming across that ochre road to the city. I want to follow him as if I had been following him for centuries. When I develop the film, I'll show it to him and if I have to we'll shoot it again, and even again, until he says, 'That's it. *Now* you see!'"

"Is this your way of telling me you're leaving? We're living here as if we were going to continue doing this forever and sometimes I wake up scared, thinking you're going to pack your bags and get a plane without even giving me notice."

Could I have told her then about you, Shechem? No, we had a tacit agreement—I was to tell her nothing and make nothing of anything she told me.

I went to the mirror in the bathroom and practiced applying the kohl that the storekeeper had given me, "As a bonus," he said, "since we haven't bargained." I think he was a little disappointed not to enter into the game of the marketplace. I had to open my eyes very wide in order to darken the lids precisely. When I looked away from my eyes, it was as if a window had been raised and someone who has always been staring at a blank wall looked out, over there, no, further, yes, there, further than she could see, felt the fresh air, remembered something, cried a little.

THE TESTIMONY OF JEREMIAH ABAZADIK
A Posthumous Autobiography

I laid *tvillin*. I got laid. I grew earlocks, wore a hat. I shaved my beard every day, even on Shabbat, with an electric razor. I fucked a woman who went to the *mikvah*. We didn't get married; she didn't get pregnant. And I sang.

I made an agreement with God: You let me sing two days for myself . . . then I got greedy: You let me sing a week for myself and I'll sing a weekend for you. I thought it could be a great song: "I'll sing a week for me, God, then I'll sing the weekend for you." Da ta da tada da da, da, da ta data dada ta daa. Don't sit under the apple tree with anyone else but me . . . Da ta data da dada daa da datatada ta daa. That was one of the great war songs. Everybody marched off to it, they couldn't wait to get into the act and contribute to the dying. But no one had the least interest in saving a life if it was a nonexistent life in one of those smoky nonexistent camps everyone said didn't exist.

My mother says that from the time I was two, I would wake up screaming in the middle of the night wherever we were . . .

—Don't ask—some things are not for you to know—some memories are like a hangman's noose—they belong to one person and only one person at a time. They're special, not like bombs or napalm which are for everyone. Napalm is so pretty at sunset in Lebanon when the fire falls like melting stars just as the blue is falling down. And cluster bombs? "Cluster bombs," they said, their eyes shining, their voices thin and thrilled, "will kill everyone, everything in a wide area, they will even kill a tree, if they can get to the heart of it." But some things, some deaths, are still private and special.

. . . My mother says even when we were safe, I would wake up in the middle of the night crying. When she picked me up, I'd say, "It stinks; it stinks." She'd change my diapers and then the sheets on the bed, but still I'd yell, "It stinks." She gave me apples to smell.

"It stinks."

"What stinks?"

"The dying stinks. The dying, it stinks. Caca."

That is what a man has left, Sybil, a private, personal death. His alone. I worked for mine. I arranged it carefully and I did it before anyone was going to take me from it, before I was going to get run over crossing the street to buy jockey shorts, or before someone shot me through my guitar as he was practicing to be a terrorist, or before they drafted me to the front or the back of my country to kill someone who on another day had given me his song.

· · ·

I asked Joseph to put Sybil's name on the list for one of the modern apartments in the Old City. A compromise. "I want to know how it will affect me to look out on the *suk* day after day, to live in a walled city. Will it alter me?"

Joseph laughed. "It will take a thousand years to get New York out of you. Maybe those who have been living in the Sinai since Moses have Moses in their nostrils, but the Russian immigrants who have settled near the Red Sea aren't breathing Moses. They're still in the Soviet Union with the great patriarchs, Khruschev, if they're lucky, or Beria, Stalin, and Molotov; they will live there all their lives. That's another form of history. As for the rest, water is water and sand is sand and the years don't affect it at all. When you, your Russian, or your Yemenite lady look out at the sea, you'll say what everyone has said since Adam, my dear: 'Oh, damn, it's going to be hot again. Look, the sunset has turned the sea vermillion; let's not fight again tonight.' Nothing, no one is going to change."

"Joseph, I don't believe you can stand behind a single thing you've said except 'Let's not fight again tonight.' "

———

Was he right, Shechem? Is it impossible for us to change? Leah turned her back on her father's gods but still she named her sons Asher for Asherah, Issachar for Sachar of Memphis, and Gad for the god of luck.

"Let's not fight again tonight, Dina. Let's make love. Wouldn't you like to know what happens to a New York woman when she fucks with a sabra?"

"Too prickly. Anyway, what good will it do, if it won't change anything, if even making love won't alter history or the future?"

Joseph said history is only those events which contribute to contemporary reality. "Have you ever watched a rabbit run, criss-crossing a field, random as buckshot? That's not history. History is a plumb line. No myth, no story, no legend. History is a set of facts that has to be respected."

"Sounds like you think history is only the straight line between the rifle and the place where the rabbit is when he gets shot."

"That's another way of putting it."

"I don't believe you, Joseph. I don't think you're so cold."

"Dina, I happen to be fighting for a secular solution for a nation state in the twentieth century. I am not a Talmudist pleading with god, I'm an attorney arguing before a variety of inefficient, un-merciful, unjust, and impossible international courts, tribunals, and commissions."

"But surely there are important and unchallengeable historic reasons for Israel to exist. Mythic reasons as well. And they matter."

"There is only one reason which is absolutely compelling."

"What is that?"

"We're here. And we have been officially here as a state for over thirty years."

"As simple as that?"

"As simple as that. It's a fact. It's the fact we work with. As much a fact as the fact that the Palestinians are here too. The rest is inconsequential."

This is the dream. Even as I was dreaming, I knew it was disappearing. I didn't have the guts to hold on to it. It faded, not as the Cheshire cat faded away but as colors on celluloid are bleached out by direct sunlight though they also depend upon projected light to be visible. The tormenter is clever: He can do his work and disappear before we awaken to the deed.

I am working during the summer for a temporary agency, the kind that sends young girls out to business firms to file, type, answer the phone. The girls work for a day or a week and then they're sent somewhere else, wherever this kind of laborer—simple, willing, accommodating, eager—is needed. I am glad to be working, have lied, as is traditional, about my age, grateful for the money. I have a Social Security number for the first time, a pair of stockings in case I cannot stop the run in the ones I'm wearing with the colorless nail polish I also learn to carry. In short, I have outfitted myself carefully to resemble the "older" women I admire in the subway, those who seem so self-possessed when they fold their left hands over the right in their laps, displaying the single-stone diamond engagement rings. In the dream I am quite young, too young to have working papers, am prettier than I am now and also more ungainly, awkward, not quite certain how a lady sits in a chair, how to smile; I am accommodating to everyone and everything.

The man in the frock coat stands over me, to check on my typing, he says. I do make mistakes, out of distraction—I cannot concentrate on this work for forty working hours—but also out of nervousness and lack of practice. But then I stay after hours without charging the company, to correct my mistakes. I am conscientious. I am working for a charitable organization, they raise money for a yeshiva in Mea Shearim and my job is to type personal letters asking for donations. I am careful not to cross my legs, to wear long skirts, and to cover my elbows. My clothes are modest, even prim. When he stands over me, he makes me uncomfortable and my hands tremble a little so that my fingers miss the keys and I have to erase the mistakes and begin again and my fingers get dirty as I correct the mistakes on the carbon copies and then the paper smudges or I forget to blow away the eraser filings and the second copy or third isn't quite legible. The typewriter is cumbersome and I must press the keys hard. My polished nails, transparent so as not to offend the rabbi, click on the keys. I have listened to this sound in other offices and understand that the long nails are required—they assure the employer through the constant tick—but, also, there is something about the impossibility of typing this way, the conflict between the limitation and the task.

As soon as he opens the door from his inner office and enters the room where I am working, I smell the sweat which is saturating his clothes. Then I feel his breath on my neck, a little moist and heavy with tea and sandwiches. Mayonnaise, soggy lettuce, kosher breast of chicken. Swee-touch-nee tea, two cubes of sugar, one rectangular, one square, two carrot sticks, a piece of honey cake. His breath is just a little fetid, just a little unwashed, as are his clothes; it's summer, noon and hot, the windows are closed against the noise, and there is no air circulating in the room. He twirls the buttons of his robe. It's a nervous habit so some are popped and the threads stand up alarmed, a bit of white undershirt peeking through the empty hole of his vest, the white of an eye. He bends closer; he says he can't see. "Shall I take it out of the typewriter for you, Rabbi?"

"No, don't bother. I don't want you to lose your place, then it won't line up correctly and you'll have to start again."

He is quite certain there is a spelling error or something he'd like to alter, or he is not sure that my phrasing is correct in the section he asked that I add. That sentence is awkward. Am I certain I didn't alter the text he gave me? He leans over my shoulder, pointing at the error. I can't see it. My vision blurs. I think it is his sweat dripping into my eyes. He drops the pencil just as I lean forward to examine the letter better, but his hand is already in my lap, looking for the pencil. He can't find it. It has dropped to the floor but he pulls me back not wanting to disturb me, to soothe me. It doesn't matter. It's only a spelling error, it won't ruin the letter, he isn't worried because he knows I'll find it later and correct it, it doesn't matter about the carbons, they don't need the spelling corrected, and it doesn't matter that he's lost the pencil, but maybe it is still in my lap not on the floor, he didn't hear it drop, his hand is on my shoulder pressing me back into the typing chair so he can look in my lap, among the folds of cloth, my skirt is very pretty, he is glad I am earning a lot of money, he thinks the minimum wage is very generous to young people and I can buy myself nice work clothes but did I think over his proposal that I donate some of my salary to the yeshiva because those boys are doing God's work for all of us, he always liked pleats, but they hide so many things. Did the pencil fall down my blouse, it was his favorite pencil, the blouse is very loose, did I know, sometimes he thinks women do not dress carefully enough, it's one of the banes of the orthodox tradition to try to instruct girls so that they will not violate God's laws. So often the mothers are lax or have forgotten all the injunctions, and what is a man to do, it is his duty, but still it is awkward, the pencil was a mechanical pencil, that is why he's making such a fuss though he's sure it isn't lost and maybe he left it on his desk, after all, but I did hear it drop on my skirt, didn't I, it has one of those retractable points that is protected within the metal casing when it is not in use, and it slides in and out very easily, but he thinks he ought to show me how to tie my blouse better, he'll look for the pen later when I get up, the blouse needs to be tighter or higher, though he agrees the style is very pretty, his mother always wore peasant blouses and now it is the fashion, imagine that. He is glad it has drawstrings, not elastic, so that they can be opened and tied tighter, no not up to the neck, but still a little tighter, there, let's see, he pats the blouse to see how it looks and lets the strings go so that it falls open and he sees that I'm upset, silly, he wants to calm me, please, it's only a spelling mistake and your blouse was not that open, not as open as it is now, but he'll fix it, no, don't touch it, he'll do it, he has to measure it, to see that it is exactly perfect, and he doesn't have a mirror for me to look in, better for girls to be without mirrors, but he can see exactly everything that he is doing, please don't cry, it's only a spelling mistake and a blouse, here, he'll soothe me, he'll pet me a little like he does his daughters to soothe me, calm me, he pushes my head back against his fat belly, relax, close your eyes, get calm or you won't be able to type and I'll just rub these little breasts, first one and then the other, you'll be surprised how very soothing this will be, just lean back in the chair, let it hold you as it is designed to do, it will catch me in the small of the back and if I raise my legs, I'll see, it will bend backwards, and he'll support me, it will be as if I'm taking a little nap and forgetting everything, I can just lie down and let him rub my little breasts, as long as I want, until I'm calm and not crying, just breathing deeply with my eyes closed, or until the nipples stand up very hard and tall and then get very soft again, it will take a little while but not too long, he's breathing hard, and rocking the chair back and forth against his thighs, and then, then, just another moment, oh what sweet breasts, we must keep them hidden but he won't tell anyone how sweet they are, as his hands rub my breasts and nipples inside my blouse and brassiere, it's too tight, it must be uncomfortable in this heat, here he'll take my brassiere off, pull my arms out of the sleeves of my blouse, no the blouse doesn't have to come off altogether, just a minute, he knows I'm so hot, I'll faint, he doesn't want me to faint, and he's unable to open the window or unlock the door into the corridor to let in air, there, the brassiere is off and the blouse is down to my waist but he pulls it up and puts my hands back into the sleeves so he can put his hands back into the blouse, the brassiere is in the wastepaper basket, he'll throw it away somewhere else later, no, he doesn't think I ought to wear it, an undershirt perhaps or a little white camisole, it's not good for the lungs, the body needs to be free, and he thinks it is OK because my little nipples don't show through the cloth because I'm just a little girl so it doesn't matter, and it is also proper for a little girl like I am always to wear white, no, don't cry, just rest and lean back against me and I'll rock you, while I put my hands in your lap, I'm sure the pencil is here, there, spread your feet just a little and we'll see, there, that's the girl, and rest against me and soon everything will be soft and then you'll be easy.

. . .

When I awakened I was terrified and wet between my legs. The bastards! It wasn't a dream. I didn't remember what I dreamed. It was another memory that the dream had brought back in the night. I was fourteen. That was the time when my life divided, when I became a woman, when the Rabbi tried to "comfort" me, when I took a lover, when Shechem was killed, when I left the tents of my mother, when I couldn't pretend anymore I was a girl or free of bitterness.

> Because the daughters of Zion are haughty,
> And walk with stretched forth necks and wanton eyes,
> Walking and mincing as they go,
> And making a tinkling with their feet:
> Therefore the Lord will smite with a scab

The crown of the head of the daughters of Zion,
And the Lord will discover their secret parts.

I stood at the window, shaking. I could see through these windows to the bronzing garden below. Now I was covering my woman's breasts with my hands as I had not been able to do then when
I was permitted only to think "rabbi, rabbi, rabbi, god, god, god,"
until he left me alone. And I was unable to leave the job until the
end of the week because I couldn't tell them at the agency and if
I quit I'd never get another job assignment, and I'd already paid
them a commission, so I made more mistakes than usual because
now my hands were always shaking and missed the keys, and it
was dark when I finally left the office each night and the streets
were deserted and I was afraid.

"Did you have another bad dream?" Sybil sat up in bed.
"Another?"
"You've been sleeping fitfully. Tell me." She motioned me to
her bed and I lay down next to her and told her the dream as if
it were a dream.
She stroked my hair as Dinah used to dream Rachel would have
stroked her hair if she had been her mother. "You're like a little
girl every time you get near anything that smacks of tradition or
orthodoxy. That must be why you're so feisty. Fear of authority,
it's that simple. Someone inside you thinks you ought to submit.
That makes you doubly ashamed. In the Sinai we'll deal with
Moses and get it over with."
"Do you really think it's Moses?"
"Of course. His story is about the struggle against authority.
That's all it's about. It considers all the forms of oppression and
resistance. Also it has defiant women in it. That's a novelty."

"Before you deal with Moses in the greater desert, I'll take you to
lesser desert." Without his jacket and without a dress shirt blousing
about his ribs, Joseph was fully the bird implied in his features. It

was in his gaze, steady, searching, focused, in his attitude of patient hovering, in the rapid pace of his very delicate body. He was constructed of little bones and his thick straight brown hair fell back from his white domed forehead like plumage.

The monastery at the Rock of Temptation is perched atop a sheer cliff. Here Christ wrestled with the Devil. Desert surrounds it, inhospitable and severe. The cliffs rise out of the desert floor as if they are a vegetation of stone, stone growing out of stone, seeding stone. Joseph, looking much like an eagle himself, took me to the base of this aerie but then insisted that I climb by myself the several hundred stairs cut into the rock to the great wooden door which would open to me if I knocked at 2 P.M. I knocked and it opened.

The monastery, imposing and dramatic as it was, did not engage me so much as a glimpse of a tall barefoot monk dressed in a gray robe who glided along adjacent corridors, coming into view, disappearing again into one of the bare rooms, then into the library, appearing again with a pot in hand, then reappearing in an attitude of prayer. Listening to the old monk who acted as guide, I learned nothing about the daily life of the monks who had chosen this completely inhospitable spot to spend their lives.

"Why did you come here?"' I asked, interrupting his monologue. I was surprised to see that my question had affronted him.

"We're a special order," he mumbled, far less articulate than he had been before, "who are dedicated to preserving this holy place. It is a privilege, of course, to live where Christ lived. It's our holy duty . . ."

"Yes, of course, but why did you come here?"

I had to repeat the question because I didn't understand why he was offended. "If I were a nun, I think it would matter to me what my daily work and environment were."

"If it did, you would have to pray very hard. We go wherever we are called," he said sternly. He was leading me again, now up the narrow stairs to the room built, he said, upon the spot where

Christ had struggled with Satan. "Those of us who are here are devoted to silence," he offered pointedly.

"But . . ." He motioned me impatiently to be quiet and so I desisted but not without apprehending that one did not come here, despite what he was saying, simply to apply oneself to the contemplative life. I studied his face as he continued, absentmindedly again, with his prepared speech. In fact, I had disappeared altogether from his consciousness and he could just as well have been talking to the walls. Still there was something in his concentration which told me that even this old, dull-eyed monk, at one time, had felt some inner urgency to place himself *in situ* of the archetypal battle of all time between good and evil, steadfastness and temptation.

What happened, I wondered, when ordinary life with all its blessed distractions fell away and one was left without any recourse but to wrestle with one's own demons.

A flash of understanding filled me with joy for the old monk. This seemingly boring old man had taken the chance to live the great drama which everyone I knew avoided as if their life depended on that. "Whosoever shall lose his life, shall gain it," weren't those the words? I wondered.

Also it had never occurred to me to think of Christ as a man, that is, in terms of his human suffering, and of everyone who followed him trying to repeat the journey in their own little lives, but as I was standing on the very spot, looking at the outcropping of rock around which the room had been built, my heart broke then for Christ, whoever he had been, that first one who had actually faced the depth of his division. Maybe his own journey had already taken him so far beyond us, beyond the collective, further within himself than anyone had ever gone, it insisted that the devil within make himself known so that he could engage in the ultimate struggle for his soul. Within himself, of course, always within. Where else? A devil outside himself would hardly be as formidable as one within. Without the understanding, that humble acceptance of a terrible vision, and then the struggle unto death, if necessary, he could not continue his work; he would have died to himself.

The old monk could have been counting spoons, it didn't matter to me. I was suddenly fascinated and hoped he would not notice how intently I was watching his expressions, the movement of his arthritic hands, the sleepy nodding of his thick chin as he talked. What longing, what monumental psychic pain, what unbearable fidelity to truth from what source, manifested itself within the psyche of such an ordinary man to condemn him, for it could be nothing but self-condemnation, to acknowledge a scale of inner torment sufficient to draw him here in order to battle it out, to reenact that theatre of *extremis*. His robe hid secrets greater than the dimensions of his squat body.

What brings someone here, I wanted to ask the monk again, but he had confronted more formidable opponents than myself and would not be diverted from his carefully rehearsed recitation on construction, finances, and furniture, designed not to enlighten me but to elicit contributions. It might not have been overdramatic on my part to imagine hair shirts and scourges, but such outward signs of suffering were unnecessary, after what I now imagined— hoped—would be a ritual forty days of silence in the dark of the spare monastery or in the blazing sun on the mountain, or within the dry barrenness of the caves scooped out of the rock which hermits had inhabited for centuries.

Friends of mine, as children, had had trouble imagining nuns squatting to piss, but I had had trouble imagining the depths of this man's prayer. But in forty days if you're a person, or in forty years if you are a people, you can strip yourself through concentration, duress, and disciplined deprivation, to the unbearable delirium of truth, wherein is revealed, without possibility of avoidance or embellishment, what you have been fated to confront: the single battle which is definitely yours. A friend once told me everything you have to know becomes known within a week of solitude and silence, if you are ruthless in refusing distraction and illusion. When the devil finally comes, he is received (I imagine) with gratitude, with such relief that he has finally appeared, made himself known so the battle can begin; the last and most lethal temptation has broken through all resistance, deviation, and denial—now you know through this envisioning, who, what, is the adversary. Even if the battle is lost (as it well may be), or avoided and therefore lost by default (as is probably most often the case), the basic need for identification has been satisfied.

I could feel the presence of the other monk below me; he was standing still, looking out the window. No one comes to these mountains except to meet the devil. No one comes to these mountains except to meet the devil face to face with one's own face: the always immanent life and death confrontation which is at the core of conscious existence.

Integrity, my friend said, becomes an obsession. It looks like madness sometimes, because it becomes so refined. After a while you can't bear to live with any impurity. You can't bear a millimeter of taint. You can't eat anything but air without anguish. You can't wear clothes because they are disguises, you can't exchange money because it corrupts, you can't speak because words distort the truth. Everything seems like a lie. Every action, each breath is scrutinized. Each second of meditation is composed of the most dedicated observance and the most ruthless observation. But this isn't really craziness. It is preparation. Finally you reduce yourself to the barest essentials. Your outer life has no hold on you, no thrall. Then you're ready for the biggest battle. The one in which you dare not be distracted. Then, *the* devil enters, dispelling all the lesser demons, and you're finally naked with your beloved. Satan! At last!

I asked the monk if he would leave me alone in the room, but he couldn't, so I assumed a meditative posture, sinking down on my knees while he turned discreetly away, occupied himself with polishing an imposing brass candelabrum which stood in a far corner of the room. I didn't expect to pray here but, in fact, I prayed wholeheartedly. It's possible that I cried. I asked for courage. I was afraid I didn't have sufficient stamina or moral fiber to undertake, let alone endure, this. I was afraid I was not taking myself seriously, was involved in a wretched little sitcom. I wanted help, needed guidance from someone who could instruct me when it was time to go to the desert, whatever ordeal that turned out to be, for forty days, whatever that meant, to do . . . whatever . . . in whatever form that demand came. It seemed the right place to pray, the doddering, but kind, monk was the best of all possible teachers, and Christ the right person to pray to. After all, if the story was right—and it was only story which concerned me, only story which had any truth to it—he knew the way, had wrestled here on this spot, and the story revealed the content of his wrestling.

Jacob, who climbed the ladder and wrestled as well, Jacob told me nothing when I asked. There was some mysterious shame in or prohibition against speaking about such things. But it was all that I wished to speak about with him.

A few minutes later, having put more than I had expected to in the donation dish, I was outside again in the brutal heat, trying to clamber up the crumbling stones, gaining neither handhold nor foothold, sliding down, scraping to a halt, and climbing up again until I reached a ledge where the sun beat down upon me. I didn't stay too long nor did I have the intention of seeing how long I could last. I was not looking for more visions than had already been presented to me; I only wanted to be equal to whatever had already come. Down below I could see Joseph sitting contentedly in the scrap of shade under what would be called a tree only in this setting. I was in no hurry to go down to him, I knew that this journey brought him a rare moment of solitude and my affection for him gave me the strength to endure the heat somewhat longer than I might have otherwise.

It would have been easy to continue to say my Satan was God.

It would have been so easy to continue Dinah's battle as my own. But I was suddenly uneasy that we had separate passions. I knew that something seduces each of us from conversing with the radiant emptiness and I didn't know—what Dinah knew so well—who was my ultimate enemy. Then it came to me despite Dinah's intensity that I—I didn't love, hadn't ever loved God, Yahweh, Jehovah enough to empower Him that substantially. It was something else. It wasn't God who was the enemy.

It was—lack of faith.

It came to me that simply, without any fanfare, visions, or hallucinations. There were no Jeremiahs appearing in the viscous air to rail me back to belief, no vision of Beelzebub inflaming the few tindrous stalks by my side, no terrifying apparitions of Anath, bleeding skulls girdled about her hips. Nothing. Only that simple thought. Not enough faith! Despite all the evidence. What an ordinary and banal incapacity. It was as if I persisted obsessively in putting out my own eyes, like a rat in a cage getting his jollies from hitting the electric shock. Well, at least I hadn't deceived myself further by climbing to the highest spot. Perhaps, I thought, it was even more awful than I yet realized, perhaps I was lacking the very capacity for faith. No faith, Shechem, not even in you. I felt a little nausea, a little emptiness, a bit of vertigo from the heat. Once again all my efforts up to this point had been superficial, only lip service and sham.

It was very quiet. Very quiet. And out of this ordinary quiet, out of the ordinary clay, the familiar and unremarkable dust, the dryness on my fingers which roughened my skin, the powdery blemishes on my legs, the few white scrapes on my thighs where I had been sliding along the crumbling stones, out of this enervating but temporarily tolerable heat, a small voice had appeared. Not the thunder booming out of the wilderness, but a sad and sobering commentary. "You don't have faith." As simple as that. It was the desert. It was the harshest voice of all. I did not know where to begin; there was nothing I could do or say.

When I came down to Joseph, I had to dissemble, to continue what was now expected of me until I could get my bearings, without dissipating the struggle in complaints or talk. I was determined to avoid my normal inclination to make a good story of all this.

"I'll be frank, Joseph, I would do anything to go mad. There is a lot to learn from madness."

"Patience," Joseph teased me. "Madness is a discipline. Sybil thinks you're mad. Didn't she chide us as we left this morning, 'Joseph, you're encouraging her worst obsessions'? "

"And I said, 'To the contrary, my life is ordinary and commonplace.' "

"You were lying. What possessed you to do that?"

"Maybe I was trying to coax her out or to trap her. 'Don't you feel the same?' I asked her.

" 'I think I do,' she sighed. 'But only to mock the drama of it.'

"Still, Joseph why shouldn't I go mad, that is, simply allow the effect appropriate to my feelings?"

"Then what?"

"Well, with a vision—madness is always visionary, isn't it?—I could more easily give up 'the faith'."

"Do you think faith is an idea or is voluntary? It's in your genes. Everything is: biology, intelligence, disease, height, appetite, dreams, history, myth. It's all there. You can't give it up like you do salt, whisky, or cigarettes."

"That's what my father says. What hope is there, then?"

"Hope?" he snorted. "Look whom you're asking about hope. There isn't any hope, there is only the triumph in the endurance of the moment. There are superb habits. That's one way."

"And another way?"

"Oh, the one you sort of covet—the pariah, the heretic."

"I refuse that."

"You refuse it because refusal is part of what you've already accepted. You see how clever we are, we create a scenario that includes rebellion and forgiveness and then there is no way to escape from the fold."

"Aren't some people outside the fold?"

"Is that what you want?"

"I'm trying to stop wanting but I would like to know where I am."

"Well, you could start by examining where you've been. What was it like on the mountain?"

"It was very hot."

"Anything else?"

"There was a monk. Not the one who led me to the room, another one."

"Yes, I know him. That one." He pointed up to the monastery and the monk who had padded alongside me in the shadows was standing behind a barred window, unmoving, staring out at us. As I left, I had gotten more than a glimpse of that cell furnished with a cot covered with a freshly ironed white sheet, of an olive-wood desk, a wall of books, and the impeccable back of the monk. Beside the window was a dark-wood carved crucifix, the Christ stretched between the four directions and the three worlds in the desired agony.

"The gossips say you don't dance, Joseph."

"I dance exceedingly well. I'll dance with you whenever you like."

I leaned against him from behind, putting my head between his shoulders where the wings might join his body. When I looked at his profile, I saw a woman and a man and a bird. Eagle, falcon, hawk-faced friend. I let the faces flutter from one to another, even encouraged them.

The monk continued to watch us through the window. "Do you know who he is?"

"Yes, just a monk."

"Do you think he's after pure sanity or pure madness?"

"What's the difference?"

"Well, I'm not sure. Sanity in the pure state is clarity and ignorance . . . and . . . well, yes, madness is the same."

"It's so much easier than you think, Dina, fast, meditate, pray, whip yourself, dance, they're all the way to Whatchamacallit."

"You don't think there's any difference?"

"I'm certainly not an adept, but I think it's in the attitude, not the act. I think we can even make love, Dina, as an act of madness."

"Maybe I'll begin the documentary with the monk. What does living on the Rock of Temptation do to his life?"

"Why don't you begin the film with yourself. What is it doing to this woman to live in the Holy Land? Rumor has it you always end up telling your own story."

"Oh, one could say I have injected a few personal experiences here and there. But not this time. This time it's got to be someone else's story. All I want out of it is to get . . ."

"To Nablus."

"Well, yes. What do you want from all this?"

"Me, Dina? I want you."

When I saw the man in his face, I saw all the sweetness about his birdlike features, but then, surprisingly, a woman appeared, the features hardened as if he had painted his mouth scarlet and his eyes black with hard lines. Then his face softened again and he was a young boy, calling to me.

We drove directly to his apartment in Jerusalem. In the old days when travel implied conflict, a man who had left the city to do battle or kill cleansed himself before reentering the fold by putting himself in the hands of the Holy Prostitute—the woman of the red thread—to wash his spirit in her body. Each woman served the goddess, Asherah, at least one year of her life in this way. The body, if you were a woman, was the temple, the temple within the temple. But it was also possible for a man to be a priest and serve in the same way. He painted his face and wore women's robes. The prophets said these men were all sodomites, dog priests, and inveighed against them.

Rachel was a woman of the thread and Jacob cleaned himself within her of his sins against Esau. After that he claimed to hate the custom but still they wanted to bring Simeon to me so that he might be cleaned of his sins against Shechem by the thread that I wore.

After the death of Shechem, I gave up the thread, and gave myself only to Joseph who was pure.

I slept with Joseph that night, Shechem. Do you understand that it was a means of becoming empty? I asked for a sewing kit because I wanted him to tie red threads about his wrist and he did, but when he asked me if I would do the same, I refused him. It didn't matter much to him anyway. I ran my hand along his hips where he was so smooth and narrow, I did not know if he was a man or a woman. It was as if we expected to be taken into each other. It was very still and quiet in the world and he made a nest for me under his down quilt and held me throughout the night. In the morning, I saw it had rained. The streets were fresh, all the dark leaves gleaming with drops of water.

"I will discover her lewdness in the sight of her lovers and none shall deliver her out of mine hand. I will also cause all her mirth to cease, her feast days, her new moons and her sabbaths, and all her solemn feasts. And I will destroy her vines and her fig trees, whereof she hath said, "These are my rewards that my lovers have given me": and I will make them a forest, and the beasts of the field shall eat them. And I will visit upon her the days of Baalim, wherein she burned incense to them, and she decked herself with her earrings and her jewels, and she went after her lovers, and forgot me," saith the Lord.

After I cut my thread and my brothers had the earrings buried, after the city of Shechem was razed, and Hamor and his son and all the men were killed and the women taken into slavery by my brothers and prohibited from worshipping Asherah, we were never clean again of war. I didn't have to curse them; they cursed themselves. After many centuries the men tried to remember something they barely remembered and they danced for the Shechina in their white silk stockings and black fur hats, ecstatic with wine and song, while the women stood behind a curtain and watched.

> In that day the Lord will take away
> The bravery of their tinkling ornaments about their
>   feet,
> And their cauls, and the amulets round like the moon
> . . . And it shall come to pass,
> That instead of sweet smell there shall be stink
> . . .
> And burning instead of beauty.
> Thy men shall fall by the sword,
> And thy might in the war.

If you've lost the way to the temple, and you have forgotten the language, and you do not remember the prayers, and you've cut down the sacred wood for toilet paper, and you don't know the phases of the moon, and the cow and ewe are confined to the slaughterhouse, and the thread is broken . . . is anything possible? Can you still have faith?

.   .   .

"On the way back from Jericho, we passed a little old man and a little old woman both dressed in black, trotting along behind their donkey, two side baskets hanging across its back filled with . . ."

"Oranges." Sybil smiled knowingly. "If I'd been God, I would have put oranges on the Tree of Knowledge for you."

"Less seductive?"

"More so. Apples don't do anything for you, but oranges, you find them irresistible."

"Apples remind me of upper New York State, winter, and rosy cheeks and sleighing. They're very energetic or healthy but oranges . . . yes." As Sybil hugged me, I felt that she was much thinner than she had been when I came, not quite thinner, lighter perhaps. Smaller and brighter. Something was burning in her. Sometimes one candle is enough to dispel darkness. The light of one small candle can be seen through the infinite dark. Sybil was burning and about her there was a mantle of impenetrable darkness.

THE TESTIMONY OF JEREMIAH ABAZADIK
A Posthumous Autobiography

When I met the whore of Babylon her hair was flaming, all of hell ablaze about her face. "You're in trouble, Jerry," I thought, "you should have listened to your mother, some things are worse than war." I went down on my knees before the apparition just to be safe. I could always pretend I was looking for something I'd lost: my life, rat poison, or a knife.

I changed countries and she followed me like any other scrawny woman hovering on the periphery of the camps, living on semen and bloodstained bandages. What did she want? Should I have dug us a portable foxhole for two where she could serve tea in a helmet and raise parakeets in nests of hand grenades? "What do you want with a man?" I asked her. "Don't you know a man is a lethal weapon? Get yourself a killer dog with a large pecker. It's safer. Love is an inflammation." I told her I had gangrene of the cock and she said she'd improve the circulation.

From the moment I met her, I started wearing my passport next to my heart. I dug an escape route through the walls of my land-lady's bedroom right into the sewers. Thank god she didn't sing, I hate stool pigeons. "I've got to get out of here," I warned her. "No one's keeping you prisoner," she smiled, her personal set of platinum handcuffs clicking like castanets. I kept silent, said the guitar in the corner of the room was a pawn for a friend; I was going to grow ferns in it.

"What do you want," I'd ask, "with a one-eyed jack?" I kept the watchmaker's glass screwed into my socket when I left work to see what made her tick, waiting for her to explode. The pendulum between my legs swung back and forth between Monday and Friday. Saturday night and Monday. On Shabbus, I took a break, allowing everything to stop. I slept from sundown to sundown in a sealed room with the curtains drawn. During the new moon, I painted the windows black. "We'll make love when time stops," I lied. I showed her the first perpetual motion machine. My tail never stopped wagging.

Jeremy, Jeremy, didn't your mother say, "Don't play house with whores and harlots. Keep yourself pure for your mommy." I looked for the clap in Tiffany's windows so that I could give her a gift for Rosh Hodesh. I bound my cock with *tvillim* to keep it still.

In the middle of the night, the slut slid in through the lock like a *dybbuk*. She pulled my spring taut and the tumblers turned about her tits until the light from her eyes fell on me like a guillotine. She got what she wanted. She said she could wake the dead.

. . .

I said nothing about Joseph at first and Sybil asked nothing. Now there were three men between us, the two dead men and Joseph. What happened in the bed to alter us so? Is it that the body establishes its own loyalties? It does it while we sleep, in an instant we are taken over, another form of possession. No one talks about it. Perhaps there are no words. Love is not the explanation.

"I slept with Joseph."

"Yes, I assumed you did."

"What do you think?"

"I'm going to advise him to fill that beautiful stoneware bowl with oranges."

"Why?"

"I wish you loved him."

"I do."

"No, not the right way. I want you to love him enough so that you'll remain here with me. I don't know how to hold you."

"I don't think Joseph will hold me. Anyway, there is my work."

"Your work is portable. You're one of the lucky ones in that respect. You could divide your time between Jerusalem and New York. Neither Joseph nor I would object. We would console each other over sad little dinners once a week, as we have in the past."

"I think you're being maudlin. Why don't you come back to New York with me half time?"

"My work keeps me here."

"What is your work, Sybil?"

The blue papers were strewn everywhere across the desk and the furniture on her side of the room. There were piles of tapes, notes, photographs, newspaper clippings, record albums, interviews, phone numbers, maps, sheet music. There was enough paper to match Jeremiah's body weight.

"For 30,000 shekels and a year's supply of *hummus* can you tell us how much Jeremiah weighed?"

"When? When he graduated from high school? He was first in his class, played soccer, and swam. He didn't have a girlfriend, didn't go to the graduation dance, said he hated the band and refused to sing with them. Voted most likely to succeed, most likely to offend—167 pounds, 76 kilos. He had a trick knee. Was advised not to play soccer. Played on the team. Weighed 175 pounds, 80 kilos.

"Went to a doctor in Boston one week before he committed suicide. Just like him to make sure he was in good health. Top condition. Weighed in at 172 pounds, 78.6 kilos. They didn't weigh the body to see if they had recovered it all. Anyway, when the spirit leaves, it weighs less almost immediately. Or maybe more, maybe afterwards it is heavy as a stone. Dead weight is impossible to carry."

"How do you know this about Jeremiah? Are you making it all up?"

"When I was doing radio in New York, who did you say was the best snoop around, rivaling Jack Anderson? What I can't find out at first, and there's not a lot, he tells me, so to speak. I use these intuitions as a lead."

"Is it accurate?"

"Perfectly."

"How do you explain it?"

"I don't. I write everything down and then I check it all as best I can. I've got to check my facts, don't I? I have to validate all interviews, so I can verify intuitions. Interviews are the least reliable but it turns out Jeremiah doesn't lie. All his associates confirm that he never lied. Not once that anyone recalls. He was pathologically honest. It was part of the cruel streak in him."

"Do you think what you are doing is odd?"

"If I did, I don't think I would continue."

"Will you include what he 'tells you' if you can't verify it?"

"Of course not. What an idea! Sometimes, Dina, I don't think you know me at all."

I didn't know what to say in the long pause between us. It wasn't the kind of silence we depended on where the two of us rested against each other, but the restless silence which occurs between strangers which is like the too familiar space created by the shadow of a man falling between two women. It wasn't death that inhibited us, it was love. It wasn't that I thought she was nuts, but love for a man, even if he's dead, is so often a wedge, a log splitter, dividing all friendships in two, the grain of the wood on one side gasping for the other side which is burning.

Dinah had faith. When I lay with Joseph, I tried to use his body to climb to faith. Jacob was given a ladder. He had it easy, I thought. But it went in the wrong direction. I needed a ladder to descend into myth. Heaven had never attracted me. Faith is simply the ability to know, to accept the reality of the knowledge. To live in the world of knowing. Faith is breath. An inspiration. I closed my eyes until I saw, really saw in my imagination, the eagle in Joseph, and then I whispered to myself, "Fly. Fly."

"Dinah followed Joseph in the desert when he was sold to the spice merchants. Did you know that, Joseph?"

"I suspected as much."

"When you consider it, what do you think about?"

"I wonder if he knew, if he felt her presence behind him at all times? Did it comfort him? Was it agonizing? He couldn't do anything to take care of her. He must have felt so impotent. He had to wonder if she had water to drink; he had some. I know enough about the slave trade to know that the dealers expend whatever is required to take care of their merchandise . . . but not any more than that."

At least we had become allies. That's what can happen in the bed. If one is conscious. Nothing need be said. One does not need to partner. One need never enter the bed again. That is what happened between Joseph and me. From then on I began to tell him anything, even in code, hoping that he understood. It happened in an instant, a silent impregnation. Afterwards we were full of each other, beginning to understand what had been incommunicable. Joseph's mind was growing in mine, and I was growing in his.

"I know what he did, it's what I would do, Dina. He chewed bits of fruit, watering them with his saliva, surreptitiously wrapped them in husks, as if he couldn't swallow, acted as if he were spitting up his food, then he buried them for her. It looked as though he was burying garbage. Somehow he had to manage this without the slave traders noticing. I don't know how he did it. I'll have to think about it: how would I do it? People have had to do this in the desert for centuries, those who have had something, like dates, have left some of them behind for someone else who was following afterwards. This sustained her when she had found nothing for herself or Asenath."

"Joseph, you're making this up to tease me. You don't believe this."

"Didn't you say I should be a novelist?"

"No, I said you should be a painter or a sculptor."

"Well, I'm trying to *see* how he treated her. I'm painting a picture in my mind, then I'm making the picture into a three-dimensional event. It's a simple rational process."

"You're impossible."

"Of course, everything is impossible. This is impossible. This is incest. I love it." Joseph made me stand with him facing the mirror. He examined every part of our bodies looking for similarities, noting even the similar whorl in our pubic hair. I don't look like a bird, but our bone structure is remarkably similar. We both have a mole on our chests just above the left auricle and our feet are similar, we have the same long toes, also the same penetrating eyes. We could have been brother and sister. He knelt down in front of me and buried his face in my breasts. "These could be mine." His skin was fairer than mine, it made him seem more delicate. I had always longed to think of a brother this way. "This turns the world upside down," he whispered. Then he pulled me to the bed and down upon him again. "Which mother shall we claim? Do you get my mother or do I get yours?"

"According to my version, Dinah, like Jacob, wants Rachel, but she gets Leah."

"On the other hand, we might consider that we have the same mother and different fathers. That's more contemporary, isn't it."

"Yes, but it's not the story."

"So, you want me to give you my mother. I don't mind sharing. Essentially I'm a democratic man." I rocked on him for a few minutes. The thought of Rachel was soothing, but Joseph, naturally, would not tamper with history.

"No, that's not the way it works, Dina, though you almost got away with it. Dinah may have wanted Rachel but . . . you can't have my mother. You don't get rid of Leah this way. We have to share the same father and the question is which father are we going to share. Do I give you mine or do you give me yours?"

"My father's name was Israel, though he changed it when he came to America. That does make him a very serious contender, Joseph."

"Well, my father's name was Chaim. That means life."

"Well, then, my father wins. He'll be so happy, he always wanted a son."

"Will a son-in-law do?"

"No no no no no, a son. Thank god your father's name wasn't Jacob, I'd be terrified if it were."

Joseph laughed, laughed so hard, he fell out of me and rolled me off him and onto the bed, his body quivering. I was annoyed and started pummeling him so he'd stop, convinced he was making

fun of me. But he couldn't stop laughing and finally when he saw
I was close to tears he tried to stop, then mounted me, still chuck-
ling involuntarily. A man in the throes of laughter is even more
vulnerable than a man weeping, and when I was pinned down—
his hands on my shoulders and his cock within me—he asked,
grinning broadly, though I could see it was not foolishness which
had attacked him but something so serious, he had been laughing
out of fear:

"What's my name?"

"Joseph, don't be ridiculous. I know your name."

"What's my name?" he repeated, sternly, laughing, both moods
at once.

"Joseph!" in exasperation.

"Dina, my name."

"You're like Rumpelstiltskin, stop dancing about with such glee.
Stop it! Stop it, Joseph ben Yacob.

"Ohhhhh!" It wasn't my voice which groaned and fell with the
weight of his full name. I shook uncontrollably and screamed and
cried and if I were writing biblically, I'd say I gnashed my teeth.

We held each other because we were afraid. And then we pulled
apart because we were afraid. We didn't know which fear separated us, there were so many between us. Incest and history were
simple fears compared with the commonplace but awesome fear
of what we didn't know and didn't understand.

"I prefer settling armed conflicts, territorial disputes, and wars.
They are much simpler, Dina, and more concrete." I watched him
shave as if shaving were a meditation. Now he was dressing, while
I lay naked on the bed, watching.

"A tie, Joseph?"

"A tie. A white shirt. A jacket. A handkerchief in the breast
pocket of my suit jacket. A vest. I'd wear a watch chain if I had
one. Don't you know that men also have their forms of sorcery?
I have a formal meeting today and that gives me a cover and I can
go out fully protected. Thank god."

"You can go to synagogue and be taken back into the fold."

"I don't think we're in that much danger."

"Then we can go to the site of the Great Goddess and get her blessings."

"Where is that?"

"Oh, there are rumors that there is one in Nablus."

"You never stop, do you, Dina?"

Joseph was checking himself in the mirror and I stood next to him, my naked body next to his dressed body; we were no longer twins. In his clothes he looked hard and wiry and I was the soft one. He turned me around and pressed my face against his chest and stroked my hair. "I want you," he said quietly.

"We could take a few minutes before you go to work."

"That's not what I want. I want you. And you?"

"I . . ." What could I say, Shechem?

"Don't answer the question."

I turned back to the mirror. "Women should be seen and not heard?"

He pulled away from me and adjusted his tie. "Don't say anything. Words lock us into positions and then we have to be loyal to our words instead of our lives. So I don't want you to give your word yet one way or another."

"Are you a man of your word, Joseph?"

"I try to be, so I try not to speak prematurely. What are you going to do today?"

"I'm going to make Sybil happy and accompany her to the travel agent you recommended. That will break the spell, Joseph, 'cause 'I'll be in Egypt before you,' " I sang.

"If I'm sent on any diplomatic missions to Egypt, I promise to stall until you return. Let the world burn if it has to. Don't say I never took care of you."

"It's not me you're protecting, it's history."

"It's only you I care about, history can take care of itself. It's the present we have to protect, from history, as a matter of fact."

. . .

When you don't have faith, you're a tourist by definition, even in your own life. Maybe, Shechem, nothing will ever come of us but the recognition of a meeting. If that happens, we can say *dayenu*, it is sufficient.

> . . . if God had led us into the desert and hadn't given us manna to eat—*dayenu*. If God had given us manna but hadn't given us the law—*dayenu*. . . .

I had been anticipating the trip to the Sinai like a tourist. That is, I intended to go there without entering it. And, of course, without knowing that I wasn't entering. Who would choose to be a tourist if she knew she was one, or if she knew she had a choice? So, initially, my intention was simply to look at the scenery, sleep on the dunes, meditate, weep a little, but it was a farce. Because I was intending to leave behind this life I had been trying to enter. I was thinking of our trip as a way of vacating.

Sybil was the unwitting partner in this. "Now that you've gotten your way about Nablus, let's put it aside and just have a good time for a week."

I agreed. "And you'll put Jeremy aside too?" She nodded. We were both lying.

I vaguely thought about Dinah as a wanderer. I thought of following her as she had followed Joseph. But the desert belongs to the Fathers and I couldn't imagine ourselves there. I didn't know how a woman alone uses that heat, that dust and sand, those severe gods, that solitude, that kind of wandering and lostness, that harshness. Then one morning, I woke up with this thought in my mind as if from a dream: I will also use the desert.

"It's just as well," Leah said to Jacob when she heard that we were both gone. I had left Benjamin to Bilhah so that I could

follow Joseph. I had wanted to take him with me, but then they would have sent my brothers after us, not Reuben this time who had saved Joseph, and we both would have been killed. "Maybe the same lion that ate Joseph will eat Dinah. We couldn't have married her off again even with her speckled flock."

Jacob could smell Leah, smell her heat, smell the wetness and was drawn to her as a bull is drawn to a wet cow. Her odor was like a potion; it left him helpless. Sometimes he was full of pity for her and cursed himself, thinking if he had loved her, she would not be so bitter. "We're too old, Leah," he grunted, "too old. Nothing will be born again, this is the time of dying." But still he held on to her breasts and imagined them as they had been most of the time he had known her, round with milk, and it seemed to him that they swelled under his fingers and were round again, were never exhausted in his hands.

She put her hands under her breasts and lifted them to him, reading his thoughts. Entering into him as he entered her, she wanted to give him something. He was afraid, as he had never been with Rachel, but as he always had done with Leah, he allowed it. That much he owed her. Otherwise every encounter between them, even if she had called him to her, even if she had cast a spell with mandrakes, would have been rape if he had not also let her enter him. She crawled into him and he cleared his mind so that she would not be injured by anything she found there. But he was able to open himself completely to her body only until the last moment when he felt her rise with her own joy, then he pressed her out. As her cries pulled his pleasure from him, he lost himself and without thinking, placed his hand flat on her mouth to muffle her voice. She bit him hard and angrily in the last wave of her pleasure which he had squashed with his palm.

Turning away from him she cried out, "Take care of Benjamin. He's the only one you have left. Without him you're in enemy country.

"I'll keep Dinah's sheep, they are mine by right. And when I die, Jacob, I'll give Dinah's flocks to Levi and to Simeon as their birthright."

It wasn't easy to enter Sinai. I had to enter it in the mind before I could enter the geography. I had to follow the specifications and directions of the inner map before I could trace our actual route in meters from Jerusalem to Eilat to Sinai and back. I had to penetrate the wall between one world and another, but I couldn't find it. Perhaps there is a deceptively impenetrable wall around each of the *sephiroth* on the Kabbalistic tree of life, as formidable as the Egyptian-Israeli checkpoints in the Sinai. Perhaps each road between one and another is as difficult as the last one. Looking at the Kabbalistic map, I was locating myself at the outer perimeter of the holy city of Netzach, which is itself on the border between one world and another, between the worlds of everyday consciousness and spirit. I had thought that I had been setting out for Tepheret since I had come to Jerusalem but then I realized I was still within the perimeter of Netzach, at one of the impassable borders. I thought I was leaving Netzach when first I had to leave for Egypt, had to climb Sinai, just as Moses had done when he arrived, from Egypt, at Netzach in the desert. I was standing inside the walled city and the walls had not yet parted like the Red Sea. When I was inside I was secretly hoping that some gallant Moses would appear, arms raised, so I could step between the red walls of water without wetting my shoes. I knew I had to leave Egypt, which is so difficult, more difficult than anything else. I had to penetrate the wall between this world and that other. Perhaps we always think we have arrived somewhere when we haven't even set out.

You see, I was, I am, already lost in time. For I was entering Sinai, thinking I was coming to the end of my story but I was out of sync, as I had not yet me, you, Shechem, so Joseph could not yet have been sold to the slave traders. When this began, I thought we were going to live out a parallel story, but time doesn't run in a straight line. And so I was going to Egypt before I met Shechem, while Dinah went to Egypt after his death. We were approaching each other in a disorderly fashion from different ends of the continuum.

If time were linear, we would have met in our story before Joseph had gone to Egypt, just before Dinah was following him there, before they had lived there and had children, before the dynasties had risen and fallen, and before Joseph had become a Viceroy and all the Israelites had become slaves, long, long before the exodus and the forty years of wandering. I was in the story, but why was I already wandering like the Israelites in the desert? I was coming out of Egypt even as I was preparing to enter it, because I had been, literally, in the Promised Land among all the ruins and broken promises.

. . .

In order to reach Sinai, you cross the Negev. In order to get to the desert, you must go through the desert. The Negev is easy. First of all, it is scrubby; in that sense it has human dimension. As with humans and camels, its beauty is not immediately obvious. Because it is so accessible, because it is soil, not sand, and because it is so familiar, it has been domesticated. Orderly confines of citrus trees and other profitable vegetation compounds bisect the terrain.

The Negev is the site of the essential spiritual conflict between the Bedouin, who wander "chaotically" living at the mercy of winds and wells (though mathematics now verifies that chaos has a pattern and plots it with computers), and those who order the environment and harness the elements. I wondered what politics would develop from the scientific recognition that order exists where despised chaos was once postulated. Invisible meridians transit the globe, indicating the movement of underground water or electromagnetic fields. The route of the Bedouin was once as precise as the route of birds. On the ground, however, the natural movements of earth, water, animals, and humans have been altered, even destroyed. Wandering is difficult now, almost illegal everywhere: the currents to be followed are interrupted by land developments, kibbutzim, even walled cities rising ghostly in the heat waves. These enclosures must be circumvented to cross from one oasis to another with the lambs, camels, sheep, and tents and soon the wanderers discover that they are willy-nilly in an enclosure created by the perimeters of the other enclosures, that what was created initially to enclose one group, in fact encloses the other. In some places, permanent villages of cinderblocks have been erected. In six months they fall into squalor, resembling the refugee camps of the Palestinians in Lebanon.

Joseph is a lawyer because he hates law. "Every law passed," he says, "is a sign of great moral failure. Every protection attacks. Every preservation inhibits." The world is full of reservations, zoos, and preserves where the few remaining representatives of anything intrinsically free are contained.

Sybil and I didn't intentionally follow any underground current in our mini Fiat. We traveled a fairly direct, maintained road. It was flattened even further by the heat pressing down upon it from a shimmering gray sky. Overanxious, we bought gasoline whenever it was available, whether we needed it or not, and filled our plastic jugs with water, drinking six ounces dutifully every twenty minutes. Going against the meridians, a traveler will feel exhausted afterwards and ignorantly call it jet lag or heat prostration. Occasionally we passed a few watering holes and the brown, ragged Bedouin boys waved at us from among the camels while the girls hid their jeweled and veiled faces in their dark linen skirts. At Sybil's insistence, I had packed my camera in the bottom of my sleeping bag so that it required too much effort to get to.

Overnight in Eilat before we entered the Sinai in commando cars, we went to some reefs with the waiter from the hotel. The sea was rough and turgid and we swirled in the sandy, gray water. Sybil informed me that the beds in the hotel were uncomfortable, that the springs pressed up through the mattresses, that the heat was unbearable, the humidity overwhelming, the food tasteless, but I was not aware of any of this. She said I was insensitive and unhealthily preoccupied. She said she was worried about me.

I lay awake much of the night trying to decipher the steady roar of Hebrew, Arabic, and English over loudspeakers as ships passing through the Gulf of Aqaba, possibly smuggling arms to hostile countries, were called upon to identify themselves. There was no symmetry between the blue of the Red Sea, the fish glistening in the depths of the coral reefs, the ammunition, legal and smuggled, the web of mines the ships must negotiate. Near dawn I must have fallen asleep long enough to dream:

I was telling a young child a story by playing a song on a two octave instrument, a cross between a flute and a keyboard. My song was inadequate and I asked my father for a story. He had a similar instrument but his was smaller. He was frustrated with the instrument or the music and I didn't realize how hard he was trying to get something right as the melody he played seemed exceedingly beautiful to me. Sybil tried to sing with him as he played. Finally my father smiled at me, defeated and kindly, tears in his eyes. With absolute resignation he said, "An ending of a story came to me as cold and far away as it is possible to be." I wanted to comfort the child but it had disappeared. Everyone was gone, even Sybil. I reached out to my father who was absorbed in the melody. I thought, "He is ready to die. The song he will learn in death is the one he's always wanted to learn."

· · ·

In the morning, Sybil said she didn't sleep at all and teased me for sleeping like a log. "Did you hear the ships passing through, the sirens, the orders to halt?" I asked. "I thought war had broken out." She smiled indulgently, "You were dreaming again."

"Why couldn't you sleep, Sybil?"

"Jeremy was restless."

I wanted only to dream. As soon as we boarded the cars, I pulled away from Sybil and the others: a young couple who were honeymooning; two American hippies; an acne scarred round-shouldered biologist from New Lebanon, New York; some Frenchmen; two Israeli families including four obstreperous children and their grandparents, additionally trying not to be distracted by the accompanying commando car charging along beside us. Their driver, Zev, was steering, shouting, chewing, drinking, pointing, whistling, while his passengers, a covey of matrons belonging to a Bavarian church choir, were cooing hymns to each other. Amit, at our wheel, blared pop music as if he were deaf. When Sybil asked, "Can you turn it down?" Amit rolled his eyes toward the choir and bellowed, "I can't hear anything over the sound of the engine." Coming to her aid, the young couple disentangled their mouths long enough to request folk songs, but Amit glared at them with scorn. Whenever the songs changed, Sybil's eyes whirled in agitation, as if spinning ahead in the grooves of the original record to find Jeremiah's voice and stop it dead. His songs were never among the selections as far as I could tell. Perhaps his suicide had become popular knowledge and he was avoided for his anti-patriotic sentiments, or perhaps his lyrics were finally understood by his adoring public and banned.

I propped my head on my arm on the open side of the car, and despite the truck's violent shaking, the din of engine, music, wind, song, exclamations, shouts, the bounce and creak of springs, the persistent flap of the canvas roof, I withdrew into my dreams and the desert. I wanted to dream with my eyes open. Amit drove the truck as if it were the leading buck in a scampering herd of antelopes. There was no road, only the sun, the rocks to guide us. Antelopes do not need roads. Sometimes we crossed other tracks but for the most part all signs of life were immediately erased by the wind.

It wasn't quite dreaming. My eyes were open. And I was aware of Sybil next to me, a copper silk scarf on her curls, the color of the sand glinting in the fierce sun. She was writing. "Jeremiah must be in a state," I whispered to her, "he was taken off to Egypt against his wishes." She thought about this for a moment, "No, I don't think he ever went to Egypt, not that he ever mentioned to me, and there's no evidence for it."

We stopped for lunch at the edge of a battle zone. Tanks were still stuck in the sand—they'll never be freed—and on a ledge another tank was turned upside down as an odd memorial to the Six Day War.

Zev got out his guitar and began singing as the gods answered my prayers and the chorale did not join with yodeling. "I can feel Jeremiah turn in me with rage every time we're near a war zone. If we come across a mine, it may be his." I stared ahead of me as if nothing had been said. Sybil may not have been aware that she'd said this aloud. I wanted to answer, "I know what you mean," but I wouldn't violate her. Or myself. After a while she knelt down beside Zev, made a makeshift rattle with a Styrofoam cup and a few pebbles and kept the beat with him. He smiled, elaborated the rhythm, she smiled, following, he nodded, the beat moved up her arm to her shoulders and head: the cobra. Everything was quivering, slightly synchronous with the heat beating off the sand. The sun was directly overhead. Sybil was glowing, the sun glinting off the mica in her eyes. Her skin resembled certain beaches flecked with fool's gold. Sometimes you can see the dark gold for several feet even in murky waters. Zev's song expanded as heat expands. He was singing to the far rocks, bouncing his voice off their vertical blue surfaces. Amit turned about and laughed; when I caught his eye, he winked at me then turned away embarrassed by his indiscretion. Zev finished his song, was about to start another when he saw the honeymooners angling toward him. He preoccupied himself tuning the guitar.

"Do you know any songs by Jeremy Abazadik?" Sybil asked quietly.

Zev looked at her carefully, scrutinized her face. His teeth clenched as if he were carrying a knife between them. He did not open them to speak.

"Are you the mysterious reporter? The . . ." he hesitated or tripped over the sentence at the outset, and then sprang over it into silence. "No more songs now," he announced to no one in particular but in time to deflect the honeymooners. "Broken string," he lied. It didn't matter to them; they steered off in another direction like two people in a sack race.

"The what?"

"Never mind."

" 'The American bitch'? That's what his mother calls me." She smiled benevolently as only an angel would smile. Run your fingers through your hair, I thought. She did. "I'm just interested in him. Aren't you?"

"I've no interest in raising the dead. I leave that to the politicians."

"Did you know him, Zev?"

"Did you?" he countered.

I didn't think she'd tell the truth, but she did. "I did," she said simply.

"Did you know him well?" Being jealous, he was interested again.

"I did."

"They don't tell that part."

"I keep my life private."

"What about his? Doesn't he have the same right?"

"He was a public figure." She lost him. Sybil knew as soon as I did it was the wrong response. Unwittingly, the journalist had surfaced, a miscalculation. It wouldn't have happened if not for the heat.

"Then you know everything, what do you want to know from me?"

Whenever we stopped, I went off by myself. If I had come directly here, stepped off a plane in Eilat, and entered the Sinai immediately, I think I would have also understood this journey as a form of coming home. Within hours of our turning away from the sea, as we left the road for the sand trails, the searing wind whipping at the canvas roof, a primitive rhythm was established by the ropes swatting the metal struts, as we bounced about in the truck. I accepted coming into the domain of the Father.

Abraham and Jacob crossed this desert. Joseph had crossed this desert as well, but Joseph walked with light steps, despite the darkness of his journey, brushed the sand off his feet in Egypt, then wrote his dreams in pictographs on the inner walls of the pyramids to remember that the shadows, particularly, had been given to him. Abraham and Jacob swallowed the light eagerly, so the Sinai is the temple of Abraham, Jacob, and Moses, it is their womb; I was in their thighs.

I walked away from our little caravan. I didn't have any water and wasn't wearing a hat. I knew I had only a few minutes to get to the top of one of the rocks and look about me before I would have to return. I found a rock behind a rock, so that when I climbed it, I had a view of the valley to the south, but I was hidden to the north and couldn't see the trucks, the toilet paper someone had neglected to bury, the direction from which we had come. It was an effort to climb. Because of the heat, I was having difficulty maintaining my balance but finally I was alone, atop a rock looking out only at rosy stone, natural temples rising dramatically out of the smooth sea of sand, unbearable heat, the assault of the sun, the desert drowning in merciless blinding light.

I was very thirsty and that pleased me and there was a red film over my eyes as I rose trembling, sometimes falling but continuing the struggle to climb higher under the point of thunderous light which fell upon the desert. I lay down on the rock and contemplated the pillow of stone.

I have been raised here, all of us in the West have been raised here; this most beautiful and blinding nightmare has incubated us. "I came out of this stone," I tried to explain to Sybil later, "this is the landscape of my psyche."

I had to slide down the stone on my ass. Amit saw me struggling from a distance and came to me with some water. He didn't reprimand me, just put his arm firmly about my waist and carried me back to our vehicle.

———

We passed through eight border checkpoints, Egyptian, Israeli, Egyptian, Israeli. The Israelis waved us through goodnaturedly, but each time we were required to get out of the car, line up before the prefabricated huts to present our papers to the two or three Egyptian soldiers sitting behind old wood tables. The men got darker and darker as we traveled further into the desert. At night, one colonel met my eye and wouldn't turn away. He examined my passport most carefully, spoke to me in three languages before he settled upon English, slurring what would normally have been a vulgar proposition to spend the night with him. He delayed our transaction though there were people in line behind me and our drivers who were watching became impatient, suspecting that he was toying with his power to delay us, was indulging the irritating prerogatives of a petty bureaucrat. There was only a cautious peace between the Israelis and Egyptians, though I did glimpse soldiers from both sides playing cards together on an overturned metal oil barrel. The colonel was very sleek, dark, and intelligent; I could indisputably read that in his face, and it was an intelligence which attracted me. I found it erotic, because it was so different from mine; in the intimacy of his mind, I would know nothing. The same would pertain for him. We would both be mysteriously wise and simultaneously ignorant of each other.

Amit broke through the line and began to argue with the colonel, gesticulating wildly, his antelope horns angled down, curved, long and sharp. The colonel turned his head, threw me a sidelong glance, intense and questioning. I didn't say anything or make a gesture. He shook his head as if unable to comprehend how I would forgo this opportunity. "I'll drive you wherever you want to go." He made a last attempt. "We have lots of petrol."

"Well, next time." He resigned himself to scanning the other papers, motioned me away.

"In another life," I murmured.

"You're a dreamer," he laughed.

In the shadows outside the shack, Sybil was whispering with Zev. I approached them hesistantly. "Watch the hippies," Zev nudged me gently. The two men were standing stiffly one next to the other, their backs to us, as if they were mechanical men, lifting their right hands, two hinged metal armatures, to their heads in sequence. "The dope machines." Zev rounded his lips and sucked the air in. Without exhaling he said in a mechanical voice, "We'll see if they share the ecstasy. If they do, can I interest you two?"

"I'm not sure," Sybil responded too quickly.

"Afraid you'll be compromised . . . as a professional?"

"What do you mean?"

"Sleuths don't smoke."

"Is that what you call us?"

"Isn't that what you two do? Where have you hidden your tape recorders?" He reached over and fingered the upper buttonholes of Sybil's blouse, leaning into her as he spoke into her collar. "Take two: Zev speaks about Jeremiah Abazadik, the legendary Israeli hero." He pulled back and held her lapels in his hands as he looked at me. "Cameras, roll."

"How do you know?"

"This is a small country, everyone's business is everyone's business. That's how we survive. Isn't that so, Sybil? Haven't you learned to do that? What do you know about me, Sybil?"

The golden hawk didn't hesitate for a second. "Your brother died in this desert. He's probably under one of the tanks where we stopped for lunch. God buried him. You were in the army, you also fought here. That's how you came to know the desert, you . . ."

"There's no god and never was one. Ask your friend J.A."

"Did you know him?" Her voice had a quaver in it like the trill of night bird.

"I knew him." Before he finished the phrase, he was turning from us. "I swore that I would only love women because then you know in advance you'll be betrayed." He leaped onto his truck and began pounding the horn to hassle the Egyptians. The colonel yelled in Hebrew, Zev swore in Arabic, and they both laughed.

"What else do you know about Zev?"

"About Zev, not much, a little more about his brother. I could tell you the number of troops he fought with, the strategy they used, the kind and size of their weapons, the date of manufacture, the names of the international cartels which sell them, the countries that buy them, the extent of the Israeli munitions industry, its relationship to the GNP, how the U.S. and Israel tie in, what ball game the Soviets are playing, the way Uzis are smuggled from armies to rebels, where the Palestinians get their arms, who is playing footsies with whom in the Middle East, and who's getting screwed—everyone."

"How do you know this?"

"The birds tell me things and then I do a lot of research."

"You never talk about any of it."

"Well, it's not very interesting, you know, even if it is all the guys ever talk about. But I have to know it to understand Jeremiah. It's the backdrop of his mind."

The colonel waved the last of the line on to the cars, filling the small doorway as Amit revved our engine violently, then the colonel shouted something, not in Hebrew, to Amit, which I couldn't understand. We roared off, the truck pitching and reeling. "Over my dead body," Amit shouted to the wind, grinding through the gears, "It's not your desert yet." One of the Israeli men yelled from the back of the car, "We won't give those thieves the Sinai, you'll see. We'll fight a three day war next time."

"You don't understand, either, asshole," Amit retorted. "No one owns the desert. No one." He pointed in all directions with an abrupt sweep of his arm. "What do you see? Nothing, right? Nothing. Are you going to fight for nothing? You want to strike the fucking rock and keep us out of paradise another thousand years?" Ahead of us, to the sides, the dark was enveloping, Amit was right, there was nothing there. Turning back we could see two bare light bulbs on naked wires suspended across wooden posts which marked the entrance and exit of that checkpoint, blinking like two lost stars.

Amit turned his attention to the wheel, then called out to me in the dark, "Dina, your old friend the colonel invites you to his house in Cairo next week; he'll extend the invitation again when we stop at the checkpoint on the way out. He says it will be like stepping into another life."

"He's not a friend, I've never seen him before." I hoped I sounded amused.

"That's what they all say." He hunched over the wheel to swallow the road, after a while he began singing. Sybil nudged me with her elbow. "I'm not jealous," she said.

THE TESTIMONY OF JEREMIAH ABAZADIK
A Posthumous Autobiography

I have two subjects: love and war. They defy the laws of gravity, they make the cocks rise without wings. The two belong together. Whenever I met a woman, I turned her into a whore, made her get down on her hands and knees on the gravel and trudge behind me like a camp follower. I imagined that she was a great tank pressing the sand up through her slow sensuous treads. I'd look into the small window at her brain, stare into the emptiness, then I'd mount the gun in her mouth and she was ready for combat.

You know the kind of woman I mean, the one who lives on the droppings of the soldiers who pin medals on her nipples. She wears an army jacket over her slouching shoulders, pouts, her mouth dark red as scabs, her eyes green as gangrene, her labia lined with confiscated bayonets.

War is a thrill. That's what my mother taught me. The Nazis had taught her. After the Nazis chased her, she turned around to get a taste for revenge. Her great sorrow was that I was her only son so she wanted to multiply me like loaves and fishes. She would have bred a battalion had god not taken her womb from her. When the doctors took it out, she asked them for it so she could offer it to Him as a burnt sacrifice. It was seared in several places and radiated a dark light. She brought me women to marry after she put her fist in their cunts to see if they were large enough for legions to pass through. After her womb was gone, I thought they should have cut off her breasts in the manner of the Nazis, with a rapier, and then she'd be just like a man without any signs to remind her of her bitter past, except for the cube of cobalt they inserted under her navel as a core which ticked like a bomb. The milk in her had become flaming aluminum gel; I lay next to her and I burned. Sometimes I thought of cutting off my balls but I was afraid that the seeds of war were planted deeper in my body and I couldn't get at them even with a grapefruit knife or a syringe. I think we should all be neutered, spayed, and gelded. Maybe that will put an end to war.

· · ·

It was past midnight when we came to the Monastery of Santa Katerina and set up camp on the sand floor within the roofless, circular stone walls. We were in Egypt. There was no moon and the stars were not sufficient for us to be able to see the outline of Mt. Sinai looming above us somewhere in the vast dark.

Zev, with his usual dexterity, opened cans, set out utensils, whistled, joked, served supper, brooded, poured wine, pranced about like Pan on little goat feet. We ate the cold supper quickly and then spread out our sleeping bags. Sybil set hers so very close to mine we would sleep face to face. "Are you lonely?" I asked.

"Maybe. If I'm not careful, I'll think that Zev will solve the problem."

"Maybe he can."

"I don't think so."

"When was the last time you were with a man?"

"In New York."

"Well . . ."

"Don't say it."

"Come here. Turn your sleeping bag around so that you can

put your head in my lap." I sat up, leaned against the stone so that I could stroke her head as she fell asleep.

"How will you sleep?"

"When you doze off, I'll scoot down and be asleep in a minute. Anyway, we only have a few hours before they wake us to make the climb. I don't know if I'm scared or excited. Sometimes it's hard to know the difference."

"Your old fear of heights?"

"Maybe that's it." We'd gone off to sleep this way so many times, one of us burrowed in the other's lap. It was as if she were my daughter this time and with all the tenderness I imagined I would have felt for the baby I never had, I let my fingers run lightly over her forehead. In a short time she was breathing deeply.

After Asenath was born, I wanted to surround myself only with women except for Joseph. Leah kept her back turned as if I didn't exist. I had betrayed her twice, lying down brazenly with two of her enemies.

"Whose child is it?"

"Joseph's." A lie. Not a lie. After Asenath was born she was Joseph's by right of dream:

I was in the tent unable to sleep because the wind was jostling the flaps. When I got up impatiently to fasten them more firmly, I saw Bonah standing outside holding a young child by her hand. The girl was invisible. Still torn between rage and gratitude, Bonah ran as soon as she saw me, leaving the little girl transparent as wind standing at the threshold. I put out my hand to her, as if I was trying to grasp water. I drew her into the tent. Then Joseph entered; I set her next to him on the divan of skins and brought them warm milk with cardamom. He took her in his lap, she was very small, and I could see her nestled in his arms by the shadow on his robes, a darkening silhouette of color. Within a short time, she began to pink, even as the day suddenly pinks into bloom, as the hidden light rises into solid fire. Then she was manifest and grasped me around my neck with tiny fervor.

"*If I had not dreamed the same dream, I could have believed you invented it to trap me.*" *He placed Asenath in his robe and carried her next to his skin as Jacob had carried me when I was first born.*

Leah had despised me even before I refused to have a son for her. Rachel avoided me because I had taken her son; she saw that Joseph would never marry now that Shechem was dead. "My only son," she said. "Why not take one of Leah's, her litters are countless. She would give you any one of them, even Simeon, her favorite, has been offered to you."

"I have been cut off from my brothers and my father forever and now you want me to sever myself from Joseph? Soon I will speak only to trees and stones. Even Bonah cannot bear to look at me. She takes care of Asenath because she is her brother's child, but without lifting her eyes to my face."

Zev, checking on everyone before he lay down, walked by us with a dim lamp which he lifted to shine first in my face and then lowered so that it illuminated Sybil. In the small light she looked like an angel. I was glad for the angel and the little bit of light.

He sat down next to me. "There's no point in going to sleep, we'll have to wake up soon." He set the lamp to his side so that we were in the dark. "Why is she so sad?" he asked.

"Aren't you ever sad?"

"We're not often sad in this country. Angry, sure, lots of other emotions, but not sad, not like Sybil. I always think someone who is sad is defeated."

"Love does it sometimes," I whispered to him.

"Is she in love?"

"I think so."

"With whom?"

I didn't say anything, lifted the sand into my palm and let it run out between my fingers.

"Jeremiah?"

"I think so."

"Everyone loved him."

"That's what she says."

"Everyone. Not the way you Americans or the British love your rock stars. Not that way. Are you in love?"

"No, not yet."

"Sounds like you're planning on it."

"Well, I think it's good for the soul to love someone, don't you think so?"

"Well, when you're a desert rat you don't think about such things. I'm not home long enough to make it worthwhile."

"Will you do this forever?"

"The Sinai goes back to Egypt very soon and then . . . who knows . . . I don't think I can live in a house anymore."

"Why not?"

"Some of the Jews in this country have been able to stop wandering, some even buy pieces of land and put houses on them and plant trees. Lots of trees, as if this is a normal country and we will be here forever. But some of us will never be able to stop wandering or to plant ourselves like a tree. Some of us go back so far we're still nomads. Some of us are as old as Abraham."

"Do you think about Moses when you're here?"

"He didn't have to leave the desert."

"He was going to the land of milk and honey."

"No, he knew the moment he entered the desert, he'd never leave. He didn't need God to tell him that, a man knows such things."

"Well, I think that you should find him very sympatico."

"Maybe. It's different though. I want to stay here. And I don't want the desert to be anything but what it is. I have friends who spend their spare time trying to think of how they can bring water in here and plant orange trees and raise bees. Others want to dig for oil. They want me to take a diviner in so that they can find liquid treasures under the soil. I tell them you can't divine unless you use a branch from a living tree in the area. Do you see anything growing?"

"A few acacia."

"I lie, saying the acacia won't work. But the acacia is better for witching than any tree because it grows on both sides."

"On both sides?"

"It's living and it's dead. Maybe I'll come to the U.S. and be a cowboy."

"I'm afraid the cowboy is pretty civilized these days, keeps his horse for Sundays, lives in an environmentally controlled ranch-style house and drives around the range in a jeep loaded with electronic equipment. It won't suit you."

"Where do you live?"

"The big city. New York, it won't suit you either."

"And Sybil?"

"The same. We lived only a few blocks from each other."

"Well, maybe I'll buy a camel and go off to the Sahara, or find a desert no one else has ever found, or maybe I'll just hang out here with the Bedouin and then disappear."

"Doesn't sound as if you need much, just emptiness."

"The hardest thing there is to find."

He got up and raised his lamp, it sent shadows bouncing along the wall. "Close your eyes. If we leave in an hour, we'll have plenty of time. When she gets up tell her I stopped by to wish her good dreams."

Sybil awakened after Zev left.

"You didn't sleep at all, you've been sitting up all night."

"The night has hardly passed. And I didn't want to sleep. I liked having this kitten in my lap."

"More like an old alley cat, Dina."

"Zev stopped by to wish you good dreams."

"Don't get up yet," she pushed herself to her feet by leaning against my shoulders, keeping me down. "I'll bring you coffee. Yogurt? A sweet roll? What would you like to eat?"

"I'm not hungry."

"You've hardly eaten and you haven't slept . . . coffee?"

"OK, coffee. Cream, no sugar."
"I know."

When we were halfway up the mountain, I stopped. I pretended it was fatigue, insisting that Sybil go on ahead. She was afraid she'd miss the dawn and I was afraid I was moving so quickly that I would miss everything, although I was concerned that the others on the tour would catch up to me and I'd be swallowed up in their chatter. Zev had taken us ahead in the small jeep he was going to use to bring supplies to the monastery, so we had a jump on everyone else, but not enough for me to be safe. Far below I could see their flashlights flickering like lightning bugs but the wind drowned out the sound of their voices.

As Isaac Luria, the Kabbalist saw it, the Divine shattered and afterwards the sparks were imprisoned in dense matter. To liberate the sparks is to redeem the world.

I couldn't create enough silence or enough time. I envied Moses all the time he had had. And Dinah, she had all the time she needed, too much time crossing the desert behind Joseph, but time enough to clear the death out of her so that she could arrive in Egypt clean. In less than twenty-four hours, I was already drying like a gourd, was rubbing white powder from my skin, the first sign of being reduced. I put everything I came across into my mouth for the dry taste, the metal, the hermetically clean sand, the old, old salt. The Israelites needed forty years, two generations to clear out memory. One generation in order to forget everything and then another generation in order to remember what was under the forgetting. Forty years in order to forget what we had remembered in order to forget. Forty years in order to remember what was originally forgotten.

And Dinah, all that time remembering. What a task. Remembering against all odds and all oppressions, inhibitions, and prohibitions. Only a little remembering makes us mad, a little more remembering and it begins to show, and soon the world says, "There goes a crazy lady." Dinah remembered for lifetimes. Sybil calls me obsessed. I'm not as dedicated as you are, Dinah. I'm an American woman, we know a lot about physical training, aerobics, that kind of extremis, but when it comes to spiritual discipline, we take a break and go to the movies.

I didn't have forty years or even forty minutes before the tourists and guides would catch up to us. I didn't want to walk with anyone, not even with Amit, who could have pointed out everything of interest because he knew this mountain the way Zev knew the desert.

I sat down against a twisted dry tree staring across the path onto what I presumed was its stone face. It was so very dark, despite the little sparks of light in the distance which were coming closer. I was barely able to see the two or three feet across, only the rough floor of the path, some pebbles about my feet, the slight sheen of my white shoes, and the patina of my own skin so that I understood that on some occasions the human being carries her own light and can see in the dark.

I erased all history from my thoughts. Shechem, you were in another country, Joseph was in Egypt, and Dinah had never climbed this mountain, had never asked for scripture. So I had no personal story to learn or destroy in order to understand. And there was no voice, either large or small, speaking to me, and there was as yet no emptiness.

Not knowing what to do, I got up again and looked at the poor wizened tree with its tenacious leaves and put my hands up in imitation. I suppose that someone watching me from a distance might have decided I was dancing. I tried to bend my arms and then my entire body to capture the shape of the tree, curving first along one branch then along another, making thorns and twigs of my fingers, sliding my spine along the very trunk, no more than a human spine itself, and reaching down as the tree reached down, as if I were as amenable to wind as the tree was.

"There is only one tree on this mountain," Amit was saying. "It's just ahead. A thorn tree. Some say it's the Burning Bush where Moses first encountered God. You can't look on the face of God, you know. . . ." Amit's voice had swollen with his knowledge and was booming across the path though he had still not come up around the bend, ". . . so God showed Himself as an unconsuming fire that was held in these very branches. The tree's so dry it should have gone up like tinder. We'll rest here for fifteen minutes and then we'll have to scurry up to the summit like goats to get there before dawn. This isn't a bathroom stop, not even for the men, you'll have to control yourself until we are on the other side."

I was already on the path, scurrying, as Amit suggested. Sybil was far ahead. Even as I rushed forward, I saw that my stride became smaller and speed was more difficult. I was walking as one does in a nightmare when suddenly it is impossible to move, as if the air is thick as mud. Something held me back, caught in my throat.

It took me two hours to climb the stone snake in the moonless dark up to the chill peaks of Mt. Sinai. I slipped several times, the pebbles sliding out from under my feet, so that finally I had to put the flashlight in my pocket and trust to my eyes to see in the dark.

My eyes accommodated quickly to the night between moons and as I approached the top, a bitter wind arose carrying dawn in its mouth. When I reached the very peak, the sun rose also and broke open upon the sharp granite, running red and orange across the sky. Someone sang out, "Hal-le-lu-*jah!*" and then we were still. It was the harshest landscape I had ever seen.

The wind scraped the wounded belly of the sky across the jagged peaks so that it bled again and again, the stain absorbed into the clouds as onto linen and then falling down from the summit, a red rain. Then there was an explosion of every form of light, until the dark was trammeled, the blood expunged, and all that remained of the sky was brilliant white and unbearable blue. I hadn't brought glasses, as if I'd known I would have the opportunity to be blinded and I didn't want to protect myself from it. I covered my eyes with my hands until I adjusted to the intensity.

Behind me someone was humming a little tune, and someone else was piping into a small flute. I couldn't turn to see who it was because the wind was so fierce, I had to hold on carefully not to lose my balance and tumble down to the ledges far below. It was very cold, Sybil and I shivered in each other's arms. Down below the wind rearranged the sand but here everything was the way it had always been. On this spot, ten thousand feet above the ochre sand floor, Moses had received the law.

The Bavarian ladies arrived, huffing and puffing. They formed a little cluster behind Sybil and myself and sang a few German hymns in Christ's name. I started to silence them, was about to say, "Have respect, you're in Israel, you know," but then I realized we were in Egypt and I didn't believe in one God anyway. I sat on my ethnocentric displeasure as on an anthill and tried to be grateful for the windbreak the women provided. They soon got bored and cold and left Sybil and me alone at the top, shivering in our thin *djellabas*. The two silver snakes I'd bought at the Rockefeller Museum, replicas of the snake goddess that had been excavated at Shechem, twisted icily against my chest.

Soon Sybil had had enough and I walked with her to the beginning of the stairs cut into the rock which would take us directly down to the monastery. As she started down, I pulled my hand away. "I'll be there soon. Zev said we'd have a few hours in the monastery itself, so I'll be down before we take off." Sybil moved to stay with me, but I motioned her away and she left and I went up to the top again. Now I marveled at the austere hermitages I hadn't noticed before which spiked precariously from the highest peaks, as over the centuries monks from different orders had competed for who could get closer to God. I looked away from Israel where Dinah had been born to look ever deeper into Egypt where Dinah had died.

Like rusted twisted knives, like the spikes of the maguey, like a trunk split by an axe, like a spear mangled in the heart, like teeth filed to a point, like a tusk thrust through the breast, like splintered bone jutting out of the skin, like thorns growing through the flesh, like bamboo rammed under the fingernail, like a hook in the eye of a fish, like the shriek of metal against stone, the dreadful peaks of this desolate range.

I was pulled down to my knees. It was for this that Shechem had been killed, in this name.

Thou shalt have no other gods before me.

I fingered the snakes the way one fingers worry beads or a rosary, wanting comfort, even power. I knew the snakes were silver, the proportions of metals carefully determined so they would shine sufficiently but not bend too much. I knew they were made by women and were not gods in themselves. But where do the gods live? And what does it mean to be a vessel for the gods? And when one shapes a vessel with one's own hands, what then . . . ? Was an idol or a replica something like a bit of the Holy Cross or the Grail which, because of its proximity to the living heart, sometimes comes alive or was it like a temple where on occasion the gods sit? And hadn't it seemed to me that one of the little Asherahs remaining in the museum glowed for a moment when I looked at it and then the light went out. Out of it? Out of my eyes?

Thou shalt not make unto thee any graven image, or any likeness of anything that is in heaven above, or that is in the earth beneath, or that is in the water under the earth: thou shalt not bow down thyself to them, nor serve them: for I the Lord thy God am a jealous God, visiting the iniquity of the fathers upon the children unto the third and fourth generation of them that hate me; and showing mercy unto thousands of them that love me, and keep my commandments.

The wind was so savage I could have been blown off the mountain if I didn't wedge myself between two outcroppings, oblivious now to the skin scraped off my hands and knees by this face of God.

And when I was ready, I cried. I cried first for Shechem and then for the *teraphim*. For Rachel and Leah, for Joseph, and then, to my surprise, for Jacob as well. I cried for Dinah. Maybe I even cried for myself. The wind was so merciless. Then I put my face down on the stone to mark my forehead on the granite. I stayed there until I knew the mountain, saw it was the back of my own hand.

Then I got up and ran, not down the stairs yet, not to the cloister of Santa Katerina, but down the steep path, until I came to the skeleton of the tree which I could see quite clearly now. It was hard to believe it was alive, it had so few leaves. It was twisted and dry and covered with spikes.

But it was a tree. And so it was god. Always had been god. Burning or not, it was god. Suddenly I knew Her name. I threw up my arms, or they flew up on their own. There was no one around but me. And She. I held them above my head in imitation of her branches, knowing, in that instant, that this was the way that Shechem had prayed, Joseph had prayed, and Dinah had prayed. Standing, in imitation of the god, hands raised in joy. Dancing. And I called out, ASHERAH!

There was a bit of green. The tree was small. I was so glad.

It seemed important to me which god I was choosing to worship. The gods are imprinted upon their followers. Jealous gods sow jealousy, vengeful gods sow vengeance, and warlike gods make war. Dancing, I thought to myself, "This God in the tree, She does no harm."

I was tired and I was afraid. I pressed my back to the narrow tree to rest against it, and after a while, I realized it was burning. It was burning as it always burned when She revealed herself, as it must have burned when Moses had seen Her, when he had protected himself from Her in the rock so that he felt only Her breath, the wind in the tree, as She went by. I sat very still with the fire against my spine for a long time.

"I'm afraid I'll forget." I was anguished. I could find no words for what I felt, for what I saw. The seeing was in my body and I had no words for it. What words I found bent away from meaning even as the lowest branch bent away from the trunk. The air was still burning with Her though nothing was different from the way it had been. There was no Word.

The words bent away, they could not say what it was I felt, was feeling, was seeing, was knowing. In that moment, the shadow of the tree fell on me, another dark, wondrous, and terrible fire. Where it burned, I could feel everything I needed to know, but where it was ash, I was cut off. When I asked nothing, it burned in me, and when I wanted words, I was alone. When I saw the tree was not consumed, I did not want to hide in the rock. It was a sign that I must try to contain the flames. I felt leaves spring from them, but the ashes took my breath away.

I must go further than this, I thought. There is nothing more atop the mountain. There is nothing on the peaks. But I could not cut the wanting of words out of me. I did not know how to stop the longing, the demand for the words I thought I needed in order to remember everything, this knowing, the feeling of it. Knowing had become manifest for a moment. It was the igneous smell of sap burning up through trees from the melting core of the earth, it was magma in the bark and the trembling branches, it was the incendiary insistence of green.

The dead tree was alive in all the worlds. It was the burning ladder, the rungs of fire descending to the blazing cyclone of animal life from vast candent whorls of air, incandescent in six dimensions, everywhere alive, also within me. Everything in me: Shechem in me, Dinah in me; I was the fiery tree. And now, yes, I was burning, was the very heart of the fire storm, the fuel, the flames, the air, combustible, incombustible, consumed and unconsumed, everything was what I was and also—how else can I say it?—everything was love.

Not wanting to think, I could not stop thinking. "This is not about belief," I was thinking, "nor faith, this is not about thought, this is not about emotions." It was another world of knowing, the sexuality, the physicality, the presence of knowing, mind both flaming cock and cunt, the great glowing slit of understanding between the worlds where knowing penetrated like a torch. I invented language without words to understand how knowing shimmered, flared with Eros, fucked, rollicked, tumbled, cavorted; all this knowing without words because it was the world. The landscape blazed with life, so it was full of the gods, it was the gods.

And then I understood. I would never have words. I would never remember in words. And so, I would not remember. But, also, I would never forget. I could see myself, feel myself, also as I would be later, when I would be lost with not being able to remember. But even as I was forgetting, I felt I would never forget. This knowing was in my genes and in the genes of my grandmother Dinamira and all the other Dinas whom I didn't know who'd come before. It was seared in us from the beginning. This knowing, this feeling, this remembering, this was Dinah. I knew, felt, everything that Dinah knew, that Dinah felt, that Dinah thought. I was Dinah, it was as simple as that.

I was Dinah and also she had passed her knowing on to me. And I would not forget, because I also would pass it on. Someone would come after me and she would have to know and I would teach her. And when I knew this, that is when I knew that I would have a child, and that the two of us together, Shechem, would be alive in her and she, also, alive in the continuing braid of flame.

Then I thought the God came again: it was the sun. It was the tree against my back. I was only a woman. A breath. It was sufficient. I will understand this forever, I thought as it faded from me and I looked up and saw that the sky was innocently blue. The sun was shining. I expected to hear birds.

I reached the top, didn't take a last look, but crossed and ran down the three thousand stone stairs onto the searing sands of the desert floor. Lizards slithered out of my path from under one rock to another, and a few wild flowers opened white, brave faces to the fierce sun.

I knew you were alive, Shechem. Somewhere. I had faith. You were alive and I had not conjured you.

The last night in the desert, Amit grasped a drum between his thighs, setting the rhythm, and Zev played the guitar. Sybil had the rattle she had made with the five white stones from the *wadi* where the Israeli tanks had foundered. Sybil's shoulders trembled, her hips undulated, her body bent forward and back with the odd loping grace of a one-humped camel. The single stick burned and the flames climbed the torch and were reflected in Sybil's hair. I stood aside to begin with and then joined her. We wound about the air, we draped ourselves about each other, shimmied through the eddies of wind. The drum pulsed, cowhide stretched tightly across the wood frame vibrated the great dark earthen moo through the desert night. We danced and danced. From somewhere far above us we heard thunder, but it did not rain. Heat lightning afflicted the granite peaks. We continued to dance.

The floor of the desert is a woman. Men and women are born from her and they return to her arms. Heroes out of the body of the Great Mother, like men born from teeth, calcium, sandstone, quartz, feldspar, granite. The pink niche, the quartz arch between the sandstone thighs, is a woman and the rocks rosy with the fading light are a woman and the sands, smooth and gentle, are a woman, and the dark is a woman, but the law, scripture, and belief from this landscape has no woman in it, is as hard as any man has ever been hard.

Soon everyone went to sleep and only the four of us were left. Then I went off by myself to the far crests of the newly formed dunes. I think Zev must have joined Sybil because he reached out to stroke her hair as he passed by us during breakfast. "Little one," he said tenderly. Amit slouched darkly about the truck and none of us could do anything to make him laugh.

When we returned to Jerusalem, the landscape had done its work. I was perfectly attuned to what didn't exist. When I walked through the streets, I saw the spaces between the houses, the negative space in the sky, the light between the leaves, the silences between sentences.

Sybil was even more silent on our return than before we left. It seemed to me I could hear fear in her breathing and also longing. "Are you thinking of Zev?" I asked when I could not bear reading her mind.

"Wouldn't life be simple if I were with Zev and you were with Amit, Dina, and we had a little duplex at the edge of the desert filled with brats and goats."

"I wouldn't mind the few brats and I wouldn't mind the goats."

"Neither would I. But I'm not thinking of Zev."

"Well you know I'm not thinking of Amit."

"Joseph, then."

"I wish I could think of Joseph that way, but I can't."

She was beginning to cry, so I got up from my bed and put my arms about her thinning neck, noticing the rings that were forming.

"I do want to marry," she whispered. Her eyes were brimming with tears. "I don't want to be single forever; I'd rather be a widow. I don't care what the world thinks, I would like the experience of being one with someone. Do you know what I mean? My soul will be too thin if I go through this lifetime without either children or a partner. Work doesn't justify a life. It's a nice embellishment, but. . . . I will be like too many people who never learn to care for someone else more than they care for themselves. You've always been harsh about those kinds of people, you accuse them of being middle-aged children, self-indulgent and underdeveloped."

"I'm just afraid of becoming that way myself, Sybil."

Her face was changing. I could see the loneliness etching itself upon it. In a while she would believe that it was this visible symptom which was itself the cause. "Look, Sybil, you're not, you never have been one of those people. I've always protected you by being sufficiently difficult so that you have to look out for me."

"It's Jeremy," she said woefully.

"I'd bring him back from the dead, if I could."

"I know. So would I. But I can't. But I can be his widow."

"A widow is lonely."

"It's a different kind of loneliness. It's not completely alone."

She pulled away from me, so I went after her. If not to hold her, at least to stand very close to her. "I don't want to lose you, Sybil. Listen," I began with new enthusiasm. "I'll stay in Israel half time as long as you want, as long as you stay . . . I promise. . . ." Sometimes women make those pledges to each other which are customarily reserved to lovers. Sometimes we manage what friendship deserves. I had not been prepared to make that sacrifice for a husband, but Sybil was my family, she was my sister.

She smiled halfheartedly. "I'm grateful," she acknowledged. "But I've never had any doubts about our friendship. But do you mind, I think I need to be alone with myself."

I took a walk. When I returned, she was busily ordering papers, labeling, placing chapters of the book on Jeremiah in manila folders. Everything was in efficient piles. Then she asked me to stay with Joseph for a few days and I agreed. When I stopped at the hospice for clothes, there was no longer any sign of Jeremiah. The papers and photographs had all been put away. Sybil's desk was clean, except for her journal, and her voice sturdy, if remote.

THE TESTIMONY OF JEREMIAH ABAZADIK
A Posthumous Autobiography

I learned a form of torture for every note and every scale. I could sing death in D# or C minor. I could see the future, synthesizers creating visual music orchestrating an entire war in full color, the noose of the deadly clarinet winding through koto water torture. Cymbals of poison rain falling across the great hairless skin drum of earth. If there had been trees in the barren land they would have died in a great dirge of bassoons and tubas sucking on the plutonium wind, another electronic miracle, all the world filled with contrived vibrations, the entire countryside electrified.

I thought it was time I get a wife. I went to the slave market because they had a clearance sale. Another war was coming and there would be a glut on the market, but they wouldn't let me sample the merchandise or even exchange it if it were defective. They said every object had a flaw, it was the nature of things, it gave them dimension. They said some of the better models came with their own airbrushes to powder over the blemishes. You could only get a service policy for the airbrushes. I wanted the top of the line, not a discontinued model. I wanted something that could be serviced, where the parts were standard and replaceable. A wife whose parts functioned smoothly with warranties from General Electric, or Lockheed, or any other reliable multinational corporation; I wanted a woman sleek, silver, predictable as a bomb. Still, as I walked through the stalls, I was thinking I would take a chance if anything struck my fancy. If she didn't satisfy me, I could always donate her for a tax deduction to the annual rummage sale of my veteran's organization.

Finally I remembered what I was looking for. The Whore of Babylon. How foolish to think I would find her in the marketplace instead of the shards of darkness. I walked the night streets with my cock trailing balls and chain waiting for a red light to go on.

Eureka! The bitch goddess. She magnetized me with her crystal cunt, her hair spun from amber. I spun in the four directions.

Do you accept? I do. Do you accept? I do. Do you accept? I do. On my hands and knees, I accept crawling in the mud, I accept groveling, I accept searching for an honest woman trained by the bomb squad to defuse anything on the planet devised by the hands of men.

.   .   .

Joseph opened the door even before I was out of the car. "Would you like a drink?"

"Bon voyage," he said, trying to be kind about the trip to Nablus. We clicked our glasses nervously.

After dinner I asked him if he had dreamed about me.

"You're not a dream, you are the real thing."

"Joseph, you know . . ." He wouldn't let me finish, wouldn't let me say that I wasn't in love with him, that I didn't have the same feelings for him that he seemed to have for me.

"We're not twins, you know, even though we were born at the same time. I don't expect you to be a reflection of me. Wouldn't that be boring."

"Don't you want anything from me?"

"No. Nothing. I'm perfectly satisfied with what transpires between us."

He asked me about the Sinai and I told him about it best as I could, including the burning bush and a dream I'd had:

"God came into the room. He was tall, stately, clean-shaven, of course—so much for Hassidic beards and earlocks—intelligent looking, wearing an impeccably pressed dark suit and a dazzling white shirt. He looked like a French banker. I knew who He was instantly. I gasped, 'There's something wrong with your head, the left temple.' He was wounded.

"He took a handkerchief from his pocket and dabbed the cut above His eyebrow. 'It's not the first time,' He said.

" 'I'm sorry,' I whispered.

" 'Yes, you would be.' He turned away, disappointed with me, I believe."

"Is that the entire dream? How did you feel?"

"Maybe a trifle touched, Joseph."

He groaned.

The phone rang and it was Sybil. She was surprisingly cheerful; chipper, Anne MacDowell would have said. "I will go with you to Nablus," she volunteered. "When will we go?"

"Monday."

"I'll be ready." She hung up.

Staying with Joseph was easier than I thought. We were so compatible, I didn't think of us as lovers.

"Sometimes when I am away from my work, Dina, I am haunted by the idea that the twentieth century is an illusion, that the entire, concrete society we've established is a house of cards."

"The old puzzle, are we awake or are we dreaming the world? But why would we dream up such a horror?"

"An important question. Why would we, Dina? Well, don't get carried away with guilt until we've proved that this is all our or your doing. I don't want you to feel too powerful just yet, although being humbled doesn't suit you."

It was a lovely weekend. When I awakened on Monday in his bed, I felt a stab of lust the way I often feel hunger after I've forgotten to eat for many hours, a sharp twist in my guts, and then a metallic hollowness. I felt lust for him the way I sometimes feel lust for my own body, the desire to put my fingers between my legs to staunch a specific localized need. I wanted Joseph the way I have wanted myself, wanting to get it over with.

"You don't have to go today," Joseph said. "Last chance to change your mind and do a good deed for humanity."

"What will you do this week?"

"I've been thinking about traveling to Mars or Saturn, I want to be out of the way when you set the world on edge. I don't like earthquakes."

Then, suddenly, I understood. "You're jealous. That's why you won't take me to Nablus. You know the story."

"I was born here, remember? I have lived all the stories. You're like every other invader pretending you can enter a territory without leaving a mark."

"I took a seminar on camping in the wilderness. I was even taught to dig up a square of grass before building a fire or digging a latrine, to cover everything up, level it, and replace the sod. Afterwards, when our trainers followed our route they couldn't find our traces."

"There's no grass in Nablus, you don't dare dig a latrine and squat down in the center of the city, and you can't hide your traces. The very air you breathe out will create commotion. It's not as if you're coming in peace."

"I'm only coming in peace."

"You say so. And you trust it because you said it; you're so damned American, always believing the naive gospel of your good intentions. And since you're not clairvoyant, you can't see what's coming."

"Are you?"

"Oh, no, but I am a realist."

"Well, Joseph ben Yacob, what would you advise me to do?"

"Stay with your own kind."

"That's just what I am trying to do. Are you afraid you'll lose me?"

"Why do you find that a laughing matter?"

I recognize this Joseph. He was always the same, that's why they put him in prison and then they made him Viceroy. First they put him in a pit and then they put him on a pedestal. They threw him down and then they bowed down. That's how they contained his power.

Joseph doesn't recognize me. He cannot imagine me. He is so far from himself. After so many years as Viceroy, it was inevitable that the dreamer disappeared. The dreamer can never be king. The king kills the dreamer without necessarily intending to. It is the nature of things. The dreamer has to live alone, wandering at night in the hills or along empty stony corridors. The dreamer can live in a tomb but not in a palace. I became the priestess. He would visit me and I would tell him stories to distract him from counting barrels of oil, sacks of grain, settling disputes. He did become lonely for his old life but it was beyond us. The desert had closed up over it so that it was lost in the sands. I couldn't go back with him because I would have had to jump over Shechem's death which sat in the middle of that life like a bloody stake. Whenever I came to that stake, it caught in my side.

I went to the hospice to pick up Sybil. We met Eli, he had red hair and approved my car. We set out for Nablus.

Millennia had not completely altered the road. It still smelled of old goat bones, even under the concrete.

Things reach a conclusion. Two parallel lines or lives meet in infinity and become one where the universe curves back on itself. For a while my sorrow was so far from its roots, it forgot itself. A woman's curse must be housed in a body, in memory, in a living story. Her curse must be personal and specific or it loses its power. After a time I became tired, I couldn't manage the burden of hate throughout the centuries and I gave it up but it was too late, the curse had gone beyond the curse, it had become a thing unto itself, the house of Levi and the house of Shechem claimed it as they had claimed and appropriated everything else, and once it was theirs, they couldn't give it up, they wrote their names on it in stone; it became the story of two men and one had deceived the other. Then it was their story which devoured me like a salt wind.

And the sons of Jacob answered Shechem and Hamor deceitfully.

Eli drove, Sybil sat beside him and I sat behind. I was happy to be alone in back with only my inner voices to answer to while Sybil chatted merrily with Eli about his family, about friends they had in common, and about politics, of course.

Because of my interest in Biblical history, Eli thought I'd be interested in a case which had just occurred in the Arab quarter. "Some people still arrange marriages for their daughters," he was saying. "There's only one way that a woman can get out of it if she wants someone else. She has to arrange a rape by her boy-friend."

"That sounds dangerous," I mumbled. I was half listening, my thoughts were on the scenery I was trying to recognize to see if I could remember having been here.

"Very tricky. The conflict is transferred to the two men, where it belongs; after all, the girl is innocent, and you don't know what will happen. Sometimes, if they're equals, the lover can negotiate for the girl without the father being dishonored."

In this instance, Shechem, the timing was off. The girl was caught with her lover before he could make his move and it was her father's tribal duty to kill her. He couldn't do it, of course, and the entire community mocked him. Eli didn't know what happened to the lover, he seemed to have disappeared from the story. One day after the villagers had provoked her father mercilessly, he lost control of himself when his daughter was late bringing lunch to him in the fields and he turned on her, battering her with a hoe. She fell down, her body twitching with the life running out of it. Her brother, thinking she was still alive, picked her up and carried her, her blood staining his white shirt, to the doctor, who said, "I don't want to have anything to do with this." So the brother took her to the police. He entered the small, square, stone building with his sister spread across his arms like a holy crimson cloak while crying out, in an attempt to protect his father, "I did this."

It was Jacob's duty to kill me, but he wouldn't. Levi and Simeon would have done it but I had already filled the air so thickly with

ashes and lamentations they could not find me. The gods of the
earth kept me safe. My brothers could not look me in the eye and
they had this much honor: they couldn't kill me from behind. If
the lamb is to redeem the tribe through the sacrifice, it must par-
ticipate in the slaughter.

Eli intended to take us up to Mount Gerezim in Samaria, where
there were the ruins of the palace of Ahab and Jezebel, after we
spent a little time in Nablus. I was getting concerned that this was
becoming a tourist jaunt, three cities in one afternoon with a
prearranged lunch, shishkabob and rice at the local inn. I didn't
want to eat, but I couldn't keep them from eating; our destinations
were entirely different. I marveled at the discrepancy between us
despite the appearances. Three Westerners on a midweek holiday.

I ordered a meal to maintain my disguise, then only nibbled,
pretended indigestion. Irritable, impatient, restless.

"Just what difference will it make to go in alone?" everyone
had asked me.

Before the meal came I paced up and down in the garden. "A
headache," I lied to Eli. If I had gone in alone, had succeeded in
getting to Shechem, then what? What if I had failed then?

"Do you like the food?"

"Oh, yes, it's lovely."

We were sitting on a veranda amid lush vegetation, partaking
of an elegant lunch, "getting to know one another" through polite
conversation. I wiped my mouth, delicately, on the pink linen
napkin. The Arab waiter watched us attentively from the shadows.
I poured tea for Sybil before she asked for it. She smiled at me
appreciatively.

"The Samaritans are very odd, more Jewish than we are in some
ways," Eli was saying. "They claim that peace enters the body of
the lamb just before the knife enters so they still smear the fresh
blood from the throat of the slaughtered lamb on the faces of their
boy children during the Passover."

Jacob had asked me to sacrifice a lamb and I wouldn't do it. I wouldn't offer him that peace, nor would I lie down like my grandfather, Isaac. When my great great uncle, Cain, offered his god fruits and grains, his god wasn't satisfied. He preferred bloodied lambs, so Cain obeyed Him and offered up Abel. But you can never please that god; that sacrifice wasn't accepted either.

Once again, Sybil entered into a slight flirtation and it did her good. The interaction was quite mild, the kind pursued by men who are expecting a first child, eager and reluctant both to disguise their jealousy and their envy and to prove that they are not completely absorbed in the oncoming domestic event. Eli fenced himself in with talk of the coming baby and then he almost leaped over the fence into Sybil's arms. It occurred to me, when I broke out of my own thoughts, that there was something maternal about Sybil now, a new deep softness, as if her womb were made of cotton wool. Still she was quite the coquette. I didn't know if my presence made her feel safe enough to play, whether it was the habit we had developed over years of being girls together, or if she also indulged herself when I wasn't present. Whichever it was, I approved it. The two of them were engaged with each other and no one asked me how I was feeling.

I was going to Nablus, Shechem, Nablus, imagine that. It had finally happened and nothing was going to stop me. This became certain when we were pulled over by the police at the checkpoint at Jericho and Eli showed the officer his papers and Sybil and I showed our passports as if we were entering Egypt again and the officer responded with some good humored warnings against falling in love with any Arabs because the Jews were jealous about their women. Then he looked at Eli and Sybil and joked, "You two look safe. It's the one in the back seat you'll have to watch out for." Clever man.

A horn blasted behind us. It was too hot to wait with the motor running while the guard engaged in philosophy. Business was pressing. "See you later, be careful, do you hear? Be careful," he called after us as Eli drove away.

When we came to Nablus, Eli was driving nervously and I realized that lunch had been a delaying tactic so we would not spend much time in the area. We were skirting the city, coming down the sides of the bowl, when he announced that we would drive directly to Joseph's tomb, some quarter mile from the main highway along a dirt road which passes through the backyards of dilapidated Arab houses. If one can use American terminology, I would say we were in the suburbs. "They're friendly," Eli reassured us. Joseph's tomb. I shuddered. Joseph had not said anything to me. Was this a joke? We were going right into a hole in the earth, a great shovel had been scraping away at the layers of time, until the gutted belly of history lay exposed with everything raw and twitching.

Joseph's tomb, unlike the site of Shechem, is under Israeli control and a young soldier waved his submachine gun genially as he recognized Eli, who spent some time each month working in the area. Sybil was visibly reassured by his presence and her relief stabbed me in my heart, even before Lev, one of the three soldiers on duty, leaped gracefully from his perch on the dome of the tomb, his leather boots cracking to the dusty ground, raising swirls of dust about our feet. "Bravo!" Sybil yelled in appreciation. I shouldn't have brought her, I remonstrated with myself—again— then I saw my regret was also a distraction and tried to set it aside. What choice had I had, Shechem? If Sybil hadn't come, who would be with Eli to distract him?

I had been afraid to ask Sybil anything, yet it was not possible to pretend that nothing extraordinary was transpiring between us. I hadn't been able to gauge her mood or response, and had to keep utterly secret, it seemed to me, my own intentions. I was afraid the slightest wind would dissolve you, Shechem, that you might fade in the merest suggestion of fantasy. I hadn't really told her why this journey meant so much, so there we were, and the tone was off. Of course, I wasn't giving Sybil any credit for being able to figure things out on her own, which she'd always done quite well in the past. Sybil and Eli were clearly having a good time. I regretted that he was married. I was preoccupied with the two of them and unable to concentrate myself.

Dear Shechem:

I have to stop here. I am distracting myself with Sybil, with irrelevant details. It is a way of looking away from the moment without noticing that it has come and gone. Fooled (by myself) once again as I had been in the beginning. Once again I am in danger of losing you.

This is what really happened. Let me live it again, as best I can, without Sybil or Eli. Imagine them in the background.

Dear Shechem:

On the way here, driving along the empty road, we passed some orchards and vineyards and ancient olive trees, thousands of years old, Shechem, so old we have to have known some of them ourselves. It wasn't as if I was riding on a donkey and watching trees go by, it was as if I were riding in one direction and history was passing by my shoulder in the arms of a great wind. In a moment, whatever I was looking forward to was behind me. But what I was going toward was so far in the past that what passed me by was my ordinary life. There were brief moments when the glimpse of the past, the mere mention of a Biblical site was so disturbing, I had to consciously clear my mind as one does in meditation. Beth-el, for example, where Jacob had first dreamed of climbing to God, and where we fled with our ashen gray sheep when Shechem was dead and my heart was broken.

Do you want to know how I felt? I felt empty inside. Flat and empty. And a little bit absurd as Sybil's presence, and Eli's, eroded everything. You can't make the dream into an outing as if it were a drive-in movie. But I had.

If those were Joseph's bones in the tomb, they were my bones as well. I didn't know which bones elicited more tenderness in me. Joseph's, I suppose. How could I contemplate my own death when I was also trying to bring something to life? The tomb is shaped like a great stone egg, half out of the ground, half under it. A blue silk cloth, the veil between the worlds, length of two bodies, color of sky, covers the top of the shell.

Joseph and I had been buried together. Later what remained of our bones were mixed together in the same vase. Moses carried us out of Egypt. He had not known that I was with Joseph. We had died as we had lived so much of our lives, with our thigh bones crossed.

We went into the tomb. Odd that Eli trusted me or understood something because he subtly motioned the caretaker out of the room after he had made some historical points to Sybil and through the archway I could see him wave at the soldiers who fell back. Perhaps Sybil had something to do with it. Suddenly she shone; she shone for me. And when she shines, she has a light which draws everything to her; she is irresistible. I was alone.

History melts. It's a thin coat after all, a varnish on a simple story and after the flesh slides off, then we're left with the same familiar bones, the basic structure, the death's head.

This was it. As it had been in the beginning. Joseph and I as close to each other as we could possibly be, raising each other, tumbling about each other and the lambs, and Shechem, there across the field and the stone wall, not far.

Oh my loves!

For days I was like a leper, even Joseph kept his distance from me. Then, looking at me one morning, he realized that I was carrying a child. Then he came into my tent and sat by me where I had collapsed after the night's vigil, sat until I awakened still frantic with exhaustion and rage. He said nothing. He brought a basin of water and a rag and began to wash the ashes, mud, and blood from me. It was the first time he had seen me naked since I'd become a woman. He tore the clothes off me; it didn't make a difference, I had already shredded them with my nails and teeth. Then he gave me one of his soft robes, though it, like everything else, was gray from the ashes which were still falling. He made me drink milk. It was from one of Shechem's goats, he said. I didn't remember having anything to drink since I had taken in wine from Shechem's mouth and the salty milk sperm from his body. He had held nothing back from me. Taking the sperm in I had thought, now I will drink you and later you will drink the milk from my breasts and we will feed each other from our bodies.

I sank down to the floor beside the tomb. The stone was as thick as the centuries. Beneath three thousand years of stone were our bones. Still they were our bodies. And outside in Shechem, not one thousand yards away according to what I had read, was a wall. If not for Dinah's brothers she would have been buried there.

And Shechem's ashes? When Joseph died, I swallowed them, lay down alongside Joseph, embraced him, as we had agreed, also drank poison, died.

At my own tomb. They call it Joseph's tomb, but it is mine as well. I kneeled down beside my own bones. If I could have broken through the great egg, I would have ground the bones into a powder again and drunk them with water from the Jordan.

So. This is the starting point. Full of surprises, aren't you, Dinah. This is also the end. In the Sinai, I didn't know if I was coming or going, but now you have brought me to the final location. And my life for eons swinging from these two poles not a thousand yards apart.

History repeats itself. Those who were recently born beside that wall are not always permitted to die beside it. Jacob's sons returned, and their children as well, the blood of the Hivites running in their veins. Dinah and Joseph's sons among them and both blessed by Jacob and the younger once again given the birthright of the elder, and still not able to live among the 'heathen', so to speak. Jacob was willing but Levi and Simeon were not. When they plow the fields for their *moshavs,* they throw the bones away, they let the bones make no claim against their land. And Jacob cannot control his sons.

I was overcome and thought to myself, "Beware of what you wish for. History does come alive."

There is no lust that compares with the lust that Joseph had for Dinah. Or was it love? It was greater than the lust that Shechem had for me because it was not the desire for the other, it was the lust that self has for self. I was precisely himself; he had no fear of me. Sometimes I think that Jacob secretly asked Laban for Leah to break that bond that Rachel had upon him. Joseph drank between my legs as if he were thirsty for sperm.

We married at the hour when the full moon rose and confronted the sun at the horizon. I came to Joseph just as the moon rose and the sun set. We went down into the bed together. We were in Egypt. Asenath was already running and speaking so my body was clean and thin again, like a young boy. We lived and we died between those two lights. Asenath remained in Egypt and my sons Manasseh and Ephraim returned to Shechem so my line extends in two directions.

I lay on the stone floor overcome with longing. It was suddenly very cold and I could feel the silk tearing in the icy air and the veil parting and a hand reached out toward me, and an even cooler hand reached out and covered my face so that I wouldn't scream, and then it was as if there were lips upon my lips, taking my breath as if we were making love, and coaxing me down into the familiar dark. I was with Joseph again. I rocked with him, breathing his cold dark air in the cradle of his arms once again as if we were in that solar barque which had taken us together to the night bedroom of the sun. I felt my body soften with oil and then tighten as if it were wrapped in linen, and the linen, moistened and then dried, shrank as skins do, so that we were as tightly bound together as healing splintered bones.

I must have been dreaming because Sybil had to wake me violently.

"I forgot myself." I embraced her warm neck.

"Praise the Lord and pass the ammunition," she sang. "I'm having a hard time with the discussion of the latest holy wars. Get up and save me."

Eli smirked at me when I exited the tomb. He would have been quite content if I had had enough and suggested we go home, but I straightened my skirt, took a sip of water from the canteen to freshen my mouth, and began walking ahead of them over the hill, avoiding the rusted car parts, torn plastic sacks of garbage, banana peel, old papers, tires.

Then, my love, I was in Shechem. I had come home. I looked about me quickly. Except for Sybil and Eli, there was no one else in sight. I didn't see you anywhere.

"Let's go in through the gate," Eli suggested and veered toward the east. The *tel* was a small knoll which protected a crater within the bowl of mountains surrounding Nablus. Now I'm careful, Shechem. Every word matters. I will not conjure anything, am warned against wizards and familiar spirits. Also I do not know the names of the gods of this place. A tree had fallen on the upper embankment, struck by lightning; its trunk was split down the middle, god's discarded compass.

If Dinah is not properly propitiated she may appear without warning and curse. Beware of the wrath of the local deities.

The pagans say that anywhere you invoke a circle becomes the center of the universe. But here the gods had drawn a circle and a circle within that circle and within that circle another circle. The *tel* was like a ravaged breast. It looked like a bomb crater, ground zero where everything had been destroyed. There was debris everywhere. "The Arabs don't take care of their ruins," Eli sneered.

I will stop pretending that I don't know anything and that I don't want anything and that I'm not afraid. I couldn't have come this far if I were totally innocent. Maybe I'm no longer even ignorant. Maybe I've come to know some of what Dinah knew when she was a girl. Maybe I've recovered something. Maybe she has passed it on, her knowledge with her power. I hadn't kept my eyes averted in the past weeks. I'd been watching and I learned something. In the desert, Zev recognized every sacred stone and maybe he had taught me to see the gods in the rocky crevices. Maybe and maybe not.

I want only to be on this land. I mutter a succession of prayers and the first is that Eli and Sybil will leave me alone. I am already separated from them so that each time they speak to me or stand beside me I'm startled. It's not as I remember it. Well, it's so small. I've been living in modern cities and you could put this entire city inside one mansion and still have rooms remaining without any past in them. Even if we had spent our lifetime with you living inside the walls with the Hivites and my living outside the walls with the Israelites, we could not have been separated. There are so many stories of lovers whispering to each other through stone walls. I know that image well. Even time is a wall. But it is transparent. I see you when I put my hand up against it, even if I cannot go through.

Here is the wall which surrounded the city or what remains of it. First, Eli takes me through the site and I go out again while he and Sybil squat down in a corner and chat with each other. I enter the city as if no one else is here but me. The oldest extant Biblical wall. Not much of a wall, but enough to know there was a wall with an entryway. Here is the flat stone which Eli says is the remnant of the temple to Baal. Baal-Berith, God of the Covenant. So now I am indeed going back in time, as Sinai was the second telling of the covenant. I bow down but only as a matter of form and politeness, as I would cover my head in a church or my elbows in an orthodox temple. But I would show Asherah my bare arms, my unbowed head, my naked body.

For they built them high places, and images and groves, on every high hill, and under every green tree.

Following the diameter from the temple floor to the great tree where the bull is tethered, you will cross through the center of Shechem, the omphalos, where one tablet stills stands. Or is it the pillar to Asherah, the stone tree, the woman with her hands raised in praise?

I prowl about restlessly like a mad woman. I don't know where to stop, how to meditate, what to pray for. I look for the spot of bloody earth where I last saw Shechem alive in my body. Here it is by the wall, no, here by the temple floor, no, closer to the south. I try the south, move in the direction of my tomb, but everything brings me back to this cricle within a circle, the diameter passing between the temple floor and the central plinth. I want to meditate but the earth is burning my feet through my shoes. I can't rest. I pace agitatedly and then realize I'm describing a circle, going around seven times, the bride circling the groom under the *chuppah* which is the silken and embroidered sky. I want to be with the bull but I'm afraid of him. Eli signals me as if he wants to tell me something about this site and I turn my back on him; I don't give a fig for his history. I throw up my hands in despair. The sun beats down fiercely. It's very hot.

A school bus pulls up to the perimeter of the site. Several Palestinians in white, blue, and gray striped *djellabas* exit the bus without turning off the engine. From the navel—a meteor could have scooped out this rough crater—I watch them march in single file above me toward some houses a few meters away. I don't know why I drop to my knees when an inner voice tells me to stand with my arms raised like a tree, but the reflex to obey Eli, who warned me not to draw attention to myself, takes over. I glance over at him. Now he is standing very straight with his shirt tucked neatly into his pants so that his gun is visible, the light glinting off it like a bullet. The men could be Hivites carrying fruit home from the fields. The first man, the leader, is carrying a great watermelon under his arm. It could be an offering, a dessert, or a bomb. They disappear into the house. Eli pulls his shirt out, covers his gun belt, turns so that he is facing the house, his back to the bus, having satisfied himself that there is no one left inside. The engine is still running. I pray. What do I pray for? I have everything.

I feel the earth as I once knew it. What else can I ask for? I begin to dig aimlessly in the sand, it will take me days to dig back to what I remember, to the temple with the clay floor and the limestone walls, to find what if anything remains of the wooden beams which held up the roof. Still I see the tents stiff with the bristly hair of goats, I hear the bleating of the herds. I remember . . .

The sun begins to angle. A young skinny Arab boy dressed in shabby jeans and a ragged shirt approaches Sybil and then me and I can't resist him. He's selling coins, "Roman, genuine," he insists, biting one between his crooked teeth until Sybil buys one for me. We take some pictures; the young boy accommodates us. This amuses Sybil. Film the filmmaker. Eli begins to explain the geography, the history, the politics. I can't turn away from him. It's become an ordinary day again. Now I'm hungry. If I had one, I'd light a *havdalah* candle to celebrate the advent of the profane.

> I was asleep but my heart waked:
> . . . .
> I opened to my beloved;
> But my beloved had withdrawn himself, and was gone.
> My soul had failed me when he spoke:
> I sought him, but I could not find him;
> I called him, but he gave me no answer.

Defeat. I have failed you. Once again in the actual living out of events, I have not been equal to the task. And I cannot begin again. I can't identify the moment of failure. Was it relying on Eli, not having the guts to come alone? Was it allowing, or asking, yes asking, wanting, Sybil to come with me? Why? So I could show her a real phantom instead of a dead one? Was it submitting to Joseph? No, none of these. It's now, it's this moment, it's a failure of the heart. A failure of the imagination. The most common failure of faith, the inability, in the moment of extremity, to stay awake in the darkness. I sit down crosslegged on the rough stone, it's uncomfortably hot against my thighs through my thin cotton pants. Good. My back hurts. Better. My skin is roughening from the constant dry wind. Great. The sun is giving me a headache. Perfect. Hunger to the point of nausea. Delight. Damn! Won't this adventure make a good story.

Maybe the land isn't sacred anymore. Maybe the land was sacred because of the temple and it wasn't that the temple was erected on sacred land. So when the temple fell. . . . This reminds me of Mycenae. Mycenae was cold. That's one of the places where history began. Like here. The site of the death of the gods and the advent of men. There were no gods there any longer. There are none here. None that I can feel. Only men watered in their own blood. History, Shechem, began everywhere in the world at the same time—the gods evaporating from the land in a mist. And the men falling like a rain of plagues.

Bye-bye, Shechem. What a big deal I made. You'd think a girl had never lost her boyfriend before. You know she didn't have a bad deal. She took all his flocks, all his money, a few servants, and everyone wanted to marry her, and then she married Joseph even though she was knocked up and after a few hard years—who doesn't have a few hard years?—she became a priestess or what do you call the wife of the Viceroy, a Lady at the very least, and she was living on the fat of the land in Egypt when her father and brothers were starving here. She was one of the great complainers of all time. Talk about not blessing your life, not being satisfied! So he died, so he was killed, what's the big deal? Everybody's being killed. All the time. Well, forgive her, Dina, she was a kid, only fourteen. That's the age when girls exaggerate their fate; it makes them feel important, gives them the sense they can have an impact on things, before they realize they're just girls and don't count and make nothing happen. Listen, some people think the story never happened, that it's just a sophisticated story describing internecine warfare.

Well, that's it, friend. Once the gods are pressed out, myth is not recoverable, and history, which may or may not be one of the great lies, doesn't serve us. It was a good try, wasn't it? I see what the Israelis mean about the Arabs treating this site like a garbage dump. Look at those damned cars rusting away. What a burial ground! And over there, under that dome, a few bags of relics, probably petrified chicken bones. Hello, Joseph, cluck cluck cluck. I think I'd like to ask those Arabs what response they have to living on a biblical site. I can just imagine their answer—they can't get off their asses to clean up these plastic bags. Adolescent girls make a lot of trouble with their runaway fantasy life. No wonder Jewish mothers are warned to keep their daughters at home, not to let them go dancing around naked in the streets. If the Jews, Jacob that is, hadn't gotten scared and run away from this site, I bet the city would still be intact, the wall would be in perfect condition, and there would be nice little families having a picnic up there under the tree.

I did the best I could, Shechem. This vessel isn't good enough. I'm sorry. I did the best I could. I give up. I couldn't manage it. Do what you want.

I hear a commotion at the rim, feel Sybil stiffen, and see Eli reach for his gun, this time holding it in his hand. One of the soldiers, I think it is Lev, is leading a tall Arab across the dry grass, pushing him with the muzzle of his Uzi. The man does not wince, walks as if there is no weapon slamming into his ribs. A gun at your back changes your posture—I know this from my own life—you either fold over or you stand straighter. Eli calls out something in Hebrew which, damn, I do not understand, and then I am impelled to my feet and am running across the grass, scrambling up the knoll, until I am level with the soldier and his prisoner and looking at them face to face. Eli is calling to me sternly, "Dina! Dina!

Come here! Dina! No! No!" as if I am a child or a dog. I can see
what Eli cannot or will not see from where he is standing. I also
stand straight because the gun is pointing at both of us and I do
not move out of the way. The eyes of the man coming toward me
lock into mine so that we cannot be moved away from each other.
We are on terra firma. We have taken the great leap over the sacred
river, though it was running fast and cold, and this is paradise
once again, the dissolve of time. What is a gun, Shechem? What
does it matter, Shechem? There's no matter. Spirit, shining and
singing, comes walking toward me in some body or other, I can
barely see its shape or texture, for all I know it is the great bull
that has come untethered and is bounding toward me with all its
luminous power. I suppose these are my arms which are out-
stretched; I only feel the wanting and the welcome in them. I
suppose these are what are called hands; I only feel the centuries
of emptiness reaching forward. I am like a great vase, a great jug,
a great vat empty of water and I am thinking, rain, Shechem, rain,
rain, Shechem, rain, Shechem. . . .

Jamine ignores Lev and his gun and comes straight toward me and
stops, the gun pointing at both of us. "Hello, Dina." In his gruff
voice, in clipped Palestinian English, slightly British in pronunciation, my name becomes Dinah. "It's me, don't you remember? I've
been waiting to see you for so long, it seems like centuries."

I can't speak. And if I had a voice what language would I cast
it in? Jamine puts his hand out to brush the hair out of my eyes
and then his fingers are wet. "Don't cry, Dina," he says softly, but
not without bitter humor, "these sabras like to stick their spines
in us, but we're desert people, we know how to survive. They
arrest us as often as they swat at flies, but we always get out
through the holes in their screens.

"Is it you?"

"Friend of yours?" Lev asked scathingly, "or are you interested in the sideshow?"

"A friend of mine," I answered.

"Naturally, he would be a friend of the American. Does he sell you oil or do you like a little terrorism with your morning coffee?" Lev planted his feet in the ground as if it had been his idea to stop and confront me. "Well, since he's a friend, by your own admission, you won't mind coming along with us to the command post, will you?"

"Do you want me to come along with you at gunpoint, or do you trust Eli to bring me?"

Lev looked down at Eli and Sybil who were staring up in disbelief. "Will you keep your gun on them for a moment, Eli?"

Eli hesitated, training and discipline reflexing in him, but he caught my eye, or maybe it was Jamine's, and didn't move forward, yelling back, "I can't do it, Lev."

"Well then, get up here and shut the damned engine, will you? And then will you bring her down to the post?"

Eli clambered up the hill, small clods of dirt falling back behind him. Sybil came up more slowly and stood by my side, she put her arm about me. "You're the man who knows embroidery." Sybil is always tactful; she was being perfect.

"Yes, many things." He walked off, leading Lev who followed after him with the gun. Eli turned off the engine, threw the keys under the floor mat. "No one steals a car with the motor idling, you don't know who's around or what may happen." He turned toward me with some annoyance. "I did want to show you Samaria. Another time. I assume you're finished here and we can go and be character witnesses for Jamine. Good show, Dina. Who knows, Sybil and I may even have to vouch for you. Is she a terrorist, Sybil?"

"She hasn't been anything else all her life."

I wanted to follow after Jamine. I didn't want to drive in a car or
be with Sybil and Eli trying to explain what I didn't understand.
In the moment I'd seen Jamine, I'd experienced a disquieting bond-
ing as if we were the intimates and Sybil an interloper; there was
a rush within me of an odd unmanageable chemistry like the kind
which calls one insect to another over miles. I watched Jamine's
long shadow. After a short while it intersected with Lev's shadow
until I could not tell the two men apart on the ground. I began to
run after them, but Eli caught my hand firmly and without a word
insisted we return to the car. We drove to the army post, passing lots of Palestinian boys in the streets scurrying about their
work, and some Israeli children playing together in the fields.
Three women, like dusky birds, were chatting as the light was beginning to change. They were behind barbed wire, patrolling the
moshav.

The military post was housed in a new cinderblock building.
By the time we got there, other soldiers were on guard and Lev
was ensconced behind a desk though still wearing his Uzi. One of
the soldiers was wearing a patch over his eye, half his face was
smashed in.

Lev saw me staring and smiled, "Quite a war wound, isn't it? But it isn't a war wound, Ms. American. It's what happens when you happen to be a kid in a bus station coming home from school and suddenly a little package of English tea biscuits in a shopping bag blows up."

I dried my sweating palms on the hips of my pants while Lev launched into a barrage. Eli went back into another room where I wasn't permitted to follow him. "Do you think he's a volunteer, looking for revenge? Ask him. Did you enlist, Shlomo? No. He's just serving his time like the rest of us. Do you know how many miles it is from here to the Mediterranean? In terms of modern warfare it's just a spit of a mortar shell from here to there. That's where your 'friend'—you did say he was a friend—would like us to be. But that won't bother you, American. Everyone in America takes scuba diving lessons, so you don't think it will be a strain to live under water. But Shlomo here won't like it. He's studying literature. Books fade in salt water, and if he has to squint to read . . . he only has one eye . . ."

"Where's Jamine Amouri?"
"We're the ones who ask the questions, American."

Sybil nudged me. She wanted to wait for Eli outside in the street, but I wasn't moving, so she went out by herself and sat on the stair before the door.

"Do you think we can close our eyes like the Jews did in Europe and walk into brand-new Arab microwave ovens? Do you know how the Jews are treated in the Mideast, why they've had to leave Yemen, Saudi Arabia, every Arab country? Why don't you find out about this before you start messing around here in Nablus? Let the Palestinians—that's what you call them, isn't it?—live in our houses in Syria or Lebanon. They're nicer, I tell you, than any of their shacks here, and they're fully furnished just like we left them when we ran for our lives. And the Arabs have so much land there everyone can have his own country. You tell me they're all not trying to exterminate us? Your friend included, Ms. American Journalist?"

"You've made a mistake." I wanted to grab at Lev across the desk, when he stood up and came toward me. I was reminded of the way guns alter men and that all my assumptions about family would be wisely set aside. I had to laugh at myself. I had been thinking that we were related, that is, we're all Jews. Without realizing it, I'd absorbed my father's belief that Jews were different, didn't commit crimes, didn't carry guns. He'd shown me the new Haggadah with pride where the evil son is depicted as a soldier. While I was thinking, he isn't really Jewish, he's carrying a gun—guns, like radiation, alter the genes, create an instant mutation—he was probably also thinking, she isn't really Jewish, this American, she's claiming to be a friend of a terrorist. Although these thoughts were going through my head, I was acting as if this were someone's kitchen and not an army command post. Is that what Joseph meant when he said I was naive, was trouble? But maybe that's the answer.

"Would you like to make peace, American? That's what you types usually say you want."

"Not a bad idea. I'm willing, Israeli."

"Then leave this town. Though some of my 'brethren' insist that you stay in Israel for the coming of the Messiah, I'd rather take the chance he'll come without you. Why don't you to go back to New York."

When Simon and Levi massacred the men in Shechem, Dinah refused to leave the city and follow her brethren, saying, "Whither shall I carry my shame?"
—Louis Ginzberg,
The Legend of the Jews

"Sorry, I'm not leaving. The army didn't bring me in to Nablus, though they offered, and the army isn't going to throw me out."

"Do you know what an army is, Ms. American? Do you know why it exists? Have you ever seen a yellow star? Do you know what a concentration camp is? Did you ever hear of Germany? Did you ever hear of Cyprus? Did you ever have to jump ship to have a country? Did you ever have anyone shoot at your children? Were you ever locked in a synagogue when the Arabs set fire to it? Now, tell me, Ms. American, about your very good friend Mr. Terrorist."

"I'm sure you've made a mistake. Ask Eli." I looked around for Eli, expecting that he was listening from the next room, but he was chatting with Sybil outside, holding back as if the original sight of Jamine on the hill had injured him, as employers often feel injured by the thieving of their maids and chauffeurs.

"Ms. American, how well do you know this man?"

"Eli can testify for him. So can Joseph ben Yacob," I lied, implicating everyone.

"Are you sure they'll testify for your 'associate'? You Americans always hang out with scum and terrorists, don't you? You think because we're a small country that we're an entertainment, some three-dimensional television screen designed for your amusement, Mideast defense, and surpluses. What's our fate today? Are we or are we not in the American interest? Where's your camera? Don't you want to put this on the evening news? Israeli soldiers torture innocent Palestinian citizen who was taking a walk to watch the sunset." He yelled disgustedly to Eli, "Do you really know this man?"

"We work at the museum together."

"He's the janitor?"

"No, he's an archaeologist as a matter of fact." Later Eli was to say that he had wanted to establish his own credentials, his own incontrovertible credibility, in order to help Jamine and I'd interfered with that process. He alleged that distinguishing a friend from a terrorist was as difficult as positively identifying an icon or dating a clay figurine or a prehistoric skull.

Shechem had never been able to go with Dinah past the far bound-
ary of the tents. He turned away from her while she walked across
the dry ground by herself. Wind picked up the underside of the
olive leaves and the light shot across the compound like arrows.
One of Judah's wives let out a long slow hiss as if to scatter the
goats. Her sons were practicing with the slingshots they used
against wolves. The whsst, whsst of leather and stone blended in
with the other animal noises, the children, the cows tearing at the
twilight grass.

Joseph arrived on the wings of the eagle the next day. When I'd
called him, he didn't let me speak before he told me he'd asked a
friend in a neighboring *moshav* to put me up. "They're expecting
you." Eli took Sybil home, I saw she didn't want to stay, and I
didn't want to press her, so I paid for the *sherroot*.

"You're treating me like a child, Joseph."

"All Americans are children."

"Everyone keeps saying that."

"Because it's true. I'll be there in the morning. Meet me at the
army post at ten."

"How did you know?"

"I already know much more than you can imagine I know. I
not only predict the future through dreams, I can read the handwriting on the wall. Try not to make any more trouble than you
have already made."

"I haven't done anything, Joseph. And I'm not a child." Joseph's
silence was eloquent. "You're the ones who are making a mess
with your war games. By the time you get bar mitzvahed you
should be able to put down the toy gun and pick up the pen, don't
you think?"

"Save the philosophy for tomorrow. I'll see you at ten."

He gave me the address, one of the soldiers gave me directions,
and when I arrived, just as Joseph had implied, I was made very
welcome: an American filmmaker, a friend of Joseph ben Yacob's!
My visit was treated as if it were a state occasion. First I was

introduced to all the kids. Then one of the men tried to convince me to make a film about his community. He went into a very sweet rhapsody over tractors.

. . .

I don't know when Joseph arrived but he was there when I drove back to the post. Suddenly there was no issue about my driving about alone. Perhaps they thought I'd made as much trouble as possible or perhaps, as I was coming to suspect, my presence was already quite well known to everyone in such a small town, and so I was protected. This time Lev did take me back to the room where they'd kept Jamine, but not without a growl.

"Why do you think he came to Nablus yesterday?" Joseph asked me as I entered.

"Why don't you asked me why I came, Joseph ben Yacob? What is it you want to know? Why I came or why they arrested me?"

"It's obvious, Jamine Amouri, why they arrested you. They arrested Hassan, your brother, last week. I interviewed him in jail."

"Were you the white knight or the executioner? Thank you, oh great attorney, for representing us when they won't let our own people have any serious standing in court."

"They'll probably make their charges stick."

"They always do. Even when they're stupid."

"Unfortunately. Especially when they're stupid, Jamine. But we're not talking justice, we're talking law."

"Sure, law created five minutes before the arrest."

"Your brother was organizing a boycott, Jamine . . ."

Jamine interrupted explosively, "Joseph, change the subject. If Hassan's your client, don't violate him and if he's not, you don't know anything and have no right to speak."

"Agreed. So why did you come to Nablus yesterday?"

"Why do you think? To watch over Dina. She'd asked me to bring her here and I refused. You know that. We discussed it. I thought, *we* thought, Joseph, it would be unsafe for her to be seen with me. But what could Eli show her? He's a nice man, but what does he know? I've lived here all my life. Except, Dina," Jamine turned to me with exaggerated condescension, "for a few years in English schools. Education is one of the forms of our diaspora, Dina."

"Joseph, you knew that Jamine was the one who'd arranged this? The two of you had discussed it, discussed me, without my knowledge? Is this true?"

"We haven't yet fallen into twentieth century barbarism in this country. We still protect our women."

"And so, not being able to stop me, you stopped Jamine from coming with me. Is that it?"

"Maybe I was jealous."

"That's a dirty trick and a patent lie."

"Well, Dina, you don't want to hear about my political judgments, and you don't want to hear about my heart, what's a man to do?"

"Who else knows that I'm here?"

"Everyone who has to know."

I was standing between the two of them while Jamine slouched against the wall and Joseph sat on the cot in the stuffy, airtight room.

"This room stinks," I said.

"Fear and sweat," Joseph said.

"Can you get Jamine out of here?"

"Oh, I took care of that before you arrived. We were just waiting for you in privacy."

"In an interrogation room?"

"It's their finest accommodation," Jamine sneered.

"Should I have been jealous, Dina?"

"Why do you ask, Joseph?"

"I'm just like any other man who wants to know if what is his will remain his."

"Be jealous, Joseph." First I put my hand on his shoulder, then removed it. "You wanted a divided woman, Joseph, well, you got one."

Now Jamine was assessing both of us with his sharp gaze. "What are you thinking, Dina?"

"Nothing."

"Are you certain?"

"I am thinking that I hate this conversation. And I would like to have a little camaraderie over lunch."

"That's a good idea. I know a little restaurant with wonderful food, if Joseph will trust my judgment."

"This is your territory, Jamine."

"That's right, Joseph, it is. So if the two of you would be so good as to be my guests. I hear you have a car, Dina, do you mind if I drive us there?"

We sat outside so everyone would see us. At a certain point visibility, not seclusion, is the only defense.

"Let's start with a drink to celebrate our meeting. How about some *arak,*" Jamine suggested.

"It's just noon."

"Coffee then, Joseph, a cup of decent Arabic coffee, not the colored water you pass off as something fit to drink." The familiar rebuke. We all laughed to be at ease with each other. Jamine ordered as I had expected although he and Joseph discussed each detail of the meal. Joseph was curious, he wanted to know how each dish was prepared here in Nablus and how this restaurant compared with other restaurants they both frequented. They were both fascinated by the minutiae of culture and I was much comforted by their absorption in the particulars of food. At times the meal became quite animated and I was alarmed because of the attention we were drawing to ourselves. Jamine was endangered on all sides.

"There's an Isreali people and a Palestinian people and both must live. In coexistence. As equals." Joseph could get into difficulties for saying that, but Jamine could be killed.

"Do you say that because the Isrealis have power or because it's right?"

"Because they have power, because it's right, because I'm weary, because I'm politic by nature, but mostly because your presence, Dina, mellows me a little. Does she do that for you, Joseph?"

"Hardly. She's always fighting with me. I have to be very tough when I'm around her." Joseph leaned his bird body back into the rickety chair. "It's been a long time since we've had a meal, Jamine."

"You didn't tell me you knew Jamine, Joseph."

"You didn't tell me he was behind your trip to Nablus."

"You would have tried to stop him."

"But I didn't. You don't trust me, Dina. I only use moral suasion, not force or manipulation."

"If I hadn't come, the three of us wouldn't be meeting together."

"Exactly."

The waiter brought us coffee in a beaked brass pot. The extraordinary is very commonplace, don't you think, Shechem? There were the three of us, Dinah, Shechem, and Joseph. Had that ever happened before?

"Are you sorry?"

Joseph took a long time to answer. The waiter brought our food, we dipped torn bits of bread into marinated eggplant and *hummus*.

"Very sorry. But since it's happened, I want to capitalize on it. Forgive the expression, Jamine, it's precise."

"Capitalize, Joseph?"

"I want to take advantage of you, Dina. That is, since we're all here together, let's take advantage of this opportunity. So we won't continue to be sorry that we are meeting—that we met this way."

I wasn't sorry. I was happy, Shechem. A young girl was dancing for the first time in centuries. I didn't touch your arm. I moved ever so slightly closer to Joseph because he had been my lover. Jamine and I sat across from each other, our eyes locked.

"It seems to me," I dared, "that the two of you are friends, not only acquaintances."

"Yes, perhaps we are, to the extent it's possible for us in this country," Jamine was smiling affectionately at Joseph. I had been right, there was a bond between them.

"What do you mean? What are the limitations? Do you mean the politics?"

"Of course, there are political difficulties, but I didn't mean anything as simple as that. Do you really want to know what happens to people in this country?"

"What happens, Jamine?"

"They go mad. Within a few months of their birth, they're damaged creatures. They'll never be sane again. They forget everything they came in with and remember everything that never happened. You'll see."

"Do you and Joseph hate each other then?"

"Yes, we do, in some ways," Jamine answered gravely.

"And do you hate me as well?"

"Probably we do. But we can't afford to acknowledge that or we'd both be lost. You're the missing link between us." Joseph seemed to remove himself as Jamine took up the conversation. Jamine leaned forward, took my hand, staring at me, "Are you and Joseph lovers?"

"Why do you ask?"

"I also want to know the borders of the territory."

"There is no territory. There are no borders." I turned to Joseph. Always the diplomat, he was smiling, conciliatory.

Jamine got up abruptly, went inside, paid the check, bowed to us slightly, took my hand for a moment, let it drop. "Until next week then?"

"Don't get shot." Joseph was not joking.

"To which side shall I look for the bullet?" Jamine walked away. His back was very straight in the midday sun.

"What did he mean, 'until next week'?"

"We have a little project we'd like to talk to you about. Give you a chance to make amends for all the trouble you've caused."

"So you're going to let me stay in Nablus for a little while."

"Well, yes. But I'll be keeping an eye on you."

"So we're all staying here for a little while?"

"Yes, it looks that way."

"Sybil?"

"She knows."

"I see."

"My clothes? Why do I feel I'm under arrest, Joseph?"

"We're all arrested, Dina, that's what you continually refuse to understand. We'll drive back to Jerusalem and get your things and then we'll go to work."

"Are you going to tell me anything else?"

"While we drive, I'll tell you what you need to know."

"And no more, of course."

"And no more, of course."

We walked out arm in arm. Joseph got a hotel room for me, with a single bed, which was clean, attractive, and safe. The owners spoke a little English and were polite. Then we drove to Jerusalem at top speed.

I have only a little time, so I need to locate myself in it. I must seem myself completely, from the inside and out, to make certain that I don't make an error, now, now, when everything is . . . when . . . I don't know. . . . So I must look at it all from their point of view, because all points of view must be considered at this crucial juncture. I am starting out in a new world and a monochromatic view, even if it's mine, won't do. If Sybil were here now, what would she say if she knew I was writing in her voice?

I haven't had a chance to speak. I've been preoccupied. Still I want to say something if only because I'm being thrust onto the sound stage of history just when my instinct is to retreat. That's how it is being a friend of Dina's. First she designs an impossible adventure, then she casts you as the assistant director, so you're also responsible, then just as she says, "Camera #1, roll," dormant volcanos erupt, a typhoon sweeps down out of the sea as a revolution begins right at your feet. She yells, "Steady, get it all, it's great footage, to hell with the script—this is our lives." By which she means, "Don't even consider getting in out of the rain, lava is good for the skin. . . ."

I agreed with Joseph from the beginning. She should not have gone to Nablus. For all we know there'll be a full-scale war before she leaves even though we were in the peace movement together. I wonder what she is thinking now. We hardly talk. But this is not what is on my mind. Why does she want to break her heart again? Why does she persist in getting involved in relationships she can't possibly consummate? Why does she attract darkness to her? It hurts me to see her going out so bravely, with so much hope, into the storm. And capsizing. Man overboard! I suppose I should ask myself why I think there's going to be a relationship when all I saw was a stranger come up to her and say, "Hello." Exactly because it looked impossible even to me. I knew that turned her on. Say the word "impossible" and Dina charges out on her white horse carrying a banner to prove she can overcome any obstacle. Where's a windmill she can fight?

I don't know who this man is. He's not anyone she ever mentioned to me except that he helped her buy a dress—the first trap— and introduced her to Eli—the second trap. Well, I wasn't exactly open to any conversations about overcoming obstacles, crossing barriers, or getting to Nablus. I wish I didn't know her as well as I do, I could reduce the entire affair to . . . an affair. Exactly. I would like to dismiss it by saying Dina met a handsome and cultivated Arab and they got it on for a week fantasizing they were solving the Mideast crisis while in reality they were making nookie. I hope that in a few days I'll write home to say, "They were turned on by danger, irregularity, and forbidden fruit. He followed her to Nablus, got himself arrested to impress her"—the third trap— "they had a fling for a few days, made the authorities nuts, alarmed her friends. It cooled off when they discovered they had nothing to say to each other and their ways of life presented too many contradictions. Listen, friends, you know Dina is an emancipated woman and he's an Arab and that's that. And even if the Muslim culture weren't so patriarchal, an Arab isn't going to hang around with a Jewish lady these days."

You will find that the most implacable of men in their enmity to the faithful are the Jews and the pagans.

Well, maybe I'll be able to write that next week, but I can't say anything now because Dina has told me nothing. I'd go back to Nablus to be with her, but my intuition tells me she has to stir this pot alone. So I stay here, though I love her.

I wanted her to come to see me so badly. In the beginning when I was here alone, I wrote her everything that happened to me, everything I was thinking, everything I dreamed. Then I stopped. One day the thread broke. One day it had made perfect sense, survival sense, to tell her, someone, everything. I wasn't real until I had set myself down on paper and then, the next day, I was afraid to tell her anything, as if there was a prohibition against speaking. Maybe Jeremiah prefers the secrecy. Dina and I always pondered the way women take on the values and attitudes, even the behavior, of their lovers. You're married and "Poof" you're a fundamentalist. Did it happen to me? I don't think I ever betrayed her. I never pretended I didn't want to fall in love and burrow into a man. The last time I'd talked about that in the same imagery, she scoured the ads until she found a secondhand elegant full-length fur and insisted I wear it to bed.

You never get to read her scripts in advance. They're written in the moment, in the camera. Afterwards someone transcribes the film so we have a written record. Even if my imagined scenario of what's going on is true, it's incomplete, the essentials are missing. We don't know anything about a relationship from the outside. Another universe entirely is enacted in the bed—I don't mean sex.

I don't know who she is, what she's thinking, because she was so strange when she arrived and became stranger yet. We won't even speak about the way she looked when she came out of Joseph's tomb. Suddenly she's preoccupied with things I never imagined would interest her. On the way to Bethlehem, she insisted we stop at Rachel's tomb. Then she suggested. . . . Suggested? Dina never suggests anything. She's always adamant, even when she's wrong. She insisted that I meditate in the tomb because, because . . . that is what barren women do. Odd that I didn't become a mother. I always expected to be a mother even when I was a girl, and prepared by bringing a particular (and noticeable) kindness to all my activities, saved spiders and moths from my mother's certain plots to exterminate all living creatures in our house who weren't paying rent. I aspired to a certain roundness of body (within the limitations of fashion, of course) was glad I had full breasts, wide thighs, and cultivated dancer's calves. I had a tendency, which I cultivated, to put my arms out to the bereft and lonely. As a child I thought that Mother Rachel would look down on me from heaven and keep me safe. And make me fertile.

It was very hard for me to come to Israel because I was leaving Dina. Sometimes I think the bond between men and women is always arbitrary, contrived. That's why we need so much law. Between women it's different. Our bodies hold us together. It's as if our natures are an invisible band and we are held firm within them gently bumping up against each other like dolphins bobbing in the sea. It's as if the body doesn't end where the body seems to end and something from me extends and wraps about her. It's as if we're one somehow. And even when we're separated, we're together and whatever happens to me or to her matters to each of us, that is, it affects us somehow. I tried to explain this to a friend and he thought I was talking symbolically or about the way ideas affect others. I meant we were the same body, we only looked like separate beings. Dina and I are married. He didn't understand that either. "Are you two lovers?" he asked me. I laughed. Why would we need to make the connection if we already had it?

That's why I left so quickly. It was Dina I had to avoid. Oh, she is always traveling, that's not the issue. I suspected I was going to something quite different and I had to jump out of my skin— and she is my skin, you see. She knew something. She knew every- thing. Even now when I don't know anything about what's going on with her, I know everything. I just don't have words for it, not even for my use. And I still have to respond as if I don't know anything, otherwise how can I continue to warn her about Nablus? A lot of good it did me, didn't it?

Now if we had been lovers, or if she were a man, we would have had it out between us about my leaving. And I'd have had to cite all the times she's been away versus all the times I've been away. We would have reduced the entire thing to an absurdity, but, actually, it would have been easier to deal with. But a friendship such as ours means that we support each other's life no matter what the hidden cost to ourselves. What if, after the charts and quasi-legal arguments, the reasoning and explanations, the analysis and tears, she'd said, "Don't go." What would I have done? Would I have remained? It's possible, even though it was clearly a call. That's how it felt. Dina understood that. She always says that women like us are blessed (and cursed, she says that too) by those events which lift us out of our lives. I am always attentive to such matters. I think it is the core of a good story to find the agency that is working behind the scene.

Now, of course, I don't want Dina to leave Israel as long as I am here. Maybe this Arab is a good thing. Maybe everything is playing into my hands. In the next months, I plan to walk across Israel so I will know it by foot, crisscrossing it from east to west as if I were lacing up a bodice. Then I worry that I may be unable to go back to the States when I will know this land so well. Intimacy is a bond, after all. I am already beginning to think that a modern city like New York is irrelevant after living here. I love this country because it is so small. I can hold it in my hand like a brooch. Hate is keeping Dina here. She loves her enemies. She's been squirming with delighted irritation from the first moment she arrived. I've seen that reaction in her countless times. Although once or twice since she's been here I thought she had a nervous disorder and wanted to prescribe shock therapy, vitamin pills, and brown rice.

Lately, I've been dreaming that my house is burning, but it isn't my house. I run into the house to save someone. Am I saving myself? Someone else? Is someone saving me?

Perhaps when winter is really here, it will help us reestablish ourselves as two women who huddle together naturally. What I like best about being with Dina is linking arms for warmth and balancing against each other as we skid through the blustery slippery streets, forming a united front against the elements. Here we're losing that natural alliance of women. It's difficult to maintain when you're not cooking together, not shopping, not doing dishes, not engaged each day in the natural round. I like being with Anne, she's almost always home, she's always happy to sit down and have a nice cup of tea. We sink into the gray goose down pillows on the couch and watch the steam of the kettle fog the squares of the drawing room windows. A bit of the world is erased from behind the pane as if we'd pulled the drapes to make us cozier inside.

Dina won't leave now, not for a long time. Maybe I'll find her an editing room in Jerusalem and she'll stay.

When she's less preoccupied, she'll accuse me of having engineered a debacle between us. It's true that things would have been different between us had we gone to my apartment in Safed. We'd have lived a normal life embedded in all the routines which reassure one that life matters. It's hard to be depressed or distant when you've got to remember to get fresh cream for your friend's morning coffee. In that moment, you're thinking about someone else and realize, unwillingly, that you're not alone, you have responsibilities to someone else. How can you be depressed? You don't have the time. Peace and quiet.

When I met Joseph and didn't fall in love, I was devastated. Then I knew no one and no thing could save me from Jeremiah. I began to envy my mother who dusted her apartment each day until the week she died and was perfectly happy. There was no shame in such attention to ordinary life. She loved every object she owned, each framed photograph, each porcelain ash tray, all the silver candelabra placed just so. The surfaces gleamed and one object enhanced the other, the light from the crystal candy dish reflecting off the silver menorah, just so.

We began to speak less and less, Dina and I. Maybe she's laying down the first colors on her internal cinematic canvas, the color of apricot paste wrapped in orange cellophane, followed by or-anges ripening, sunsets, candles, amber beads, umber pantaloons of Yemenite women, men converging so closely as they pray, one mass of swaying bodies. No, I can't pretend anymore she's making a film. Why did she need to go to Nablus? Why didn't she stay here? Why didn't she just go off with that Egyptian officer in the Sinai for a few days if she was hungry for Arabs, or take Amit for a romp through the dunes? They are both perfectly harmless. I would even have given her Zev, if she'd shown the slightest interest. I gave her Joseph, didn't I? That's the equivalent of the shirt off my back.

It's been so satisfying for the two of us to live together in this little room with our suitcases under the beds and the few drawers divided between us and the closet partitioned with the dressing gowns, robes, skirts, blouses we've always shared hanging in the middle again. At home, our closets were always confused. Some-times I'd look for something of mine to wear, not even something specific, but anything of mine, and it would seem to me I couldn't find anything because all my things were at her apartment and all her clothes were at mine. It didn't matter. We both had enough and it's silly to make a fuss about what you're going to wear except that I like things that shine more than she does. I like silks and satins and glitter. The only time I envied something Dina had was when she bought a pair of gunmetal boots. My feet are larger than hers. I couldn't get my feet into them.

I'm chattering to myself as a distraction. I'm worried about her. The truth is, this time, I don't have the faintest idea of what is going on. Joseph is in Nablus with her. She tricked him, but she won't listen to his caution. She hates caution. I think she's allergic to it. Just who is this man who said hello to her? He really could be a terrorist. She lied so blatantly, saying Joseph and Eli were going to testify for him. Eli is really a sweet man. It's lucky she didn't say I knew him. She knew I'd faint away. He could be a terrorist. He could be using her while Eli and Joseph are cautious about stepping on her toes. Dina, what a stew you're cooking. Jeremy's no use to me in this. He has been utterly silent on the matter.

Sybil's voice is easy. I've known her all my life. But Joseph, brother or not, is another. Certainly, I know as well as anyone that we can't take our brothers for granted, can't assume we know what they are thinking and certainly cannot sense what is in their hearts. But I have to know what Joseph is thinking and he, being a diplomat, unlike myself, is exceedingly careful about what he reveals.

I would prefer if it were possible to simply file a brief about this matter. The style suits me and while there is always the danger of being misunderstood, still it seems that the clear presentation of factual material creates the ground for understanding, if not agreement.

The facts are as follows. Dina Z., an American filmmaker, came to Israel in the fall for the purpose of personal research while she also engaged in pre-production work on a film for American television regarding the way residents relate to the Biblical sites they occupy. In the United States there has been a recent understanding of the limitations of American history and a concomitant desire, as people there put it, to discover their roots. This leaves some of us with a slight anxiety, as you may well understand, as Americans find it difficult to distinguish between their roots and their trunk, as if everything that has given rise to them, the roots, the water absorbed by the roots, the earth surrounding the roots . . . belongs to them. Naturally we wonder if this supposedly inner exploration is going to end up as another kind of conquest. Americans exhibit a restless expansive quality which they call openness but which I think has to do with developing large surface areas. When you live in a small country you've got to dig down deep, but they've not had that limitation and so they spread themselves out quite thin. When they get to their geographic boundaries they just ooze out onto all the surrounding surface areas, oceans notwithstanding, until they come to some absolutely impenetrable barrier and then they improvise. Actually, I think the substitution of imperialism for colonialism is quite ingenious. You take everything and don't have to give anything back, not even a lousy government.

I'm digressing. Dina Z. was also looking for her roots. Whether due to culture shock or the inability to adjust to a different culture, or, as I said, the American tendency to think that everything outside the self must become the self rather than to understand that the self must conform to what it encounters, from the moment she arrived, she showed signs of disturbance, irritability, and impatience. She treated the country, the people, and its government as if they were her reluctant employeees and she complained bitterly that she could not get them to do her will. She seemed to have no respect for the laws or customs of the country when they did not conform to her sense of law and justice, to the procedures which she would have found accommodating or convenient, or, to be straightforward about it, when they prevented her from doing what she wanted to do. On several occasions she openly challenged the existing authorities as if their legitimacy depended on her approval. Westerners, since Locke, despite the lip service they give to God, have the tendency to believe that they have invented law and are therefore its arbiter. Though not a native of this country, or perhaps exactly because she was not a native or a citizen, she assumed that she was exempt from our laws. Patronizing is the best word to describe her attitude. Yes, patronizing, exactly. She patronized us while we found her adolescent. She was exhibiting in middle age the kind of rebelliousness usually associated with late adolescence and which we treat, in women and men, in the rare instances when it appears, with a few arduous months of training in the army and some difficult duty at the borders. In one instance, she came close to being arrested after creating a serious disturbance during a major national religious celebration. It seems that she tried to interrupt the prayers with a long lecture on the separation between church and state.

You see, the dualism that characterizes the fashion of rational thought which formed Dina's mind cannot encompass the paradoxical coexistence and juxtaposition of "national" and "religious." She was raised in the dualistic orthodoxy of the separation of church and state, a concept which others, many of our citizens, find naive. She would say these believers are unenlightened and they, in turn, might kindly note her lack of consciousness and pray for her gradual understanding of the nature of reality. In her wildest behavior she has had the audacity to try to take them on in their own territory, asserting that there is a distinction between church and G–d and that she has a direct telephone line to the deities. They believe the same thing in the singular. At the Wall, only her American press credentials, her incontrovertible good looks, and a sudden sobering or acquiescence on her part prevented grave consequences. Some of us were asked—how shall I put it?— to look out for her, because any incident in a country of this size can have international repercussions.

I met Dina Z. through her longtime friend and my recent acquaintance, Sybil Stone, who had taken up residence in Israel two years previous. Sybil was researching a book on the life of Jeremiah Abazadik, a folksinger of great renown, whose untimely accidental death was a cause of great sorrow to the nation. Abazadik had sojourned in the United States in order to recover from the stress of Isreali life, the constant alert, the defensive wars, the deaths of so many of his friends in the Sinai and Golan through military *and terrorist attacks. Abazadik's friends had prevailed upon him to refrain from active duty by serving his country through singing for the troops, acting as a cultural liaison between Israel and other countries, assuming a diplomatic rather than military function. There are many soldiers but only so many angels. It was not Abazadik's inclination to eschew any risk so when he didn't heed this request, he was simply refused any positions in the army. His rank became ambiguous, he was given no assignment, his bed was requisitioned: there was nowhere for him to be. He tried to become a private again, but this was refused as well. They say he had once for a short time been a private and had even assembled mines. The latter fact makes his death even more lamentable. After his R & R, he returned to Israel and was on his way to visit a friend serving in the Golan when he took a shortcut through a restricted area—it had been a mine field—and accidentally blew himself up.*

Without declaring his death a national holiday, all of Israel came to a halt when his death was announced. Men and women cut their clothes and wore black, though technically, the rite of kria *is reserved to family members. "It was as if song itself had died," one commentator said.*

It is not clear whether Ms. Stone had met Abazadik in the U.S. but we know that she had read about his death in the newspaper and being a journalist, she was intrigued by his story and, feeling the urgency of recording the life of such a spirit, she came to Israel forthwith. At the time of this writing, we can say that she is the foremost expert on his life and that we await her opus with much anticipation. Upon publication, Abazadik's music will be reissued as will some posters and other memorabilia. Ms. Stone disclaims any financial interest in the project other than meeting the basic expenses and so the proceeds will go toward the rehabilitation of Israeli soldiers wounded in the wars since 1948. This information was released by Mrs. Abazadik, Jeremiah's mother, though, some say, without consultation with Ms. Stone who has remained silent on the matter. The name of the publisher of the book has not yet been announced.

Naturally, since I had had some meetings with Jeremiah Abazadik, Sybil and I also met. She is so thorough an interviewer and researcher that it is no exaggeration to say that she has spoken with everyone who ever met Abazadik, or has made appointments to interview them. Everyone except his mother, that is. Ms. Stone has managed to collapse an entire lifetime into two years. Some say she is so diligent, she will interview the dead. We like to glorify ourselves; such attention clearly feeds our national pride.

But Abazadik is another digression. Back to the task at hand. I enjoyed meeting Sybil and we became friends, entertaining each other from time to time. She served as an amiable companion and eased the tedious ceremonies which are so common to diplomatic and governmental life. Energetic, attractive, and intelligent, she was just the right woman to accompany a weary minister on state occasions. The task served her, as well, for it provided her the opportunity to further her research in style. Of course, we had a great deal in common and spent a few private moments together as well. I like to think I distracted her a little from her labors and even brought a little mirth into her life.

So it was not surprising that I would be one of the first to meet Dina Z. though it was disconcerting to find the two women so alike and so dissimilar. Their resemblances are natural; after all, they have been friends for years and admit to sharing the most intimate details of their lives. This leads, in friends, I'm certain (though I've never had such a friendship—men rarely do), to the same assumption of common habits of behavior and thought patterns which one finds in married couples. I've never been married either, so all my conclusions are suspect as they have no validation from direct experience. I don't believe that proximity creates similarity; I think resemblance derives from the inclination to strive for consensus in emotional life. I was grateful for the opportunity to observe their behavior together, thinking that from this vantage point, I would learn a great deal about a dynamic which could only be useful to me in my work. You could say that my life work is the study of consensus. I am familiar with the dynamics of conformity. There has been much study of conformity; it doesn't interest me. Fear is its essential element. But what provokes two distinct beings, who are not motivated by fear, to sing the same note? Imagine if one could isolate the pleasure principle of harmonics and apply it to political life. Imagine, for example, if Israelis and Palestinians were motivated to cultivate their differences while at the same time—singing. . . . You see the point!

Also, I was not disinterested in the opportunity to study the national characteristics of Americans so closely. Or American Jews. Or American Jewish women, who are also of considerable political influence and therefore strategically important to my country. I have known many Americans; however, few, if any, were so open about their inner processes. We know that personality, like fruit, is influenced, if not determined, by the soil in which the tree roots. That is the thesis of Ms. Z.'s film. So, their national as well as individual identities engaged me. I am an anthropologist, or sociologist, by curiosity, not training, and am fascinated with the origins and transmission of culture.

You can imagine my dismay when Sybil seemed to withdraw more and more from our company and thrust Dina into it. Almost immediately after Dina's arrival, Sybil became increasingly preoccupied, until finally Dina seemed to have taken over her role altogether. While both women were fully absorbed, even obsessive, about their work, it seemed to energize Dina, while it seems to me it has consumed Sybil, of late. I would say Sybil has vanished under it, has disappeared as important documents are swallowed by the sheaves of trivia which surround them. To resort to a medieval vocabulary, let us say that Sybil was becoming possessed by her work while there was no such atmosphere about Dina. If anything, one would have to say that Dina is the possessor. Which is not to say that she does not suffer from some very serious delusions. She has so much energy and determination, I sometimes feel her body is insufficient to contain her. She needs to enter into everyone and everything. When we made love—I think this is relevant and hope you will not think I am vulgar to raise it—I deliberately tried to be very tender with her because I was afraid of arousing those violent feelings which, for her own welfare, she ought to contain. I tried to calm her with my lovemaking, to caress her, to dispossess her of the fierce intensity which, I admit, I was pleasured by, though I thought ultimately it would only do her harm. When she went off with Sybil to the Sinai, I hoped the sun would burn the furies from her, melt her down. It had been Sybil's idea to go, but by the time the little diversion was upon them, Sybil had become quite silent. It was as if coming together on this land, they had nothing to say to each other anymore.

Now we come to the issue at hand. I have met and even worked with Jamine Amouri on several occasions. He is far from what one would call the typical Palestinian, if there is one. He is a very unusual man. I don't think this is the place to discuss politics, but let me say that he is what is called a moderate by some, a traitor by others, a terrorist by many, and even, by some, a sort of secular saint. I think of him as a very shrewd, rational, highly decent man. Personally, I think his philosophy is radical, but that is probably because it agrees with mine to some extent and I like to think of myself as honorable and unique. Earlier than most, he'd come to see that an independent Palestine, free of both Jordan and Israel, was a workable compromise, maybe even an opportunity, though the gross reduction in land is for the Palestinians a grave situation—as it is for the Israelis—being as they are an agrarian and nomadic people, with a rapidly increasing population. While the Jews have had to become urban people over the centuries and have returned to the land only recently and in Israel, and do not have such a high birth rate, nevertheless, endangered as they have been everywhere, they are adamant about needing one country where all Jews might eventually live as Jews. Amouri understood, as I do, that what seemed like conflicts specifically between our two countries were rather the broader consequences of modern life. Sometimes there is, in reality, given the whole picture, no single one to blame absolutely, except . . . uh . . . fate.

Amouri always discussed the issues of independence and self-

*determination within the context of economic democracy and po-
litical development, by which he certainly did not mean a laissez-
faire state. He had a unique attitude toward the Soviet Union, the
United States, and a few other superpowers. He detested them all.
I use the past tense advisedly. Things change so quickly in the
Mideast, I am reluctant to assume that anything exists now just
because it existed before. I haven't spoken with Amouri for some
weeks. I don't know what he is thinking. Since we spoke there
have been hideous attacks from both sides. Any one of these events
could change one's attitude entirely. However, when we were in
contact, Amouri did not seem inclined to fight to replace the Israeli
military authority, loathsome as it was to him, with a new or an
old Arab oligarchy. Again, some people called him a Marxist,
others an anarchist, others a fool. The way he differs from most
people in the area, Arab or Jew, is that he seemed to have an
almost physiological disinclination to value a military solution for
the area. Sometimes he seemed to recognize its necessity, but even
then, he said, he, himself, would not participate. This brought him
and me together, though with enormous suspicion and distrust,
having come to the same position from such very different tradi-
tions and circumstances. Sometimes he insisted they weren't very
different at all. We were both odd birds. Our affinities made life
quite difficult for us. We didn't see that any relationship would
bring us any personal satisfaction, to the contrary, it would surely
bring us quite a bit of grief and alienation. But, as he is an honorable man, he agreed, despite the acrimony—let's be honest: the
threats, attempts on his life, isolation from his family which came
to him from his community and from mine—to negotiate with me
on occasion, also as a kind of minister without portfolio. So we
came to a rather remarkable—underground—working partner-
ship. We always met unofficially, though sometimes as unacknowl-
edged representatives of our respective governing bodies. You see,
in our country, even a cup of coffee is a matter of state. What
really happened is that two men found it convenient from time to
time to hammer out some alternatives which were not yet possible*

to imagine from a governmental perspective. When we'd come to some refined understanding between ourselves we took it back to our constituencies. You see, this allowed there to be real discussion of various peace alternatives, as well as identification of the real-politik impediment, as well as the imagining of a peaceful solution, all of which are impossible through official channels. We were both dangerous and indispensable to our respective communities, conflicted and diverse as those communities are. I judge our value to both peoples by the fact that they haven't killed us off yet.

At one point we came to a logical extension of our activities: I urged Jamine to invite me to spend some days in Nablus speaking and living with various families. He wasn't enthusiastic, though it was his idea that his people would benefit from Israelis experiencing Palestinian daily life as a way of understanding the context of Palestinian demands. We didn't get very far but I did spend a few days in Nablus, under quite a bit of secrecy. The experience informed me. I dare say my heart opened a little though I cannot with certainty trace the impact of these experiences upon my thinking. Nevertheless, reason prompts me to suggest that they may not be inconsiderable.

Ruefully, I must admit I had as great or greater difficulty finding homes which would welcome a Palestinian as he had finding homes that would welcome me. Of course the Peace Now people would welcome him, but that didn't seem to be the point of this undertaking. When I made the request of some of the new settlers at the border, they told me in one way or another that if they let him in they would expect to awaken in heaven and look down to see themselves in their beds with their throats slashed or their bodies broken apart. Their descriptions were so vivid, Amouri imagined that this would in fact be his *morning fate. Finally we persuaded a few who did not claim that cooperating meant they were retarding the advent of the messiah—a more grievous sin is not possible to imagine—though I was dismayed that it was more difficult for me to bring him into Israel than it had been for him to bring me into Nablus. Still, that is because we avoided the Peace*

Now advocates, not wishing to speak to the converted, and there is no similar group in Palestine. There are a few pacifist Arabs in Israel but to advocate such beliefs is paradoxically to threaten one's own life. Still, Jamine was courteous and also benefited from the exchange even if he was slightly embittered and self-righteous (justifiably or not—who can tell?) that more hospitality was extended to me than to him. My friends claim this is because the Palestinians knew I would not shoot them in their beds. But, I must ask them, why do they assume such a thing? It has certainly been the Palestinian experience to be mowed down in their homes. Then my friends say it is because it is in the Palestinian interest to accommodate me, as we're the ruling government, while the Israelis, by accommodating, only have something to lose. (As this is exactly what the PLO says on the other side, I sometimes think that the first stage of economic cooperation might be to have a single disinformation bureau to write propaganda—programming the computer to substitute one or another proper noun as needed.) These same Israeli friends say a Palestinian state is a giveaway, that the Arabs will gain what rightfully belongs to the Israelis, and the Palestinians know it and that's why they were so nice to me. I frankly think there was an imbalance because by avoiding those Israelis who have declared themselves, we avoided those, and there are a considerable number, who welcomed the opportunity to make some rapprochement, who see it in their real interest. On the other hand, as Amouri is quick to point out, anyone who took me into his home did so at more than considerable risk to himself and his family and any close associates. All those lives were risked. And this must also be appreciated.

Amouri is an honorable man. You have to be if you are willing to stand between everyone, to please no one, to be alone in your integrity. Such a man is Jamine Amouri. When Dina called me, I already knew exactly why Jamine had been arrested, if I was not certain which faction had engineered the event. There are dozens of groups who would think it advantageous to have him arrested on sight. He would have been placed under house arrest long ago, even as a favor some Israelis might extend to their Palestinian cohorts, had they not been afraid that his reputation would increase sizably through such an event. As a matter of fact there are quite a few groups who would like to have Jamine arrested exactly because his reputation would increase, but the IDF is not inclined to cooperate with those factions. They don't know the extent of his resistance to entering the political arena. The majority in both our countries believe that the political call, in whatever form it comes, may not be refused. Men like myself and Amouri—all men, as a matter of fact—are not allowed the right to pursue a life disentangled from public affairs.

A simple phone call sprung him from jail; this confirms my theory. As many want him out, or neutered, as want him in.

Dina Z. knew nothing of our relationship. I had never mentioned Jamine to her, knowing full well she would pursue him mercilessly. When she found him, without my help, I decided to be quiet about it. When he called me, I was noncommittal, though he knew, everyone knew, she and I had been closely associated. Personal ethics prevented me from imposing my attitudes upon him. Also, I wanted her to see me as an ethical man. I hoped he wouldn't be fool enough to help her, so I was relieved that he'd found Eli to solve the problem. It never occurred to me that he would follow her to Nablus. There is no question that if I'd suspected that, I'd have done whatever was in my power to stop them both. Short of forbidding it, that is, short of asking the authorities to intervene. Had I suspected he'd follow her, I probably would have accompanied him—would he have let me?—or followed him. Who knows, I might have precipitated the very explosion I've been seeking to defuse. I had thought that not telling Dina Z. about Jamine was the best way of keeping her away. I was afraid that her presence would create an incident. She generates tension as a natural course. I was right once again.

I dare say this is only the beginning. We're in for trouble. My thought then is to gain something from this for our side in the interim.

"Do you recognize yourself in these pages, Joseph?"

"Not at all."

"Are you sure?"

"Quite."

"How about Sybil?"

"I'm not sure. She certainly wouldn't have referred to the Koran."

"You're right. She wouldn't have. My mistake. You understand, don't you, I'm trying to see the back of my head."

"You're not doing a good job, Dina, you don't have the right vantage point."

"Someone could tell it this way."

"Yes, that's true. But not me."

"Am I being too hard on you?"

"Yes, I think it's unfair. But it's as unkind to you as it is to me, so I don't take it personally. If I resent anything, it's that you don't seem to have noticed that I've actually invited you to stay in Nablus. That, in effect, the disagreement between us has been resolved."

"Clever, diplomatic Joseph. You've gotten exactly what you planned all the time. There I will be in a few hours, with my camera, all my permits in order, including the implicit, if not also the specific, approval of the army. Let's not talk politics. I feel outwitted."

"You got what you wanted."

"Did I? Joseph, have you and Jamine ever had a personal conversation?"

"What do you mean?"

"Never mind. What is going to happen to us?"

"It's your story, Dina. I don't know. It's a little easier to bear because neither I nor Jamine know what's coming. I like to hope that we'll all stay friends."

"Is that impossible because we've been lovers?"

"Oh no, that's the easy part. It's because we've been acquainted in Israel that makes everything impossible."

"I've finally got it, Joseph, the difference between us, it's not as great as I thought."

"Maybe there's no difference between us."

"Don't be absurd, Joseph. It's only that I think myth is acting inside of me and you think that none of us can escape the impact of history."

"Maybe, it's something like that."

"Why don't you ever get angry?"

"I like to be unique."

"Joseph, your answers make me wildly angry. You're so placid, accepting, accommodating, careful, diplomatic."

"How about loving, can you put that in your analysis?"

"Are we going to continue to be lovers?"

"I don't think Jamine has the capacity to share you or any woman. I think you are going to have to deal with another temperament altogether, one much more possessive."

"Well, he is being dispossessed."

"You can make a political analysis of it to soothe your modern soul, but I don't think it will hold up. There are cultural or racial or religious differences among men—am I offending you?—and you're going to be up against some of them. Frankly, I can hardly wait."

"Bitter, Joseph, bitter. What about Jamine? Am I right about him, Joseph?"

"Well, you're a little romantic, a little naive. It's more complex than you know."

"Well, Joseph, I'm not certain I'm going to be lovers with Jamine."

"Aren't you? We'll see. It's not up to you, you know."

"What do you mean? It is my body."

"Spoken like a true feminist. Is it your body? Nothing belongs to us anymore, Dina. Nothing. Nothing. Nothing in this world."

"Nothing?"

"Ask Jamine, Dina, he knows better than anyone else."

"Well, it's my life, I'll do with it what I want."

"I guess you're scared." He was so very tender with me. "It's not your life, either. You know that; you've known that since you've come here. It wasn't even your idea to come. Like the rest of us, you're a victim of circumstances. Even your passport doesn't relieve you of that."

"Circumstances?"

"A catchall phrase, it serves all parties."

PART III

*And when Shechem lay under her, both static and decaying, so
quickly exuding the yellow sheen of death, and when she burned
him and he turned to ashes which she inhaled so that her lungs
were the color of him, and when she was birthing Asenath, and
Shechem breathed with her, as if he were a storm, and when she
was dying herself, her bones grinding into Joseph's bones but on
the bed of Shechem's bones, and when they were all dead, their
genes swimming back together to the sacred pool, she dipped his
name in honey and pressed it onto her tongue and the scent of
Shechem was on her forever. Even when Joseph held her and closed
her mouth with his tongue, she breathed Shechem into him. But
as she was his sister, he took her as she was, saying all the love
that was in her enriched him thousandfold.*

Dear Shechem:
    You exist. Praise the gods.

For so long, I have been writing to a dead man, but now whatever
I say is to someone who is alive. I am afraid to write anything
down because it may come into existence. But being superstitious,

I am also afraid that anything I write down will disappear. Surely we would have had a cup of coffee even if I hadn't written any of this.

I have been living with you, Shechem, perfectly these last months. Why should I trade that perfect love for the morning sourness of your mouth, your surly temper, your irritability, physical aches, the impossibility of your hopes, your bitterness and frustration? What do I want with a man without a home, without a country, who may not even have a right to his own body? How do we share it then? How can I live inside of you when you don't have a deed to your own flesh, when all your real estate is mortgaged?

I don't know who you are. For all I know you kill my brothers, machinegun them down in airports or throw bombs at Edka to destroy the little ragged vest she got as a hand-me-down. Maybe the shoe is on the other foot, maybe you've been beaten up by Edka's uncles and your youngest brother was murdered for wanting to stay on your own land. Can you forgive my brothers? Can I be certain you won't revenge yourself on me? Why should I open my heart to this? Here on the page everything is clean. Neat, elegant black characters on crisp water-bonded paper. You become everything and anything I want.

What was your original dream, Dinah?

It was, Dina, that we married, that we were initiated into the mysteries, that our flocks were sacred, that we had a daughter, that we visited Joseph in Egypt, that Joseph married Asenath, that she was the thorn that stuck to him, that there was no famine, no unending winter, that there had been no loss, no curse, nothing withheld, that we lived in peace, that my name meant 'well', that he drank from me, that I rested upon his shoulder, that my brothers had no blood on their hands, that our names survived, that we lived as two banks of a river holding a single stream, that we were as a single stream, carving the two banks of the river, that we were

*water in the desert, that we were all the forms of water. That we
didn't begin the wars.*

I'm sick of politics. I want to live with a man. I want to have a
kid. I don't want him to die. I want an end to the wars.

I continue the book, Shechem. Even though you're alive. Even if
you were sitting in the next room, reading, or brushing your teeth,
or writing a speech, I'd have to continue. See how alike we are,
despite culture. Your toothbrush, mine, only the colors different.
I have a black brush. I like it a lot; I give you the blue one. I put
it next to mine in the cobalt blue vase. I scrub the sink. I lay out
fresh towels. The flowered sheets are clean. There is, always has
been, only one world. In it there are square rooms, whitewashed
apartments, clean windows which open to the evening breeze, to
catch the church bells, the call to prayer from the minaret, the
men walking to synagogue just before the sun goes down. This
must be the foolish reverie of any adolescent girl dreaming about
entering an apartment with a little key. Anywhere in the world,
the same: the sofa, the little table with magazines, the same, the
bowl of fruit, the vase, the same, a candle . . . You know how
it goes, a man, a woman, it's so simple, they don't even have to
talk.

But you're not in the next room. I would never recognize your
house. Even the ordinary objects of your life are so different from
mine. I fantasize that you are free—deprived?—of the willful illusion of middle class life, the deception of straight white walls
and electric ovens, the imposture of couches and chairs. The shirts
we wear have a different weave because the source is different,
the woman who made your shirt is very different from me.

You walked out of the cafe. Your back was (seemingly) effortlessly straight. I imagine that it's smooth, and somewhere, unexpectedly, I'll find a mole, or a swirl of hair, an old scar, something,
which will tell me that the skin is thin after all, that a bullet can

enter here. Your shoulders are square, swimmer's shoulders or those of a gymnast, or of a man who uses a shovel.

You just got up and walked away, through the heat and dust, through the brilliant light smearing in the powdery street. Watching you walk away, I was thinking that if you were shot in the back, you would not flinch, you would not fall down. I was imagining a bad movie. This is not the first time I've watched you from behind. I followed you in the *suk*. Before that when you walked out of the office, I also walked behind. There is something different about your posture here in Nablus. You walk at the same pace, neither hurrying nor dallying. Maybe you know what's under you. You walk away from me like a man who knows the land. Your feet bend to it, (seemingly) effortlessly, while my brothers insist the land isn't yours.

We didn't offer to drive you back to Jerusalem. I drove back with Joseph. At the hospice, he held me briefly before we separated. We both wanted to bathe. We were going to drive up in tandem. "Because of the equipment," I said. "The American needs to be mobile," he teased me. There was no discussion; I didn't ask him in. Still, I don't pretend that Joseph did not hold me, did not caress my leg. He did.

· · ·

Where are we, Shechem?
Here, Dinah. Between.
And how long will we stay here?
As long as necessary.
I can't see you or feel you.
Nor I, you.
How do you know we're here together?
I have faith.
What are we waiting for?
To be born again.
Will we be together this time?
We'll see.

Is there anything we can do?
Have faith.
Will it make a difference?
That is what is said.

      .   .   .

Sybil was seated in a chair facing the door like a mother waiting for her wayward daughter to return. "Did you have a good time?"

"Surely, Sybil, you're not mad that you had to drive back with Eli alone?"

"I enjoyed it. He's a dear man. I'm glad he had a gun. I was worried."

I groaned melodramatically. "I thought I maneuvered your departure together rather deftly. He was relieved, don't you think?"

"Archaeologists are more accustomed to dealing with stones."

"Listen, archaeology causes a lot of controversy in this country. He must like conflict."

"Everything, Dina, causes controversy in this country, according to you."

"Well, isn't that true?"

"I suppose it is. What do you think my book on Jeremiah will do, support the war effort or undermine it?"

"Both. What do you think?"

"I don't think about it. Do you judge me for that?"

"I don't judge you, Sybil."

"Are you leaving?"

I'd started packing the smaller suitcase so she'd know I wasn't leaving the country. I wasn't packing hastily but carefully, the way one packs for a lover, imagining the color of a blouse, purple, turquoise, brilliant red, against his skin, sandalwood, meerschaum, amber, the feel of silk on his palms.

"I let you go off with Eli without any sign of objection, without a single word of complaint."

"He is a married man." Sybil was curt.

I felt like I'd been slapped and the surprise of it inspired me to honesty. "I want to tell you about Jamine."

"I don't want to hear it."

There was no humor on Sybil's face, instead a rather grim expression was frozen there. Her eyes went cold as she stared beyond me and shuddered as if it had suddenly started to snow in the hallway outside the door. "I don't want to encourage you, Dina." And that was that. She picked up a book on Israeli folk music and turned from photograph to photograph, then shut it with a slam and a sigh.

"Would you like me to help you pack?"

"I wouldn't want you to violate your principles, Sybil." We'd always promised we'd never let a man come between us.

"I'll pretend you're going to be with Joseph."

"I will be."

"Not from the looks of the clothes you're packing. Would you like this blouse, I find I'm not wearing it lately." She was folding a satin shirt, the color of apricots.

I didn't know, Sybil, how to ask you to stay with me when we were in Nablus and I didn't know how to ask you to go back with me against Joseph's advice. So I said nothing. I took the blouse. You laid in a long skirt, two simple dresses which, as they say, "travel well, don't need ironing," and a shawl alongside the khakis, jeans. "We don't know the fashion politics. It can't hurt to be able to dress like a woman, if necessary. It's as good a disguise as any, Dina. Take the nice robe, and a few nightgowns."

"The West Bank, Sybil, not the Hilton."

"OK, take the flak jacket and your gun belt."

"That's even worse."

"Take this." It was an ordinary, pale blue, well worn, therefore soft, man's shirt. The collar buttoned down with tiny pearlized buttons and there were faint white stripes running vertically through the fabric. One of her lovers had worn it and she had slept in it and it had fit each of them perfectly and they had held each other in it, so it conformed to both bodies and both embraces. She took it off the hanger and folded it inside the satin blouse "to keep the blouse from wrinkling."

"Whose is it?"

"Don't worry about it; it's the perfect solution."

"How many times, Sybil, have we done this together?"

"Do you mean how many times have we sent each other off? Thousands. I like the other packing better—the film, tape, mikes, and batteries part. That's easy."

"Because it's already done. I just have to load up the car when Joseph gets here." She came into my arms and we held each other. I stroked her hair and then she pressed my face against hers. "Will you be all right, Sybil?"

"So, Joseph is going with you. Yes, I'll be all right. I was alone before you came."

"But Joseph was with you then."

"I was thinking that you're probably really lost. Now that you've won Joseph over to your side, there'll be no one to protect you." She became conciliatory and maternal. "If I'm lonely here, I can make a phone call, do an interview, or go out to dinner or I can sit downstairs with Anne and gossip about the guests. She makes me feel secure. I used to crochet as a young girl, I may take it up again. And if these don't work, I can always spend a few hours meditating. Or do you prefer me to admit that I'm learning to pray?"

"You, Sybil?"

"Living in Israel, one may as well do as the Romans do."

We closed the suitcase together. Then I waited and she said it, "Call when you figure out what you've forgotten and I'll send it. Better yet, give me an address, I'll just send it when I figure it out."

I gave her the name of the hotel. "Listen, Nablus is only a few hours away."

"So is hell."

"Sybil!" She looked genuinely contrite. "Jump in the shower," she pushed me toward the bathroom. "If you don't tell them how *we* prepare for war, I'll come in and scrub your back. Maybe I'll even do your nails. In the meantime, I'll put the Tampax in your suitcase, next to the Gucci designer sack of plastique. That's what you forgot. When you get cranky next week, just remember why."

"I always forget."

"I know you do. How's your Arabic?"

"As fluent as my Hebrew."

"You'll be a great success."

This was the known world again. Sybil had offered to come into the steamy shower and scrub my back with a loufa. I went off dutifully like an obedient child cheerily reciting what I knew to give me courage. I knew how to load a camera. I knew how to conduct an interview. I knew how to develop black and white film. I knew that I had a good eye. I knew how to pack for another country in two hours. I knew the names of all the American presidents and quite a few revolutionaries and poets. I knew how to make chicken soup and damned good *hummus,* yes, that too. I knew how to talk about film, how to interview heads of state and people in hiding. I knew that the Garden had one meaning for a Christian and another for a Sufi, and another altogether for the worshippers of Asherah. I even knew how to make love, how to raise the cone of desire, praise, and gratitude which makes the crops grow. I knew there were things I didn't begin to know. I knew things I couldn't begin to utter because I had no words and I knew them because Dinah knew them and she put the knowing in me. And I also knew that I had had to go to Nablus when I did and that now I had to go back there again, although it occurred to me that if Sybil said, "Come, climb into bed, I'll sing you a lullaby," I might have done it and stayed with her forever.

THE TESTIMONY OF JEREMIAH ABAZADIK
A Posthumous Autobiography

I looked for a whore and found a washerwoman. When I took
her to war, she scrubbed the tanks, hung out the white dishcloths
like a sign of surrender, painted the guns, polished the mortar
shells. She brought a mop to the foxhole, made us douche before
we could hide out for dear life. She perfumed the latrines with her
own aromatic shit before she made us pray. She even made the
dead one wash his hands before he sat down to eat. "Look," she
said, "I always wash my cunt before grace." When I put on my
kittel, she smiled and ironed the white shroud. Knowing her proved
I would have been dead in a week if I'd taken a wife. When she
scrubbed the carrots, I dreamed it was my cock. Wherever there
was a hole, she put in water and salt. Cock, cunt, tit, and ass, she
would use anything to make a soup. She dipped three times. There
was never any blood. When she was tired, I plucked the chicken
and stuffed it with my own ramrod. Kosher is kosher. Dead is
dead. Soup is soup. Then she washed the corpse. Haven't you
heard enough? I'm sick unto death. You'll have to let me go.

I bought an icebox for my bones, so she could trim the fat and
hang me on a hook to age, eat me a bit at a time as she sucked
my sperm on ice. Didn't she need a man that would last? Haven't
you heard enough?

These are my last words. You take them down. If I had had a
son, I would have changed my name to Abraham to make the
sacrifice.

And you bring flowers to my grave.

I'm sick unto death, Sybil.

.   .   .

"So this is what you want, Joseph, a simple story: An American
woman comes to the West Bank, is drawn into the Israeli-Arab

conflict, has the naive belief she can ameliorate the tension somehow, agrees to make a film with an Israeli and Palestinian man in
which each side is intimately revealed to the other. Something
between an autobiography and a documentary. And Jamine
agrees?"

"Jamine agrees."

"You don't want me to simply follow us around, you certainly
must want to add a few juicy incidents with the IDF, the PLO,
some Arab farmers, some illegal Jewish settlers. What else? Some
Jordanians, Syrians, CIA agents, Russians, a peacenik, an agron-
omist, several stalwart Druse." I was nervous, and so I was on a
roll. Joseph tolerated my rant. "More? Oh yes, the Lebanese of
all persuasions, Christians on the way to Bethlehem, U.N. peace-
keeping forces, a few terrorists, saboteurs, nuclear physicists, mul-
tinationals, militarists, all of that, so we can make box office. Why,
you could keep me here for years trying to get it all down. Is that
your plan?"

"You've left out the great romantic love story, Dina."

We were at the checkpoint waiting for the Israelis to let us
through. Everything had been arranged; it seemed I had papers,
permits, letters of introduction. Joseph was frighteningly efficient,
my permits even had my photograph attached to them. "What a
terrible use to make of my photo." I interrupted myself. "I thought
you were going to keep it next to your heart."

"When you leave me, give me another." He paused and looked
at me sadly. "You think everything is a game, don't you, Dina,
affairs of state and affairs of the heart."

"I care for you, Joseph."

"I know you do. It just isn't enough, is it?"

I thought I should go home right then. Perhaps I would find one
of my old lovers perfectly satisfying after all. Maybe this was only
a mid-life tear. I could take up domestic filmmaking, champion
the neighborhood, work small, vote, write to my congressmen,
stay out of trouble. Like Sybil, I could (should!) learn to crochet.

I saw what was coming. I was already so torn that I imagined saying, first lying in bed with Joseph, and then another time lying in bed with Jamine, not remembering that I had said it, "If a war breaks out, I will have to stay here, on this side."

"What's your dream for this, Joseph?"

"I don't tell my dreams and I don't play in futures, Dina. We're going to do an honest piece of work. That's all, and then we'll see what comes out."

"Another one of your impossible tasks, right?"

"Right."

As we drove back to Nablus, and later as we walked together through the city, and even later as the three of us met and then when we were actually at work, shooting, I gathered myself together, and remembered what it was I knew how to do, what I had done again and again, what I was still able to do, what skills remained to me. I made lists in my mind: "I know how to read landscapes and faces. I know how to read what is said and to show what isn't said. I know how to pick figs and what it means. I know how to judge the produce that comes across the Jordan, how to reveal a state of siege in the quality and quantity of oranges, in the condition of the road, in the numbers of patrols, the twitch of a hand . . .

In the beginning, it was my job to watch. I knew nothing; *that* was my great gift. I tried to record my innocence, later, if I tried to recreate it, it would be contrived. I watched myself, I watched us make the film. I caught Jamine on film. I trained Jamine's younger brother. He was old enough that some of the settlers were afraid he'd hidden a bomb in the camera, but was young enough to pay attention to the image and not the talk. The Palestinians weren't any more trusting of me and so we achieved a balance. Soon there were the three of us on film, separately and even together, for eternity—which stretches in both directions, if you think in linear time, or in all directions, if you believe—or for as long as film lasts. We were indiscriminate with the film stock, I recorded everything, a casual walk through the city—"Anything may happen"—and the subtle rancor between Joseph and Jamine as jealousy and conflict developed, because we were working together, because they were men, because their cultures demanded it. A quibble over food. Irritation in a restaurant. A squabble over an interview, scheduling, a shot. And then a heartfelt talk. Their hands clasping. A slap on the back.

Sometimes I went out alone. There were other things I wanted to show. The dust hovering over the land, so astonishingly yellow even next to the Jordan, not the yellow of mustard growing on green hills, not the sharp yellow of that weed flower, not the yellow of buttercup or scotch broom or forsythia, but another yellow, the yellow of the picked mustard flower, when it dulls when the life seeps out of it, the yellow that no blue can turn to living green, the yellow that seeps into uniforms for example, the yellow that tints the tank, that is essential to camouflage, the fuller yellow of the liver spreading through the body, leaving its mark, before the loved one dies. I wanted to show that yellow dust on the fruit, in the crevices of our hands, a mask on our faces, covering the brown wings of birds, the larvae of insects, yellow swarming in the air like locusts so that everything existed in a soft haze, every brutality and cruelty falsified in that yellow light.

We filmed the working on the land, the building and the tearing down, the mutual rage. We filmed the dust and the well, drinking in cafes, pissing and spitting into the dust, the dark plug swirling for a moment before it dried. Orchards, where the water seeps in slowly, stealthily, drips steadily from black tubes wound like snakes about each tree, and the trees bear more fruit than anywhere else for miles around, and the air is cleared, miraculously, a column of blue air reaching upwards, by the tinkle of water, and everyone eats. Jamine said these orchards no longer belonged to his people, others said, as they had eons before, this was proof that the Palestinian god is unable to manifest miracles. We filmed everything I laid my eyes on in my innocence, and everything they pointed to with their knowledge. Amazingly, we were fair, though only I tried to be neutral. After a while, of course, I didn't want it ever to end. I thought to myself, magically, "As long as this film is being made, there can't be a war."

And once, Shechem, I followed behind Jamine. He was walking away from me. I saw you so clearly, Shechem, all the times of walking away collapsed into one single shot which had to serve for all. I practiced in my mind so that I would know it when I saw it, your confidence with the land, how it supported you, but then I saw something else, something I didn't want to see.

Your voice, Jamine, was simultaneously seductive and ironic, slightly mocking, yet intimate. You looked at me, your head tilted slightly. Obviously, you had turned around, you were no longer walking away, you felt me watching you and you knew what I knew, so you were forced back to talk to me. We stood there, you staring at me, and you asked, "What is it you see, Dina?" Your voice, your tone was practiced under a clever veneer of anger, precise as porcelain, the finest cloisonné of perceptions and responses, arch bitterness, worldly resignation, with even a touch of detached amusement embedded in the most developed sarcasm and intellectual weariness. I'd come to find this stance familiar. But when you asked me this way, in this tone, I couldn't tell you. Could you ask me another way? Could you be curious? Could you trust me? That is, could you acknowledge that I might see something you hadn't intended for me to see and that I wouldn't do you harm?

The tone of your voice might have been anger, deep sarcasm, or deep disgust. Certainly taunting. I heard the phrase "What do you see, Dina?" again and again in my mind in every possible intonation but I couldn't hear it the way I had to hear in order to answer you.

I waited a long time. There was a deep silence within me. I knew why I couldn't hear what I needed: I didn't trust you to say it that way. I waited, then, a long time, and practiced hearing it.

Then you turned to me and stroked my face so gently and asked in a very quiet voice, "What is it, Dina?"

Then you knew what it was I saw and you were as moved by my seeing it as I was. I didn't have to tell you. I could simply put my hand out to your cheek in the same way, or put my finger against your lip, I could even have kissed you, but so gently, you would barely have felt my lips. Then, because it didn't matter, I told you.

"I see your suffering."

By which I meant, "I see your suffering, my love."

You nodded, you touched my shoulder, you turned away, you walked from me and I saw it all, your strength, your anger, your astonishment, your disbelief, your humiliation, your suffering. You disguised nothing for me. You let me see it all. You walked away and I filmed your back.

In the middle of the shoot, Sybil called me home. It's only a few hours drive, she reminded me. That's all she said. She sent a type-written page like the ones I'd seen in her journal about Jeremiah Abazadik. At the top she'd scrawled some sentences about mileage, directions, speed limits, as if I'd never been in the country.

THE TESTIMONY OF JEREMIAH ABAZADIK
A Posthumous Autobiography

Good-bye. Sybil.

Even death sings.

Bye bye Sy Bil, I'm off to see the wars.

My mother was right, when I was born she saw my cock stand up and said, "Praise. This boy's a soldier, look what a shooter he's got." She was crowing, "Cock-a-doodle doo."

I always liked a battle to the death. They beat their swords into plowshares. Their spears into pruning hooks. I beat and I beat and I beat.

My heart broke. That's the truth, harlot. I never stopped going off to war. I put your ring around my cock, as a marriage bond. Ring around the rosy, and we all fall down. They said it was a plague. All that dying; it was contagious.

So they made a war. And we made a war. It's not the first time, Jerry. Wars are like weather, they blow hot and cold, they come and they go. So we made a war. So you think it's the first time? What's the matter, you didn't read the Bible? When you read that Book, you *daven* in one war and out the other. For God, everything is good, the cow is good, the tree is good, the rain is good, the mud is good, the cockroach is good, the man is good, the plague is good. A plague on all your houses. The war is good. Who am I to make judgments?

Hello, Sybil. I want to tell you something. It will break your heart, too. I'm making a war on me for making a war on someone else. I can't forgive myself. I also made a war. I can't forgive, Sybil, I can't . . .

.   .   .

When I came back to Jerusalem, Sybil was wearing a black dress, the color she claimed she never wore. It was oddly becoming

because it slimmed her hips which had become even wider. There
had been no way that I could telephone her, so I simply set out
when I received the letter, still, she was waiting for me at the
entryway as if I'd just gone around the corner for milk, bread, and
eggs and had dallied for the newspaper.

"Where were you?"

I didn't understand.

"The tea is getting cold." She ignored my little overnight case
and led me into the drawing room. There was no one else there.
On a cart by the pale yellow and gray couch was a teapot, two
cups, a few cakes. She poured. Miraculously, the tea was not ice
cold. "I thought you'd never come."

"I came as soon as I got your letter."

"Where were you?"

"I was in Nablus, Sybil. You know that. I'm making a movie.
Remember, you didn't want to come."

"Did you ask me?"

"Maybe I didn't."

"Maybe you did. I forget." Her skin was ashen, it had turned
gray, as if the lime poured on the dead had seeped into it.

"I forgot where you were. I looked all over for your address.
Then I thought perhaps you'd gone back to the States. Joseph
wasn't home, either. He must be on a mission."

"He's with me, remember?"

"No. I forgot. I'm forgetting everything. Maybe it's better."

"Better? How can you dismiss me that way? You are forgetting
everything, including me, my life, my circumstances. Don't I exist
for you anymore?"

"No more than I exist for you."

We were having tea. The brew was warm and spicy enough to
be comforting after a long drive. How could something be wrong?
It took me longer than it should have to believe that she was
serious, to see how grieved she was.

"I'm here, Sybil, I came as soon as I got your letter."

"Are you? It's hard to know what's here and what isn't."

I took her hand and we sat quietly. I didn't know what to do so I prayed as hard as I could that no one would walk into the room, and if this is a proof of the efficacy of prayer, my faith was rewarded: we were left alone. Finally, I took her in my arms, surprised by her weight, by her leathery bulk.

"It's all over and Jeremy is dead," she said after a long time, crying without tears, heaving great soundless sighs. "He's dead. An accident, they say. They say he stepped on a mine. Some say it was suicide. Now it's too late. There's no hope." She wiped her dry eyes with a black handkerchief, a piece of unhemmed black cotton which looked as if it had been torn from the sleeve of an old dress.

"You sent me a few pages of a manuscript."

She shrugged. "He died. I had had the hope that we would have something together. He couldn't step out of his life."

"He did the best he could." I was slightly nauseated by my facile words. I was looking for the "therapeutic" response and hated myself. Grief is grief whenever it comes. It must not be assuaged.

"You knew he was dead. He's been dead a long time. You've known for a long time." I tried to be as gentle as I could. My responses were as hopeless as hers, so I let myself say anything and reached for her hand. "You'd read the articles; in fact, that's what brought you here."

Sybil looked directly into my eyes. She did not seem mad at all, only broken with grieving. "Everyone has another chance, Dina. Oh, you must have been thinking I was truly mad.

"Let's go upstairs now. I didn't want to go to our room directly. I had to tell you here. It's too close up there."

"Are you ill, Sybil?" Her walk was lumbering, careful, she favored one hip.

"I couldn't save the child. You understand. We're too old to have children, it seems. That's what the doctor said. It wasn't more than a few weeks." Now her stare was cruel. She was warning me. Or perhaps it was a threat. I do not like to say what I thought at the moment: it sounded like a curse. "Well, where were you?"

"Was it Zev's?"

"Where were you, Dina?"

"Does it matter? I didn't know, Sybil. If I'd known, I'd have come immediately. What can I do now, Sybil?" I looked directly into her eyes. "I would have been here, if I had known. You have to believe that."

She led me up to our room and I saw why she hadn't wanted me to come in right away. At the foot of her bed was a small wooden box and, as proscribed, all the mirrors were covered with black cloth to protect us from the pull of the dead.

"And the manuscript, Sybil?"

"It won't bring anyone back to life, will it?"

O daughter of my people
Gird thee with sackcloth and wallow thyself in ashes
Make thee mourning, as for an only son,
Most bitter lamentation:

THE TESTIMONY OF JEREMIAH ABAZADIK
A Posthumous Autobiography

This is my swan song:

> You kill
> You sing
>
> > You sing
> > You die.

Do you like my song? I haven't written the music yet. It will be a dirge.

That's all there is to the song. A chorus that all the angels will sing.

There isn't much vegetation where I exploded, not much rain to hurry things along, but still, within months, I'll be part of the weeds and scrub. This burial in the dust is more than good enough for me.

By the waters of Babylon. I met a woman in Babylon. I loved her and I didn't let her know. Every whore in Babylon wants you to give her a son she can send to war.

I stepped on my own mine. How lovingly I'd made it and then how lovingly I'd planted it the way you plant orange trees in the desert, or a child in an empty womb, asking for a miracle. I knew this one would grow. "Wait for me, *bubbele*," I whispered to it, "I'm coming back for you."

When I set that mine, I set my own clock running.

How much money are you making on this story of my life?

I died clean. I didn't leave a wife or a child.

You kill
You sing

You sing
You die.

You kill
You die.

You die.
You sing.

You sing.
You sing.

. . .

After a week, it seemed to me that Sybil had recovered. By which
I mean that the outward signs of her inner anguish and loss vanished. She spoke curtly of her late period, the intense cramps, and
busied herself with the routines of normal life. When I tried to
speak with her, she said, "The living are living, the dead are dead."

"As simple that?"

"As simple as that."

"You sound like Joseph."

"Good, he's a smart man."

She began thinking about the book, but differently, it seemed
to me. Now she consulted me about details. She was considering
a photobiography interspersed with a series of interviews. Sybil
would have to add very little of her own. She had certainly put
her journal away and would say nothing to me even about the
pages she had sent in the mail. When I brought them up cautiously,
she said, "I was raving for a while."

"His mother is not going to get a single penny," she proclaimed
triumphantly. Mrs. Abazadik still refused to communicate with
Sybil in any way, after the first letter she'd sent.

"Will there really be any money in it?"

"What do you think?" Sybil answered me indignantly. She fixed me with a cold dark stare. She was wearing an umber velour shirt. It was beginning to be cold in Jerusalem. She looked like fire, my old Sybil. "I'm giving half the profits to Peace Now. Wouldn't you? That's what he would have done. But *after* my salary and expenses. And they're considerable. For example, tonight I'm taking you to dinner. And that's on the expense account."

"Will you come back to Nablus with me?" She shook her head, sparks flying from her hair. Joseph, it seems, had talked to her about how delicate our work was. "God knows, I know about delicate work. You finish it and then when you're ready, maybe I'll be ready to go back to the States with you to dust my apartment and help you edit."

We spent an entire day cleaning our little room, polishing the furniture, washing the windows, the mirrors. Her face was ruddy from the effort, a patina of sweat across her forehead. She was luminous, thin, so it seemed to me, after only a week. She was my Sybil again, my golden cat, my sphinx. We bought her some wide copper bracelets, one for each wrist; I admired her as we walked through the old city, the brown cloth of her skirt flouncing about her calves like a flag. She ate honey cakes, tore at thin sweet rolls of apricot paste, dipped into bags of dates as we walked through the streets of the old city, sucking at the sweetness. It was as if we'd never been separated from each other.

The last night we indulged in one hot, thick, sweet coffee after another. Wrapped in sweaters, we were seated out of doors, despite the chill in the air. Shivering, delighting, I braved the issue again:

"Can you tell me anything?"

She stared at me a long time. When her chin quivered slightly, she looked away. "No." Another silence. "I can, but I won't." She looked up at me, the coffee steaming her face. "No. I would, but I can't."

We got up to walk. The night was literally perfumed with all the spices of Arabia. It was very quiet. Most of the stalls were closed. The city dwellers were hidden away in their rooms in the secret labyrinth within the walls which neither of us had really ever entered. We could hear the murmur of voices, but it was a murmur only, as of the wind around a corner of stone, or an underground river rushing steadily and invisibly beneath our feet. Sometimes we heard a high-pitched tone, a child crying or a woman's voice, just an instant of a familiar sound, and it fell away like a falling star.

"Can you tell me anything, Dina?"

I thought I could. I opened to the torrent of words which had been waiting so long only for this question. The words tumbled up into my throat, but as I opened my mouth, they vaporized like so much sulphur and steam.

"I can't either." Because I couldn't? Because I wouldn't? Because I shouldn't?

"That's right," she said, taking my hand, and we walked home.

"Joseph, are we dreaming?"

"No, we're in history. We have to be. We wouldn't have invented this if we'd been either conscious or sane."

"Nothing changes in history; things only happen; it's always the same. The intractability of the first cause. If we're only in history, we're lost, Joseph."

"But what have you been dreaming, Dina? I miss hearing your dreams."

"I don't dream anymore. I haven't been dreaming since we returned to Nablus. Except sometimes, like Sybil, I do dream of having a child. And you?"

"Yes, Dina, sometimes I dream of that as well."

And unto Joseph in the land of Egypt were born Manasseh and Ephraim which Asenath, Dinah's daughter, bare unto him.

In time Joseph grew distant from Dinah. Asenath was no longer a child but not old enough for marriage. She didn't interest him at this time and he thought it was proper that Dinah raise her, particularly, as he said, "She isn't really my child." It was after

Dinah bore their sons, Manasseh and Ephraim, that he began to
dream about tribes and blessings and so turned wholeheartedly to
the affairs of state. He ignored the ceremonies they had practiced
together. He began to look north. His dreams of earth became
dreams of territory. He remembered the dream of the sheaves of
wheat bowing to him and laughed aloud with pleasure. One day,
at the time of the dancing and the sowing, Dinah reminded him
of Rachel and the gods. He turned to her, his mouth twisted,
saying, "Let's not talk of these things." He was looking at his two
sons and at the sons of his brothers and he saw a long line of sons
stretching to the horizon covering the earth. Like an army of ants,
she thought. When she expressed this, he smiled, saying, "I am
my father's son. My life must show respect for his name. He has
given my sons their blessing."

"They are my sons, too, Joseph," Dinah said.

"Then the blessing is a covenant between us all." He looked
away from her; she saw his heart was breaking. But after Jacob
had come to Goshen and had gone home again, and after Jacob
had blessed Manasseh and Ephraim and given them Dinah's por-
tion, without even her leave, and after Jacob had died, then the
heaviness of Jacob came upon Joseph.

Sometimes Joseph and Jamine left me to myself and then I walked
through Nablus without causing the riot Joseph had given me to
expect. Often someone wanted to sell me something, but otherwise
my presence was not disruptive. I wouldn't say the city was peaceful, but I had acquired some limited peace of mind which subdued
the constant melancholy which accompanied me as I walked about.
As if I had known the city in the old days, I ached for the trees
which had once been here and were gone and on the outskirts I
felt injured by what seemed to me the flagrant bounty of the Israeli
orchards compared with the Palentinians'. When I was alone I
thought of Asherah of the sacred grove; when I was with Joseph
or Jamine, these thoughts fled. The new orchards formed a green
fence, they were a commercial enterprise. You could not enter the

grove to pray or pick an orange unless you owned the land. Between interviews, I filmed the trees—the ancient olive groves which had been there even from Dinah's time, the new orchards and the sandy fields of scrub where the trees had been cut down.

But ye shall destroy their altars, break their images, and cut down their groves:

She knew he saw what was coming and he had no means to resist it. He did not have it in him anymore. He had lived too long among his brothers. And Dinah praised the day when they had sold him to the spice merchants and she cursed the day he had forgiven them, that he had embraced Simeon, who had, against Reuben's protests, determined to kill Joseph after he had killed Shechem. She prayed to the gods by herself and she kept the rites. One day she took him outside and she said, "Look, They're there," pointing to the wind and the trees, and all the places where she saw the living gods, each being numinous with life. But he turned to her wearily. "I don't see it anymore. The affairs of state are tedious and God is very far away."

"Where?" she asked.

"There." He raised his hand but it was too far for him to reach, and though she poured the living water over him, he felt nothing. She left him alone. He called Levi's sons to him and asked them to study all the names of God to call God down to him. He put the priests between himself and God, "as a living bridge," he said. He wondered if they should continue to rule together, saying, "Though your gods are only images, they distract me from the serious business of living. Also it's not fitting that I elevate my dishonored sister and wife over my brothers when I am living in the house of men."

Likewise, thou son of man, set thy face against the daughters of thy people, which prophesy out of their own heart; and prophesy thou against them.

While we were working in Nablus, Joseph held me to him tightly, but within the embrace, I felt him desert me. He was so attentive, particularly before Jamine, I was embarrassed by his solicitude. He was like an adolescent boy courting a woman for the first time, as if he were bringing flowers to the beloved whore who had initiated him. But she was the whore; later he would go on and marry another kind of woman. He was exquisitely courteous and respectful, particularly about my work, acquiescing to all the decisions I made without challenge. Then he became reticent, unwilling to shape the film, he said, cautious about his influence, he said, and prejudices. I was forced to bend toward him, in the direction he had originally maintained. I found myself advocating the Israeli viewpoint to be sure that his point of view was also included. I hadn't known that he'd had such a strong bias until it seemed to be my charge to protect it. After a while, it was as if Jamine represented one constituency and I represented another while Joseph stood between us, smiling benevolently. He was clever, Joseph. I admired his skill as a diplomat and my heart sank.

I was restless when we slept together, couldn't remember my dreams, couldn't separate the dream from the nightmare. "It's inevitable when you work with such concentration that you won't remember your dreams. The psyche can only handle so much input." Joseph was not at all concerned that his dreams had also disappeared.

When Dinah was in Egypt she was taught the art of music and when she was sufficiently advanced as a musician and knew the sacred songs and their power, she was taught the secret art of making her own instruments. She could not make the vessel until she was familiar with the contents which it must hold. It was not the vessel which must shape the song, but the sweet demands of the song which determined its proper house. Then she was taught how to wrap bodies in white linen and ointments. She learned the rituals of the caretaking of the dead and she added this knowledge to the knowledge she had of the caretaking of the living which she had learned from the daughters of the field. So she knew all manner of healing, healing of the living and balming of the dead.

From the time of Shechem's death, Dinah carried his charred bones with her in a wrapping of linen that had on it, for all the years afterwards, even though she washed it again and again, the smudge of ashes, as a constant sign; it could not be washed clean. When she opened the linen and saw the bones and the dark ring of ashes, she would weep again, as if she had never yet wept and then she put the ashes to her mouth, and a sweetness came to her, as of love.

    After Joseph had reconciled with his brothers, he bound himself tightly most tightly with Levi and Simeon. It was when Dinah saw him embrace those who had killed Shechem that she took the bones and she laid them out carefully in order. She counted them, and then again, to be certain that she had each bone. All the bones of the skull, the delicate bones of the hands and the feet, the ribs, the hip bones, the jaw, nothing forgotten, nothing lost, nothing broken. When she laid them out in the sand, there was one bone missing, but not a bone, only the appearance of a bone, the part of him she had sucked into herself, the bone through which he had joined her. In her mind, she remembered the feel of that bone, she remembered it with her cunt more than with her hands or her mouth, she remembered it as a horn growing alive within her, as a white horn, yielding and flexible, penetrating her, as an ivory horn, smoothed, polished, and full of heat, carved exactly to the inner circles of her body. The ascending spirals of the horn pointed into the descending spirals within her until the two circles were spinning flames from the great double horn of light.

    She laid out the bones, and she cleaned them white of the ashes and hollowed each one of them carefully. Then she placed them on the sand until she had constructed the shape of a man. The man was hollow. From each of his bones, Dinah made a flute and tuned each one perfectly to its proper sound. Then, beginning with the feet, she blew into them, she sounded each bone, she sang the song of each bone. One by one, she passed her breath into his entire body, all the time going back in her mind, bone by bone and note by note, singing into and through his ashes, into the burning and the fire, blowing the note through the corpse which appeared to flesh his bones. She blew each flute, each note, through his translucent corpse, singing him back through time. The first note sang him into his death, the next note entered into his dying. With flute and song she progressed backwards toward the red line about his neck, the scabs, the full crusts of blood, singing toward his death rattle, toward the astonished sound gasping for air, toward the last easy breath, the notes clearing the dark spirits, singing through even as far as his stare of disbelief. That was where she lost courage, where she faltered, at his astonishment, his disbelief, his incomprehension that life was flowing out of him as the universe was destructing. He could not set it right. She was not certain she could pass through that barrier, the force of it was so strong, it took her own breath away. She almost died herself, but now he had breath in him and that air entered into her. Her breath was in him and his breath was in her; their living love for each other was only moments away. She leaped toward it, grasped it, breathing and singing. She sang into the next bone, going back further, bone by bone until his pellucid skin pinked. He was smiling, she was blowing the sweat fresh on his brow, the hairs upon his chest, her eyes staring into his lucid eyes.

She played their living bodies joined, moving in the oldest dance, the coming together, the parting, the coming together, the parting, breath by breath, enacting the day and the night and the seasons, the moon and the sun, the living and the natural dying. In her mind she brought the cries to his lips, played each bone until she ended at the crown and he was whole. She set down the last bone and mounted him in deed, on the bone which was no bone, but light. Time stopped. She gave herself to their embrace. She became light too. And the light of her hands and mouth penetrated his body through every pore, through every hollow bone. He glowed and a spear of light gathered itself at his crown, shot through his body, pierced his heart which was beating in light, and spilled into her out of his living bone where they were joined.

When she came to, it was raining. She gathered the bones into new linen and went home. That night she slept alone; she could not sleep beside Joseph. In the morning, she did not tell him her dream.

And Saul disguised himself, and put on other raiment, and he went, and two men with him, and they came to the woman by night: and he said, "I pray thee, divine unto me by the familiar spirit, and bring me him up, whom I shall name unto thee."

And the woman said unto him, "Behold, thou knowest what Saul hath done, how he hath cut off those that have familiar spirits, and the wizards, out of the land: wherefore then layest thou a snare for my life to cause me to die?"

. . .

Jamine stayed somewhere in Nablus with his relatives, Shechem, while Joseph and I slept together at the hotel. Joseph made sure that Jamine knew that; it was the only example of spitefulness I saw in him. I confess I liked him more because of it. Not because he focused on me, it wasn't only vanity, but because it made him human. He was no different from his brothers, he also believed that you and I should not be together. We can say it was personal—I was his lover, his sister, after all. But it wasn't personal—it was racial at its hidden core. He did not think one of my kind should mix with one of your kind.

"But you, Joseph, would marry a Palestinian woman. That's what you want, isn't it? A woman as divided as you are."

"Yes, I do. I would prefer it."

"I remember how you told me how far I was from your fantasy, that you didn't want to marry an American Jewish woman who could understand nothing of your country but, ideally, you wanted a divided woman born of parents who lived on opposite sides of the Wall, who had been conceived in no man's land in a foxhole."

"Exactly."

"Why then does it seem right to you that I should never be with a Palestinian man?"

We were in bed. The conversation was, we both agreed to the lie, entirely speculative.

"It's not about right. That's not what I mean. It's neither about what is right nor just. That's not at issue, because what you say is both right and just. It's what I believe, Dina."

"Have you always believed this? Do you mean it's what you feel? Have you been lying to me all along?"

"No. This belief, feeling—whatever you want to call it, there's no difference between them—has just come to me. I'm grateful to you for the lesson."

"What has happened?"

"I watch you carefully while you're working and are unaware of my observation. You go into a Palestinian house and your face changes. Someone offers you a piece of chicken cooked in the Arabic style and you taste it and take it in and you're never the same again. You learn an Arabic word as if you're being reminded of something you'd forgotten. After I make love, I can take a shower and wash the smell of the woman off me entirely."

"I've seen you do that, even with me."

"But whatever enters you, you make a part of yourself, and you stink of it forever."

"So, Joseph, my great peacemaker, only Jewish men can mate with Palestinian women, is that it?"

"I don't think so. I think Jamine must feel the same way that I do about his sisters. I think he must also want to protect the womb. For the first time in my life, I understand why we've been taught for centuries that we must stay apart. I think he and I think exactly the same way on this matter, shameful as it is. We are going to have to find another door to peace."

So he loved me, as a way of keeping you and me apart. It made it easier on him, the loving. It made him forget what he'd wanted when he thought he had been looking for a wife. I understood why he'd never married. Loving me allowed him to think he was acting like a rational man. As I said, his irrationality delighted me, but liking him more didn't cause me to love him any more than I did.

· · ·

In the few Palestinian houses we entered, I was waited upon with exquisite attention. Courtesy is still an art in your community, Shechem. This reinforced the great distance between us all. The informality among Joseph's Jewish contacts created another kind of breach. Whatever was calculated to draw us together, in fact set us apart. Even if audiences rave about our film, I will know that I failed to achieve something I wanted, what mattered most to me—that the film impress us first. We were the film's first subjects, and it did not serve us as I'd hoped. Though after a day of shooting, we were most often bonded with our subjects, among ourselves there was more of an uneasy truce than a trusted alliance. In part, I think it was due to Jamine's intrinsic manner—he was always a little cool, even aloof—and also to Joseph's unconscious withdrawal; perhaps that too was strategic, though he claimed he wanted to disappear so that something unknown might develop. It sometimes drew me to him, but it also cut the film in two. If I had been allowed to be the common ground, another tone might have emerged. I had wanted to ignore the content, to mute the litanies from one side and another, until the stories emerged, the language careful, specific, but familiar. Familiarity was the essence here, the effect of storytelling. We are moved not only by the details, but by the way the words wrap us into a known world. Story demands repetition, is repetition. We all long for that moment of insight and recognition—yes, we understand, we see. Story holds familiar images repeating a known history. In story, unique details become transparent and shining kernels containing within them everything we need to know. That's what I wanted. And I wanted us to swallow those kernels and become whole. I wanted Joseph and Shechem to become brothers again.

I thought that if we listened long enough and edited well, it would be evident that each story was a variation on every other story. We all had the same history; we were already sharing the same ground. The same story which lay under the feet of Joseph's cousin's hate was also the foundation for Jamine's aunt. When the Arab farmer who, like Esau, had sold his birthright, had sold his land for a pittance before he even understood what papers, deeds, and contracts meant, told us his story, it sounded exactly like the story of the Jewish shopkeeper who'd had to flee Syria leaving everything behind. These stories which made enemies could, I thought, create bonds. This did happen to the three of us. I did see Joseph's heart open toward Jamine's people and Jamine move toward Joseph's kin. But that did not bring them any closer to each other. I knew that we would be the catalysts for real alliances when we could bring the people we were interviewing face to face to speak their grief, but they were not yet ready for that intimacy. Hate, after all, is a great balm, sometimes it is all one has left. The best I could do was to get all the stories on film, edit them for their similarities, and pray that everyone would see. The next step would be to bring the participants together in the same room, a kitchen, preferably. Telling family stories, while cooking a soup, who could be thinking of war? Jamine, Joseph, and I were equally intractable; we didn't risk telling our stories to each other. I think we didn't want to bond more than we already had.

. . .

Sometimes I met Lev in the streets. When I was with Joseph, he tipped his head respectfully, but it was pretense. I could see the mockery on his face. Joseph ignored him; Lev was just another fanatic serving his time in the army like everyone else.

On the few occasions when I encountered Lev as I wandered through Nablus alone, during the midafternoon rest, his respect disappeared.

"How's your terrorist, American?" he greeted me.

"You're the terrorist," I answered, unable to ignore him.

"Be careful," he warned, "we know every move you make. The government says it's our job to protect you, American."

"And who's endangering me, Lev?"

"In your case, American, it's your own self." He muttered a prayer and continued on his rounds.

. . .

I had the opportunity and excuse, Shechem, to scrutinize Jamine for days. I had to keep an eye on him because he was translating the Arabic while Joseph translated the Hebrew for me. I couldn't pick up everything in innuendo and gesture. So, to know what to shoot and how to focus, my eye would fall on Jamine as much as on the speaker. Sometimes I listened only to the music, one voice impassioned and melodic, followed by his voice—steady, deliberately monotonous, cool. The translations were only for me; Joseph, Jamine, and his brother were fluent in all languages, yet, as I think of it now, Jamine was the one who made certain that I understood every word spoken exactly. His particular kindness, the careful translation of each word, the attention paid to the finest distinctions of meaning and tone—Joseph agreed he was masterful—set us even farther apart. The old paradox: if you step halfway to me and then half the distance and then half the distance again, you will be coming toward me, unsuccessfully, forever. Every time he reached toward me, I realized how very much I didn't understand.

There were the three of us—Jamine, me, Joseph—sometimes in the midst of his family and friends, sometimes among Joseph's kin. Jamine drew me close to him, knew how to do it without moving a muscle, without a single overt glance, without a surreptitious word, but he also kept a distance between us. Should I have determined to leap across the barriers imposed, which, Joseph assured me time and again, were innate and inevitable, Joseph restrained me by his presence. He assured me in every possible way that any move I made to connect with Jamine meant war. I said that was an impossible contradiction. He agreed, asserting it was that very contradiction of this country which I had been re-fusing to acknowledge since I arrived.

I continued to sleep with Joseph, returned with him at night to his room, not to mine. When we made love, it was as if I was pulling myself about myself. Throughout the night, he held me, no matter how I shifted from one side to another, he extended his arm and folded me into himself. He comforted me and his bony hands stroked my hips and thighs, slowly, lightly, hypnoti-cally until I fell asleep. Just at dawn, I left his room for my own down the hall so that I could begin the morning alone, also so I could wash him off my skin. But you knew, Shechem. You could smell him.

One evening, asking if I was cold, Jamine carefully draped a shawl about my shoulders without his fingers touching me at all. I leaped toward him in that infinitesimally small space between my skin and his hands, but by the time I moved he'd agilely moved away.

Did Dinah approach you, Shechem? Did she circle you in the field until you lay beneath her so that between you it was certain that you had never enacted a rape?

Did it mean also that I would have to move toward Jamine, that he had come, by my design—or so I was accused—as far as Nablus to meet me, and then I'd have to go the rest of the way? Was he impatient with the contradiction between my willfulness on the one hand and my innocent posturing on the other? Was he tired of my ignorance? Or was he wary of being accused of rape? Did he refuse to touch me because he thought I belonged to Joseph? Was it property rites we were enacting once again?

Between Jamine and Joseph, I found the abyss that lies between desire and need, between passion and comfort, between other and brother. Maybe it was also that Dinah was attracted to one man and I was attracted to another and the two of us still in one body. After all, I watched Jamine, seemingly with more curiosity than desire, and I still slept with Joseph. I craved the impersonal chem-istry of his body wrapped about mine. During the days, Joseph looked at me sadly, watched me out of the corner of his eye as I watched Jamine. But at night Joseph always seemed confident as he led me to his bed. He watched me drawn to Jamine, but sat silently, smiling, encased in his elegant, studied, trained, scentless detachment. When we made love, he knew I was less with him than I'd been, though he also knew I couldn't do without him. Dinah had not mated with Joseph by default. She had also been drawn by the tremulous eroticism of his lean white body, tantalized by his faint, tender caresses, the barely felt strokes, the rhythm intermittent and startling, his motivations hidden, the sexuality of an eagle, darting, swift, random, inciting, disappearing, his mouth, damp, tender, evasive, his breath like a spring breeze, sudden and elusive. Throughout the nights, he wrapped himself about me, as if to encase me in feathers, feeling and not feeling.

.   .   .

Against my will, I began to believe in another kind of magic, as we spent day after day taking testimony. I began to believe less and less in talk, ideas, and images. I began to give credence to an intuition that the magic lay between us, that it was for the three of us to perform some act of reconciliation. But as I watched Joseph detach himself from us, it left Jamine and me to see what was possible between us, to see, after all the pain which had divided us for centuries, if we could come together again and transform all the forces and divisions which pulled at us, so another history might be implied.

I believed this out of despair. Because I saw no alternative. Because of Joseph's growing reserve. I didn't know how it might be enacted, we were drifting further apart with each story.

.   .   .

One evening, as we were carrying the equipment to the car, Jamine bent over me to open the door and whispered, "Let us spend tomorrow together, as we're not filming. Just you and I."

"It seems rude." I was trembling.

"Considering the crimes we've been discussing so politely today, rudeness hardly matters. Allow me to compensate for the rudeness by extending the hospitality of my people to you outside of our work setting. It will be a courtesy for you to accept."

I had had enough courtesy and hospitality. I had had enough talk, had heard enough to make me despair for millennia. More than anything, I would have liked to prepare a meal for us, to stick garlic cloves in a leg of lamb, baste it with wine and rosemary. Even a single, independent, American woman needs to wield a paring knife or toss a salad every so often to remain sane. But I didn't know where or how he lived and I didn't dare ask, and I wasn't certain I would know how to shop in Nablus. Still I wanted to make an offering.

But I said, "Yes, Jamine. Yes." Joseph had other friends in Nablus and business to attend to, was glad for the free day, and so Joseph and I separated from each other very early the next day.

And when Shechem, the son of Hamor the Hivite, prince of the country, saw her, he took her and lay with her, and defiled her.

In the distance, the women were dancing about the fire, flames leaping into the night between their dark shapes so that it seemed to Dinah as she lay in the grass, her head propped up on her hands to look past Shechem's face, that the women were dancing in the fire, but were not consumed.

Moses would descend from Dinah's line. He was to be the son of the daughter of the daughter of the daughter of . . . Asenath, who was to be the daughter of Dinah and Shechem, who has just been conceived. It was not only the thought that came to Dinah, but the awareness of a point of light, the first instance of a star crossing the firmament. Usually, when a star is born it takes eons for its light to reach us. It is born so far away that despite its longing and determination, it cannot reach us faster than the speed of light. Between the conception and the destination lies the darkness of the universe. Stars are always born beyond us, we are given the time to prepare ourselves to receive them. In this instance, however, there was no moment of darkness, no unknowing. The light reached her in the instant of the birth of the star. Dinah stared into that fire admiring the women dancing within it. At first, it was as if the fire was falling upon her, as if she was within it herself, and then it was as if the fire was within her. She let herself dream. Then she could not tell the difference between herself and the fire.

In the distance, she could hear the coronet, flute, harp, the sackbut, psaltery, and dulcimer; Shechem's sisters were gifted in music and had promised to teach her to play the flute, but Leah feared the music as much as Jacob did and Dinah could not bring herself to practice stealthily when each breath was praise. Shechem was asleep but she did not want to be asleep. His breath was music to her. In the darkness, he had given her oil and opened her legs, so gently, for her own hand to enter her own body; he had led her in, so that she would open her own door. Before she broke the hymen entirely, she wanted him, and only then, when she'd asked, did he yield to her, and she removed her hand and he followed her inside. He moved so carefully, so quietly, with such small motions, with almost unbearable sweetness, that she felt as if she was awakening from a long dream, and took the initiative again, moving toward him, urging herself upon him, until there was no space between them, but only the rhythm of the double breaths of their bodies. When she gasped, he made a ring of her anus about his small finger, and slipped his tongue into her mouth, so she was sealed and all the magic enclosed between them.

He awakened just as the moon rose. Together they watched it drive across the sky leading the small white lamb clouds to a newer darker pasture. In the instant of her pleasure, in the instant that Dinah was known to Shechem, Asenath became known to her. Perhaps Shechem knew because he smiled, though they did not feel the need to speak about it. Dinah determined to name her daughter Asenath because she felt the thorny prick of sperm and egg entering her womb and the wound of that thorn and its flower would be with her forever.

They were only children. They were each only fourteen years of age.

Dinah hoped her mother, Leah, would not notice her absence. Leah watched only for her sons, assumed Dinah was with the handmaidens or scampering about with Joseph, whom Leah despised. She enjoyed saying he was a soft boy, womanish. "Puling," she called him and lost no opportunity to call Jacob's attention to Levi's squat, muscled frame and Simeon's long hairy arms. "Look how these sons resemble you, but that boy of Rachel's, how do we know to whom he belongs?" She was tireless in her imprecations. Dinah's brothers, most especially Levi, and Simeon whose great passion was livestock, would not look for Dinah, they took no more notice of her than of a goat whose deformity prevented them from either breeding it or eating it.

Joseph, however, knew where she was. Since they'd been born, they'd been bound with an invisible thread, as if the cord of their mothers had been tied to a yet more nurturant cord which did not fall off, which fed them both in tandem. In addition, she had told him a dream that morning and so she knew he was seated on the ridge where the new olive trees had been planted, looking down into the shadows where she lay with Shechem, attentively holding her safely in his mind which was the same as casting a protective darkness over her as the lamb clouds crossed over the moon.

Jamine and I drove north out of Nablus past Jacob's fountain which, they say, never casts a shadow on the summer solstice. It was a blissfully ordinary day. Two people driving in a car, chatting. We could have been in the south of France, even in Iowa, mildly drawn to the anecdotal, finally exchanging simple stories about our lives: where we'd been born, who our friends had been, how we'd liked and hated school. When Jamine looked like he was going to launch into the kind of diatribe he called a teaching, I put my fingers on his lips and he kissed them. I felt myself tremble so I stretched out my legs, slouched against the seat, and forced myself into a semi-reverie, watching the scenery pass. Occasionally little pillars of dust before or behind us announced the presence of another car or cart, but for the most part I felt as if the two of us were alone in the universe. I did not feel the need to say anything to Jamine, not even about you, Shechem; he either knew everything or it didn't matter. Now and then he identified a house or a landmark, but mostly we allowed the silence to be about us. Maybe, I thought, after so many years, the gods had granted us this solitude.

Jamine told me the names of his other brothers and sisters, there were six at the time who were still alive. The youngest one and I had become quite friendly during the shoot. Two brothers and one sister, he said, were fighting with one branch or another of the PLO.

"Fighting?" I repeated his words.

"Affiliated," he said.

So the day passed. In the late afternoon, we had a large meal and then just before the light began to fade, Jamine stopped the car by the side of a field so we could walk a little before the sun set. He got out on his side, and I inhibited my reflex to get out myself, but waited for him to come around, which he did, and formally open the door, extending his arm to me. I took it and winked. He smiled at me, the pose of the approving teacher, and led me down a dirt road. It was pleasant. Small houses were in the far distance. The sun was going down slowly, a white ball of light. The sunset would not be spectacular. The fields were small, carefully divided, tidy.

Soon Jamine stopped, and with careful expertise slipped between the barbed wire so that he was on one side of the fence and I was on the other, then he reached out and pulled me to him, roughly, so the wire was between us, and it pressed into my thighs, and his also, I imagined, and tore the silk blouse I was wearing.

He looked at the rip, but not with regret.

"Silk is rather elegant for such a poor, rough country."

"A natural fabric." I shrugged. His grip was strong and the wire did cut into both of us. I saw that, and I began pulling away, "Jamine . . ."

"Come closer, Dina."

"Jamine!"

But he silenced me, his fingers on my lips this time. "Don't speak, Dina," and pressed my head against his chest, his fingers firm but tender upon my hair. We stood that way a long time. The sun went down. A breeze came up, as it does, at the moment of setting. He released me. There was blood on his shirt. I began to speak again, but he silenced me.

"Let's not speak at all." He led me back to the car and we drove silently to Samaria, where Eli had wanted to take me, up the rough road to the ancient ruins built by Ahab where he had lived so many years with his Phoenician wife, Jezebel, who had reintroduced the worship of Baal and Asherah.

He knew the old man and his wife who were the caretakers of the site and ran the souvenir store, selling old coins, stones, sodas. I sat outside under the standing Roman columns, feeling the stone draw me back through the years, not far enough, trying to loosen the tension on my body. Let everything go, I instructed myself as he chatted with his friends. As politeness would require that he translate, I preferred to sit by myself, without inhibiting his talk in whatever languages he chose. For a while I pitched stones with a young boy who informed me in pictures, hand gestures, and some rather expressive sounds that he tended the goats. Then he ran off and I was alone again. The air was very fresh. Before I became impatient, Jamine strode out of the little shop where they also slept, excusing himself with as few words as possible. I understood we were still not to speak and didn't press him.

He took a few blankets from the car, a small basket, and motioned me up the hill. All he said was, "Careful as we climb the hill. Hold on to me. We'll be able to be alone for the night. It's very peaceful here, and there won't be any tourists until after ten though the young boys may very well drive the goats up to pasture about dawn." He didn't say all that at once, but intermittently, as I walked through the dark behind him to the top of the hill past the ruins of the palace were Ahab and Jezebel had rolled, roiling the displeasure of the high priests. Here, as everywhere else, there were only a few stones left to indicate the palace and the temple. The grand columns are Roman; history has played here again and again.

He walked confidently and I stumbled behind, unable to see where I was going, entertaining the dark thoughts that he had done this a hundred times, that this was the favored trysting spot, that I was one of a succession of women, but then I tried to bring silence to my mind, knowing I was using these thoughts to distance myself. I was watching his back again, wondering why I was following him so "obediently." It rather surprised me that I made no protest whatsoever, did not even demand the protocol of flirtation and seduction even though it wasn't lust I felt, not even passion, as I followed. It was impatience, apprehension, fear, that dried my mouth as if I'd never been with a man before, as if I didn't understand what we were going to do, as if I couldn't conceive what it meant for a man to enter my body, as if I had never been entered, as if I were a young girl, innocent, uncomprehending, and afraid.

In the earlier, self-induced moment of jealousy, I had managed to reduce Jamine to a mere man with a firm, small ass, fine shoulders, the musculature of a well trained horse. Although these qualities have, in fact, never interested me much, his craggy, animal features and an irrefutable musky tension were a momentary distraction.

I reached out toward him, caught his belt behind, his hand reached back, grabbed mine, quickly pulled me to his side, and embraced me to steady me against him. The strangeness between us fell away.

Coming toward us with the momentum of a large boulder crashing down a mountain, I saw two other beings equally in the dark, stumbling similarly toward their first meeting. Jamine and I fell on each other, we collapsed on the first bit of grass under an olive tree, didn't even spread out the blanket, but grasped at each other as we sank down, desperately. I thought, as we fell down, down, that they also fell upon us, that history became a single point and the boundaries of our so-separate bodies dissolved. I am not certain we took off our clothes, perhaps they also vaporized with our flesh.

If only it had been that easy.

Jamine threw the blankets down and stood by the tree looking down on to the little bits of lights in the fields below us, or up into the sky toward the other lights.

I waited a while and then I came to him and he turned around and looked at me with his hands on one of the low branches as if it were holding him up. I suddenly knew he couldn't approach me and so I stood there, some feet from him, and began to unbutton my blouse. He watched me. I dropped it to the ground. It was cold. It didn't matter. I began to unbutton my skirt. His face was overcome with sadness.

"Don't you know who I am, Dina?" It was as if there was a wall between us, a very old wall that was still standing through the centuries, a wall that had managed to withstand every conceivable onslaught and condition and still continue standing. I was sure my heart would break. I hoped my heart would break before his broke. I didn't think I would be able to bear that. "What fantasies do you have that make you think that this is possible?" Jamine's voice was kindly. What an old fashioned word. Still, it was.

I began to walk toward him. He didn't say anything, but it seemed to me he recoiled slightly. I understood then that he wasn't waiting for me to approach him. He didn't stop me, but I wasn't to go forward. He didn't say anything aloud. I heard him, though. He did want me to come to him but taking a few steps across the ground on a cold night was not the way it could be accomplished.

I had only the most primitive grasp of what was being asked, what it meant, and what was required. Yet even as I was thoroughly perplexed, in another part of myself I began to understand. I heard him very deep inside of me and I tried to walk toward him in the way he meant; I didn't move. I even took the blouse and wrapped it about my shoulders against the chill. We stood staring at each other. Inside myself, I was walking toward him over the great distance of thousands of years of wandering and thousands of years of forgetting.

"Don't you know who I am?" I don't know if Jamine had actually spoken those words again. I had to turn away from him in my mind, that is, I had to turn away from my own mind, the ridicule of my thoughts, from the insistent skepticism, to plunge through the dark vortex of myself where the indomitable Adversary within, the absolute inability to believe, ruled supreme in order to penetrate the impenetrable wall, beyond which stood a young boy named Shechem. He was fourteen, a shepherd and a farmer; we had loved each other.

Jamine looked into my eyes. I knew that if I walked toward him a great peace would descend on us. I knew that and I wanted that peace more than I had ever wanted anything in my life. It was there, waiting; he knew it too. I had to lose my life.

I stood there. I buttoned my blouse not to leave but against distraction and put my shawl around my shoulders. I bent down and picked up Jamine's jacket and handed it to him, but he shook his head and so I dropped it.

The passage is always too small and treacherous. I could know nothing, I could take nothing with me. I had no allies except . . . Dinah, and so I prayed to her. I prayed to her for the first time for my own life and she must have felt pity for me, because I passed through that wall of disbelief to look up and see the young boy. I saw you, Shechem, not as I'd been imagining you, because in truth I'd been imagining a man, but I saw the boy—you were so young. I saw this boy, Shechem. I remembered.

I wanted to leap forward to embrace you, but I couldn't.

Then I knew what it was, what was holding me. I felt them grab at me, all my fathers, my own father, and Jacob and Moses, all of them, grabbing at me, and I couldn't move. It wasn't that you, Jamine, stopped me, hopeless about the ridiculousness of our situation—an American Jewish woman really expecting to have an inconsequential love affair with a Palestinian Muslim in the middle of a state of siege.

"Don't you know who I am?"

Nor was it you who stopped me then, Shechem.

"Don't you know who I am?"

No, it wasn't you. They reached out and they grabbed me. No, that is not quite how it was. They didn't grab me, they were me. For all my words and actions and love and wanting and hope and vision, Shechem, for all my rage and heresy, for all the centuries they had betrayed me, we were still in one skin, I was still part of them, and, therefore, they were alive in me.

It came to me in terror that if I stepped toward you, if I made the slightest move, it would mean that I would be annihilating them. You and I would become one being and all the centuries of separateness which had defined us would dissolve. Therefore they also would dissolve in that moment. I couldn't do it. I couldn't do that to them. They were my fathers. I couldn't kill the father.

I don't know what words they used to call me to them, to myself. Maybe it wasn't words, all the words I seemed to be listening to did not contain the anguish, or the warning I experienced. They forbade me. I understood 'forbid.' Language regained its power, became the thing itself. I was immobilized.

If I left, they said, if I walked toward you it was the same as if I had cast them into the gas chambers, into the showers, into the ovens.

I couldn't do it. I saw it all, everything you were asking, you wanted me to leave them and to walk into your house, into your smells, into your garbage, your bed, your language, your mutterings, your way of waking in the morning, everything odd and unfamiliar and dangerous. That wasn't it. It wasn't that I was going toward everything wretched. That they could have survived. Still I distracted myself with these small fears, counterpoising them with my great hates: Levi and Simeon; Jacob, who pretended to be innocent, who had not only married but loved Rachel, the priestess, while betraying her gods; Leah, the collaborator, whom I despised; Abraham, who'd been willing, happy, to kill his own son; Moses, who brought law and more law and more law, who had cursed his sister, the prophetess; all of them who had destroyed my own gods, cut down the groves, had forbidden my words, my language, my knowledge; all of them. I focused on my rage and the betrayal; still they held me and I couldn't cut them off.

If only there was no promise in our joining. If only I didn't believe in the peace which was looming at the end of it. Peace and dissolution.

"You must not," they said. "Anything but this heresy." In the camps, ovens, showers, defeated, demoralized, destroyed, still they had become stronger; in their destruction, they had found their own faces. They had never lost sight of who they were.

My own father, my very own father forbid me. I loved him, Shechem, I loved him.

You stood there, unmoving. I don't know what you knew or what you saw. I looked into your eyes. You looked at me. I couldn't do it for love, not for the kind of love that we dream exists between a woman and a man. You see, love would have been easy. I had to do it without the easy ecstasy, without that drug, that intoxication, that oblivion.

"Hello, Dina. Don't you remember? Don't you know who I am? It's been so long since I've seen you, it seems like centuries."

Didn't I remember? Didn't I remember that peace, in the beginning?

Then I saw it all. I don't know what I saw. It wasn't now and it wasn't the past. I saw It, the Two of Them, I don't know how to name Them.

I saw Them, together, the Two of Them, as They had been together from the beginning. Coming apart and joining, the rhythm of the breath and of sex and of seasons. It was like waves in the sea of wheat, the coming apart, the joining. Sometimes They were One and sometimes They were separate. But it was one and the same. They were not divided from each other. They were one and the same.

Then as I watched, I saw the universe sundered, wrenched apart, grinding and grieving, a division more terrible than death, the world broken in two, forever, without any possibility of joining, as if half the world had been ripped from itself and banished.

I couldn't say anything. I looked into your eyes again and then I began. I didn't know how to do it, but I began to flay my skin from my body, not to remove my clothes alone, but the clothes of the body itself. As I tore my skins from me, my eyes held by your eyes, you didn't move, you were infinitely patient.

I thought I heard you speak. Your lips didn't move. Both your arms were up holding on to the branches. You said, this is the real moment, the real story. To step into the understanding of this moment, into its very heart, you have to pierce through your beliefs and your history and your loved ones and everything familiar, until they do not hold to you in any way and when you are that naked, you will remember that we are lovers. You will come to me as if you are going to Shechem, as if you are Dinah, now for the second time. We are not two people coming together in the flesh, but history, the entire past coming together and altering, you must be willing to do this, to alter the past, even at the risk of erasing it, them, you, me, because the moment we come together, we inevitably erase everything that has come before, everything that has prevented our joining for centuries. There will be peace. Are you brave enough?

Was this the sacrifice then that I had feared for so long?

I began. I tore my fathers from me, and Jacob from me and Leah from me and all my brothers, even Levi and Simeon, and I tore the desert from me and Sinai and the tablets, and all of history, skin after skin, I stripped myself until I was completely flayed. I was clean even of the camps, Shechem, yours and also mine, all our massacres and clean even of my father. I cannot describe the pain, so much pain the blood was a balm and poultice.

Then, Shechem, what was hardest, what was so hard, I tore . . . I tore . . . Joseph from me. Even Joseph. You left me nothing. Joseph whose hands covered me again and again, who had held me, in two lifetimes, so tenderly, so protectively, who had fathered Asenath, who had given me everything, who was like my own, my brother, my own body. I loved him so much; I tore him from me, with my own nails digging into our flesh.

Then there was nothing left of me.

I walked toward you.

You took me in your arms.

You were weeping. That's when we fell down and they fell into us. That's when we fell into ourselves.

There is only one night in my life. There is only one night in all my lives. Once a friend folded a piece of paper into a fan she called 'time' and threaded a needle through the folds, saying this one point unites all the folds. When the paper is folded, it is as if time folds and one point exists in all the folded lives, the same point in all the lives. There was that night, Shechem, when all our lives came together again in one moment. I walked toward you. You took me in your arms. You were weeping.

That's when we fell down and they fell into us, that's when we fell into ourselves.

. . .

I wet my fingers in your mouth and ran them down along my body that there would be no intimation of force or rape and placed my own fingers in my body, opening the wet gates to you as you said, "Open," in three languages and pressed your tongue into my mouth, your cock slowly sliding into me, and then pulling away and your hands entering me, and my body opening beyond you as the universe opens and takes the stars into its nothingness. All the time you insisted my eyes be open and yours stayed open as well, and we were falling into the darkness, into the no light at all, nothing shimmering, no reflections, falling into nothingness, and each time you nodded to me so that I knew you were with me, that I was not alone. Once we plunged so fast I had to dig my nails into your back to hold on, and once your teeth broke through my skin at the shoulder, but we did not flinch, knowing we would have fallen away from each other had we let go because of the speed of our fall.

I lost my breath and when I caught it, I asked desperately, "Are you with me?" immediately regretting the question because it drew me back so sharply to myself and I had to fall even faster to reach your gasped, "Yes," to catch up with you before we were centuries away from each other again. We caught each other and we fell through all the pain and grief of repeated deaths and separations, through rapes and assaults, through passion and desperation. In this beginning, there was no tenderness between us, there was no time for it, we were being slammed between the folds of time. I was afraid of breaking, but the body does not break when it yields.

When you actually spoke your first words, Jamine, you were so cruel. I think it was your voice which seemed to mock me as I lay under you, the precise icy intonations of English which you used well but begrudgingly, as if you had practiced with it in your mouth until it became a weapon.

"Well, Dina," you said, "this is what it looks like, you see. The Jewish American lady is finally fucking her Arab while she is thinking she'll teach him peace, thinking she'll ease the wild man with her white thighs. She's been waiting, watching him, studying him, so that she'll know when and how to alter him, how to captivate him, how to make him dependent on her. That's what she's been doing. She pretends to yield to him, all sweetness and openness, while every minute she's setting her trap. But he is a good lover, he knows the art of it and she'd been waiting for that too, for she's read how skilled we are at eros."

You, Jamine, whispering all this in my ear. "But I know your spots, lady, yes, I know them. That's what you hope and that's what you fear. Because when I touch them, I may make you forget everything, all your traps and all your intentions and you will yield then, yield totally without hope to your infidel, your beloved. I warn you, be on your guard, Dina, because I make it my business to know how to know you. I practice this ritual. Be careful, I feel you weakening. Now when I pinch your nipples, it hurts you, still, you are trying to overcome it, your resolve is oozing from you with only your nipples in my hand, you give yourself to me as if I were a lion, yes, a lion, or a wolf, or God. You've lost yourself, you let the pain be, the pull on the nipples is not tender as you imagined it, it is forceful and yet you take it in. The snare drops out of your hand, my teeth enter you, you forget yourself and yet you cannot forget that I am here, I won't let you. I am moving along your body and you are giving me everything, and I won't let you forget that I am taking everything, that there is nothing here you can hide or keep from me. This is what my hand is telling you now, on your nipple, what my mouth is telling as it follows my hand, as I take you into my mouth, as I make you flow into me, as I part your legs, as my hand enters you, as I take out your diaphragm, and you don't protest, and I throw it away, as I feel even your womb under me in its preparation of opening and acceptance; even your womb is mine.

"Still, I am determined not to give you pleasure. Not yet. Pleasure is the door that allows you to open so easily, too easily, to me, and I must feel your body opening not from pleasure, nor

desire, nor need alone, but from grit determination, from the necessity of your being, your need to submit, to yield, to overcome
yourself, to join with me, no matter what, at all costs. My fingers
enter you now as explorers, they touch every part of you, they
grope through the darkest places, the smallest spaces, to memorize
the caves and caverns and the hidden places. They uncover you,
and they know you.

"Every part of your body, exposed to me. Does it pleasure you
to be so deeply known?

"I claim you. This body is mine."

. . .

I am lying. Because I am afraid. There was never any cruelty. You
were never bitter. You were more tender than I was able to dream.
You said, "This is what I promise you, Dina. In this exploration,
I take nothing from you. I will use nothing that you do not offer
me, I will use nothing against its nature. I will not bombard you,
I will not desert you, I will not destroy you. I will tend this garden
in the way it teaches me to tend it. I will listen with my hands and
with my heart. I promise you this.

"And I give you my body, as well. My body to die in you and
to be brought back to life. That is what my hand is saying. It is
telling you that it knows the gift and it is taking the gift. It is
making certain that you know this, that you are not unsure. I am
here with you, within you, have taken you exactly as you gave
yourself, all of what you gave. You are the gift.

"But, also, I claim you, for the first time, now, and also again,
in front of all your brothers and your fathers, whom you have had
to cast off like living cloaks, cloaks which cling to the skin, so the
skin comes off too and lies like so many old hides in the corner
of those fields which were both of ours thousands of years ago.
My hand is not tentative. My hand is confident, as absolute as if
it were touching itself, and my mouth is confident and absolute
and does not lie. I claim your breast, these mountains, your belly,

this smooth plain, your mouth, this lake, your thighs, these mead-ows, your cunt, the most hidden caverns, the veins of metals under the earth, the secret waters, and I claim your uterus, the soil, the seeds, the seasons, I claim your heart, the forces of the wind, I claim it all, but not as something that belongs to me, nor as some-thing that I possess, nor with any claims you may not equally make on me. This is my stake, and this is how I stake my claim. My cock in your hand and now in your body, I enter into you, fully naked, without fear of how you will use me. I also lose myself in you and I offer myself up to you completely, also a living sacrifice.

"This is what I say when I claim you, I mean:

"She has offered herself to me and I have heard her call and I accept what she has offered, and I will cherish her and the gift with my life. I have heard her call and I am willing to be part of her. I join you, I ally myself with you. I also give up my will to you. I will learn your seasons and the time of the sun and moon."

I lay there wondering—why didn't you have to bleed, why didn't you have to bleed, too? Until I looked down at your body and saw the dark fresh line around your circumcision and that covenant you had made with me.

We left our skins, the layers of my hymen, our circumcisions, lying there, tattooed and scaly with our history, for some other leviathan to put on.

.   .   .

I slipped down between your legs and I licked at the line of blood around the glans where you were sore, and I put your cock in my mouth and licked at you, to ease you with my tongue. Your hands were on my hair, and you were muttering. At first I thought it was prayer, then I began to hear the words . . .

". . . you have had to come to me, Dina, so naked, with nothing, no present, no past, and I am coming to you, as you were, so full of hate, of politics, full of my mother and my father and of the ancient houses, so full of war, so well trained for killing, so full of the land and of the mud, and of the loss, of Islam, of the *chador*, of pride, of hate, of domination, conflict, victory, and defeat, of famine, drought, sand, so full of being a man, of hunger, of trial, of density, of the sword, of my sisters, my brothers, of the camp, our robes, of Mecca, of the goat, of our manners, our way of speaking, of our smell, of poetry, of diplomacy, of mathematics, of visions, of ivory, of horn, lamb, cheese, of olives, of Bedouins, of ruins and ashes, of camels, of rugs, of dust, and I ask you to take me in, to take it all in, and as you are taking it in, suck at me, suck, suck me through these, suck the myth back into me, suck our past back in and our innocence, and my clean soul, suck it back into me as you suck out my semen, suck it back to us from such distances, from thousands of years ago, suck that cleanliness, suck in those dark gods we were, that boy, that light . . ."

You stopped me and pulled me up on to you and we joined again. "I can feel the light coming, Dina. I can feel it white and searing like the great moon rising in us and returning us to where we were, the ecstasy which is coming, this is the sign of our union, the leaf, the pillar of fire, the convenant of the fusion of our hands interlacing and of our dissolution . . ."

Then there was another voice that joined his,

"*. . . through this hollow bone of light that is the body stretching back through the centuries . . .*"

or we were four voices,

"*These are our bodies, these twisting, interlacing, hollow snakes of light, mouth to mouth without beginning and without ending, slipping into one another, skins of each other's bodies, entering and dissolving and reentering, our bodies of pulsing light and the humming darkness singing, these bodies, born again and again,*" *emerging and remerging, and reemerging, these our bodies filling with luminous seeds from our land of our milk and honey."*

It was true, exactly as Dinah had believed, a great peace fell upon us, which neither of us had ever experienced. We looked at each other in wonder before we fell asleep. The peace was with me even in my dreaming and I wondered that you, an Arab, a Muslim, a Palestinian, had led me to peace. My father would not have been able to believe this.

And his soul clave unto Dinah, the daughter of Jacob, and he loved the damsel and spake kindly unto the damsel.

We awakened in the middle of the night. I was frightened and pulled away from you and though I would like to believe it was the stones, the accumulated dampness, the live and biting earth which brought me to my senses and tore me out of your arms, I don't know what it was. You tried to comfort me, pointed to the stars brilliant between the black leaves of the grove, whispered to me while tracing some words in Arabic on my belly. I didn't want to ask you to translate, tried to read them from your fingers, could and couldn't. It tickled, I tickled you back, laughed at your circumcision. "Of course," you said, "both Jews and Arabs." Soon we were tumbling about, then you rolled on top of me, your hands in my ribs. I exploded in laughter, couldn't bear your weight, couldn't dislodge you. You were smiling at my struggles, not understanding I was helpless. You pinned me down, playfully, without any effort. I couldn't speak. Without warning, a terrible rage welled up in me and, hands flailing, I reached desperately about me, dug my fingernails into the earth, found a stone, and smashed it upon your shoulder. You sat up abruptly, letting go of me in pain, but then instinct led you to reach for me immediately and hold me as we wept.

I tried to catch my breath, found myself shuddering with each breath as children do who have been crying too long. I didn't understand what was shaking me. If the moon were full, I could easily explain this lunacy. But it was not full and it was not waning. It was a waxing moon, two days from fullness; everything was propitious.

You stroked me, comforted me, whispering, "Dina," or was it "Dinah"? How do you spell it in your language? Then you smoothed the blankets carefully so we'd be more comfortable, folded our clothes into pillows, covered us, drew me to you again, and we fell asleep once more.

I awakened first when the sky was not black but deep blue, the moon sinking toward the far hills. As I reached toward you, I didn't recognize the brown arms extending from my shoulders to embrace you at the small of your back where you were so tender and young. I pressed up against you, my cheeks against yours, your beard softened and your arms thin, delicately nicked from the butt of rams and goats. My arms were also thin and my breasts which were once full now scarcely budded under your chest. You approached me differently. I could feel you holding your weight back so you wouldn't crush me, and as careful as you were, you were also hesitant and awkward, filled with adolescent shyness, so I didn't know whether to look at you or hide my face in your shoulder. But you pressed my face back when I buried it, stroking my hair, looking at me with disbelieving eyes. I think your eyes also filled with tears.

I could hear the fragile tinkle of a bell as, somewhere, one goat shifted and nestled against another. I was so young, Jamine. I knew nothing. I could keep nothing from you. There was nothing to keep. The leaves rustled slightly, I listened to the soft brush of our bodies against the cloth we lay on. I tried to memorize the sound of your breathing, the taste of your breath, the exact pitch of your sweat. I thought, how lean a young boy is, how smooth, how soft. It was not the beauty of your body, nor my body, not these nipples hardening for the first time, nor the trembling that I felt inside me, nor the gentleness of your rough fingers, not even the hint of dawn coming in the rising breeze, as if spring were awakened in autumn, which evoked my cry, "Shechem, Shechem," but an indisputable tenderness that awakened in the heart of the universe. When our bodies opened, the world slipped in with us; it was as it had been in the beginning, the earth and sky mating gently without anguish or war.

Dinah was singing. A little song. A lullaby. Rocking us in it. We rocked and rocked as the gods must have rocked before creation, for centuries and eons and then just before the sun rose, I tightened gently about you . . .

Shechem! Shechem!

The tremors in my belly, milking the white seeds from your body, opened the horn of my ovary. The small moon floated out of the clouds. The offered white seed insisted itself into the heart of the egg.

A moment of double ecstasy; as Dinah had felt the prick of sperm and egg, I knew that we had made a child. I am not lying to you. As you sank down on to me, the sun coming up over our shoulder, my womb curved up, my hips beginning to shape themselves into a bowl to hold the two fused halves of our child. Even when we separated, we would never be separate again. We had made the union; the world was set right. We heard the goat bells; the young boys were awake, preparing to come up the mountain. Sinking into each other for a last moment, we sighed joyously.

"You filthy Arab pig." Lev stood above us pointing his bayonet.

There stood my brother, the emissary, the angel of God with his holy bayonet, blessed and dedicated. We both leaped up. I grabbed for the blanket to cover myself but we were both entangled in it, and so I found myself standing naked between you, Jamine, and Lev, the seeds of our love-making spilling down my legs. Though you tried to push me away, then tried to cover me, the accident of my nakedness was suddenly fortuitous, because Lev looked at me in horror, and when I wouldn't cover myself, he was forced, by his own beliefs, to look away.

You grabbed my shoulders more forcefully to move me aside so you could face the gun directly. I was not concerned with all the issues of honor and shame provoked by my behavior. Setting my legs firmly apart, I resisted you with some superhuman strength, managing to maintain my position and cover your heart, Jamine, by remaining between the two of you. Maybe the two of you looked away unable to bear the sight of me. I don't know; I don't care much. I fought in the only way I knew, with my nakedness. Also I had our child in my belly with all her promise of life and I had to protect her by establishing my own ground. It didn't matter to me what it might mean to you to be protected by a woman. I erased the sound of your heart beating, the smell of our double rage, my own fear, a life of habits and instincts, all of it was erased from my consciousness. I erased that first horrid glimpse of Lev's triumphant grin, also his bayonet, which was already limp in his hand. I saw nothing and heard nothing and so I could stand there.

My hands were on my hips. I even forgot I was naked. I thought the incident was over, except for the abuse. "How dare you," was what I intended to say, but, "Lev, I beg you," were the words that came from my mouth. I let my hands fall, supplicating him.

"You may be a whore," Lev snarled, "but any pig that rapes a Jewish woman, even an American Jewish woman, deserves to die. Even if she's a whore." But in the moment of seeing me naked, it had turned to bluster. He could not look at me. His God prohibited it.

If he had heard me, my request had hardened his heart further, but as the three of us were standing looking each other in the eye, Lev could not kill in that way. He could have managed stealth, even a knife in the back, but he couldn't kill eye to eye. He heard the Commandment and he could not transgress it.

Looking away from me, backing away from us, his face distorted with rage, the triumph that had enlivened him seeped out of his face, but he was unable to kill. I smelled his defeat turn venomous as he began to slink away. I felt dark forces invading me too.

Now, I wanted to kill too. If I had had a gun . . .

Of course, I expected Joseph to come down from the hill where he had watched this wedding between us, but he did not show himself. Maybe his heart was broken. I hadn't intended to abandon him so totally. In my imagination, I had hoped that the three of us would be together somehow.

So, I expected Joseph, not the goat boy in his scrappy gray clothes clambering up the hill toward us, drawn by the sound of voices, alert as any boy is to argument. He scampered off as soon as he saw you and Lev, yelling at us that he would get his father as there was trouble. Lev turned to stop him; it was too late. The boy was a friend of yours, Jamine, could not believe that you would be the trouble. Lev had already lowered his gun and, reading the wind, he was off also. Joseph still did not appear. He had not protected me in his heart.

· · ·

We were silent in the car again but it was a different silence. I could feel you seething, your frustration as you muttered in Arabic.

"I wanted to kill him," I said to you.

"That's no surprise."

"It is to me. How does one live with that desire?"

"The wanting doesn't matter. It matters only what you do."

"That's not good enough for me."

"It will have to be, Dina."

· · ·

I was not surprised to find Joseph waiting for us. He looked so cold, so calm, and ready to take care of business. Lev, being a hothead, had made the incident known to everyone important, especially him.

"I hope the two of you slept well, until you were interrupted, that is. I hear the night was cold in the mountains."

"Don't be an ass, Joseph."

"Well, naturally, I was called before things got out of hand. Got out of hand *again*, Dina!"

I never had appreciated the extent of Joseph's gift for diplomacy. I'd always seen him as a maverick; I'd failed to see his affinity for the work. It wasn't only that he enjoyed the precarious game of getting to it and found the highest stakes, the most important round, where he could play. The Pharaoh must have recognized his gifts immediately. If it was only that Joseph told dreams, he would hardly have qualified to rule; he would have made Joseph High Priest not his Viceroy.

"Would you like to go back to the hotel, Dina, and wash up before we get to work? We do have a film to make this morning, and I, for one, would like to request that when we meet again at ten this morning, that no matter what kind of hangover you have, we look like a team. We'll have to work very fast, very efficiently, double up on our schedule. When this gets out . . . Even if you decide to be discreet, which I strongly urge, Lev probably won't keep his mouth shut. So I don't think we'll have a film permit for very long, or people who want to speak with us." Joseph put his arm around my shoulder—brother? father? lover?—and turned to Jamine as we walked off. "I hope you appreciate your victory."

. . .

I don't know what you thought, Jamine. I don't know you well enough even to imagine it. You are not a hothead, however, and whatever you thought and did, I know you thought it and did it with the utmost, not caution, but deliberation. I didn't expect you to consult me about it and you didn't.

. . .

We finished the movie. That is, we got enough footage so that when I returned to New York, I could edit it. We didn't get everything. It's a good film. I was gratified that you both trusted me to edit it. Despite everything, you both know that I'm fair, and Jamine, you know that I love you. I call it *Beside the Ruins*. I couldn't consult you regarding the title. Joseph found it sufficiently ambiguous to be intriguing.

.   .   .

I pressed charges against Lev after we finished shooting, against Joseph's express displeasure. What did he think I would do? The military commanders asked me to reconsider and threatened to keep me from working in Israel again. I won't bore you with the bureaucratic haggling, it's familiar and exists in every culture. I was adamant, countered with a useless threat to go to the American Embassy. We agreed to talk when I was calmer. My threats were idle. I simply wanted time. If I had gone to the Embassy, they probably would have been harsher with me than the Israelis. I was counting on gossip to get me what I wanted. I put in a telephone call to Sybil. She was very reliable. A few casual words here and there in the middle of her normal conversations. By tea time, enough people in Jerusalem knew about the incident so that some kind of hearing was unavoidable.

When this broke open, I was asked, as expected, to leave the West Bank. Within a few days, you, Jamine, were also ordered out of the territory and knew you had to leave the country altogether.

Why do I repeat this to you? Don't you know this story? Is your version so different from mine?

.   .   .

The last nights, Joseph and I continued to sleep in the same bed. Why should I have slept alone? I hadn't been in the bed in my room once since I'd come to Nablus and I was too shaken to initiate it then. But, after you and I had been together, Joseph and I didn't make love again. Nor did you and I. The last morning in Nablus, he and I examined our bodies again and laughed this time. We were really so alike, we were indeed like brother and sister.

"It's hard enough to marry a sister," he chuckled, "let alone a twin." So I knew he forgave me. Forgave us.

I asked him when he intended to be serious about getting married.

"After I'm sixty. Twenty years from now, I'll settle down. I'll still be old enough to have a child and too old to make serious trouble. Just the right age for a man to have a family."

"That gives me just enough time. By then I'll have just the right woman for you." I didn't say more than that. He knew what he knew.

Before I drove back to Jerusalem, I went to the ruins again and knelt at the stele, put my head to the ground, not in humility, but for the energy of the earth, tried to feel the old times under my hands. Joseph waited for me, his back turned, at a discreet distance.

At the tomb of Joseph, three new soldiers watched me nervously but said nothing. I insisted that Joseph come into the tomb with me. There we were together, the live ones and the dead ones. It was very still.

•   •   •

This, Shechem, is what happened:

There was an "in house" hearing. I'd wanted to have Lev charged with attempted murder. The military settled for "harassment," or "incitement," or "conduct unbecoming an officer." They read my affidavit in court. It was taken in Jerusalem as I was packing, "with all due regrets that the witnesses could not be present." You were . . . where, Jamine? You delegated Joseph to speak for you. He agreed. He is a gentleman. So it was known to all that you had not been allowed to testify and that the real facts in the case would never be known publicly, through that tribunal at least.

The military had enough reason to bring in some judgment against Lev, after all he had certainly broken discipline, used his rank and position inappropriately, had, all in all, made a lot of

trouble for everyone. They trod a fine course between demoralizing
the Israeli soldiers, outraging the orthodox, and alienating me, and
thereby American media. How the Palestinian population might
respond was of no real concern. Perhaps they relied upon you to
cover your ass, to say it was a lie that a Palestinian had been
fucking a Jewess.

Lev argued his own case. He touched his *kippah,* he bowed his
head, his eyes shone.

The judges—military officers—did not find him innocent nor
quite guilty, and they didn't quite pardon him. They did say he
was overzealous in his duties. They didn't forgive him and they
didn't exonerate him. They didn't publicly applaud him. The
judges suggested that he was suffering from severe emotional strain
and exhaustion, and ended his duty on the West Bank with a light
sentence. Maybe they gave him solitary so he could meditate. Lev
was considered a good soldier and, for most of his buddies, this
was much in his favor.

They sent me a notice in New York. Sybil promised to send me
the newspaper accounts but didn't, or there were none.

· · ·

This, Shechem, is what I imagine happened:

I imagine that Lev was called to argue his case before God. He
did not have a lawyer represent him. In Judaism you don't need
an intermediary, not even a rabbi. Since Job, it's been possible to
go directly to the source. Anyway, Lev is of the tribe of Levi, so
he is his own priest.

Before God, Lev did not argue law, he argued faith.

He argued that he was an instrument of the wrath of the Lord
who had descended upon the inhabitants of Shechem on account
of their wickedness, that they had persecuted the children of Abraham, that they intended to push them to the sea. He said he was
a general in God's army, that he intended only to defend His name.
He said that they would be overrun if they were not vigilant. That

the heathens had sought to do unto Sarah and Rebekah as they did unto Dinah, but the Lord had prevented them. Lev said that Dinah was a fool, a harlot, like mother like daughter, a green calf, that she would feed her sons spoiled milk, that their bones would curdle. Lev said when a calf is sick, you must cut it out of the herd. Still, he said, he was also protecting her. Lev said it was proper to kill one's enemies instead of waiting for them to slaughter the ones God had chosen. He was pure of heart. Lev opened his robes and showed God his circumcision. He said that it was not sufficient to cut off one's foreskin without cutting oneself off from evil and idolatry. Lev said the foreskin was the false god which hooded the living truth. He shook his cock in God's face crying, "This is a bond between us."

Because God knows all things, He did not call any witnesses against Lev. But as I insisted that I be heard, I was permitted to speak. So the two of us, Lev and myself, faced each other in that small room built of cinderblocks where Jamine had been incarcerated. There were two windows in the room, opposite each other, and the light coming in formed a small quadrangle on the floor which divided the room in two. I did say that Lev and I faced each other, but I do not know if he ever saw anyone but God.

After I told my story, exactly as I've told it above, I sat down on the patched plastic seat of the rickety aluminum chair. Lev paced up and down. His uniform was wrinkled and stained with sweat.

God asked me if I had anything else to say, anything I might have forgotten which was pertinent to the issue. I took my time before I spoke. Then I told Him:

"I was in my innocence. I was full of love. I was awakened brutally. In that moment, I knew what it was to want to kill to protect what I had so recently gained, to protect what I had come to love more than my life. I don't know how I would have acted if I had had a gun, but I do know that for a minute I also wanted to have a gun so that I could kill Lev. I never would have thought that was possible. I am ashamed."

"What's your judgment?" God asked.

"We aren't very different from each other, are we? I have to forgive him," I said.

. . .

Dear Shechem:

This is the end. Something, Shechem, was to be rewritten, something was to be retold, something was to be relived. Somewhere at the end of the journey, something and someone would be altered. I thought it would be a simple task—I would recreate our history and also avoid its consequences. I simply wanted to bring our story to another conclusion. I had to tell it so that at the end, Shechem, you wouldn't die and I wouldn't remain alone.

At the end, you didn't die, Shechem. The book is finished. At the end of the book you are living.

I didn't write it, of course. It was written on me, as if my flesh were a page. In the beginning, I had the illusion that I had a choice about words. In the beginning, I was even beguiled with the thought of conjuring. That's how I was drawn in.

I came to a road which I had not chosen and which I did not recognize and I could not go back. There was a wall and somehow I had to pass through it. Somehow I did, I suppose. For here I am, on what seems to be another side of the wall, with the wall behind me, though I can't see it anymore. I had to break my heart open and pass through it.

I don't mind being alone. At least I don't mind it as much as I minded loneliness when I started out. I don't mind it as much as I imagined I would mind. Alone, I'm not without the past, am I?

Also, I have us on film. So, for me, you will always be alive and with me, somehow.

And Dinah the daughter of Leah which she bore unto Jacob went out to see the daughters of the land. When Shechem the son of Hamor, the Hivite, prince of the country, saw her, his soul cleaved to her and hers to him and he brought his sisters to dance and

drum as they lay together. And he loved Dinah. And she loved
him.

Then he spoke unto his father, Hamor, saying, I love this
damsel, get me this damsel to wife.

When Jacob heard that they had lain together, he was grieved.
And Hamor communed with him, saying, "The soul of my son,
Shechem, longeth for your daughter. I pray you give her to him
to wife. And make ye marriages with us and give your daughters
unto us and take our daughters unto you. And ye shall dwell
with us and the land shall be before you; dwell and trade ye
herein, and get you possessions therein."

And the sons of Jacob answered Hamor deceitfully and said,
"We cannot do this thing, to give our sister to one that is uncircumcised; for that were a reproach unto us. But in this will
we consent unto you: if ye will be as we be, that every male of
you be circumcised, then will we give our daughters unto you
and we will take your daughters to us, and we will live well with
you and we will become one people."

And Hamor and Shechem came unto the gate of their city and
communed with the men of their city, saying, "These men are
peaceable with us; therefore let them dwell in the land, for the
land, behold, it is large enough for them.

And unto Hamor and unto Shechem hearkened all that went
out of the gate of the city; and every male was circumcised.

And it came to pass on the third day when they were sore that
two of the sons of Jacob and Leah, Simeon and Levi, Dinah's
brethren, took each man his sword and came upon the city boldly
to slay all the males.

· · ·

But Dinah saw them coming and she met them at the gates of
the city and she said unto them, "This is the third day of the
pledge and the day of my marriage, why do you come to my
wedding with a sword?" And Dinah berated her brothers sor-
rowfully, saying, "Shechem and I have already been married

before the gods and now we will be married before all our broth-ers and sisters and there will be no swords among us."

And the two brothers were ashamed and they left their swords outside the gates of the city as she requested.

When Jacob learned what they had planned he was grieved and said, "You, Levi, shall give one half your portion of your inheritance to your sister and you, Simeon, shall give one half your portion of your inheritance to Shechem, for you wished to take what was theirs for yourself."

But they said, "How can we live with men who are not like us?"

And Jacob reminded them of what his God had said: "And if a stranger sojourn with thee in your land, ye shall not vex him. But the stranger that dwelleth with you shall be unto you as one born among you and thou shalt love him as thyself."

So it came to pass that the Israelites and the Hivites lived together in peace and became like one people.

And Dinah and Shechem lived a hundred and eighteen years and their daughter Asenath lived also a hundred and eighteen years and Joseph took her to wife. When Dinah and Shechem died in Egypt, Asenath buried them together. Before they died, they asked that they be buried in the old way. Therefore Asenath put their bones in the earth and planted a tree on their grave.

As the tree grew, peace grew also in the land about the tree. But when the tree was almost grown, lightning split the trunk midway into two limbs. From a distance the tree appeared like a woman, her great wooden green arms stretching up to heaven, a single root plunging into the earth.

Good-bye, my love. What else is there to say? Only, good-bye, my love.

Documents

Mr. Jamine Amouri
General Delivery
Cairo, Egypt

Dear Jamine:

Once again, I saw it as if it were a film.

I remember the very last minutes we spent together as if I'd been the witness, not a participant. I play it back to see what you saw. A woman, divided by the sun and shade, so that one half of her face is in darkness, tries not to squint as the sun glances off her cheek. She is speaking to you the only way she is certain you will understand, that is, with the eyes. I deliberately filmed it in my mind because I was afraid that this would be all I would have, ultimately.

In the film, we are standing facing each other in an arched doorway. The cars are waiting, three of them, yours, mine, Joseph's. The engines running. Joseph has the discretion to move to the other side of the street, to give us a moment together. He and I drive back as we came, in tandem. He and I will remain friends.

You and I cannot ride back together. I am willing but you, both

367

strategist and soldier, think you are responsible for my life. I think you are taking my life with you as you go. I think I have just come alive.

After I finish a film, I run it back slowly frame by frame, watching it, without sound, from end to beginning to be certain the narrative action is smooth in both directions. Is this because I have been trained not to believe in time? Do we go on now or is this the end of the movie? Have we done our work? Or must we proceed in reverse altering each frame, century by century, until all the necessary changes are made and the two of them who insisted themselves upon us are redeemed.

Without them, we would not have met . . . again. I'm grateful.

Joseph forgave his brothers because their cruelty was his means. It happens again and again. We were not spared.

May I call you Shechem, just this once between us. Dear, dear Shechem.

Now, Jamine again. I know this name as well. Jamine. The flower in it, the pervasive night scent, the heart explodes and behind it the wind follows fresh and empty.

Is it enough to know you've alive? Dinah also recedes from me, becomes an other, is almost merely a story. Is that because she is at peace?

I see your face perfectly just as it was. You're saying goodbye to me. Your hand strokes my hair, then you touch my face. You take the dark side and the light side between your two hands, one shadowed and one illuminated. You lean forward; I take in your breath.

I cannot see our bodies. We do not dare to touch more than this. It is as if our bodies disappear, as if they know each time they have met in another body, and each time they disappear from each other, each time she has seen him die.

This time you didn't die.

I realize, belatedly, how innocent and foolhardy I was. It is the consequence, as Joseph frequently informed me, of being an American. You seem to have agreed. Naive and self-absorbed. Maybe

I'm being too kind. Maybe I was stupid. I never believed that you would die again, because I was so arrogant about my own power. I risked your life, all the time I was thinking I was protecting you.

But, Jamine, there's something else, which you also know. On the other side of the wall, there is another system of ethics and strategies. I trusted Dinah. She led the way.

Perhaps we've put an end to it finally. How do we give them a proper burial? I'm afraid to do it.

I'm afraid that we will meet casually someday, find their bones, bury them, say the proper prayers in several languages, throw dirt on them. First, I will use the shovel, then you. They will be together just as they wished to spend the centuries of their old age beside each other. I think they originally hoped for their graves to be forgotten, to turn back to the soil, but together, as a cow and bull turn back into the manure and grasses.

So we'll bury them somewhere, beside some wall that will resemble the wall at Nablus. Since I don't know when we will be able to return together, if ever, we will have to find a knoll with a single upright stone marking the remains of a temple. That won't be difficult. There are many ruins. Then we will look at each other in disbelief as our history and myth drain from us and we become so very ordinary, seeing our bodies flatten, the sparks receding, extinguishing like lightning bugs at the coming of dawn.

How will it be? Will we reminisce over a coffee afterwards? Will we be polite, affectionate, promise to write, agree to meet again in twenty years? Shall I watch for your publications and activities, read the obituaries faithfully? Will you see my movies regularly, holding some other woman's hand, telling her nothing? Will you forget we have a child?

I memorize the moment we said good-bye.

I say, "I want you to learn these words and when you say them, in whatever lifetime, we will both remember. They're very simple. Say, 'It's me, Dina, don't you remember? I've been waiting to see you for so long, it seems like centuries.' "

You say it to me. You say it in English, you say it in Hebrew, you say it in Arabic, in Aramaic, in French, in Ladino. You say it silently.

I say, "I remember." You don't say anything else. I add, "See you . . ."

You don't say anything else.

That's where the film ends.

Is the story over? Did we do our work? Are you still alive?

Love,
D:

Herald Tribune, International Edition, August 14.

A daughter, Asenath Z. Amouri, was born to the noted documentary filmmaker, Dina Z. Ms. Z. has been working on a film for NTS in Israel. She returned to New York in order to have the baby in the U.S. She was accompanied by her friend and associate Sybil Stone. The whereabouts of the father is said to be unknown.

The New York Times, August 14

Prizewinning documentary filmmaker Dina Z. gave birth to a daughter, Asenath Z. Amouri. Ms. Z. returned to the United States some months ago when difficulties developed around the filming of her soon-to-be-released documentary, *Beside the Ruins*. It is rumored that the father of the child is the Palestinian activist and archaeologist Jamine Amouri, who as persona non grata in Israel has often been associated with members of the PLO. Amouri had been reported shot, possibly killed, in a border incident in Lebanon this year. Ms. Z. refused to comment. The Israelis deny any knowledge of the incident.

Hollywood Reporter, August 21

When documentary filmmaker Dina Z. returned home from Israel some months ago, it was not because she had finished post-production work on her new film for NTS, *Beside the Ruins*. Yesterday, it was revealed that the father of her daughter, born last week, was the noted Palestinian archaeologist who was allegedly killed in an ambush near Nablus this winter. Ms. Z. has refused all interviews. The film is scheduled for release late this fall.

WESTERN UNION CABLE

Dinah Z.
14 Greenwich Mews
New York, N. Y. 10011

Visa difficulties solved. Meet you September 17. Cairo. No American hotels please. All is well. Nile still rising. Bring the dress. *Ana bahabik Salaam*. Peace and love.

S.

Mr. Jamine Amouri
Hotel Mabaruk
Cairo, Egypt
(Please hold for guest's arrival)

My love, I'm on the way. We're on the way. Sybil says she'll try to live without Asenath for six months. Or she'll join us after a while. How lucky Asenath is to have two mothers. This child compensates Sybil for all her grief.

You see, despite your apprehension, the test was right. It said all would be fine. The doctor had also agreed I was not too old to have a child.

We have a daughter, as you said we would. The test could have told me that, but I didn't want to know in advance more than we already knew. Are you relieved? Your letter was so fierce. How did you put it? You were afraid to have a son, Abraham is too strong in you; the same in Arabs as in Jews. Yes, so many centuries of Abraham.

I hope you're right about daughters, though I find the irony difficult, that in this century it may be easier to learn not to sacrifice the daughter than the son.

It's hard to tell, my love, but everyone says she looks exactly like

US.

Love,
D.

"Shechem, my love, it's done, everything as it should be.
Why   isn't   there   peace   yet?"

"Miracles, Dinah, work themselves out imperceptibly with the
rhythm and form of history, that is, very, very slowly."

"And in the meantime?"

"We live our lives as best we can, each time better than the time
before."

When there is no Sabbath, it is said that it is not possible to cross the river to Grace and Gan Eden. But if one must cross the river, then one finds the narrowest way, for it is also not possible that the path to the Gods is entirely closed, but only that it is so narrow that without mystery it cannot be traversed.